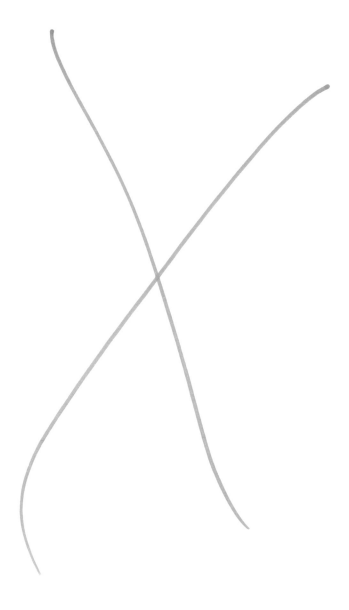

Rough Edges

Books 1-3

A SMALL TOWN FIREFIGHTER SERIES

USA TODAY BESTSELLING AUTHOR

ASHLEY ZAKRZEWSKI

Cover by Zakrzewski Services
Formatted by Zakrzewski Services

CONTENTS

ADORE ME

ADMIRE ME

CHERISH ME

ADORE ME

BOOK 1

1

DAMON

Thick black smoke and flames reach the sky, the compound crumbling to ash before my eyes as the fire truck screeches to a halt. Everything but the thumping of my heart goes silent. Even if we put it out, the destruction is inescapable, with the fire spreading across the entire complex. Individuals are standing off to the side by a couple of ambulances, coughing uncontrollably with soot smeared on their faces.

The chief instructs us to prepare the hose as a screaming child comes from behind me. When I twist around, a little girl of about seven is scrambling out of the building, black streaks down her face. My heart plummets as I scurry over to her, plucking her up, struggling to get away from the tumbling debris. "Are you okay?" I ask, examining her body for any signs of cuts or burns.

"My mom... She's still inside..." She sobs. "Please. Help her."

"What apartment?"

She stares at me. "I don't know."

"First floor?" I ask, requiring at least that, and she nods. "I'm gonna find her."

Before wasting any more precious time, I pass her off to the paramedics and dash inside to find the young girl's mother.

Upon entry, there are two floors, the top one is missing pieces of the roof already, but I don't let that deter me in my search. This is my job, and no one is dying today.

The crashing of debris is deafening, making my ears ring, and my throat is on fire from the dense smoke taking over the corridor. This building might come down at any point and trap us both inside.

"Your daughter is safe," I yell. "If you can hear me, make a noise."

It's hard to hear over all the clamoring from the fire, but my eyes shut, battling to take notice of anything that can point me to recovering the girl's mother. *Nothing.* Proceeding to scan through apartments, I tremble. This structure is massive. She could be anywhere and I'm running out of time. I need something, anything to help me locate her or neither of us will be walking out of here alive today.

The once-sturdy frame, damaged by embers, is deteriorating before me, allowing mere minutes to locate her before it will all come plunging down. Sometimes, in situations like this, my life flashes before my eyes, as cliché as that sounds. Every life is worth saving, and I can't leave someone behind, even if it means my death.

My body swiftly moves through two more residences damaged by excessive smoke soot, seeking to expose the woman, but no luck. She isn't responding to me, and that isn't a good sign. Is she unconscious? "Bang on something... anything."

The attempt to drown everything out around me to concentrate fails until I pick up a clang coming from the next apartment. *Finally.* My biceps flex as I force the debris off her and take her in. Under the soot and wide eyes, she has a delicate bone structure that would be beautiful under other circumstances. Green eyes peer up at me, frenzied.

It's Tessa.

She suffers no obvious injuries. The smoke is closing in on us, with no clear path to get out now. What the hell are we going to do? I'm not letting that little girl grow up without a mother. We are getting out of here.

I search around the apartment for anything that she can manipulate to protect her nose and mouth. "Use this." I jab a ragged towel from the floor into her hands.

She presses it against her nostrils, gasping for clean air, her eyes searching mine for instructions.

"I'm gonna get you outta here," I say, scooping her into my arms.

Ash coats her face. "My... my..."

"Your daughter's outside. Safe. Come on."

Debris is falling all around us, and for a minute, I don't expect us to make it out until we reach the foyer and the paramedics charge us. Not even thirty seconds later, the structure where we were just at comes crumbling down. Any more hesitation from either of us, and we wouldn't have made it out alive.

The little girl is whimpering, standing next to my brother Liam. Today, she almost lost her mother. That's something that will remain with her. As it does for many people, even those beyond her years.

Once the paramedics have Tessa, I saunter over to her daughter to reassure her everything is going to be okay. I crouch down in front of her, bringing myself to her level.

"My name's Damon. What's yours?"

"Emily..." She sniffles.

"Your mom's gonna be okay, Emily. I couldn't have saved her without your help, so thank you."

Her arms wrap around me and my heart breaks. She reminds me of the one thing I may never have, but have always wanted. *Children.*

"Let's go see your mom." I accompany her over to the ambulance where the EMT is examining Tessa.

Thankfully, she has no cuts from the debris falling on top of her, but will have some bruising. The worst thing is all the smoke she inhaled. That's the most dangerous thing about fires. It can decrease lung function, and a lot of people suffocate due to the lack of clean air.

When I shift around to head back to the truck and help the guys with the hose, Tessa clutches my arm.

"What's your name?" she says, her voice scratchy.

"Damon," I reply, holding out my hand, gazing into the green eyes before me. She must not remember me. Maybe that's a good thing after our incident. She works at the local grocery store by my house, and a couple times I tried to work up the courage to ask her out, but I talked myself out of it.

"I'm Tessa. Thank you for saving me and my daughter." Her hand reaches out to shake mine.

A smile takes over, and I reply, "It's my pleasure, ma'am. Glad to see you're going to be okay. That little girl needs you."

We exchange a smile as I walk away, heading back to the truck, to receive an ass chewing from my brother.

"You should have waited, damn it. What the hell were you thinking? You could've died, just like Dad," Liam yells.

His face is crimson, and I know what he's thinking. *Don't be a hero.* But I can't help who I am. Yes, there were consequences to think about, but the good exceeded the bad. The chance of us not making it out of a building is high, but we can't let that stop us from attempting to save people.

"I had it," I reply, clutching the hose and ripping the fire a new one.

As it sprays over the structure still tumbling down, my mind drifts to Tessa. My brothers didn't know about my crush on her. There must be a reason fate brought us together today, right?

Perspiration drips off my forehead as I twist the hose off, and the boys assist me in placing it back on the truck. The fire is out, but the destruction is still happening, with debris continuing to fall. The crowd has become bigger around the destruction, with people stopping their cars and taking in the scene.

"Let's head back to the station," Liam calls out, hopping into the driver's seat.

Winter is the worst season for fires in Grapevine because of all the objects left plugged in like heaters, or even burning candles. Sometimes it's defective wiring, but there is always an investigation.

Luckily, we haven't hit winter yet, and the leaves are still crunching beneath my feet as I stride to the truck, savoring the breeze for longer. September in Texas isn't too bad with the temperature being in the sixties. We get a couple of months in between scorching hot and the chill of the forties. Every once in a while we will have some snow, but not very often.

After leaving the complex, my mind always assesses if there's something I could have done differently. Either better or quicker. My brothers sometimes tell me I'm too critical of myself, but every second counts. If we were a couple minutes later, Tessa could have died and left behind her daughter. I tremble thinking about it.

After removing our gear off the truck, I head inside to the break-room, and my mind travels back to an idea I've been throwing around.

We sit down at the table, and I chug a bottle of water to help relieve the burning sensation in my throat. "So, I'm thinking about purchasing some property."

"For what? Like another house?" Liam asks.

"Not for me, but every week people suffer misfortune, leaving the scenes of fires with only the clothes on their backs, and most of the time they end up in shelters. What if we could help them instead?" My arms cross and I lean back in my chair.

"I'm listening. You know I'm down to help."

"We aren't wealthy by any means, but purchasing some property and offering it up to the community sounds like something Mom and Dad would do," I respond.

My father left instructions for his life insurance to be split into three accounts for me and my brothers. One thing my father always said was, "Being a firefighter is amazing, but you should still go to college." So, the contingency on the account was we would gain access after obtaining at least an associate's degree and reach twenty-one years old.

When my mother passed, her life insurance was also placed in these accounts with instructions to use toward retiring early so we can enjoy our lives.

That's what Liam and I have been putting our money toward instead of spending it on useless stuff like our younger brother, Aiden.

"You think we can find something that isn't too high? I can chip in one hundred thousand dollars. The rest I have in a fund to build interest."

"If we can get Aiden to agree to pitch in, that's plenty. I can't imagine we couldn't find a property for three hundred thousand dollars in Grapevine."

This is something we can operate as a family, to facilitate aid in our neighborhood after witnessing the tragedy strike family after family.

I draft up a text to Aiden and edit it twice. He has issues with money, so I'm not sure if he will be able to go in with us.

Me: *Got time to meet up tonight at Dixie's and have a beer?*

Liam challenges me to a game of poker to waste away the last hour of our shift, and I'm not one to back down. He always acts like he's so good at it, but he needs to learn to not show his cards. I laugh every time.

"So, did you see who that girl was you saved?" he asks.

Of course I know who she is, but how does he? "Yeah, Tessa. Why? What about her?"

"I almost asked her out earlier this year, but decided not to."

I am not competing with my brother over a girl.

"It's those eyes, I bet. Got me too."

I try hard not to show him any kind of resistance because he likes competition, and Tessa doesn't need us fighting over her, treating her like a piece of meat. Liam isn't a womanizer like Aiden, but he cares too much about looks. Honestly, for me, of course I want them to be attractive, but it's more about who they are and what they bring to the table. In twenty to thirty years, we will both be older, and it's more important that I have someone to talk to and share things with in my life than basing my decision off their looks.

So instead of hearing more from Liam, I try to change the topic. "Hey, you know there's that set of duplexes over off Dupont. Been a for sale sign for months now."

"If Aiden wants in, we can go see it. Mark can find us a good deal."

I lay down my cards and smile.

"How do you do that every time?" he yells, rising from the table, almost knocking it over.

"Keep your cards hidden and I won't beat you."

My phone vibrates against the wood table.

Aiden: *Meet you there at five.*

Things between Aiden and me haven't been great in recent years. It started when our mother passed. With Aiden being the youngest, he was used to receiving special treatment, but Liam and I didn't hold back. He needs someone to make him realize when he's messing up, just as Dad would do if he were still alive.

After our shift ends, we head to the bar and chat about the various properties we've seen for sale around the neighborhood. Mark is the agent that helped us find our homes, so he'll be the one we enlist to help us find the perfect property.

"You think Aiden will go for it? He might not have enough cash left..."

When he turned twenty-one and got access to his account, he dropped his money on luxurious items like an enormous home and an upscale Audi instead of saving or investing it. Liam and I are wiser about our wealth. We each acquired a fixer-upper house and set the rest back in an interest account for retirement. When it comes time, we both wish to live comfortably.

Aiden didn't really have a plan. When we asked about how he's saving for retirement, he laughed at us.

"I'm too young to think about retirement. I haven't even lived yet."

His materialistic aspects of living will be his downfall. Those elements don't mean crap when you're sixty-five and need to pay for your medication. Until then, all we can do as his brothers is wish for the best.

I pull my red Honda Civic up to the bar and unbuckle my seat belt and turn the car off. "Let me talk with Aiden. You know how he can be sometimes."

Liam nods, agreeing to let me take the lead as we head inside.

When the doors open, I regret my decision to meet here, forgetting it's open mic night. I can hardly hear Liam when he tries to talk to me.

"Over there." He points where Aiden is thrashing his hands around, trying to get our attention.

"What's the big occasion? We haven't done this since what? My twenty-first birthday..." He bangs his beer down.

Fuck. Already? His eyes are glazed over, and he is already slightly slurring his words. It's only five on a weekday. How can he already be this drunk?

"Now hear us out. We wanna buy some property and use it for those who don't have anywhere to go. Just another way to support our community," I explain. Even though my brother enjoys having money to fall back on, he has a heart. Just like Liam and me, there's a reason he followed in the family's footsteps. Helping people runs in our blood.

Aiden's eyebrows rise. "Well, what do you need from me?"

"If you want to go in with us, we can split the cost three ways. How much do you have left in your account?" Normally, I wouldn't ask such a personal question, but he might not even have enough to help.

"Around two hundred thousand dollars, I think," he responds, taking another sip of his beer.

That's it? When he turned twenty-one, there was over a million dollars in that account. Has he really been that foolish to spend so recklessly? I resist the urge to yell at him; it isn't my place.

"We would split the cost, but until we decide on which property, there's no telling how much it will be."

Aiden's age encourages him to make crazy impulse decisions, and not consider the repercussions. "Screw it, I'm in."

The three of us clink our beers together. Our family has been around misfortune enough.

"What about that estate over on Dupont?" Aiden chimes in.

"I'll call tomorrow and see if we can look at it. We should see several properties before we make a decision," I reply, snatching my keys. "I'm heading home. We'll talk more once I've spoken to Mark."

It's been an exhausting day, but it's only a little after six, which means it's time to head home and find something to eat. The quiet gets to me and for the last two years, my solitude is going to work to break up the depression and silence. I try not to let it get to me anymore, but sometimes it sneaks up without me knowing it.

As I pull into my driveway, Tessa creeps up in my mind, reminding me of our last interaction. I'd been trying to rustle up the courage to ask her out, but always fell short. It was a Thursday, my day off, and I decided I was finally going to do it. When I walked into the grocery store, there she was, checking someone out, and so I acted like I was shopping until she was free, only instead of paying attention to where I was going, my ass knocked over a display of Cheez-Its. They all went tumbling to the ground, and everyone in the store came to stare.

"Are you okay, sir?" Tessa asked, laughing. "I keep telling my boss we should move the display to the side, but no one listens to me."

She began to pick up boxes, and I helped her. "I'm so sorry about this. I really need to watch where I'm going."

It took about twenty minutes to get all the boxes picked up and put back together on the display. I don't really say much, still embarrassed, but I wasn't going to run out of here like a little girl. However, my nerve to ask her out was completely lost.

Maybe today is a sign that I should buckle down and just ask her. Maybe it's a way of fate telling me to stop being a pussy and go for it.

2

TESSA

*H*ow are we going to recover from this? We can't afford to stay in a motel with only a hundred bucks left in my pocket until next week. Working part-time while Emily's in school doesn't bring in a lot of money, but as a single mother, I do what I have to.

"Mama, I don't wanna go." She coughs into the crease of her elbow.

"I know, baby, but we should. Just to be safe," I say, holding out my hand.

The ambulance takes us to the emergency room, and we go directly to a patient room that's bleak and sterile, where we remain, hands interlaced, waiting to see a doctor. I'm not leaving her side, even for a second. Not after coming so close to losing her. The fear of being on that floor, fire all around us, and nothing I can do to save her is something I never want to experience again. Attempting to wipe the tears from her eyes, the soot on her face smears, leaving more black streaks across her face.

The door opens, and a nurse comes inside. "I'm Angela. Dr. Ward would like us to run some tests. If you would follow me."

Emily grabs my hand, and we walk together into an all-white room with machines. She clutches my hand.

"Just do what the nurse asks, and we'll be out of here in no time. And then we'll go get ice cream. Okay?"

She nods and takes the nurse's hand as they run the test on her, and then we switch. After Angela takes us back to the patient room, we wait for the results.

"Here. Let's get you cleaned up," I say, grabbing a couple of paper towels and running them under water for a minute before wiping away all the black. "Much better."

I wrap up next to Emily on the hospital bed, pondering where we will go from here.

My way of life since having her has been tough, but I constantly push through and make certain we have food to eat and a place to lay our heads. Now, with the apartment out of commission, that isn't the case, and I'm feeling as if I let my daughter down.

There is no one for me to lean on in my time of crisis. My mother lives thousands of miles away, so our only other option is to stay at a family shelter. If we owned the house, then insurance would kick in and help us, but we only rent. I doubt our cheap landlord is going to shell out anything to house the families from the fire.

A knock sounds on the door and the doctor comes in. "It looks like you girls should be fine besides some coughing spells, which are an effect of the irritation from the smoke. Tests show no prolonged damage to the lungs, which is splendid news."

"Are we free to go? We need to get our things in order so we have somewhere to sleep tonight."

"Of course. Here are your discharge papers. Follow up with your family doctor next week. If the coughing persists after a week, come back and get checked out."

As we wander out of the hospital, Emily tugs on my hand. "Mama, when can we go home?"

I don't think it has settled in that we didn't have a home to go to. My head sinks, and I try to keep from crying because I don't know where we will go. I must keep it together in front of Emily. She's only six years old, far too young to have to fret about something like this.

"Let's run some errands before we get ice cream, baby."

First stop is to Goodwill to get some clothes that don't reek of smoke.

Luckily, there is a twenty percent off sale on blue tags, and I ransack the place, hoping to find some good deals. The hundred dollars I have must be spent wisely, especially not knowing how long we will be without a place. Most racks have little to no sale items left, but I find some things for both of us.

As I make my way to the front, I see an old suitcase and look to see how much it is. Eight dollars. My logic is we'll need something to lug around our items in, so I pick it up and add it to the clothes on the counter and pay.

"Can I have this, Mommy?"

She holds up a doll, missing some of its hair. I almost say no, but she will need something to play with, and my heart gives in. "Of course, baby. Put it up here."

As we exit the store, holding our only possessions inside of a suitcase, things become clear on how the rest of this year is going to go.

"It's ice cream time."

Emily grabs my hand as we stride to the next block over. The little diner is just what you would predict, booths attached to windowpanes, giving a pleasant view of the town hall across the street. Old Coca-Cola memorabilia are on the walls. It has a couple of people inside, and we take the booth farthest away from the exit.

"What can I get y'all this evening?"

"Mint chocolate chip, please," Emily responds.

Ice cream always helps make her feel better. She comes back with a double dip of her favorite and I observe as she inhales it. "Slow down. You're going to get a brain freeze, sweetie."

"Those aren't real, Mom." She rolls her eyes.

I take the time to step away and a young woman confirms a spot is open.

"Mommy, can we go home now? I'm done," she begs.

Shaking my head, I explain, "The apartment's in awful shape, kiddo. We have to find somewhere else to stay."

"Where will we go? To Grandma's?" Tears appear in Emily's eyes.

I glance over to see a drawing.

"What's that, sweetheart?"

"A picture for Damon. Can we give it to him?"

I rattle my head. "I don't know. It's almost seven."

"Please. I worked really hard on it."

Showing up unannounced at someone's house seems improper, but maybe he wouldn't look at it that way. Emily will simply beg until I say yes, so we might as well get it over and done with. Plus, he might enjoy knowing that we admire him for what he did today. Grapevine isn't too big, with a population of around ten thousand or less. The residential neighborhood isn't as substantial as you would expect, but plenty of thriving businesses set up shop here.

A couple days after the first time Damon came into the grocery store, I strolled past his house on the way home from work, but he didn't recognize me. So, I already know where he lives.

"Let's take it to him. But then, we must go to where we're staying tonight. Okay?"

A grin takes over as she plucks the picture and sprints for the exit. We stroll hand in hand for the next six blocks. There, on the corner, is the refurbished house that belongs to Damon.

"You ready to give it to him?" I ask. "That's his house right there."

Emily is quick and gets to the door before I'm even on the porch.

Knock. Knock. Knock.

A voice resonates from inside. "Just a moment." The door opens and Damon crouches down, his white t-shirt hugging his broad shoulders. *Pull yourself together.*

"Hey there, sweetheart. What can I do for you?"

"This is for you…"

As Emily reveals the picture, I recognize the three of us and my hero written across the top. "It's beautiful. Did you do this all by yourself?"

Emily nods, drifting in for a hug.

At six, it astounds me how compassionate she is for others.

Damon's eyes close, welcoming her. "Well, thank you. Would you like to come in and put it on my fridge?"

Emily doesn't hesitate to walk inside before glancing back at me. "Come on, Mama."

As they turn into the kitchen, I gape at the interior of the home. It's refreshing. There are light-blue walls, and nothing you would conclude a bachelor's home to look like. From the guys' houses I've seen, it's usually sort of chaotic and not very vibrant. Damon's definitely has a woman's touch. *Is he seeing someone?*

"Whoever decorated your house did an outstanding job," I say, scanning around.

I make my way through the living room to the kitchen to see Emily using a puppy dog magnet to hang the picture.

"Now you'll see it every day," she says, glowing.

"I'll never take it down. It's not very often I get a hand-drawn picture. I'll treasure it."

Emily clutches my hand. "We can go to the shelter now."

My cheeks burn hot, and I avoid eye contact until he invites us to stay for supper. I can't remember the last time we had a true home-cooked meal. Damon might just be offering, but not actually want us to stay. It's the polite thing to do when you have guests show up around dinnertime. Or at least that's what my mom always used to say.

"Can we?" Emily asks, tugging on my blouse.

My stomach rumbles and answers for me, causing me to blush. I haven't eaten since breakfast. Food has been the last thing on my mind. I've been more focused on figuring out how to get through the next few weeks.

"If you show me where the stuff is, we'll set the dinner table."

He points to the far cabinet, and when I open it, I notice some china inside on the top shelf. Why would a man have china? Is it his mother's? I grab three plates and set the table.

Afterward, Emily goes back into the kitchen to observe him cook. He drags over a chair so she can relax on the counter and watch.

"Have you ever helped someone make dinner before?" he asks.

"Mama doesn't let me. It's dangerous."

"Well, maybe, this one time... she'll trust us. I won't let you get hurt. I'm your hero after all."

His eyes flick over to me as Emily sits on the counter helping him prepare dinner. First, he puts the chicken in the oven to bake it while the water is waiting to boil, and then he puts the pasta in. They both watch the water bubble, and they stir it every couple of minutes as they wait for it to be done.

"Now for the sauce," Damon says, unsealing the jar and dumping it into the pan.

Emily is savoring every minute. Usually, it's just me and her, so it's nice to watch her interact with someone new.

Once they're done, we each carry a dish to the table and take our seats.

"Ladies first," Damon says, prompting us to make our plates.

Emily doesn't waste any time, stacking the pasta on her plate while licking her lips. She chuckles and then digs in, shoveling it into her mouth.

"Slow down, sweetie. We don't want you to choke," Damon says.

The last time I had chicken alfredo was when my father was still alive. It's not a meal I can afford to splurge on. Yes, the meal probably only costs eight dollars to make between the pasta, chicken breast, and sauce, but that's a lot when you only have fifty dollars to buy groceries for a week. Living paycheck to paycheck isn't pleasant, and sometimes we fall short with just enough for bare essentials. We spend many nights eating ramen noodles or chili with crackers. Anything to scrape by until my next paycheck comes in. I hate that we have to eat such unhealthy food, but it's what I can afford, and it keeps us fed throughout the week.

As I enjoy my meal, my eyes dance around to look at him without being so obvious. Of course, I remember him from the grocery store, a regular customer. Although, I haven't seen him since he knocked over that display.

He isn't a bad-looking man at all, with a distinguished jaw, almost chiseled to excellence, and the five-o'clock shadow. Let's just say he's way out of my league. I've had a crush on him since the first time he came into the grocery store. Of course, I've never mentioned it, because why would he want a woman like me? Plus, there's my rule about not dating firefighters or police officers. The chances of them dying on the job are too high, and I never want Emily to go through the pain and suffering that I did when I lost my father to his job.

I can remember it clearly, the day my father died.

It was only a few days after my sixth birthday when he leaned down to give me a kiss before heading out the door to the fire station. When the phone buzzed just a couple of hours later, my mom fell to the floor, weeping frantically. When I asked her what was wrong, she didn't answer. Her eyes just scanned over me. Of course, I was too young to notice the signs of grief and loss then. For two hours, I remained on the floor next to her, my head on her chest, trying to calm her down, but nothing worked.

The buzzer went off, and I dashed to the door, opening it to a man in Daddy's uniform. "Can I help you, sir?"

He knelt down. "Is your mommy here?"

She paused behind me. "What now?"

They made some sort of eye contact and she asked me to go to my room for a minute. I obliged, but I left the door open so I could hear.

"Ma'am, I'm sorry for your loss. We wanted you to know, he died a hero, trying to save a family from the fire, but he didn't make it out in time. If there's anything we can do at the station to help you, please reach out to us."

That day followed me for years. Being so young, knowing my father was never coming back home, killed me. All the father-daughter dances I missed or parent-teacher conferences held where they would ask if both parents were coming. Every time it hits just as hard as the first.

"Who's the pretty woman on the wall?" Emily points.

A choking sound comes from Damon. "That's my late wife."

So, that solves the woman's touch on everything. He was married.

"She's beautiful."

Emily asks to be excused from the dinner table and asks Damon where the bathroom is. "Down that hallway, second door on the right."

After she shuts the bathroom door, I apologize.

"She couldn't have known. No big deal." A drop of condensation rolls past his finger as he tilts the glass to his lips, taking a drink, before clearing his throat and finishing his food. "Married for eleven years. Right out of high school."

From the raspy tone of his voice, I can tell it still hurts. "You don't have to tell me. Honestly, it's none of our business."

His demeanor changes after this, and sadness fills the room.

After a couple minutes of silence, I round up the three plates before heading to the kitchen to give him some space.

"I'll dry," he says, following behind me.

Emily takes a seat on the couch and turns Animal Planet on in the living room.

"So, what made you want to become a firefighter?" I ask. It kills me knowing that he goes against my rule, but he never came in wearing any type of uniform, so how was I supposed to know? Couldn't he have chosen any other job? I look into his eyes as we continue doing the dishes, glancing back and forth.

He grazes his chin and looks up at the fridge to a picture of a man in uniform. "Runs in the family for three generations. My brothers are as well. We like to help people."

Damon is someone I could grow to admire. Better than most, I recognize the risk of being a firefighter, and death becomes the consequence for several of them. Why did I have to crush on a firefighter? Literally, it can be anyone else, but no. Then he saves me and Emily, making me like him even more. What the hell am I going to do?

"Have you ever thought about changing your profession? Doing something less dangerous?" I ask, being selfish and hoping he would say yes.

"Not at all. I'm happy to put my life on the line to save people."

Emily is giggling away in the living room and enjoying herself. I know staying at the shelter is going to be unusual for her, but we won't be there forever. Eventually, we will find somewhere we can afford or they will rebuild the complex. Until then, we must go with the options put in front of us.

Damon stops and twirls around. "So... not to be extremely forward... but I have an extra bedroom."

My eyes open wide, overwhelmed by his offer. "Oh no, we couldn't impose like that." It would be a better environment than the shelter, but inappropriate.

"Your choice. I wouldn't feel right if I didn't at least offer a comfy bed. You could stay here as long as you need. No need to pay anything. My wife believed in helping people too and she would invite you in if she were here."

This could be an excellent opportunity to get to know him better, while also having a place to stay. Damon is a good man to offer his extra room, but would he expect anything in return?

As we return to the dishes, I reflect about it further. What am I getting myself into if we stick around here? Damon's hot, and I could already tell he has many noble qualities even after only being here an hour. How much else would I learn about him? Do I take the chance and accept his gratitude?

The more I contemplate it, it's better than staying at a shelter around many individuals we don't know, and I bet the bed is more comfortable too. I'll play it by ear, and change course if we need to after tonight.

"Would you like to stay here with Damon for a little while?" I ask Emily. If she feels uneasy about staying in any way, then off to the shelter we will go.

"I wonder what he makes for breakfast... Waffles? Pancakes?"

Damon's eyes dart over at me. "Continental breakfast for one morning only."

He makes his way to the back of the house while we sit in the living room watching TV.

"I made the bed up for you."

"You didn't have to do that. We could've done it," I say, getting off the couch and instructing Emily to follow. "It's bedtime, sweetie."

"Sleep good, kiddo. See you in the morning," Damon says right before Emily goes in for a hug.

I clutch the suitcase on the way to the room and then get both of us into something more appropriate for bed. Emily changed into a pair of plaid pajamas we bought earlier, and I changed into a pair of sweats and a t-shirt from Goodwill before sliding under the comforter that is as soft as snow.

"I'll stay here until you fall asleep. Mommy's not tired just yet."

Sleeping in a new place might cause some issues, but between my fingers running through her hair and the bed itself, it doesn't take long before she's snoring, which shows how secure she feels here. Damon somehow has magic powers. "I love you, baby girl."

I slither out without being caught and find Damon relaxing on the couch in his pajamas. He stretches, causing his shirt to shift, letting me see a bit of his toned stomach. I bite my lip, wondering how good my hands running down his chest would feel. *No, don't start. You are not getting involved with Damon. You can't.*

3

DAMON

*B*efore Carol passed, we would cook meals together, experiencing that mutual love. On holidays, our home transformed into a restaurant with our families blended together to enjoy our cuisine cooked to perfection. That was, until she became sick.

We discovered each other early in life, the first day of junior high, to be specific. Carol was standing up for another student, against a big eighth-grade boy. He was enormous and didn't have any apprehensions about attacking a girl. I walked in between them and tried to talk him into going away. He swung at Carol, and I laid him out.

At first, she was furious with me, preferring to deal with it herself. She eventually warmed up to me, after not looking my way for a couple of weeks.

We became best friends until high school. That's when she came forward about her affections for me, and we'd been together ever since. Most people warned us we were foolish when we became engaged and married at nineteen, but nothing came between us. Sure, we had our fair share of setbacks, but doesn't every marriage? She was still my best friend and soulmate.

As the years rushed by, we acquired a home and remodeled it. That was her thing—cooking and decorating. We chatted about having children but delayed until we were a little older. There was no rush.

"I love you. I'll see you after work." She kissed me goodbye, as she always did.

I went to work, arrived home, doing my normal daily routine. When she arrived through the front door, I could see something was off. Her face was blotchy, like she had been sobbing.

She sank down next to me. "I had my checkup today... They discovered something."

"What? Just tell me. You're terrifying me," I replied, my eyes big with worry.

She settled her palm on top of mine. "I have breast cancer..."

I moved her close and let her sob into me, causing my shirt to become damp. How could this happen to her? The woman I love? My knuckles turned white, and I looked up to the ceiling, questioning everything. Why would he take away someone so young, someone who has believed in him her whole life? Carol had a full life ahead of her, kids and grandbabies. They diagnosed people every year, but no one ever thinks it would happen to someone they care for.

After the diagnosis, I remained by her side and took some time off work to take her to consultations to figure out treatment strategies. The news wasn't what we desired.

"After studying the scans, it shows we did not reveal it in the earlier stages. As you can see, it's spreading and quick." The physician waited a minute for us to process the information. "She will need to start chemo next week."

My knees hit the floor, palms together, urging for God to pardon her.

This lingered on for months, and we hoped it was working. Within six months of the diagnosis, she was hospital-bound.

The day the specialist came in, and without a word, we both knew what he was going to report. They tell you in therapy to prepare yourself, at least mine did, for Carol's possible passing when we first found about about her cancer, but how does one really prepare for their spouse's death emotionally?

"Just give it to me straight. No sugarcoating," Carol said.

"You have limited time left. We would prefer to send you to hospice where you can be more comfortable."

That was the day when I had to brace myself for when I wouldn't have her in my world anymore. My wife was going to die, and there was nothing I could do to save her.

On her last day, she was exceedingly frail, but surrounded by family. All I could do was be there for her in the last hours and let her see I truly adored her. More than she would ever realize.

Once everyone left, I seized her palm and wept. Her breathing was becoming shallow. "When I'm gone, don't turn into a recluse. You deserve to live a long, happy life. Even if it's not with me by your side."

Tears dribbled from my eyes. "I don't know what I'm going to do without you. You're my entire world."

"Don't shut out love. One day you'll find someone who can love you, even after I'm gone. Don't run, embrace it. I want you to."

"No one will take your place. Ever."

This was not the conversation I preferred to have with my dying partner. How could she even be thinking about me with someone else right now?

That night around midnight, Carol's lungs took their last breath with me by her side, her hand intertwined with mine. My forehead rested on her bed, asking for God to bring her back, just let me have one more day, but he had bigger plans for my Carol.

I lingered in my room for weeks after her death, not bothering to venture outside even to check the mail or get groceries. My life headed down a suicidal path, where I sank into a deep depression, not showering or getting out of the bed most days. My brothers would come over and check on me, try to get me to at least come out, but I never did.

After two months, I went back to work even though I wasn't ready. The silence in our home was forcing my depression to worsen, and all it achieved was causing me to miss her even more.

I have never looked at a woman like I did with my wife. Until Tessa. I'm not sure what it is about her that draws me in. At first glance of her walking through the grocery store, I wanted to get to know her, what makes her tick.

The sound of a door shutting brings me back to reality.

"Mr. Damon?" Emily calls out, coming out in her plaid pajamas. Her eyes light up at the smorgasbord of breakfast items. "You made all this?"

I nod, seeing her smile, and take a seat at the table. Her eyes are bigger than her tummy when she puts a mountain of food on it.

"You sure you can eat all of that, kiddo?"

She thrusts a chunk of sausage in her mouth and nods.

Tessa strolls out, hair up in a messy bun, and yawning. "Please tell me there's coffee."

"Of course. Fresh pot in the kitchen. Mugs are in the cupboard above."

She walks off, half asleep still, and then comes back with a cup of joe and sits down next to me.

"Wow, you didn't have to make all of this. It's too much."

The pleasure of having people in my home, a home I thought Carol and I would raise our children in, is immense.

"I've got to get going. Enjoy your breakfast, ladies," I say, emptying my coffee into the sink and heading to the living room. "You guys stay. No rush. Just lock the door when you leave."

As I snag my coat, Tessa approaches me. "We'll be out within the hour. Again, we appreciate you letting us stay here last night."

"Stay as long as you need. It's no trouble. My number's on the fridge if you need anything," I counter, pushing on my coat and heading out the door.

It's not how I imagined our first night together to be, but that's okay. Once she finds a place, and I get to know her better, then I'll ask her out.

On the drive to work, I wonder if they will be there when I get home. Their presence is driving the silence away, which gives me some tranquility. It's also a nonchalant way for me to get to know more about Tessa. She is beautiful, and for her to be sleeping across the hall from me has me dreaming vividly of events that might happen.

As I walk into the station, everybody is throwing me strange looks. I look down at myself, inspecting my shirt and pants for a stain or a piece of paper saying kick me or something. What the hell is everyone staring at?

"You look chipper, brother," Liam suggests. "What's gotten into you?"

"Had some company staying over."

"Staying over? Like a woman? I never guessed I'd see the day."

Jesus, lay off already. Liam and Aiden are constantly trying to get me to date, and I can only express to them in so many polite ways to back the fuck off. "Not like that. It's the mother that I saved yesterday with her little girl. They had nowhere to go. So I suggested the extra bedroom, no big deal."

I've never discussed my crush before, and thank God. If I had, they wouldn't let up on me now, knowing she is staying with me. Sometimes it's better to keep matters to yourself.

"Once we decide on a property, they can stay there. Or do you plan on keeping them there with you?"

"Of course not. I'll call the Realtor now," I reply.

I dial Mark's number, hoping he can tell us what the asking price is, and if there are any other properties we should look at around the area. After the pleasantries, we get right to business.

"What's the cost for the duplex property on Dupont?"

"Let me see." He is fumbling with some sheets. "Shows two hundred fifty thousand is the asking price."

"Can you meet us there after work, around six? We'd like to see it and talk before making a decision."

"Sure. See you then," he says before hanging up.

I text Aiden.

Me: *Tour of Dupont property tonight at six.*

We don't need to rush a decision and buy the first thing we look at. Mark has a few properties he thinks we will like, and he'll show us the other two tomorrow.

My phone starts buzzing against the table with a number I don't recognize. "Hello?"

"It's Tessa. Did I catch you at a bad time?"

I look around, seeing Liam clearly trying to listen to our conversation. "No, it's all right. What's up?"

"What time will you be getting off? I'm gonna make dinner."

"Around six, but I'll be home closer to seven thirty. No need to cook me dinner."

"You're letting us stay with you. The least I can do is make you dinner after a long day at work. It's not a bother at all. See you later."

Liam's eyes are piercing through mine. "She's preparing dinner for you... seems like a keeper. Ever think maybe she could be..."

My jaw clenches. "Don't make assumptions. I'm helping them get back on their feet. No need to make this into something it's not."

I try hard not to give Liam any indication of my feelings toward Tessa, because he will never let it go. Plus, I'm not really sure about them right now. Sure, she's gorgeous, but there's more for me to know before I decide to ask her out. With her living with me, it makes it easier to get to know her and Emily, without having to take her out and risking broken hearts.

Liam finally lays off the girlfriend bullshit and pulls out the deck of cards and starts shuffling. "Why don't we play some gin rummy to pass the time?"

I nod. Normally, we play poker but the rest of the guys are in the bunkers taking a nap, waiting for a call or the end of our shift, whichever comes first.

Before we know it, it's almost six, and I've beat Liam nine times and about to make it ten. "Done getting your ass beat?"

Liam lays down his cards on the table. "Okay, maybe you beat me today, but not the next time."

Everyone begins to gather their stuff and head out the door. "That's a wrap, fellas," I say, striding out to my car.

It's time to go take a look at the duplexes and even though I know it's a process, maybe we can acquire something soon.

Liam and I head over in separate vehicles to Dupont, finding Mark outside waiting for us. Aiden's car is already parked.

As we stroll through the duplexes, it's clear there are some things to be corrected. There is hardwood throughout, which is a plus for me. They each have two bedrooms, which will be suitable for a family.

"Do the appliances come in the transaction?" I inquire.

"Indeed, they do."

Appliances are expensive, so that will save us a ton of money. "Let us discuss, and then we'll get back to you. What time would you like to show us the other properties tomorrow?"

"Let's say seven. That work?"

In unison, we reply yes and take off toward our cars and head back to our respective homes. I look forward to spending time with Tessa and Emily. It's how I imagine my life would be, having a woman and child in the house, even though it's not Carol or my child. It's nice to come home to someone after being alone for so long, just sharing the basic things like meals and downtime.

As I open the door, the aroma swirls around my house, hitting me. There is nothing like a warm meal waiting for you. I take my coat off and head for the dining room. The table has pork chops smothered in bell peppers, onions, and mushrooms.

"Wow, you've been holding out on me. It smells unbelievable," I say, walking into the kitchen.

"Mama made it just for you," Emily says.

"You really didn't have to do this."

"It's the least I can do. Just enjoy," she says, sitting down next to me at the table.

Over supper, Emily asks many questions about my job. It's nice to see she takes an interest in what I do. Another thing is taking notice of how Emily reacts to things. It shines light on how she is raised. So many parents don't focus on teaching their kids how to be well-mannered and productive citizens, and they end up being little turds, but not Emily.

"Why did you become a firefighter? Aren't you scared?"

The question is hard to answer coming from a child. At young ages, children think of us as heroes and want to be like us. If we tell them how scary it is, then that might change. So I keep that part to myself usually, and give them a more direct answer, sidestepping the actual question. "It's dangerous, but someone has to look after the people in our town and keep them safe. It's up to me. My father and grandfather did it before me."

"My grandpa died trying to help. Right, Mama?" She looks up.

"That's right, sweetie."

There are many things I'd love to know about her, and we have nothing but time.

"I think your father would be very proud of you for saving us," Emily says.

His wish was always for me to take after him and keep the family legacy going here in Grapevine. When I was old enough to join, it's the first thing I did.

Once everyone is done eating, Tessa and I clear off the table and do the dishes again while Emily watches TV. I catch myself peering at Tessa. What was her life like before the fire? Being a single parent has to be rough and exhausting. Where is Emily's father? What transpired there?

"Carol did a fantastic job decorating this place," she says, breaking the silence.

I clear my throat. "When she passed, it didn't feel right to change anything. Decorating was her passion, and I can't imagine taking down her work." Silence lingers for a few moments, because I don't ordinarily talk about this sort of thing with anybody. "It's been years, yet still seems like yesterday sometimes. I wake up expecting to discover her next to me... but then I remember."

Her eyes flick over to me, radiating sadness. "I'm so sorry. If it's any consolation, I wouldn't change a thing about this house. It's perfect the way she decorated it."

There is so much I'd like to know about her, and maybe it's time I start asking questions.

"So where's Emily's dad? I realize you mentioned he wasn't in the picture, but is that new?" I ask.

"It's a long story. Chris couldn't handle the responsibility of having a child. He left when she was two. Last year, he started calling around Thanksgiving to visit her, but I refused. She deserves better than a father who wants to come in her life every couple of years."

What kind of man does something like that? Just up and leaves his kid. Emily is better off without that son of a bitch. If I ever have children, they will wish for nothing and never wonder if their father loves them.

"So you don't get child support from him?" I ask, realizing how direct that question is and probably shouldn't have asked. Not every dad pays it, and sometimes it's the mother's decision to file. At least she's not one of those moms that keeps the kid away because of some stupid reason that has nothing to do with Emily. Women like that irritate the piss out of me.

"Nope, I don't want anything from him. We are better off."

"I'm so sorry. She's such a great kid. His loss not to get to know the amazing girl she's become because of you."

Just being around Emily in the short time I've known her, I can see she is a wonderful, sweet, and intelligent little girl. Tessa has done a great job all by herself at raising her to be independent and thoughtful.

"Yet sometimes, I feel like I'm failing her... not able to provide her with things. Her whole life we've struggled. Good jobs are hard to come by."

My heart can't stand it. Tessa is doing the best she can under the circumstances. My mom struggled after my dad's death with us three boys. It was chaos because the home was never the same. She was used to having someone to experience the hard days with and had no one. "You're raising her to be strong and independent. That counts for a lot more than... trivial things."

"I know—I just wish I could find a better job. Something so we don't have to live paycheck to paycheck. Hell, sometimes I can hardly afford ramen. Bills just keep stacking up. It's a never-ending vicious cycle."

"Don't beat yourself up. You're a great mom."

I want her to comprehend how marvelous she is. After Chris left, she stayed and provided for her baby. That meant something. As an adult, I don't reflect back on what we had for dinner, but rather the times I got to spend with my parents and how loved I felt. Emily is healthy, and that's all that should count.

"You're doing your best. Ramen is better than nothing to eat at all," I say.

She is being overly harsh on herself, and that means that we need to switch the topic.

I send her into the living room with Emily while I dish up three bowls of ice cream.

"Hopefully you all like mint chocolate chip," I say, handing them each a bowl.

Before Emily and Tess began staying here, I didn't look forward to coming home to an empty house. But now it's full of laughter, and I wouldn't want it any other way.

4

TESSA

*H*ow did he know that it's my favorite flavor? Maybe he's just able to read me well. As we devour our ice cream, I can't help but wonder what else there is to know about him. I've heard about his wife, but what about his parents? Did he grow up here?

In the back of my mind, I know it's trouble getting to know Damon, especially when there are already feelings involved, but I can't help it. He's intriguing. There aren't many good men left out there, and maybe I can overlook his profession. The man did save me and my daughter, so maybe I can cut him some slack.

I look down at my phone, wondering why my mother hasn't reached out yet. Usually she calls to check in every couple of weeks. Would I even mention the fire or living in a stranger's house? Probably not. She will think I'm batshit crazy. Instead of waiting on her to call me, I attempt to call her, but she doesn't answer.

To say our relationship isn't the best is an understatement. When she does call, it usually consists of her trying to convince me to move back to Oregon. *Like that's ever going to happen.*

We continue watching Animal Planet until about nine thirty when Emily's eyes fade. So I cart her off to bed before she falls asleep on the couch. It didn't take but maybe five minutes for her to snore a symphony. As I lie back on my pillow, a million things run through my head, causing me not to be able to sleep. How long can we stay here without overstaying our welcome? If Damon refuses to let me pay rent, then would it be enough for me to save up to get another place?

Maybe it's time I consider moving back to Oregon, even though I don't want to. *Hell no.* Getting away is the best thing that's happened to me, and going back would be a mistake.

As if in a daze, my phone rings and I look at the clock to see it's almost midnight already. What the hell have I been doing for almost two and a half hours? *Mommy* slides across my screen as I decide whether to answer it. Surely she realizes what time it is.

Before my father passed, it was always me and him against the world. Me being a daddy's girl always got to my mother, I think. Of course, after his passing, she tried to make more of an effort to keep up the things we used to do together like fishing, baseball games, and watching the Super Bowl every year.

"Hey, can you hold a second?" I say, whispering into the phone so as not to wake Emily. The bed squeaks as I get up and head for the bedroom door. *Crap.*

"Mom?" Emily says, half awake.

"I'll be right back, sweetie. Go back to bed."

I close the door softly behind me and head out into the living room where I see Damon sitting on the couch doing his usual. "What are you still doing up?"

"Couldn't sleep. Everything okay?"

"I'm going to take this call outside." I open the front door and close it behind me, letting the breeze twirl my hair around. It's not too bad outside, maybe sixty-five.

"Ma? You still there?"

"Yeah, sorry for calling so late, but I saw a missed call from you. Everything okay? Still working at that supermarket?"

It never fails; she always has to comment on my employment, wanting me to find something better, but without a degree it's hard to do. Most jobs around here pay minimum wage, or a little above. It's not like I have a whole lot of options in front of me.

"Yes, Mom. Part-time. It's hard to find a full-time job that works around the schedule with Emily; you know that."

"If you moved back to Oregon, you wouldn't have an issue at all. I'd watch her so you can work. Hell, I could take her to school and pick her up."

The offer is nice, but as she knows, Oregon isn't where I want to be.

"Not gonna happen, and you know it. Why don't you move down here?"

It's a stupid question because I know the answer. The house my parents bought when they first got married is something she would never move away from. It's paid for and holds all their memories. "I'm not moving."

"Okay, then. When are you going to come visit? Emily is gonna forget who you are, it's been so long."

She scoffs. "Wow, way to make me feel like shit, Tess. You know I can't afford it yet. I'm saving up and when I have enough, you'll be the first to know."

The conversation doesn't get any better before the call ends.

My mom knows Oregon is the last place I want to be. The whole point of going to college was to get away from that small-town life and find somewhere better. Sure, Grapevine isn't much bigger than my hometown, but it's somewhere new and I find that comforting in its own right.

I'm surprised when I go back inside to find Damon still up watching TV. When does he sleep? Maybe he has insomnia or something.

"Would some tea help?"

"That would be nice, thanks."

I still don't know much about this man, but the more I find out, the better a man he becomes in my eyes. If my mother ever meets him, she will like him. He reminds me of my father.

"You know, I can change the channel if you would like to watch something else." He yells from the living room to the kitchen. "How about the Travel channel?"

I dunk the tea pouch in some hot water. "That's fine. Hopefully I can fall asleep soon so I'm not grouchy in the morning."

Coming back into the living room, I set the cup of tea down on the side table and take a seat on the couch. His eyes slide over to mine and remain there for about ten seconds. I can't take mine away, even though it feels sort of awkward. It's not like he is crushing on me, not with his late wife still on his mind. Not that I blame him. If I had been with someone for that long and lost them to something as horrible as cancer before thirty, I'd feel lost and broken too.

Maybe he isn't staring at me, and it's all a dirty daydream. Wouldn't be the first time.

"Who was calling so late? Her dad?"

I break the stare and look down at my phone. "My mom. I don't really want to talk about it. It's the same thing on every phone call. I love her, but I'm not moving back to Oregon."

It wasn't just the fact Chris cheated on me there, but the town we lived in was small, like seventeen hundred people. Everyone is always in each other's business, and nothing is a secret there. *Nothing.*

"So that's where you're from. What city?"

"Cannon Beach."

The only thing I miss about it is waking up with a view of the sandy shores and the blue water. I'm not sure how my mom puts up with the small-town drama there, but it was enough for me to want to get far away and never go back. Eventually, I would like her to move closer to us, especially as she gets older and might need help. I'd never say that to her because she'd kill me, but it's true.

"I wish. Never even been to the beach before. My parents never really had time to travel with us, and then as an adult with my job being as demanding as it is, just never got around to it."

"Have you ever been outside Texas at least?"

"Never. I'd love to go to Europe at some point, but I'll probably have to save that for when I retire. I've heard it's not worth it unless you go for at least a week."

I'm in the same boat, really. Besides Oregon and Texas, I've never really been anywhere. Sure, I drove down here from Oregon so I passed through some states, but I didn't actually stop and enjoy them. So that doesn't count.

Maybe I should use this time to get some questions answered. "So, you don't have any kids?"

"Nope. Carol and I decided to wait, and then she passed."

"I just figured you did with how great you are with Emily."

"Maybe someday. If I'm lucky enough."

Damon is someone who would truly be a wonderful dad. Some men you can tell by the way they interact with children and he is wonderful with her. He's very timid, and he doesn't seem to lose patience with her even when she's asking a million questions that are none of her business.

"Well, here's to getting your wish," I say, raising my cup of tea to clank his.

His eyes study me for a minute, and an urge to kiss him takes over, but I don't. I don't need to go making a fool of myself. After a couple seconds, his eyes avert back to the TV and I take a deep breath. *You are not going to make a move on him. Be a good girl.*

He goes back to watching the show, and it cuts to a commercial and he turns back to me on the couch. "Not to bring up a wretched conversation from earlier, but you're doing great with her. Don't get yourself down because of some obstacles that have come up. She won't remember that, only the time you spent with her. You're a good mom, Tess. Really."

I know he wants me to believe that, but in the back of my mind it could be better. Some decisions I made when younger ruined it for me as an adult. If I would have finished college and got a degree, it would be easier for me to find a better job right now, but I didn't, so I'm stuck working at a store or as a receptionist. Something I already have experience in. How the hell am I going to find a job that pays more than minimum wage doing something like that? For now, I'm stuck working part-time in the local grocery store for a sexist boss who thinks just because I'm a single mom he can talk to me like a piece of trash.

"How's that tea?"

"Making me sleepy, that's for sure," he says, taking a sip before setting it back on the side table. "What are your plans tomorrow?"

Tomorrow is my last day off, and I don't really have much to do. Probably tidy up around the house, so he doesn't have to, and maybe some laundry. "Nothing really. Why?"

"Just wondering. I'm off and didn't know if you planned on staying in or going out to do something?" He picks at his fingers. "I mean we could go out and do something fun with Emily."

I nod and take another sip of my tea. He wants to take us to do something, and maybe I'm reading too much into this, and his glances, but I think he likes me. My inner schoolgirl squeals. I'll test the waters later, but if things keep going like this, maybe I'll work up enough courage to ask him out when we find a place. Emily has a strong bond with him already, and my brain is giving me intense dreams about what a night with him would be like, so it only makes me want to experience it, at least once.

"We should both get some sleep before Emily wakes up and stomps through the house demanding breakfast." I laugh and so does he.

I crawl back into bed, causing it to squeak again, almost waking her up but only causing her to stir. It's around three in the morning and she'll be up in a matter of a few hours. My eyes shut, giving up the fight to keep them open.

5

DAMON

"All right, little one. What's for breakfast today?" I ask.

Cooking has been our system of bonding since the first night. We both seem to enjoy it and sharing my passion with someone makes it that much more enjoyable. Who knows? Maybe Emily will grow up to be a famous chef one day because of our time together.

"Hmm... Mommy likes omelets... with bacon in them... Can we make that? Like a surprise?"

"You got it!" I hold out my hand. "Let's get started. I'm surprised she's not up already."

But I'm not. She didn't go to sleep until after three in the morning and is probably dead to the world right now. Unlike her, I can't sleep when someone is moving around.

Emily gets the eggs and bacon out of the fridge. Since Tessa's still asleep, I let her help as much as she can without burning herself. She cracks the eggs, and I secretly fish out the minor fragments of shell when her attention shifts elsewhere. No need to spoil her excitement.

"Mommy is going to be surprised."

"Surprised about what, sweetie?" Tessa asks, pausing in the corridor to the kitchen in her pajamas, her hair everywhere.

These are things I enjoy, getting to know her on a different level. I get to see her at some vulnerable moments, like when she first gets up, no makeup or anything done to her hair. The real Tessa.

"It's about time you got up. We made a special breakfast just for you. Take a seat at the table."

Emily laughs as Tessa walks by pretending to sneak a peek. "No peeking, you cheater."

We conduct some last touches, adding cheese before closing the omelets and administering them on plates. "I think she's going to love these. Good thinking, Em."

Tessa's eyes are closed, awaiting the unveiling. "Oh, my. I wonder what it could be."

"One of your favorites." Emily giggles.

A mug of coffee transpires in front of her. "And I notice how you like your coffee. Two creams and a spoonful of sugar. Drink up."

An ordinary day off for me consists of tidying the house, watching TV, and being deep in my thoughts. With them here, I won't be doing that. Why should we stay inside this house when we can go out and enjoy some fresh air? Emily has a love for animals and this could be a great trip if Tessa agrees.

"I was thinking maybe we could take Emily to the zoo. Get out of the house for a little while."

An outing will provide an easier way to get to know them better while we have some fun. My brothers aren't exactly biting at the bit to hang out with me, and it's no fun doing things like this by yourself. Emily has never been to a zoo before, and today is the perfect opportunity with it being a high of sixty-seven. I still treasure our family trips to the Dallas Zoo to this day.

"Can we, Mama?"

"That sounds great, actually," Tessa replies.

A smile resides on my face, thanking my lucky stars she agrees.

We all exit the dining room to get dressed for our joint adventure. I quickly throw on some jeans and a t-shirt and head to the living room. They are already waiting for me. We pile up into the car and begin our journey to Dallas. It's a thirty-minute drive from the house if we don't get caught in bad traffic. When Emily's eyes spot the big Dallas Zoo sign, a gleam appears from sheer excitement.

"Oh my gosh. We are here. Thank you, Mama."

Tessa turns to me. "I really appreciate this. You've done so much for us. I don't know how I will ever repay you for your kindness."

Why did she feel the need to? I like having someone to do things with...

The things we have in common make it easier to open up to her. The fact her father was also a firefighter, and both of ours passed under the same circumstances, connect us on that level. She's a single mother, and my mother was for a couple years after my father passed. I might not know firsthand the struggle she faces, but I can understand from a child's perspective.

Tessa needs someone supportive on her side, and it can be me. Raising a child by yourself is hard, and not having anyone to turn to is even worse. With her mom living all the way out in Oregon, she has no one.

Emily gets out of the car and snags my hand. "I wonder what animals they have here. Monkeys? Tigers? Sharks?"

"You're in for a treat. I used to come here when I was your age with my parents. My favorite part is the penguins."

"Penguins, really? Did you like it?"

"I loved it, and so will you."

We spend most of the day with Emily attached to my hip. Every chance she gets, her hand is in mine. I figure it's a security thing and don't mind. It's been a while since a male role model has been in her life. I'm glad I can be that person for her.

We linger at the gorilla exhibit for a solid hour, just observing her laugh. It's hands down her favorite part. When we try to move on to the next one, she mopes. So Tessa and I grab a bench and let her enjoy herself. We chuckle, watching her talk to them like they are best friends, wanting to know if they are hungry, what they play with, and if they all get along in there.

"You know you don't have to repay me for anything, right?" I sit my cup down on the ground. "You wouldn't begin to understand all you've done for me in just the last few days."

Her eyes peer into mine. "What do you mean?"

"Before you two came along, I wasn't my best self. Losing my wife really took a toll on me." I don't want to make eye contact with her because sympathy isn't something I prefer. "Depression has been an issue. Living in that hushed house by myself, regularly being reminded of her everywhere I turn..."

"I can't imagine." Her hand settles on top of mine, causing a rush of warmth through my body. "Is there anything I can do?"

My honest answer is to just be around. It's been nice having someone to talk to and do things with after Carol passed. Yet, how could I ask that? Live with a guy she hardly knows just to help him curb his depression over his deceased wife? That's just too much of a request. "Keep me company for as long as you can. I know someday, you'll find a new place, but I'm delighted for you to stick around as long as you need."

God, I sound so desperate. She probably considers me as this poor broken man who needs mending, but that's not it.

"I'm ready to go home now," Emily says, yawning.

The wind has picked up, making the sixty-five-degree weather feel like the fifties. I wrap my jacket around her shoulders, and we head to the car.

Our eyes meet. "Listen, I know that tough times come and go. But for you, they've been every day since losing your wife. I won't say I know how you feel, because I couldn't possibly... but I'm here for you. Just like you've been there for us."

I hold her gaze, thinking about how great of a woman Tessa is, and there's still so much to learn about her.

On the drive back, Emily falls asleep. *Poor girl.* All that walking must have worn her out.

After the short drive home, Emily snuggles up on the couch to watch her Animal Planet special. When I head into the bedroom to change, I see four missed calls. Two from the Realtor and then one from each of my brothers.

"Mark, sorry. I was out. Got any news?"

"Great news, actually. They accepted. Closing on Tuesday."

"Just let me know the details. See you then."

I haven't mentioned this project to Tessa. The sooner the duplexes are ready, the closer it is to them leaving me. After today, I'm not prepared for that. I'm not ready to be alone again.

A knock on the door sounds "Dinner's ready."

Emily and I rush to the dining room, taking our seats, waiting to see what she has come up with this time. I don't mind keeping the fridge stocked for us, and having a home-cooked meal is well worth the time in the store picking out all kinds of ingredients. One of these days I'll make her my dad's famous California pasta.

Is it weird that Tessa and I are getting close? In such a short amount of time, I can already see myself with her. Maybe it's because we are living together, and the common ground we share. Almost like we have known each other for longer.

"I've got some great news I'd like to share." My chest tightens, and then I begin to second-guess my intentions. I don't want to tell them because that means they will be moving out, and being in this house without anyone will drive me mad. Yet, that's not something that should affect her decision to stay or go. I'll deal with my depression when it comes. Until then, I'll just enjoy the time I have left.

"Really? What?" she asks, passing me the bowl of salad.

"My brothers and I put an offer in on a set of duplexes. We close next Tuesday."

Her eyes dart at me. "I didn't take you for a rental property guy."

"Not in the slightest. It's for those like you two... people who lose their homes and have nowhere else to go."

At that moment, our eyes link, and it's like we're talking to each other telepathically.

"That's wonderful. You truly are an amazing man."

These last few days have been the best. What am I going to do when my house is quiet again? When it is just me for breakfast and dinner? It's been amazing having someone to share my love of cooking with, spend my days off with, and just laugh.

The conversation continues over dinner with her asking when I came up with the idea to buy property, and when I tell her right after her fire, she drops her fork.

"You aren't doing this just for us, are you? I mean it'll be months before the complex is ready, but we can find somewhere else to go."

"It's for anyone who needs help after a tragedy, not just fires. I told you. You can stay as long as you need."

She picks her fork back up and goes back to eating.

I want to caress her, and maybe even kiss her, but can I? Does she even want me to? Sure, I'd love to touch her skin that appears like silk, or feel her lips against mine, but the last thing I want to do is make a fool of myself. Am I truly ready to move on? Without being certain, I shouldn't lead her on. Tessa is a girl I'd only get one shot with, and I don't want to mess that up.

After dinner, we go through our nightly routine: dinner, dishes, and then a little TV. Emily ends up falling asleep on the couch.

"Listen, about what you said earlier. I'm glad we could help you out, just like you did us... but I can't help but feel like there's more to it. Us staying in your home, taking us on trips..."

I know where this is going. My chest tightens, and my palms begin to sweat, trying to choose the words carefully before I speak. "Confusing for both of us. I love my wife. A part of me always will. And despite that, I think about you. I know it's wrong, but I can't help it."

Her eyes drop to the floor. "It's not wrong. Moving on is natural; it just takes some time. And you shouldn't do it before you're ready."

There is so much I want to say, but it's better to wait until Emily is in bed so we can talk freely. "Let's finish this after she's in bed."

She looks at me and nods. "Of course."

Tessa is a beautiful woman, and as much as I'd love to feel her body against mine, the thought keeps crossing my mind that it might be too soon. How the hell am I supposed to know if I'm truly ready?

Her hand is placed on top of mine, and her eyes bore into mine. "Emily's getting very close to you. It worries me because you could leave at any moment, and she doesn't deserve to go through that again."

I inch closer, shaking my head. "I would never leave her. That's not the man I am." My voice cracks. "Even if we never become a couple, I'd always be there for you both."

Hearing Tessa voice her fears makes me think about everything in a split second. Maybe I haven't shown her the kind of man I am, but I intend to now. Emily will always have me to lean on, no matter what happens between Tessa and me. That little girl has been through enough, having her daddy skip out on her, and that's one thing she will never have to worry about with me.

"That could confuse her, though. That's what I'm trying to avoid."

Tessa looks around, almost like she's trying to hold tears back. "Emily. It's time to get ready for bed, honey. Let's go."

She gets up from the table, and I reach out for her hand, caressing it. "I'm sorry. I don't know what to say."

With tears in her eyes, leaving pale streaks on her cheeks, she walks away toward the bedroom and shuts the door.

Fuck, did I just majorly screw up? *Just make a fucking choice already and go with it.* At this point, I have no way to know if things will work out between Tess and me in the long run, but I'd be a coward if I didn't just admit my feelings.

About twenty minutes later, after leaving me stirring in my thoughts, she comes back to the table, tears gone.

"Sometimes she just doesn't want to go to sleep." She pours herself a glass of wine.

I place my hand on top of hers. "Listen, it's not always gonna be a struggle. Eventually things will get better for you two."

Could I see myself being that person she can trust? Yes, but is now the right time to bring that up? Putting myself out there, being vulnerable, is something I don't usually do, but maybe this time it's the right thing. "I would like a shot at being that person for you."

My chest rises and falls, waiting for a response from her, but she stays silent. Her eyes peer into mine, and then she responds.

"I thought that person was gonna be her dad but he bailed. And I thought maybe I was just meant to be alone. Almost every relationship I've been in ended because of him cheating or worse. I'm not sure if I'm ready to be in a relationship again, to put my heart on the line."

"Why would any man ever cheat on you?" I raise my voice, but I don't mean to. It makes my knuckles white hearing that come out of her mouth. She's beautiful, smart, and a wonderful mother from what I have seen. It just doesn't make any sense. No woman ever has to worry about me cheating because I have enough decency to end it if I'm not happy. If I feel the need to go somewhere else for sex, then whoever I'm with isn't the right person for me. End of story.

She stares at me with her luscious green eyes, almost piercing through me. A woman like her should be bursting with self-confidence, and Tessa just isn't. Whoever these guys that hurt her before are, they're fucking idiots. They have broken down a good woman.

The urge to be close to her sets in, so I lean in and kiss her. Not hard, but soft. As our lips part, a sigh escapes her throat, leaving me wanting more. I've been waiting patiently for this to happen. She has a surprised look on her face.

"I'm sorry. Maybe I shouldn't have done that." Even though her lips taste like honey and the scent of lavender body wash throws me into overdrive. "Forget that happened."

"I'm not sure I can," she says, staring at me. "Can you?"

My fingers caress her jawbone lightly. "Nope."

Our lips crash together again, and this time I don't stop there. My chair scoots closer, squeaking across the floor, and I pull her into my lap and place my hands on her hips. Fuck, does she feel good. My tongue slides effortlessly down her neck as she runs her fingers through my hair.

At that moment, a glimpse of Carol comes to mind, and my eyes start to water. Why am I seeing her right now? While kissing Tessa? Is my mind trying to tell me I'm not ready after all?

Fuck. What am I doing? Stop, you idiot. You're ruining everything!

I push her slightly off my lap and back into her chair.

"What's wrong?" She looks like I just ruined her whole evening. "Did I do something?"

Fuck. Why would she think that? She's perfect, it's just... Would Tessa want to share my heart with someone else? My head is spinning and I guess I take too long to answer because she gets up and goes to the bedroom.

What did I just do?

6

TESSA

This is exactly what I have been afraid of, getting close to him, and him not being emotionally available. It's like he wants to, but who knows. Why did I put myself in this position when I know he still loves his wife? Grief is a tricky thing, especially when it's your spouse, and the last thing I want to do is push him to move on before he's ready. Yet, the way he stares at me, and then kisses me, shows he might be more ready than he thinks. The subtle touches, the intimate glimpses into my eyes, those mean something. I guess it's best for me to be patient, get to know him on his terms, and hope that one day he'll be able to let me in. Yet, I still have these doubts that maybe we are overstaying our welcome or putting too much pressure on him.

The next morning, we wake up later than normal, and Damon has already left for work. Maybe it's for the best. We should discuss what happened last night, but later. If we aren't on the same page, I don't want my entire day to be ruined. I'm already going to have to deal with my ass of a boss, and that's enough.

"Em, it's almost time to leave. Can't be late." I raise my voice from the living room, using the dustpan to scoop up the dirt tracked in from Damon's boots.

Nothing can prepare me to go back to work today. The days off have been great, but my boss is an imbecile. As frequently as I wish to quit, it's my sole source of income, and we are already without our own place to live. No need to make matters worse.

"I'm dressed, Mama," Emily says, striding out into the living room in her pink leggings, a long-sleeve princess shirt, and fuzzy jacket picked up from Goodwill.

We lock the door behind us and head toward the school. Emily is always wanting to skip half the way, and this morning I just have no energy. I've got to start sleeping better.

As we reach the school, Emily hugs me. "Have a good day, Mama."

My walk to work leaves me deep in my thoughts. What is going to happen when we move out? Damon seems adamant that he will be around, but to what degree? He says he thinks about me, but is he really ready to move on? All I know is, he's the first good guy I've come across in three years, and he truly cares for Emily.

The automatic doors open, and I walk inside, knowing my day is about to get significantly worse.

"Where have you been?" my boss, Kevin, asks.

"My shift doesn't start for another ten minutes," I say, striding past him to the back room. His favorite thing is to bring up the fact I'm a single mom and need the job. Why does that give him the right to be an asshole?

"No, you were expected to be here at eight thirty. When's the last time you looked at the schedule?"

Admittedly, it was on my last shift before the fire when he put it up in the breakroom. Shouldn't he alert us if the schedule changes? How else would I know to be here at a different time? "Monday. It said nine. Haven't had a shift since," I counter, walking away.

"Well, it changed. So you're late. Again. If you can't be on time, then I'll find someone else to replace you. I don't accept tardiness; you know that."

I want to spit in his face, because he barely shows up except to yell at his employees. He is a complete bastard and I can't wait for the day when I don't have to see his sexist ass again. "And how was I expected to know it changed, huh? If I wasn't scheduled until now?"

"Not my problem. I don't appreciate your attitude."

I saunter away and defy the urge to flip him off while clipping my name tag on. Why does he have to be such a complete asshole all the time? He wonders why he can't keep employees; this is the reason. I punch my time card and make my way up to the register and drown him out.

"Excuse me, ma'am. Could you tell me where the chips are?" a male voice says.

"Aisle eight," I respond without looking up.

"You're Tessa, right? You remember me from the fire?"

I glance up at him. "Oh, Liam... Damon's brother."

"You and your daughter still staying with my brother? He driving you crazy yet?"

Maybe I can pick his brain about Damon, if I had time. "He's been a great help."

"Yes, you've had quite an impact on him. He seems happier with you two around."

Over the intercom, Kevin says, "Get back to work."

Liam laughs. "Have a good day. Don't want to get you in trouble."

Are you freaking kidding me? Tonight, I will start looking for another job. One that offers a little bit more money too. That would be a blessing. The only problem is I can only work during the hours of school because childcare is too costly. They really screw single parents over. It doesn't make any sense to send the kid to daycare for a hundred and fifty dollars or more a week when that's most of my paycheck, if not all. So after paying them, we wouldn't be able to afford to pay rent, insurance, or anything else.

The next few hours fly by, with no more communication from Kevin. I'm still in shock that he came over the intercom system to yell at me in front of customers. Who the hell does he think he is? Even Liam seemed put off by it.

At two thirty, I sneak to the back, clock out, and head to pick up Emily before Kevin can complain. The fellow employees hate him just as much as I do, but they're in the same position as me. They can't afford to lose their jobs, so they take it, making Kevin think it's okay to talk to us and treat us this way. Maybe we should stand up to him, make him realize he can't.

When I pick up Emily after school, the whole way home she tells me about the new girl at school from California.

"She talks different, Mama. Even dresses in all black. Is that normal for people there?"

"It might be. I've never been there. Just make her feel welcome, baby. She'll need friends to help her adjust."

When we get back to Damon's, I scan the paper, seeking to discover something that will work. I found an ad for a receptionist, but it doesn't include the hours or pay. It's worth a shot since I have experience, and anything is better than dealing with Kevin any longer than I have to.

I punch the number to the office into my phone and hit the call button. It rings a few times before a lady picks up.

"Good afternoon, thank you for calling Grapevine High School. This is Harper."

"Hello, do you know if the receptionist position is still open?"

"Yes, ma'am. In fact, he's doing some interviews today. Could you swing by around four thirty?"

"I'll be there."

A squeak escapes. I might actually get the hell away from Kevin. That is a blessing in and of itself. But wait... who would watch Emily? She couldn't go with me, but how unprofessional would that be.

Me: *Will you be home at normal time?*

This isn't something I'd normally ask anybody to do because it's my responsibility, but this could be monumental for us. I trust him with her, and we already stay in the same house. They will probably sit around watching TV in my absence anyway.

Damon: *Yes. Everything okay?*

Me: *Got a lead on a job. Wants me there at four thirty.*

Damon: *Say no more. You can take my car.*

Now that Emily is taken care of, what the hell am I going to wear? After the fire, I don't have much. Rummaging through my suitcase, the only thing I really have is black dress pants and a white blouse. That will have to do for now. There is not enough time to walk to the thrift store to buy anything else.

"Where you going, Mama?" she asks, looking over my outfit. "You look pretty."

"I might be getting a different job, sweetie."

I hope this goes well, and maybe even pays a little more than the supermarket did. Anything to get ahead of where we are. I am sick of taking two steps backward all the time. I'm just waiting for my big break.

The front door opens, and he tosses me the keys. "Good luck. We'll be fine. They will be lucky to have you."

The business is only fifteen minutes away, and I make it early to fill out an application. I have experience from a couple years ago, before accepting the supermarket job.

When I turn it in, they request me to stick around to talk to someone. Nervously, I play with my thumbs until a man comes out and calls my name. It has been a while since I did an interview, and I hope I don't tank it. *Deep breaths.*

He takes me back to his office and begins asking basic interview questions, which help me calm down, knowing I've been asked these same ones a million times.

"Your experience makes you a good fit. May I ask why you are wanting to leave your current job?" Lex asks.

I didn't prepare for that question, even though it's valid, but I can't tell him the truth about the way my boss treats us. "The hours aren't the best, and I really need better pay."

There are more questions about the software I've used, a basic typing test, and then it's almost over.

"One last question... Are you able to work nine to three?"

A smile takes over my face. "Yes, I just have to be off to pick up my daughter from school. So that would be ideal."

"Could you start tomorrow?" he asks. "I know you typically are supposed to give a two-week notice at a prior job, but we are really strug-gling right now. If you need two weeks, I'll understand."

"Nope, I can most definitely start tomorrow. I'll notify my boss tonight, but if you don't mind me asking, what is the salary?" I cross my fingers, hoping it is more than nine an hour.

"Oh, of course, sorry. We would start you out at twelve an hour. Does that work?"

Twelve dollars an hour? I can't even believe it. "That's perfect. I'll see you tomorrow at nine, sir. Thank you so much for the opportunity. You won't regret it."

I walk out of the office with my head held high, shoulders back, excited about the new adventure I'm embarking on and the raise that will be a welcome addition to Emily's and my life.

After some debating between just not showing up to work at the supermarket, I decide in person sounds much more fun. He needs to know I won't be returning. It feels like a good slap in the face after all the crappy things he said to me just earlier today. No more sexist jokes, single mom insecurities, and no more lingering eyes. He is a bona fide creep to the tenth degree.

I park in front of the market, and I begin to go over what I want to say. This is my chance to get out everything that has been bottled up for the last two years, and give him a piece of my mind. Profane language and a middle finger sound great, but I want to be classier than that. The car door opens, and I slam it behind me, marching through the automatic sliding doors, straight back to his office, and walk in without knocking. No one really knows what he does in there, and for a second I'm worried I might find him fondling himself like a pervert.

"Excuse me. You don't just walk into my office without an invitation. What the hell has gotten into you lately?"

Oh, he didn't even know the half of it.

"A lot, actually. I'm sick of the way you treat me. You're a complete ass who takes advantage of women. Yes, I'm a single mom, but I have more balls than you ever will. Fuck you!" I say and walk out of his office feeling proud, even about using the vulgar language.

He follows me. "What are you talking about? How do you plan on feeding that kid of yours? Huh? Don't be stupid... no one else will hire you."

A laugh escapes as I turn around to face him. "Actually... I got a new job today. Paying more than you do and more hours. Plus, the boss isn't a complete asshole and perv. Have a nice night, Kevin."

He's still talking to me when the automatic doors open and close, and I don't give a rat's ass what Kevin has to say at this point. He isn't someone I have to deal with anymore. And I couldn't be happier about that.

Pulling up into Damon's driveway, I take a minute before going inside. My life has gotten better since meeting Damon, but that might not be directly correlated. I found a friend, saved up some money, and now I found a new job that will make a huge difference in the way Emily and I live going forward. I still feel the need to thank him.

The front door closes behind me, and Emily runs up to me for a hug.

"How did it go, Mommy? Did you get it?"

I try to hide my smile to throw them off my scent, but I failed.

"I take it you got the job?" Damon asks.

"I start tomorrow, and it pays more. I'm still in shock. Thanks for watching her."

He embraces me, and my feet lift off the ground as we twirl around and celebrate.

"See. I told you things would get better. Just gotta believe in yourself," he says before placing a kiss on my lips that leave me confused once again.

Why is he doing this? Just last night, he pulled me in and made me think he finally realized he's ready to move on, and then he pushed me off his lap and rejected me. The utter shit feeling after that caused me to get no rest.

I push away from him and migrate to the dining room to eat the lasagna Damon prepared, and then go through our nightly routine. Once done, I explain to Emily that things are finally looking up for us, and soon we will have our own place again.

"But why would we leave here? It's a perfect place. We are both so happy here..."

I've been worried about this happening, with all the bonding those two have done together, but we can't stay here forever. The last thing I want to do is overstay our welcome. "This wasn't permanent. Only temporary, sweetheart."

"But... then how will I see Damon?"

A tear falls from my eye. "Well..." I look over at him.

"You don't have to worry about that. It's not like you'll never see me again, booger. You can come visit me whenever you want, plus we will have to go to that zoo again. Right?"

Emily nods.

My heart breaks, realizing my daughter is attached to him. But Damon also has a bond with her that is beautiful to witness.

I**t's** my first day at my new job and I'm ready for a fresh adventure. This will be something new and exciting for me. Normally I sleep in until six thirty, but I find myself wide awake at five.

I'm determined to do the best I can at this job, so it can possibly turn into a full-time gig down the line. Eventually, I will need to work more than part-time to be able to afford the things I want to provide Emily.

A door opens, and now that I know Damon is awake, it's time for me to get up and move around. I want to make breakfast this morning— nothing major, just bacon and eggs. But anything to continue to show our appreciation for his hospitality.

"Good morning, how'd you sleep?" I ask Damon, holding out the cup of coffee I made for him.

"Better than I normally do."

I miss having someone to snuggle with and keep me warm in the winter months. When Emily's father left, the first few weeks were lonely, even if I hated his guts. Sleeping in our bed just wasn't the same without him. How lonely Damon must feel sleeping in his bed all alone?

I make myself a cup of coffee and get the items out of the fridge for breakfast. Damon sits in the living room watching the news while I cook.

"Good morning," Emily says, walking out of the bedroom in her pajamas and making her way to plop down right next to Damon on the couch.

"Breakfast is served. Eat while it's hot."

We gather around the table, some of us more awake than others.

"So, will you still be able to pick me up from school?"

"Of course, same as always."

I'm lucky the job hours didn't extend until after school. I have no one else to pick her up. Even though Damon would kindly do it if asked.

"All right, breakfast was delicious, but duty calls. Good luck today. And have a wonderful day at school. I'll see you after work," Damon says, giving Emily a huge hug before walking out the door.

Not too sure what to wear today, I throw on those same black slacks and white blouse.

"How do I look?"

"Beautiful," Emily replies. "What about me?"

"Gorgeous."

We head out the door and to the elementary school to drop her off, and then I continue on the road to my new job.

As I walk in the door, Harper greets me. "Good morning, Tessa. I'll be training you. Have a seat."

There is some paperwork that I have to fill out first before getting started on learning the ropes around here. The phones are easy to learn, and the computer system isn't that complicated. It seems this is going to be easier than I thought. The environment isn't toxic like the supermarket and having a boss that isn't a complete prick is fantastic.

Harper is around the same age as me, maybe early thirties, I think. She asks me some questions to get to know me, seeing as we will be working together. I find out I'm actually her replacement because next semester she is taking over as the chemistry teacher. Apparently, she moved here from California and has been helping out as the receptionist until the teacher position starts.

"Don't worry. Lex is very nice and isn't gonna be up your ass. As long as you do your job, you will barely hear from him," she says.

After December, I will be by myself up here, so that gives me some time to learn the ropes to make Harper feel okay about leaving me unattended.

I am her shadow today, watching her send faxes, answer emails and the phones, and greet each person that comes into the office.

Around eleven, we break for lunch and talk some more.

"So did you major in chemistry? Just wondering why you would choose chemistry as your subject of choice."

Harper replies, "It's actually quite an interesting subject, although I would have been okay teaching biology or earth science too."

I don't see a ring on her finger, so I assume she is single. "Any kids?"

"Nope, haven't found the right guy yet. Maybe someday. You?"

"Yeah, I have a six-year-old girl named Emily. We've been on our own most of our life, but I just started seeing this wonderful guy."

"Details. Come on," Harper pushes.

She seems so cool, and it's nice to have someone to hang out with and talk to. I never really have had time to socialize much. "He's a fire-fighter, tall, dark, and unbelievably handsome."

"Sounds like my kind of guy. He got any hot brothers?" she asks.

"Yeah, two. Don't know much about them yet though."

"Well, let me know if they are looking. But none of that friends with benefits or sex on the side stuff. I'm not that kind of girl."

She cracks me up, and even though I've only known her for the day, it feels like we are already friends. Maybe we will continue to hang out even after she moves to teaching. Until then, I'll just enjoy lunch and gossiping.

The rest of the afternoon is slow with barely any visitors. Three o'clock rolls around and I thank Harper for training me, give her my number, and head on my way to pick up Emily. Even just the walk feels different, like I'm finally going somewhere in life.

"Mama!"

Emily is always so happy to see me and I hope that never changes. We hop and skip back to Damon's house, where I change into something more comfortable and join Emily on the couch to watch some TV before he gets home and we plan dinner.

The little times we have to spend together mean the most. In six or seven more years, when she's a teenager, she won't want anything to do with me, so I have to take advantage of it while I can.

"I'm home," he says, coming in the door. "How did your first day go?"

I smile. "Perfect. I think I'm really going to like it there."

He goes to his room to change and comes out in dark jeans and a button-up.

"What are you getting all dressed up for?" *Not that I mind, he looks scrumptious.*

"Well, I'd like to take you out to dinner to celebrate. So, you two better go get dressed."

At first, I want to say no since he has already done so much. "Are you sure? We can save money and just eat here."

"I'm not hard-pressed for money and would like to take you guys out. Don't worry about it. Just have fun."

Damon blinks hard when we both come out. I put on a black dress, and Emily a yellow one.

"Wow, I'm one lucky guy."

In the car, I catch him glancing down my body, taking in the dress that hugs my shape in just the right way. It's these subtle glances that leave me anticipating more from him. His eyes keep taking me in, even walking into the restaurant and when sitting down at the table.

"So, let's use tonight to get to know each other better. Like... What's your ideal career?"

"I don't really know. When I was younger, my dream was to become a kindergarten teacher."

"Interesting. I could see that. Where do you see yourself in ten years?"

Why is he asking so many weird questions? "Hopefully with a stable place to live, a good job, and maybe married." Once I say it out loud, I figure how cliché it sounds. Every girl dreams of the perfect man and marriage.

"I don't think there's anything wrong with wanting to be married... as long as you are with the right person and they treat you well." He looks over to Emily. "What about you, little one? What do you want to be when you grow up?"

"Just like you. I want to help people."

Damon seems shocked by her response and even sheds a little tear. "Wow, I'm honored."

"I think you and Mommy will be married in ten years... at least I hope..." Emily explains.

We look at each other, seemingly awkward now. "I don't know about that, sweetie."

Our eyes lock on each other, wondering if the other is stepping back. I honestly don't know what Damon wants at this point. He's so hot and cold, and I can't get a read on him. One minute he's kissing me, then the next he's shoving me off. *Make up your fucking mind already.*

"I know, but you're both so happy... I just wish it could stay that way..."

Emily is a young girl, but she is intuitive for sure. I couldn't refute that since staying with Damon, she seems happier. Hell, we all are.

Will Damon choose to move forward or keep rejecting me?

7

DAMON

Today, October 29, will always hold meaning in my heart. It's the day I lost my wife and I take it off every year. It normally has me stuck on the couch for the first few hours, remembering all the great times, and then mourning her loss all over again.

"Good morning." Emily runs out of the bedroom.

"Morning, sweetie."

I'm not as chipper as I normally am, and I think she can tell. Instead of asking me what's wrong, she crawls up on the couch and hugs me. How can anyone be depressed with her around?

Tessa is in the kitchen making breakfast and hasn't asked either. Probably for the best. It's going to be a long, hard day for me.

"Breakfast is ready."

Sitting down at the table, I am not in a lively mood. I try not to show it too much because I don't want them to worry.

"So, you're off today, huh? Got any plans?"

Well, I guess that cat's out of the bag. Lying isn't an option. "It's the anniversary of Carol's death."

Silence takes over the room, and everyone eats without speaking a word. I didn't mean to make them feel uncomfortable.

"If you'll excuse me."

I make my way to the bedroom to get dressed so I can run my errands before going to visit her.

"I'll see you guys later. Have a good day at school, Em."

As I get into my car, my chest begins to tighten, old memories of Carol and me seeping into my brain. How we met. Our wedding and honeymoon. Some of the happiest memories I had with her were by my side. Why did she have to be taken from me so early in life? We were supposed to grow old together, raise our kids, and then spoil our grand-babies. Except none of that happened because cancer decided to take her so young.

I back out of my driveway and head to my first stop, Paul's Bakery. They know me pretty well there, as I used to go there every Sunday and get a blueberry scone and surprise her for breakfast, but now I get it to take with me. Next, Stella's Flower Shop for a new arrangement to put on her grave, and they have it ready for me so I don't have to wait around. Carol was well loved in the community and volunteered her time to many organizations in Grapevine.

The most surreal moment is when I pull up to the cemetery and memories begin to flood my mind, of her funeral, seeing her lowered into the ground, knowing it was the last time I would see her. Tears leave behind streaks on my face as I try to man up and keep it together. Hesitation hits me, like it does every year, whether I should visit or not. Many people say visiting a grave of a loved one only dredges up bad emotions, but to me it's the one time a year I can converse with her like she's still here with me. *You can do this.* I open the car door and shut it behind me, then walk to her grave, placing the box with her favorite scone and the flowers on top.

"I really miss you, darling. Every day."

I like to think that she can hear me in the afterlife and watches over me. Carol truly was my best friend.

"The pain of losing someone you love never gets easier. Even after these past few years. My heart hurts like someone is squeezing it, trying to rip it out of my chest. What I would do to have you back in my arms... just for a few minutes."

I take a seat on the grass next to her grave and unravel everything that's going on in my life.

"This year has been tough. Everything reminds me of you. And every day I wonder what my life would be like if you hadn't passed. How happy we would be... probably with kids running around the house. Oh, how I wish you were here..."

Sometimes I think about how different my life would be if she were still alive. Would we have had kids? How many? Would we still be happily married? Everything in my mind points to a solid yes, but life sometimes throws you curveballs. I like to think that Carol and I would have beat the odds. Together forever.

"I've got someone living with me... a single mom who lost every-thing... Her daughter, Emily, is the sweetest girl. You would love her. I'm trying to keep my promise to you, but it's harder than I thought. Having them around has helped with my depression. Having someone to come home to and to share meals with."

Sharing this wouldn't upset her because on her deathbed, she told me not to be a recluse and let others into my heart, but it's harder than she thinks. My feelings are growing for Tess, but I don't know what to do with them. It's like my body wants her so badly, but my mind is screwing me. When we kissed the other night, I saw Carol in my head and it ruined the moment for me.

"I know I promised you I would open my heart, but I don't think I'm ready. I still love you. With all my heart. How could I fall in love with someone else? Open my heart to someone when you still have it?"

I know she can't respond, but it feels good to talk to her about it. Let her know I'm still thinking about her.

"I love you, baby. Always have, always will," I say, walking back to the car.

Things have changed since last year, and I believe Carol already knew that. I like to think she watches over me from up there. So she must know about them and how my heart has expanded since the fiery disas-ter. When Emily mentioned going to a shelter, I couldn't let that happen. Those are last resort places, and they had me. No way was I letting them sleep on a cot when I had a perfectly good bedroom for them to occupy until she got back on her feet.

Looking back, maybe I didn't see the bond already starting to form on that first night, but it crept up on me until I couldn't deny it. They make me feel at home, and I haven't felt that way in my house since Carol passed.

The drive home is silent until my phone rings.

"Hey, what's up?"

"You ready to sign the paperwork? I can come by and pick you up. I wasn't sure if you were done visiting Carol or not," Liam asks.

"I'm done. Be home in fifteen."

Liam and Aiden are already waiting for me when I pull up. We ride together in Liam's truck, drop by the bank to get our money orders, and head to see Mark. We are ready to take on our new adventure together as a family.

"Can you believe we are actually doing this?" Aiden says, sitting in the back of the truck. "I never thought I'd do something like this, but that's what I have you guys for, to keep me grounded."

"I knew we would do something good with the money... just not to this capacity."

Liam is quiet.

"You okay over there? You haven't said a word," I ask, looking over at him.

"Just got someone who could really use a place right now. How long until tenants can move in?"

"Well, technically, it's livable once we turn on utilities. So, by the end of the day tomorrow, maybe," I answer.

Liam worked a fire two days ago where a woman lost her child and dog. She desperately needs somewhere to stay and has no one.

"Good. I'll swing by the shelter tonight and see if she's there," Liam states.

Liam pulls up to Mark's office and parks, then we jump out of the truck. *This is it. No turning back.* Once we sign these papers, we will officially be property owners.

"Hey, look who it is... the infamous Jackson trio. Haven't seen you boys in a while. How are things?" Mark says, gesturing for us to have a seat.

We all look at each other before Liam responds, "We're just ready to get this up and running. Let's get down to business, shall we?"

Mark pulls out the paperwork, and we each take our turn signing.

After we hand over the money, he dangles the keys. "Here you are, rock stars. Enjoy."

We leave in a hurry to make it down to the utilities office to get everything turned on and ready to go for tenants.

"Hey, uh... so we didn't think about something," Aiden says.

"What?" Liam asks.

"Furniture. The people that are going to be staying won't have anything. Maybe we should get at least some basic furniture in and go from there. The last thing we want is for them to be reminded of all the things they lost, right?" Aiden responds.

My brother is showing the kind side to him we haven't seen in a long time. It's refreshing to see, and it makes me smile.

After getting the utilities scheduled to be turned on tonight, we head to the Furniture Outlet.

The duplexes already have stoves, microwaves, and refrigerators, so that's off the list. We decide on getting bedroom sets for each duplex, since it's cheaper than buying separately, and a kitchen table plus chairs. We want these people to feel at home when staying here, even if it's for a little while.

"Can we have these items delivered? We just bought a property and have some families that really need to move in tomorrow that have lost their houses to a fire. We'd like the furniture to be there before they move in," Aiden says, pulling out his debit card.

"Of course. We can have it delivered tomorrow morning. Will someone be available at the property between eight and ten?"

"Yes, I'll be there. That would be perfect," Aiden responds.

He's off tomorrow, and he can get everything settled while we are at work.

More money is spent than we initially expected, but whoever moves in will have everything they need. Liam even offers to give Aiden some money to pick up some essentials for the duplexes tomorrow like linens, cups, plates, and bowls.

Liam takes us back to the house to grab our cars and we head to the bar. This requires a celebratory drink. A drink turns into two. The memories we share of our parents have us smiling and laughing. The way our mom always used to wake us up an hour before we needed to be up because it took forever to get out of bed. Or how our father would take us fishing every Saturday he had off, and we'd spend the whole day fishing and joking around. Things like that, we really miss.

"I think they would be proud of us today. You know how they always wanted to make a difference. Well, their money helped us do that," Aiden says.

"Cheers to that."

All the bottles clink.

I wonder what Tessa and Emily are doing right now.

Me: *I'm out with my brothers. Just signed the finalized paperwork. Duplexes are officially ours!*

Tessa has become like my best friend, and it's nice to have someone in my life that I can spend time with. Now I can see where this can lead for us, and with her living in the duplex, it will be easier for her not to feel obligated to say yes when I ask her out.

Tessa: *Congratulations. Looks like you will finally be able to help people like you always wanted. Proud of you. Carol would be too.*

I love that I can talk about my wife with her. Aiden and Liam always tell me it's time to move on. They just don't understand what it's like for me. All those years spent with Carol, happy, dreaming up our future together to have it all taken away. How do you move on from that? From the person you thought you were going to spend the rest of your life with?

"Earth to Damon." Liam claps his hand down on my shoulder. "You still here?"

I laugh. "Sorry. I guess I'm a little tired is all. Been one hell of a day."

Aiden can go out and party after work until three in the morning. I can't. I'm the oldest and I'm normally asleep by ten. My brothers like to refer to me as the old man sometimes. A little joke between the three of us.

"You better head home... Is Tessa still staying there?"

"Until the duplexes are ready. Sure is."

"You guys getting close?"

"I know what you are referring to, and no, we are not sleeping together." When will my brothers give up? "I'm gonna head out. My eyes are getting a little droopy and start time comes faster than you think."

I promised Emily we would watch the Animal Planet special on monkeys. No way am I going to disappoint her on possibly her last night with me.

"I'm home. Just in time for... monkeys," I say, taking off my coat and hanging it up.

"We were just waiting for you, bigshot. Saved you a spot right here," Tessa says, patting the seat next to Emily.

Nights are just as they have been since they began staying with me. Lots of laughter and smiling. What am I going to do when they move into the duplex? My nights will go back to just me and *Chicago Fire*. What a sad world that will be.

AIDEN: *All right. They helped get the furniture into the duplexes. That's done. I'll go ahead and put all the stuff up before I leave. It'll be ready for your friend and Liam's to come stay tonight if they want.*

Me: *Thanks, bro. I'm glad you were off. I'll let Liam know.*

Liam and I are sitting around the table, playing cards.

"It'll be ready to go tonight. Might let your friend know."

He gets up and pulls the phone out of his pocket. "I'm gonna call her now. Thanks."

I'm not looking forward to the conversation when I get home, telling Tessa that it's finally ready for her. I don't want her to think she has to leave, but I don't want her to feel like she has to stay. It's like a teeter-totter... already trying to balance between the two. I don't want to lead her on, but I don't want her to leave either.

Then there's Emily. I can't fathom not having her around every morning and night. It truly brightens my day, and I want it to stay that way.

Liam comes back to the table. "She'll be there around seven tonight. I told her I'd meet her there with the key."

"Well, it's quitting time anyway. Go home and shower first."

"Planning to."

I head home to have the dreaded conversation.

"I have some news... Where are you?" I ask, my voice carrying from the living room.

Emily replies, "In the kitchen."

The aroma of whatever concoction Tessa has cooked this time and the laughter from Emily make me stop for a minute. This could very well be the last night I get to enjoy this, and I'm going to soak it in.

"How was work?" Tessa asks as I sit down at the table.

I shrug my shoulder. "Uneventful, but the duplexes are officially ready."

"We're leaving?" Emily asks, staring up at her mom.

Tessa brushes her hand through her hair. "It was going to happen eventually, sweetie. We can't stay here forever. It's just not logical."

"I didn't say you had to leave. You're more than welcome to stay here as long as you like. But if you feel you need to go somewhere else, the duplex will be there waiting for you," I say, keeping my eyes focused on the floor. I can't make direct eye contact with her because then she will be able to see how much this is killing me inside.

"Please. We can stay. He just said so," Emily says, running over to me and engulfing me in a hug. "I never want to leave. Damon's my best friend. Why can't we just stay here forever?"

The tears start leaking from everybody's eyes. I wish nothing more than to have them next to me all the time.

"Emily, why don't you go get ready for bed and lie down so we can talk for a minute."

She stomps off to the bedroom.

Tessa wipes her eyes and takes a drink of her wine. "Listen, we have both enjoyed staying here, and your company, but I can't keep going down this road. Emily's becoming attached to you... and so am I..."

Without words, her body language and glances tell me all I need to know. "Tess—"

"No, please. Let me finish." She cuts me off. "I know you're not ready, and again I understand. But I can't keep waking up in the same house as you every morning and going to bed every night with you in the next room. It would be easier if we were living separately, more like friends, since that's what you want to be."

I want to pull her close, apologize for my idiocy, and tell her how every time she smiles at me, my heart beats faster. "I completely understand. You and Emily have completely brightened up my life since you stepped in it..."

"And..."

"I guess what I am trying to say is..." I can't find the right words, so instead I get a little bit closer to her, and say, "I'd like to show you."

My lips touch hers and there isn't time to stop. Even though I've been in denial, this is exactly what I need. *Her.*

"You should think about this," Tessa says, easily backing away.

"What do you mean?" I shake my head.

"Are you absolutely sure you want to be with me? No more rejections. You have to open up to me all the way, and let us in. For all three of our sakes."

Right now, all I can think about is getting closer, rubbing my nose along her neck and taking in that sweet lavender scent. Her beautiful green eyes captivate me, and I can't seem to get enough of her. I keep asking myself if I should back away and give it some time to see if it's just us living together making these feelings appear or if she is supposed to become a huge part of my life. I hope for the latter because Tessa is one hell of a woman. Just thinking about someone else touching her makes my knuckles turn white.

"Tess, it's you. Ever since I saw you in that grocery store, I haven't been able to stop thinking about you. It's time for me to move on and follow my heart."

It is only moments later that she begins to scoot closer on the couch to me. *Come on, a little more.* Her eyes keep darting from my lower half to my eyes, and I can tell she is obviously thinking along the same lines as me.

What am I waiting for? Just fucking do it, you pussy. Get in there and get your girl.

My lips land on hers as they part and invite my tongue inside, leaving my hands caressing her back as they skim down her spine.

She inches closer, practically straddling me now, and I put my left hand around the back of her neck, making it easier for her to move on top of me as we moan in unison.

"Are you sure you wanna do this?" she says, almost out of breath.

Instead of replying, I put her on her back, tear my t-shirt off, and climb on top of her. "I'd like nothing more than to feel you quiver around me tonight."

A low squeal escapes her throat as I begin kissing her neck, then slowly downward until I reach her breasts. I lightly bite her hard nipple and look up at her. Without saying anything, she removes her shirt and bra, leaving me breathless as I stare at some of the most beautiful boobs I've ever seen. Too big to fit in my hand, but I bet they'll fit in my mouth. And so I do, sucking and licking, throwing her into a frenzy.

"Don't stop," she says, slightly pushing me downward.

"I think I know what you need," I say, kissing from her breasts to her belly button.

"And what is that?"

My reply is simple. I pull her shorts and panties off and bite the inside of her thigh. She arches herself up, taking in the scene of me licking her clit, and throws her head back. "Fuck."

Without stopping, I hand her a couch pillow to put over her face, knowing it's obvious she is going to be loud when I fuck her in a minute.

My tongue circles her clit, and my nails dig into her thighs. "You're getting close. Do you want to come from my tongue or my dick?"

She removes the pillow and squeals. "You. Now!"

That could mean either, so without clarification, I slide my sweatpants off and ease into her, hearing her let out a breath as I enter. "You are so wet, Tess."

I leave one hand gripping the pillow in front of her face, and raise the other one above her head as I go nice and slow, working up to my max.

"Tell me what you want, Tess. Anything, it's yours," I say, sliding in and out of her with my eyes closed, enjoying the sounds of her moans.

"Faster."

"Is that it?" I say, picking up the tempo as requested. She grips the pillow harder, and her thighs begin to tremble. "Not yet."

"Don't stop. Please!"

The tempo picks back up, in and out, as I savor the feeling of her walls clenching around me. It almost sends me over the edge, but then she writhes underneath me.

"I'm sorry. It's been a while," she says, removing the pillow from her face. "Let me take care of you now."

She slides her naked body across the couch and then sinks to her knees, her tongue circling around my tip. My head flies back. "I knew you couldn't stay away for long."

She smiles, looking up at me through her lashes. "I'm gonna make you come so hard."

Just hearing the words escape from her mouth nearly have me, as she goes back to claiming me, all of me in her mouth without any reflex. *Fuck, this girl is like a magician. No one has ever been able to deep-throat me. Kudos.* It's just what I need to erupt all over her. "Fuck, Tess. Where have you been?"

"Right under your nose the whole time."

I pull her into my embrace, her head on my chest and my fingers going up and down on her arm. "Do you think this could work? Like really work?"

She looks up at me. "We won't know until we try. Plus, after that, I'm not giving up on us so easily. I want that for the rest of my life."

8

TESSA

Today is Halloween and one of Emily's favorite holidays. After what happened yesterday, I will need to think long and hard about what that means for our living situation, but it's on the back burner until tomorrow.

"So, are you excited for tonight?" I ask Emily.

"When are we going to get my princess costume?"

"After breakfast. Make sure you eat," Damon replies.

We haven't had a chance to really talk about what went on last night, but right now my focus is on my daughter and making this a great holiday for her. Every year we usually find her a costume at Goodwill, almost always a princess, and then I dress up too.

"What are you gonna be?" she asks, looking straight at Damon.

"Oh, you want me to dress up too?"

"You and Mom could be. Hmm. Maybe Cinderella and Prince Charming? Mommy looks pretty in blue."

Her reference only makes me laugh, and then Damon is staring at me. "That's a great idea. We will see what we can find."

After breakfast is over, we all get dressed and head out to obtain costumes. There are too many to choose from at this point, but Emily finds an Elsa dress and falls in love with it.

"Can I get this one? It's perfect."

"Sure thing. You want to help your mom and me find one?"

She nods and heads over to the adult costume section, which has a lot more to choose from than the kids. Weird. As she is sifting through, I see a lot of inappropriate costumes, but she doesn't even notice, and then she comes across this blue princess dress.

"This one." She grabs it off the low rack and hands it to me and then continues to look for something for Damon.

There isn't really anything Prince Charming like, so she settles for a Robin Hood costume.

"Please tell me I don't have to wear tights."

"It's part of the costume. Get into the Halloween spirit," I say, laughing, imagining him and his junk in some spandex.

He shakes his head and takes the costume only to make Emily happy.

After checking out, we go home to get some cleaning done before heading out to go trick-or-treating.

"How much longer until we leave?" Emily asks.

"About an hour, sweetie. Just waiting on the last load of laundry to be dry so I can fold it."

This will be her first year having someone other than me to celebrate with, and the fact that it's Damon makes it all that more special. All he wants to do is make her happy, even if it means wearing green spandex for a few hours.

Emily puts on her dress and twirls around, staring at herself in the mirror. And then I do the same. My costume could have been a size up to be more comfortable, but I wouldn't dare complain in front of her.

"How the heck do they expect men to walk in these..." I hear Damon say from the other bedroom.

"Having trouble in there?"

"They are so constricting. How do women wear these?"

Emily and I go to the living room and wait for him to be finished, and when he comes out, I try to hold in my surprise. The costume is sexy, but he is right. The leggings are really tight, and you can see his junk imprint through them.

"Maybe you should take those off and just wear jeans underneath?" I say, wondering if he noticed.

My eyes just keep staring at his bulge, giving me flashbacks of last night. His hands all over me, making me scream and beg for more.

"You should definitely take those off. Best for all of us." I wink at him.

He comes back out wearing some jeans underneath the Robin Hood top, and it's much more appropriate for children. "Perfect."

Emily tugs on my hand, and we walk out the door and down the driveway. His neighborhood has many houses with their lights on, even though it's not dark yet; there are plenty of kids already going house to house asking for candy.

Damon and I watch as she walks up to the door by herself, and after a couple streets her bag is already full.

"What's our rule?" I ask.

"Once a bag is full, we head home," she replies, head down, walking back toward Damon's house.

I might be a Debbie Downer, but no kid needs multiple bags of candy.

Damon and Emily hold hands as we trek back home. Then we start supper. We keep our porch light off so we don't confuse any trick-or-treaters.

"So, how was your first Emily Halloween experience?" I ask, adding the milk and butter to the potatoes.

"I didn't have to wear the tights, so it was better than I expected." He laughs.

With Emily in the living room on the couch, now might be a good time to discuss our living arrangements. The duplex is our best option and will give us the space we need to relieve some of the pressure of living together.

"About the duplex."

"You've decided?" he asks, running his fingers through his hair.

His eyes are searching mine frantically, almost like he might never see me again.

"I think it's best if we stay somewhere else. Us staying here has made you open up, and while that's great, if we are gonna see where this goes, then it's best if we live separately."

His eyes close briefly, and then Emily comes in.

We drop it for now because it's not something we need to discuss in front of her.

"Let's eat," I say, taking the dishes into the dining room.

He doesn't need to worry; us moving out doesn't mean I'm going to stop seeing him. I'd love nothing more than to see where this can go.

After dinner, he carries our suitcase to the car and comes back in.

"Are you ready to go? Anything else you are forgetting?" he asks, lingering by the front door.

Emily is crying, and maybe I've made the wrong decision, but we have to move out eventually.

The short ride over is silent except for Emily's sobbing.

As we pull up to the duplex, he hands over the key and carries our suitcase inside.

"Please let me know if you need anything," he says before closing the door behind him.

My mind is scrambling, going back through the time spent with Damon. *The best fucking sex of my life.*

"Mama, are we going back?"

"No, honey. We'll stay here. It's nice, isn't it?"

Hell, it's nicer than our old apartment by a long shot. The bedroom set is charming and out of our price range. How much he cares is one of the things that really drew me to him fast. I didn't meet many people like that.

"Mr. Damon is nice. He got this for us. We should thank him."

"Maybe tomorrow. Go in there and try to get some sleep."

"No TV?"

Emily has a nightly routine, watching Animal Planet on the couch. "Sorry, bug. Want to color until bed? I didn't forget them..."

"No, I'm feeling tired. Good night, Mama," Emily says, carrying her blanket to the bedroom and shutting the door.

After a few minutes, I can hear my little girl sobbing in the room.

A knock on the door startles me.

"It's me. Can we talk, please?" Damon says.

I close my eyes and let out a soft sigh. "Come on in."

Damon looks around. "Emily in bed?"

"Yes, she's not too happy with me right now."

He takes a seat on the couch, brushing his hands together. *Just spit it out.* "I need to talk to you."

"It's okay. We had sex. It doesn't have to mean anything," I say, offering some distance between us.

"No. That's not it. I'm trying to find the right words," Damon says, shooting his fingers through his hair. "The night Carol passed..."

"That's the whole reason we're here instead of at your house. Your wife was your best friend, lover, and the person you thought you would die next to..."

"Let me finish. The afternoon of her passing. She made me promise something."

"What?"

"Not to run away from love or from someone who can help open my heart again. Honestly, I never thought I'd meet someone like that. Until I first saw you. Tonight opened my eyes to realize how much you and Emily mean to me. The thought of losing you pushed me over the edge. My life would never be the same without you. The two months you've been here have been the happiest I've been since Carol passed."

I don't utter a word or move a muscle. I just stand there like my feet are bricks of cement. Did he really just say that? Am I dreaming?

"I don't expect you to come back to live with me. If we are going to start a relationship, then we should do it the right way. But I want you to know I'm all in."

I still don't utter a word.

Damon makes his way to the front door, opens it, and says, "Good night, beautiful."

I want to run after him, but I don't. It's a gigantic step for him, and even more so, moving on from Carol. I know how much he still loves her and that he always will. And I will never try to make him forget about her. She is a huge part of his life and the reason he is the man that I like.

A man like Damon is worth waiting for, and I know in my mind that eventually we can have a happily ever after. But rushing it could have detrimental consequences too.

WHEN MY ALARM goes off at five thirty, I haven't slept a wink. A part of me also wonders why it takes us leaving for him to admit his feelings to himself. But then, thinking back to how his life was before we came along, he was alone.

Sitting on my couch, drinking my cup of joe, I miss him. Even the interaction with him while drinking our coffee every morning or the conversations over breakfast. It just isn't the same without him around.

Sitting there, I know he will be awake by now. I pull out my phone and start typing him a message. I delete it twice and begin writing again.

Me: *I want to give you some time. You feel you've made your decision. I get that. But...*

Me: *Emily is young, and she really likes you. I have to think about her feelings in this too.*

She's young and it has already broken her heart when her father left. As much as it pains me to say, I don't want her to lose another man in her life. Maybe that's why I've been so put off about the idea of even dating in the past. It's rough, and you never know if it will last. But with Damon, there isn't a doubt in my mind. We mesh so well together already, and there is a friendship in place.

Damon: *I understand. But I know what I want... It's you two... without any doubt.*

Tess: *100%?*

I sit on the couch waiting for his reply, but nothing. Did he need to think about it again? The clock shows six already, which means I'll be getting Emily up in a little under an hour.

I hear a brief, quiet knock on the door. *Who the heck is here so early?* I open the door to find Damon with a box in his hands.

"What are you doing here?"

"I brought breakfast," he says, placing the donuts on the counter.

"Listen." He gets closer to me, putting his hands around my waist. "I'm going to say this again. You are what I want. I can't lose you. Please know how serious I am."

I look into his eyes and curl my hands over his shoulders. "I needed you to be sure."

He pulls me in for a kiss that is sweet and passionate. Our eyes remain closed as we explore each other's hungry mouths. Shivers run through my entire body from head to toe, and I can't imagine that every kiss could be like ours. It isn't too wet or too dry.

As he pulls away, it steals my breath. He leaves me wanting more.

The clock shows six fifteen and since he brought donuts, we have about half an hour until we have to wake up Emily.

"Where you going? We've got time." He pulls me back in for another kiss; this time his hands wander down my back.

"But I barely know you." I laugh.

"Would you like to get to know me more?" he asks, his voice filled with desire.

As I nod, he starts inching me toward the second bedroom, luckily not knocking down anything on our way.

He quietly shuts the door, and we proceed to the bed. "Right now, I just want to focus on you."

My nightgown comes off over my head and into his hands as he raises an eyebrow when he notices I'm not wearing any underwear.

"Were you planning on me coming back this morning? 'Cause you look prepared."

But before I can respond, he's between my thighs, giving me the pleasure I have been missing. Yearning for. My body relaxes while his tongue moves faster.

"Use the pillow..."

My face is covered now, but I know it's only a matter of time until I combust from the overwhelming sensation burning in my stomach. As his finger pushes inside of me, making me moan, it leaves me writhing around, begging for more.

"I want more." My voice shakes.

I can feel the buildup coming, and as much as I want to let go, relax and enjoy, I can't. He should get to feel the same pleasure as me.

"I want you."

Instead of complying with my request, another finger is inside me, working in sync with his tongue until I'm on the cusp. My entire body tenses.

"Don't. Let it come. Please," he says, his voice growing deep.

"I… am… gonna…"

A loud moan, even through the pillow, erupts as I tighten around his fingers.

"See. You gotta let go," he says, lying down next to me.

The euphoria of an orgasm is like seeing stars on the ceiling. I still wonder why he didn't give me what I wanted. He deserves to receive pleasure, and especially after what I just experienced. It's nice to have someone who didn't just think of themselves for once. There have been men who were only worried about their release in the past, and Damon is definitely not one of those guys.

I sit up, a hand on my forehead. "I can't believe I just did that with her in the next room. What if she heard me?"

He laughs, looking at his watch. "I'm sure if she did, there would be a knock at the door, but it's time to get her up."

We both get off the bed, and he hands me my nightgown.

"I'll go get Emily up. She'll be excited to see you."

Walking out of the bedroom, I'm happy. It's like an instant light, and I can see how happy we can be. We could have this amazing, joyous feeling around all the time.

I nudge Emily. "It's time to get up, sweetie. Someone's here to see you and brought breakfast."

Her eyes fly open, and she is off the bed in a jiff.

"Damon. You're here," Emily says, running to him. "I missed you."

He looks at me. "I missed you too. But I'm not going anywhere."

This changes things, but for the better. He finally decided, and he chose us. Sure, there is always a chance it might not work, but if you go into every relationship thinking that way, then how will it ever succeed?

We share a bond I haven't felt with anyone before. And it isn't just sexual. His heart is enormous. That is what I like so much about him, his sense of caring for others, and not only himself.

Then, of course, his immediate bond with Emily. She never takes to strangers like she did with him. They are best friends from the first hug, and that just overwhelms my heart.

At first, I questioned my decision about moving into his place, but if I would have declined his offer, and we stayed at the shelter, I never would have gotten to know this wonderful man. Emily would have never experienced the incredible bond.

She sits eating her blueberry glazed donut with Damon, while I get ready for work, slipping on a pencil skirt with a blue blouse. That'll do.

"All right, it's time to head to school," I say, heels in hand. "Never been late, and never will be."

"I'm off. Can I give you a ride?" he asks insistently.

I nod. It is better than walking barefoot until I get to work. There is no way I'm walking the entire way in heels.

After dropping Emily off, I want to talk about this morning.

I bite my lip, thinking about this morning, and his hand brushes against my thigh.

"Whatcha thinking about over there?" he asks, smiling.

I don't reply. Honestly, all I want is to pull over and screw him in this car right here and now.

"I've been thinking since you drove her to school, and I don't have to walk to work, we have twenty minutes to kill." My eyes still focus on his hand.

"Oh, really." Damon licks his lips. He didn't revert to his route. "I think that's not enough time for what I'd like to do next."

Shudders run through my body. I pout a bit, but get over it when we pull into my office's parking lot.

"Thanks for the ride, stud," I say, bent over into the rolled down window.

"I'll be here at three to pick you up. Don't have too much fun working today." He winks and drives off, leaving me wishing I had the day off too.

Why am I acting like a schoolgirl instead of a grown-ass woman? Is this normal?

"Good morning," Harper says. "The principal would like to see you."

I haven't had the pleasure of meeting him yet. He's been out on vacation. I put my bag down underneath the desk and head to his office.

The door is ajar, and a middle-aged man sits behind a mahogany desk,

"You must be Tessa," he says, standing up from his desk to shake my hand.

"Nice to meet you, Lex. How did the vacation go?"

"Oh, you know, never long enough."

Casual conversation is fine, but surely he didn't call me in here just to shake my hand. He could've just come to my desk for that. How can I leave without seeming rude?

"Glad to have you on board."

I turn around and walk away, back to my desk, where Harper is waiting for me.

"See, I told you, he's super chill."

Harper and I talk about our lives, childhoods, and exes to pass the time while processing all the faxes and paperwork. I monitor the time, hoping it will go by quicker so I can get the hell out of here. Harper makes the job that much more enjoyable, but right now I just want to get home and see Emily and Damon.

Thirty seconds to three, I start gathering my stuff to head out the door.

"Dang, girl, you in a hurry for something? Must be that hot man you got waiting at home for ya, huh?"

"You know it. See ya."

My feet scurry to Damon's car and shut the door. "Thought today would never end."

"So, how was work?" he asks, putting the car in reverse.

"Same as every other day. Made a new friend at least. Harper. She seems cool."

His hand rests on my thigh. "That's great. You need to have a girl-friend. You want to invite her over for dinner sometime? Or go out for a girls' night? I'll watch Emily; just let me know."

Damon is seriously one of the best guys I've ever met, and so supportive in everything I do. To be willing to watch Emily while I go hang out with a friend is sweet, and more than Chris ever did.

We pull up to the elementary school, and Emily starts waving her hands around when she sees Damon's car.

"You came to pick me up. Does that mean we are going to watch TV tonight?"

What is it with that girl and TV? I guess when you go so long without it, and then get it, it's hard to go back. She is obsessed with Animal Planet. I might just surprise her and buy a TV for the living room if I can afford it with my next paycheck.

"We could if that's what you guys want. You are welcome at my house anytime. You know that."

We hightail it out of there and head back to the duplex. I think about asking if he wants to stay for dinner, but decide against it. I don't want to seem clingy. Is it if we have spent the last two weeks together in the same house?

"So, I was thinking. Since we mutually decided this morning"—he smiles at me and continues—"maybe we could all go out to a nice dinner. With my two girls."

My heart flutters. *His two girls.* I like that.

Emily is too young to understand. He wants to take us out on a date. A smile begins. "That would be great. I'll need to change."

"Don't worry. I'll be back at six to pick you both up."

He seems like a different man. Maybe he did truly open his heart to us, and this is what our future looks like, full of happiness. That's all I can wish for.

9

DAMON

This can't have come at a better time, especially since I'm off today. After dropping Tessa off at work, I try to come up with something special to do with them. She deserves someone who will be there one hundred percent and from now on that will be me. My heart is open, and it feels damn good.

Before Tessa came along, I used to tell myself that it would be like cheating on my wife, being with another woman. It just didn't seem right, but now I understood what Carol meant. I was doing exactly what she told me to avoid, being a recluse, not letting anyone close to me, and even pushing away my brothers. *No more*. The glimpse of happiness I feel already, in one day of being open with her, proves that Carol was right. I've been missing out on so much these past few years, and I will never let it happen again.

What about that one restaurant? Chateau? It's a nice restaurant that opened up two years ago but I've never had anyone to take. Some might find it weird I'm going on a date with Emily and Tessa, but they are a package deal, and I don't see a problem with that.

In fact, I'm over the moon excited about being able to stay in both of their lives, possibly for good. Emily needs someone, and from the beginning I've become that person without even realizing it. I can't imagine not being a part of her life now.

Tessa: *Just wondering... what should we wear? Not sure where you are taking us.*

Me: *Something you could wear to work. Or nicer. Up to you.*

Honestly, I can't wait to see her regardless of what she is wearing. I have gotten so used to having both of them around, that when they aren't it feels foreign. Almost like something is broken and I need to fix it.

Tessa: *See you in 15.*

I pull on my black dress pants, blue-striped button-up, and leather shoes. It isn't often I get the chance to dress up, so I'm taking full advantage. My hair is slicked back. *Ready or not, here I come.*

Pulling up to the duplex, my choice to wear a dark-blue shirt proves to be smart as you can't see the sweat. It's just Tessa, not some stranger who is going to ask me a million stupid first date questions. *You can do this. Just enjoy yourself.* My chest rises and falls as I walk up to the door. I knock, and Emily appears before me.

"Wow, you look beautiful," I say, picking her up for a hug. "Where's your mom?"

She's still getting ready, and that gives me some time with Emily. She shows me how she can finally write her full name in perfect cursive. For being six, it's better than mine by a long shot. I applaud her for a job well done, then her mom comes out.

My jaw drops. There she is, in a red silk dress that hugs her shape. How will I be able to keep my eyes off her tonight? Maybe that's her intention since I declined her advances this morning on her way to work. She is getting her payback, making me want her so badly. A little bit of drool slips through the crack in the corner of my mouth. *Calm yourself. It's not like you've never gone out with a beautiful woman before.*

"What do you think? Nice enough?" she says, spinning around. "I figured something new would be nice for a change."

I don't reply, but instead get off the couch and plant a kiss on her cheek, which makes Emily giggle. I'm not sure when Tessa will tell her that we are "dating," but that's her decision. Until then, things will remain casual in front of Emily.

The clock shows six thirty and we have to get going before we end up missing our reservation. I pick Emily up and place my hand on the small of Tessa's back, feeling the silky fabric with my hand. *So soft. Just like her skin.* This only makes me picture her, clenched palms filled with sheets of the bed earlier, trying to keep herself from being too loud while I enjoyed being between her thighs. I shake my head. *Stop thinking about that. Not right now.*

Being the gentleman my mama raised me to be, I beat her to the car so I can open it for her and let her slide inside, the dress sliding up to expose a bit of her upper thigh. The same thigh I kissed this morning while she moaned. I can't wait to hear that sound again. Her softly asking for more, and the way her body writhed underneath my touch is exhilarating.

My eyes keep venturing over to her legs while driving, wondering when I'll be lucky enough to experience kissing her silky skin again.

"Wow, this place is pretty. Look at the lights on the trees," Emily says.

Our first date is supposed to be magical, unforgettable, and something to tell our grandchildren one day because I have no doubt this will work between us. Even though I haven't known her very long, she is the most real person I know, not to mention kind, intelligent, and one hell of a mother. *Please don't fuck this up.*

Chateau is candlelit inside, with lanterns hanging from the ceiling for added romantic effect.

"Wow, it's so… beautiful," Tessa says, taking off her coat while looking around.

My eyes are fixed on her. She is a sight to see in that dress, and the smile that has been plastered on her face since seeing me only made my heart flutter more.

When the waitress comes over to take our order, she does a double take, realizing Emily is sitting with us. What? Why is it so weird that we are all dressed up and out to a nice dinner?

"What can I get for you?" she asks Emily first, and she orders the chicken tenders with French fries and a Sprite.

Tessa and I both order the prime rib, with loaded mashed potatoes, and a salad.

"How funny." She chuckles.

"So, this is nice, isn't it? Instead of sitting at the house eating. Bet the food is better too. I guess we will see."

While we wait for the food, Tessa begins asking me questions, which I expected, since this is a first date and normally when you get to know a person. She wants to know more about my parents.

"They must have been great people, with the way you turned out. I wish I could have met them."

My mother would love Tessa and praise her for being a single mom and doing such a wonderful job raising Emily all by herself.

"My mom was all about us boys. Never missed a game or practice. She was very involved in our lives. My dad, well, he worked a lot. Not that he wasn't there for us when he could be."

Our waitress drops off our food, and we all begin to dig in, but that doesn't stop the questions.

"And your brothers?"

She's met Liam, from the day of the fire, but not Aiden. He is the one I will have to worry about the most. He's not the type to think about things before speaking. "Liam, the one you've met, he's just trying to figure out what he wants. Aiden is more of the playboy type, revolving front door, and doesn't have any clue on how to be a functioning adult."

Tessa's phone rings, and she pulls it out, examining the number, and then sets it down on the table where it continues to ring.

"Everything okay?" I ask because of the sudden shift in her demeanor.

"Just someone I don't want to talk to," she replies, tucking a hair behind Emily's ear and smiling. "Plus, I'm here with you two. They can wait."

For the next several minutes, it's quiet besides the constant vibrating of her phone, and something just doesn't feel right. Why wouldn't she just answer the phone? Her cheeks are red, and the conversation has halted, becoming one-sided while she continues to pick at her food.

I decide to get the check and take them home. Something is obviously bothering her, and she has a phone call to return. If she wants to talk about it, then I'll listen, but I won't pry.

On the way from the restaurant, Emily talks about a special on

Animal Planet that she doesn't want to miss Friday and asks if she can come over to my house to watch it since they don't have a TV.

"Of course."

Tessa hasn't said anything since getting in the car, just picking at her fingers.

As we pull up, a man is standing outside their duplex. Who the hell is that?

"Emily, stay in the car with Damon."

"You know him?" I ask, eyebrows raised.

"It's Chris," she says, shutting the door.

That's why she has been acting so weird. Her ex has been calling and texting her, but how does he know where she lives?

I hand my phone to Emily so she can watch videos of monkeys, and I can focus my eyes on them to make sure that if there are any signs of trouble, I can get out at a moment's notice to step in. Or would she want me to?

I can't hear what is being said, but both voices are being raised. Chris is getting closer and closer to her, and I don't like that. If he so much as lays a hand on her, I will lay him out.

Then I see him point toward me. *You got a problem?* I don't like that she's standing outside in the cold in that dress. She must be freezing.

When Tessa starts crying, I open the door. "Are you okay?"

"This isn't any of your concern. She's fine," he responds.

"I don't believe I was asking you. Tess?" This guy doesn't know me, and I'm not one to start anything, but I shut the door behind me, and just stand there, not getting any closer.

"I mean really, Tessa, who the hell do you think you are? She's my daughter. You can't keep me from her. She deserves to know me. Stop letting your feelings for me jeopardize your judgment. You're a better mother than this."

Rage fuels through me, and my knuckles become white. Who the hell is he to talk about her mothering skills? He hasn't been around in how long? Then he shows up and starts talking like she's a horrible mother for not letting him see her? You've got to be kidding me.

"Don't act like you're innocent. You haven't seen her in what, four years? More? Hell, I couldn't even tell you it's been that long. You disappear and then all of the sudden expect me to just let you walk right back into her life? Fuck you. That's not how it works. You could easily walk right out of her life again tomorrow. I will not put her through that again. You should leave."

Good girl. Tell him exactly what you have been holding in all these years.

"You're telling me I can't see my own daughter, but you will let that dude be around her? How well do you know him? Huh?" he says, waving his hands around. "You fuck him while our daughter sleeps in the next room, I bet, huh? Really classy, Tessa."

Yeah, he should really leave me out of it.

"I think you should leave before I call the cops," Tessa says.

He starts walking toward me, and Tessa tugs on his jacket. A part of me wants to run toward him and just knock him off his feet, but I don't want Emily to see that.

"Leave," she says, holding up her phone with 9-1-1 clearly dialed. "I'm not playing."

Chris locks eyes with me and starts walking backward. "Okay, I'll leave. But next time you see me, it'll be with court papers. I will see my daughter, whether you want me to or not."

Tessa comes back to the car and gets in. "I'd really rather stay at your house tonight. Now that he knows where I live... he will keep coming back."

She seems pretty shaken up, and all I want to do is bring her close and comfort her and assure her everything will be okay, but can I? A court battle is something that would go on and could be detrimental, but what judge would side with Chris after being out of Emily's life for so long and the abuse? Texas is pro-mom and tries to keep the children with their mother unless otherwise proven unfit. Tessa is anything but an unfit mother. Everything revolves around her daughter, and she does what's best for her at all times. I can't see a judge taking Emily away from her.

As we walk in the house, Tessa turns on the TV for Emily and covers her up with a blanket. "Mama's going to talk to Damon. I love you so much." Tears are beginning to form in her eyes.

10

TESSA

I'm trying not to cry thinking of how many different ways this could go. What if Chris gets a lawyer and we have to go to court? Even with the money I've saved, it's not enough to hire an attorney to fight it. The first thing they will look at is child support and probably ask why I never filed for it. Who the hell would want to take money from Chris? He would be given visitation and honestly I wanted to hold off on that for as long as possible. If I am honest and tell them everything, things I haven't ever shared with anyone, then maybe they won't. Everything is swirling around in my head, so much that a headache is coming on.

I know that he called, but never in a million years did I think Chris would show up at my house. Matter of fact, how the hell did he find out where we lived? This stumps me because literally no one knows. Why would he show up in person after all these years? I've been clear that Emily isn't someone that he can just come see and leave for months at a time with no contact, and then show up again. I make the decisions for Emily's well-being. She deserves someone who wants to be in her life and steps up to the plate. Not just when it's convenient for them.

Damon sits down with me at the table in silence. I want to talk to him about it, but I'm stuck in my head with a million things swirling around.

"Are you okay?" he asks, his hand falling on top of mine. "That's all I wanna know."

My head shakes before dropping it to the table. What the hell am I going to do? I can't afford a lawyer. Can he? I have no idea what his life is like now, without us. Maybe he's just bluffing.

"I... don't know what to do... or think. Was he being serious about getting a lawyer?" I scramble together my words. "I can't afford one. He probably knows that so he's trying to scare me into letting him see her. It's not going to work. I'll keep her away from him as long as I can until a judge tells me I have to."

Damon sits there quietly, just listening to me ramble.

"I can't even fathom what it might do if she sees him, develops a bond, and then he bolts again. The first time was hell, she cried for months, asking when he was going to come back..."

Going back to that day isn't something I like to think about, but I do.

I just got home from work, a double shift at a diner the next town over, and was exhausted. He watched Emily while I worked, but he always complained, like it was too hard for him. We had been fighting more lately, but when he drinks, things tend to get a little out of control.

I took my shoes off at the door and hung up my coat. "Where is she?"

"In bed," he replied, drinking a beer on the couch. "Don't wake her. It took me an hour to get her to sleep."

It had been a long day, and all I wanted to do was give Emily a big hug. He had been an asshole for months, but having a kid was hard. It wasn't meant to be a cake walk.

"I'm serious, don't go in there," he said, standing in the hallway.

I opened the door and went inside anyway. He wasn't my boss. I could do what I wanted.

The next thing I knew, bangs throughout the house were heard. If he didn't want her to get woken up, then why the hell was he being so damn loud?

"What the hell? If anyone's going to wake her up it's you," I yelled, noticing a bag packed by the door. "What the hell is that?"

"I'm done. This house is miserable, and I can't do it anymore." He picked up the bag and opened the front door.

"You're seriously going to leave in the middle of the night?"

"You leave me no fucking choice. I've been telling you to quit that job for weeks... yet you refuse. I can't keep watching her for eight to twelve hours a day after I get off. I'm exhausted, and she does nothing but cry most of the time."

As much as it pained me, I hoped he would come back. For Emily's sake. But he didn't. I tried calling for weeks but he didn't return a single one. Him being gone meant no more bruises, and people at work were starting to ask questions.

Everything went downhill. I couldn't find anyone to watch Emily while I worked, so we lost the apartment, and I lost my job. It got so bad I almost called my mom to go stay with her, but then I found the receptionist position for a dentist office, and things began to look up. After a couple weeks, I got a new apartment for just the two of us.

Sometimes I wonder what would have happened if he didn't leave for good that night. What if he would've stayed? But then I realized that we weren't happy and couldn't stay together just for Emily. She's the reason I stayed and took whatever he dished out, because I didn't want my baby girl to grow up without her father. He never harmed her, but that didn't mean he never would have if he stayed.

Damon brings me out of it, rubbing my shoulders, seeing me grimace at the bright light over the table.

"I'll grab you some Tylenol and we can go lie down," he says.

I'm not in the mood for anything tonight. Sitting here, I'm emotionally and mentally drained.

"Don't worry. I just want to hold you. That's all."

Damon, even in this horrible situation, is there for me. He could have run for the hills, with Chris showing up. But he didn't. That spoke wonders for his character.

He leads me to his bedroom, and we get under the covers, and I lay my head on his chest, still in my red silk dress. Lying in his bed with him feels normal. Like we have done it a million times before.

"I'm a good mom, right?" I'm trying not to let him get into my head, but he is. He's making me doubt myself, and why should I? Who potty trained her? Who was there for her on the first day of school? Who helps her with her homework? Who feeds her every night? "Like you don't think there's anything he could use... that would make me seem unfit..."

"No. You literally do everything you can to support Emily and give her what she needs. You have a place to live, a decent job, and have been by her side the entire time. He can't say that. I don't think you have anything to worry about."

I nuzzle into his chest, and a soft sigh erupts from my throat. Not everything is about sex. Intimacy has many layers, and this is just one of them. Just being there, present with the other person, and showing them you care, even with a subtle touch.

"Mama," Emily says, shaking me which wakes Damon up.

Crap. I didn't think we would fall asleep.

"Oh my goodness, I fell asleep. Good morning, sweetie."

"What are you doing in here?"

"Damon and I were up late talking. Guess we fell asleep. Sorry, sweetie."

Emily smiles and pulls at my hand. "It's time to make breakfast. My tummy is growling. Can't you hear it?"

I look back at him with a smile and get out of bed. "We better feed this girl before... she eats us."

He follows us into the kitchen as we rummage through the refrigerator.

"Cinnamon rolls. That's perfect," Emily says.

Damon preheats the oven and opens the rolled package. "Here you go. Put them apart for them to grow on this cookie sheet. Then when they're done, we will let you ice them up."

"Why don't you go get dressed while we are waiting on these to be done," I state.

He gets the coffee started and sits at the dining table. "Sorry..."

"No need to be sorry. You didn't do anything wrong. I didn't plan on falling asleep either."

The question looming in my mind is, what are we going to tell Emily? She must be wondering why we were in the same bed.

The oven beeps, and I slip the cookie sheet into the oven and set the timer for twelve minutes. They will be done and cooled before we will all need to leave.

"Has he tried calling you?" Damon asks.

"I had twelve missed calls from him when I checked my phone this morning."

He isn't going to leave me alone. Why did he show up now? After all these years? Maybe because of the holidays approaching? His parents weren't very happy when he up and left us. For the first year, they kept in contact with me, but stopped after that.

"Maybe you should go down to the police station. See if there's anything they can do. Just don't think he's going to let up, and you don't want him showing up at your house in the middle of the night."

Once the oven beeps, and we ice them, Emily and Damon sit down to eat while I get dressed.

Emily doesn't waste any time before digging in.

"He just keeps calling me. Ugh. Why won't he stop?"

We all sit around the table, eat breakfast, and then head out. It's time to take Emily to school, and then drop me off at the high school on his way to the fire station.

Harper must be able to tell something's wrong because the first thing she asks me is if I'm okay.

"Just a long night. Emily's dad won't stop calling me. He showed up at my place last night out of the blue. Wanting to see her after years of nothing. Jackass."

Her hand lays on my shoulder. "Keep your head up, girl. Stick to your guns. You're the mama. Have you talked to the court about rights?"

"No, I haven't ever thought about that, really. He chose not to be around for years, so there was no need for that."

"Well, you might need to start. It can't hurt anything to at least find out what his rights are, and what you can do, you know."

"Good point. I'll call tonight after work. Thanks, girl."

Work is a whirlwind, but it keeps me busy so I don't focus on Chris all day and debate whether to tell Emily he's in town. Am I a horrible mother if I keep it from her? Maybe she won't want to see him anyway? But what if she does?

As soon as the clock strikes three, I'm out the door and into Damon's car.

"How was your day?" he says, kissing me on the cheek before pulling out.

"Busy. But I think after we pick up Emily, I'll go down to the police station."

"You want me to come with you?"

"If you'll watch Emily, I'd like to go on my own. If that's okay?"

He shakes his head, smiles, and pulls up to the curb. Emily isn't in her usual spot. Maybe she is late getting outside. We wait another five minutes, and still no sign of her.

"Where is she? She's always right here waiting for me."

I get out of the car and go talk to the lady who is standing with some of the students.

"Have you seen Emily? She's usually right here."

"I'm sorry, I'm not sure who that is. Who is her teacher?"

"Mrs. Drummond."

"You might ask her. She's over there." She points to the front of the school.

My feet quickly carry me over to the teacher. "Where is Emily?"

Mrs. Drummond looks at me with wide eyes. "What do you mean? She's already been picked up."

"By whom?"

"Her father."

11

TESSA

*M*y heart sinks, and it's almost as if a sixty-pound rock is pushing down on my chest, as my worst fear is coming true, and I should have seen it coming. He has been so adamant about seeing her. Why didn't I think about this? Of course, he would show up at her school. My daughter is out there somewhere with him, and that scares the living hell out of me. I don't know anything about the man he has become, only the man I knew. And that man isn't someone I want to have her.

Mrs. Drummond looks at me; my face is hot. "Are you okay, miss?"

"How could you let her leave with someone other than me? My daughter has been kidnapped!"

The teacher looks around, and bystanders are now looking my way. "She said it was her father, ma'am."

"You just always take a child's word for it?" I yell, practically running back to Damon's car. "Take me to the police station now."

"What?" he says, putting the car in the drive. "Where's Emily?"

"He took her. Hurry!"

Skid marks are made, and he steps on it all the way to the police station. I try to take deep breaths, calm myself down, but how the hell can I do that? Sure, I know who she is with, but not where she is. They could be anywhere. Why would Emily leave with him?

Damon pulls up to the station, and I don't even wait for him to put the car in park before I am out the door and running inside. "I need to talk to someone now." My voice carries throughout the station.

"Ma'am. Calm down. What's going on?"

"My daughter's been kidnapped. I need to speak to someone now."

"Where was she last seen?"

"At school. Her father showed up yesterday, haven't seen him in years. Demanding to see her. He took her. I need her back, please," I beg and plead. "I need my little girl back."

The female officer sits me down. "Listen, I understand you're upset, but we need some more information. Can you take a deep breath?"

"Yes, I'm sorry, I'm freaking out."

"Okay, now can you give us a description of your daughter? You said the man was her father? Do you have a custody agreement in place?"

What the hell did a custody agreement matter? He hasn't been in her life for years, and now all of a sudden, he shows up at her school without even mentioning it to me. "No, we don't have a binding agreement through the courts yet."

"Okay. Let me call and see if there is something we can do. Typically, in these situations, unless they are withholding the child from you, there's not much we can do since he is the biological parent. How long has she been with him?"

"Since school was let out. Please go call someone, I need my little girl back." I hand her a picture of Emily and wait for her to return. What am I going to do if he keeps her? Who cares if he's the biological parent? She doesn't know him. I don't know him.

Damon's arm drapes around my shoulders. "I'm so sorry you're having to go through this. I wish there was something I could do."

This is the type of a man I want in my life, and he just keeps proving he's a better man than Chris could ever be. Why the hell did I ever even sleep with that jerk? Not that I would ever want Emily out of my life.

Damon pulls me into his chest and runs his fingers through my hair, trying to keep me as calm as he can. I can hear his heartbeat and even though he's putting on a good front for me, it's beating crazy fast.

The officer starts walking back over to us. "Okay, we can't do anything until after twenty-four hours. Now, since she's not technically missing, but with her father, we can't do anything unless you can prove he's intentionally keeping her from you and that would be handled in civil court."

It's boiling up inside me, and a scream erupts from my throat. "Are you freaking kidding me? I don't fucking understand. My daughter is with a man that she hasn't seen in three plus years, a man who abandoned us. You're telling me, basically my choice is to sit around and wait to get her back?" This is unacceptable! She could be out there hurt, starving, or God knows what, and they want me to just wait until he calls me?

"Officer, let me explain something again. This man hasn't seen his daughter in years. He abandoned us when she was a baby. And then he just showed up yesterday demanding to see her. Now that he has her, he could run off with her... Waiting that time frame, it's just not acceptable. By the time it's been that long, they could be anywhere. How are we supposed to find them?"

"I know it's not ideal. I'm a mother too, but that's how the law works in this particular situation. Once she's back, I would get with a lawyer to see what precautions you can take in the future. Form a binding agreement within the courts so he can't pull something like this again. If you have not made contact with him after twenty-four hours, then we can step in and charge him with parental abduction."

Do they not realize how much can happen in twenty-four hours? What if he forgets to feed her or leaves her home alone? All these scenarios start flying through my mind, and my stomach is in knots. "I'll be back in twenty-four hours then. Not a minute after, and then I expect you guys to find her and bring her back to me."

Damon tugs on my shoulders, maneuvering me out to his car. "I know you want her back, but the police can only do so much right now, like she said. Tomorrow, we will come back and get Emily back home with us, okay?"

I'm not furious at him, he did nothing wrong, but I don't want to leave the station. Twenty-four hours is too long to wait and Emily could be in danger somewhere without me there to help. As her mother, it's my job to protect her, and I failed. The signs were there; he wanted to see her so bad. I should have picked up on that and put precautions in place. *Damn it*, I tell myself, hitting my forehead and leaning forward in the seat. *Why the hell didn't I see this coming?*

Damon's hand flies over and grabs mine tightly. "Don't hit yourself. This isn't your fault. We'll get her back."

Most of the night is spent with me calling Chris every five minutes and not letting up. Eventually he'll get sick of me calling and either answer or turn it off. The only way I would get him to answer me is to bug the crap out of him. He always had a temper, so I wanted to focus on that. After the three hundredth call, he turns his phone off and it goes straight to voicemail. *Damn it*. He isn't going to bring her back to me. Something in the pit of my stomach knows if it were up to Chris, I'd never see her again. He told me his parents want to see her, and without him saying it, I bet that's the only reason he wants anything to do with her right now.

Chris's parents are not very smart and remind me of those parents who could never believe their child could ever do anything wrong, like ever. Even when he was eighteen, and still getting in trouble, they bailed him out of jail when he would get public intoxications. How the hell did they expect him to learn any kind of consequences if they just bailed him out of everything?

When Chris left, he tried to get his parents to believe I wasn't the same person he fell in love with, and my focus was on work, not Emily. They kept in touch for a little while after that, but then no communication, just like him, for years.

We move to the couch, and Damon tries to keep me occupied with some TV, but it doesn't work. My phone is glued to my hand, and I continue calling and texting him. Emily is probably wondering where I am, and he's spreading some lies about me. She's never been away from me this long.

We both end up falling asleep on the couch in the wee hours of the night when our eyes just couldn't stay open any longer. Nightmares take over, seeing Emily trapped in a warehouse, screaming out for me, but I'm nowhere to be found. I'm not closing my eyes again until she's in my arms, period.

"We've only got an hour until the time is up. Do you want a sandwich or anything before we head down there?" Damon asks, making himself one to tide him over until later. "You really should eat something, anything. It'll help with your energy level."

He's right. No one knows what will go on today after going back down to the station. Especially after last night. "Okay, I'll take one."

We sit at the dining room table, but it's missing Emily. Normally, she's chatty when we sit down to eat and always making jokes. It really kept meals interesting with her here. But now, it is just us, and neither of us say a word while we eat our sandwiches, preparing for what will come next.

The twenty-four hours are up, and I still have heard nothing, so Damon and I arrive back at the police station. The woman from yesterday isn't on duty anymore.

"I need to speak to someone about my child. Her father took her from school yesterday, and we aren't able to get ahold of him. They told me to come back after twenty-four hours."

The man behind the desk jerks up and grabs another officer. "He's familiar. She filled him in before she left early this morning."

The officer extends his hand. "I'm Officer Jeffords. You still have not heard from the father about her whereabouts?"

"Correct. Can we do something now? I just have a horrible feeling she's in danger, and I can't shake it."

"I have the picture of her. Emily, right?"

I nod. "Please help me get her back."

His eyes are sympathetic. "We'll do everything we can, ma'am. An amber alert has been issued and we will start searching for them now."

All I can do is cry. Damon tries to hold me, but I push him away. Right now, I want Emily in my arms. To know she's safe.

"Is there anything I can do?" he asks. "I don't know what to do."

My mind is running all over the place. Why would Emily have gone with him in the first place? He abandoned her. But she's a child who just wants to see her daddy. I have to remember that. It isn't her fault he shows up and talks her into leaving with him. She knows not to go with strangers, but technically he isn't one. I fidget and cry for the next few hours with no sign or word on Emily. They try to talk me into going home, but that is a no go. I'm not leaving. The police are out looking for her everywhere, but I have no clue where he would take her.

I pull out my phone and look him up on social media. He lives in Houston. "Sir, he may have left the city. It looks like he lives in Houston. They could be there." My tears start up again. What if they can't find her? What if we never get her back?

"We issued an update to go out statewide. All hands on deck to find your little girl."

I watch plenty of stories of kids going missing, and the investigators always say that if they aren't found within the first forty-eight hours, then it usually doesn't end well. He is her father; surely he won't do anything to harm her.

"If she got away from him, where do you think she would go?" Officer Jeffords asks.

"His house." I point to Damon.

"You should go back there, just in case she shows up. We'll call if we find anything. I promise we are doing everything we can to find Emily."

As much as it makes sense to go back to Damon's, I don't want to leave. If she gets separated from Chris, she will go somewhere she feels safe.

"Tess, I think he's right. She's always felt safe at my house. It would be the place she'd go," he says, staring into my eyes, knowing how much I don't want to leave.

We hightail it out of there and get to the house as fast as we can.

"Emily! Emily, are you here?" I yell, running up to the house, looking around. But there is no sign of her. My baby hasn't come home. "I'm going to sit here," I say, claiming the chair closest to the door. "Just in case she comes back."

With everything going on, I totally forget to call my mom. How am I going to break the news that Chris kidnapped her granddaughter? She was a big fan of his back in the day. As I pull her up in my contact list, I take a deep breath, not knowing how this is going to go.

"Honey! I was going to call you tomorrow to check in. How are things?"

My voice starts to crack as I say, "Not so great."

"You sound—what's going on?"

"Chris showed up two days ago demanding to see Emily. He threatened to take me to court, and then without me knowing, he picked her up from school, and we haven't seen her since, Mom."

"What do you mean you haven't seen her? Where is she?"

"He took her and we have no idea where. The police are looking for them but haven't gotten any leads yet." I explain everything to her and try to stay as calm as I can. My mom was my rock when Chris left, even though she can't help me financially. She talked me off ledges multiple times and made me believe I could provide Emily the best life.

"I'll let you go in case the police call. Keep me updated. I'll pray."

She hasn't seen Emily since Thanksgiving three years ago. Shortly after, she lost her job and could barely make ends meet like myself. "I love you, Mom." I reply before the line goes dead.

Damon brings me some soup, but I'm not hungry and can't even think about eating right now. How much longer can I sit around and wait? Hell, I should be out there helping them find her, searching every place in town. Surely someone has seen her. They had to stop to eat or get gas at some point.

My biggest concern is why the school let her leave with him. They obviously had never seen him before, and wouldn't they have found that odd? Aren't there rules in place to keep the kids safe and prevent things like this from happening? After this, I'll call a meeting with the school board to discuss their rules because I don't want something like this to happen to another mother.

My eyes are getting heavy, but I can't bring myself to allow them to close. What if I missed a call, a knock on the door, or something leading to Emily? Nope, I'll just make a pot of coffee to keep me awake. I can sleep once she is home and in my arms.

The warm coffee does the opposite of what I hope for, and when my eyes open it's dark outside. Where is my phone? I search around the room but can't find it.

"Damon?" I yell, trying to find him.

"I'm in the dining room."

When I walk in, my phone is sitting in front of him, and he's drinking a cup of coffee.

"I was looking for that. Did I miss any calls?" I jerk the phone away from the table.

He frowns in response. "No calls. I stayed up, just in case. You needed some sleep."

Ugh. When the hell are they going to find her? I can't continue to sit around idly waiting. I'm going crazy.

"Here's your coffee. Have a seat."

No, I'm not going to sit down. How is that productive in finding Emily? Where is she? The police have probably already canvassed the entire city looking for her with no luck or they would've called. No more waiting around. I dial the non-emergency number to the station.

"Grapevine Police Department."

"Any news on Emily? I haven't received anything for hours, and I really need to know something, anything."

The officer replies, "Officers are out at the hotels with her picture and a call was made to Houston PD to check the residence of the father."

It's been hours, why haven't they done that already? Couldn't they have checked his place hours ago? I'm really starting to doubt our police department's capability to handle this situation promptly. They could be in Canada by now. "Keep me informed."

Damon talks to his chief and takes the day off; that's just the type of man he is.

We move to the living room, and put on some westerns to help pass time, trying to keep our minds occupied so we don't just sit and worry about Emily. Our bodies snuggle under a fuzzy blanket, and my head is on his chest. I feel safe and protected.

About twenty minutes later, there's a knock on the door.

Damon jumps up. "I'll get it. Stay here."

12

DAMON

*B*efore opening the door, I pray it's Emily, let down when it's only Aiden standing on the other side.

"You about to hit me?" He flinches.

"Sorry, it's not a good time. I wasn't expecting you." I open the door wider for him to come inside. "We're kinda in a crisis here. What do you need?"

"Wanted to check in on you guys." Aiden says, putting his hands up. "Jeez. Is that okay?" His eyes shift over to Tessa. "Nice to meet you. You must be the famous Tessa my brother raves about."

He sits on the chair and I join her back on the couch.

"Liam called and told me what's going on, since you didn't bother to. I was worried about you guys."

"It's been a long night, and it's going to be an even longer day. Don't have time for sarcasm right now."

He nods, mutely apologizing. "Do they have any news at all?"

Tessa shakes her head, and I can see her eyes starting to water.

"Well, if you have a picture, I'd like to help. Go around to the local places and see if anyone has seen her. You never know, worth a shot at least."

I'm surprised at my brother's offer.

I motion for Aiden to follow me into the dining room where I explain the scope of what is going on away from her. We are both too close to the situation, but she is more than I.

"We'll find her and bring her home. Too many people out looking for her right now. I just wanna help however I can."

Maybe my little brother is finally growing up a bit, and that makes me proud. A couple years ago, I wasn't sure he'd grow up at all.

"I'll take this photo and show it around. See if I can get anything. I'll call the police first if I find anything and then you."

Aiden heads out to search for Emily while we stay at the house. She might come back here if she's still in town and can get away from her dad. It's worth a shot to stay here just in case.

I try to keep Tessa calm for the next few hours, but it's hard. Each passing hour means Emily is possibly farther away, and that scares both of us. She won't eat and won't sleep. All she does is constantly check her phone to see if she has any messages.

My phone rings, and Tessa picks hers up fast. "It's mine," I tell her, seeing Aiden's name scrolling across my screen. "Hello?"

"So I already called PD, but the gas station on fifth said that she and a male came in around midnight last night. Got snacks and gas."

Damn it. He's planning on taking her somewhere outside of Grapevine, which isn't good news. Tessa is going to freak out. "Okay, thanks for calling."

"Who was it? Did they find her? Is she okay?"

She is frantic, and taking my time to tell her probably doesn't help the situation. I take her hands in mine and say, "She was seen at a gas station last night with him. Buying gas and snacks." As much as I want to lie to her, I can't. But I want to remain hopeful that they will get her back.

"That asshole's running away with my daughter. Who the hell does he think he is? I just..."

Another phone call comes in, but this time on hers. She answers the phone, and a look of relief comes across her face. *Is it good news?*

"Okay. And... should I... Thank you."

She doesn't turn to look at me, just stays frozen in place for a few minutes. "They found her at his place. Alone. Bastard left her alone while he went to work like he hadn't done a damn thing wrong."

She's safe! Relief washes over both of us knowing she's going to be home soon and in our arms. These last thirty-six hours have been excruciating and I never want to experience this again.

"The police have her and will be dropping her off to us."

Aiden will be thankful to hear the news so I grab my phone.

Me: *They found her in Houston. You can come back now.*

This situation could have ended way worse, and I thank God it didn't. We will never let her out of our sight after this, and the school board is going to hear all about it. This shouldn't have happened in the first place. There are supposed to be rules in place to prevent this sort of thing. I don't want any other parent to have to go through what Tessa just did.

We wait outside, not caring how cold it is. Emily will have questions when she gets here, and Tessa will answer them truthfully because that is just the type of mother she is.

"That must be them!" she shouts, seeing a cruiser coming down the street. Her smile is back, and she's practically jumping up and down.

Emily jumps out of the car and runs straight into Tessa's arms. "Mama, I missed you. Please don't be mad at me."

"Never, honey. I'm just glad to have you back." Their hug ensues for a good couple of minutes before breaking apart.

My turn. I swoop her into my arms. "You're home, doll. We missed you so much."

After going inside, I leave them alone for a minute and start the homemade chicken noodle soup for dinner. The weather is getting colder, and soup is just what it calls for tonight. The house will go back to normal and both my girls are safe and sound. Just the way it should be.

Will they go back to the duplex after this? No way. How will they ever feel safe there again?

"How was it seeing him?" Tessa asks, hoping for some more information. She isn't one to scold her daughter, but she's curious how the situation has been for her. Did she get scared when they left Grapevine? When he left her alone at his apartment?

Emily was happy to see him, but he didn't like watching Animal Planet like I did. "Daddy didn't like Damon. Why not?"

To a child it might not be obvious, but to me, Chris wants me far away from Emily. He didn't want his daughter taking a liking to some other man that can provide her with more than he ever could. Love and stability.

"Your daddy doesn't want anyone else in your life, including Damon. But he doesn't get to decide. You do." She leans over and tucks a strand of hair behind Emily's ear. "I would never force anyone into your life, and you seem to really like him."

"So, I can still watch Animal Planet with him?" A smile lights up Emily's face.

"Of course, sweetie."

Chris has a problem with me, but what man wouldn't. Most guys don't like others being in their kids' lives. Usually, they have to prove themselves to be a good fit, but not me. Anyone would be a better fit than that guy.

"All right," I say, going into the living room to join them. "Who wants to watch Animal Planet?"

The three of us spend the next half hour watching a special on lions. It's so great to have her back in our arms and out of danger. She might not be my child by blood, but that doesn't matter. My heart can't imagine if this is how I feel about Emily, how strong of a bond would I form with biological children?

The timer goes off, and dinner is ready. The aroma of the soup carries through the whole house, making our stomachs grumble with hunger. We decide to eat in the living room tonight, snuggled up on the couch, just enjoying each other's company. These last two days have been emotionally and physically draining, and tonight we will all be able to sleep peacefully.

Before taking Emily to bed, Tessa explains to her that we are dating. Her reaction is priceless. She almost seems more excited than we are, if that's possible.

It's officially out in the open, and I don't have to be careful about what is said around her anymore. A weight lifts off my shoulders. It warms my heart to know she has no qualms with us being together.

"Hey, don't run off without giving me a hug, goob," I say when she tries running to the bedroom. My arms around her, I say, "I'm so glad you're okay. Happy to have you home. Good night."

This is her home, whether Tessa decides to go back to the duplex or not. I will always consider my home, theirs. And one day, I hope we can get a new home for us to make memories together. One with a backyard, two stories, and a bigger kitchen.

"Just wanted to say good night." Tessa sneaks back out and kisses me. "I'll see ya in the morning."

The focus tonight is on Emily; after the scare, we want to savor every moment we can.

THE HOUSE IS QUIET, and I sleep like a bear during hibernation. Hell, I even thought about calling into work today, they'd understand, but I don't. Liam already covered for me yesterday, and I don't want to take his day off from him.

The girls are still asleep when I leave for work, and I can't dream of waking them. So I just prepare some cinnamon rolls and leave them iced on the counter.

Once I get to the station, everyone wants to know what the hell happened. The guys know about Tessa, but not that we are dating. It seems like everyone is happy for me, finally moving on and finding a woman.

When Aiden shows up, late I may add, he doesn't look so great.

"Out late again?" I ask, laughing at my brother clearly hungover.

"Of course. I'm young, it's what we do." He laughs, pouring himself a cup of coffee and sitting down next to me. "How's Emily and Tessa?"

"Better now that they are both at my house. Safe and sound."

The conversation takes a different direction. Aiden wants to know if things are serious between the two of us. I don't know how to answer. It's not like I'm going to ask her to marry me next week, but I can see myself married to her one day. "Serious enough. Why?"

"It's just that it's your first relationship since Carol, and as girly as it sounds, don't really wanna see you get your heart broken is all."

Aiden worries about me, even before Tessa, even though he didn't always verbally express it. "Neither one of us wants to get hurt. She has a daughter to think about, but things just fell into place. I'd protect both with my life."

"That's what I'm worried about."

No need to. I can take care of myself. The situation with Chris isn't something either of us were expecting to happen. And after what he did, no way a judge will give him custody or even think about it for that matter. He really screwed himself when he took Emily.

Aiden wouldn't understand because his last relationship was in high school. If you could even consider a relationship at that age real. I mean the feelings are, but normally relationships deteriorate after graduating. It was a fact of life, except for Carol and me. We were the lucky ones that flourished after graduation. Aiden really couldn't be giving me relationship or women advice since he hadn't had either in years. All he cared about was getting laid. Even though there was so much more for him to have. One day he'll realize it, and it will come back to haunt him.

"There's no need to worry about me, brother. You can't find happiness unless you open your heart to it. If anyone knows that, it's me. Think about it. If I didn't, they would have walked right out of my life, and I'd be moping around the house, back to depression again. Don't you want someone to go home to?" He's still young, but as he gets older, he will realize having someone to share life's moments with is the biggest joy of all.

"Honestly, yes, but women are crazy."

I chuckle and slap his shoulder. "Not all of them, just the ones you take home. Change your standards, and instead of buying them drinks and taking them home for sex, take them out to a nice dinner and have actual conversations."

13

TESSA

*A*fter the weekend is over, the fear of dropping Emily off at school sinks in, and I don't know if I can do it. Chris can show back up at any time. And what's to say the school will make sure she doesn't get taken by him again? My heart can't handle that again.

Instead of Damon taking me to work, I decide to be dropped off with Emily and have a conversation with the school administration. They have to do something to make sure this never happens again. Rules need to be followed and implemented, end of story. Or I will never feel safe leaving Emily.

The principal isn't in yet, so I wait for her. My boss understands what's going on, and said it'll be okay if I'm a little late today. I'm glad they are so understanding, but they kind of have to be after a situation like Emily's. As much as I need the job, she comes first no matter what. This is about not only her safety but the other children. The school needs to take responsibility and fix the flaws within their system. Parents shouldn't have to worry about things like this happening while in their care.

I sit in the chair, watching kids come and go from the office, wondering what I am going to say exactly. There was no need to come across as a crazy mother who is bashing the school or anything. But they need to understand the severity of their actions. They are the protectors of our children while out of our care. This means they should be keeping an eye on them, and that didn't happen with Emily. In fact, they utterly and completely failed.

When the principal finally comes into the office, I quickly introduce myself. "I was wondering if I could speak to you privately. I'm Emily's mom. I'm sure you heard about the situation last week."

"Yes, of course. Let's go into my office." She looks caught off guard.

I follow her inside and shut the door.

She maneuvers behind her desk, sits down, and folds her hands atop the desk. "I'm so sorry for what happened. The teacher feels terrible, and even asked Emily multiple times if she knew she was supposed to be going home with him. We've never had a situation like this, and thought you just forgot to call and let us know someone else was picking her up."

Not an excuse. I don't give a crap that it's never happened before; it happened to my child. No amount of excuses is going to make me worry any less. "Whether it's happened before or not, my daughter was kidnapped, under your school's watch. That's unacceptable. Why do you send a form home to fill out who can pick the children up, if you don't follow it?"

The principal starts to answer, but I cut her off.

"Who lets a child go off with someone they've never seen pick her up before? Your administration needs to do something, fix something, or this will happen again. And I'd rather not take action against the school."

The principal's face grows red. "Again, we are so sorry for what happened. We have a meeting tonight at six with the faculty and the administration to discuss it."

I really want to go off on this lady, but I decide that's enough for right now. "My daughter is not to leave with anyone else but me ever again, unless you see my face and I say it's okay. I've already told Emily to wait in the office for me every day, until I pick her up, so something like this doesn't happen again."

I storm out of her office and out of the school, madder than hell.

The chilly air outside quickly makes me regret not getting a ride from Damon. It is around forty degrees outside and the coat I am wearing isn't really meant for this kind of weather. Power walking seems to help a little, but not enough. I shiver all the way to the office.

"Sorry I'm late," I tell Harper, taking off my coat and sitting down. "Had to take care of some things."

"I heard what happened, girl. Why didn't you text me? I would've helped you look for her. How is she? Did they put him in jail?"

I fill her in on the details and get to work. It's bad enough I'm late, so I don't want to get behind on my work too. Especially after Lex being so kind about me coming in late. This job is going to be the only thing helping me to pay for the lawyer to help me keep Chris away from her.

After a while, when I get caught up, he calls me into his office.

"I just wanted to say I'm glad your daughter's home safe. I'm not sure what your plans are, but I wanted to recommend a lawyer. He's a friend and handles family cases. Of course, it's up to you who you use."

I take the card and thank him. It's the next step. Even though it'll cost me a fortune, I need to be certain that Chris can't come near her again. If it takes a couple thousand dollars to do that, then so be it.

Back at my desk, Harper hands me a stack of faxes, and I get back to work. Things are piled up and need to get done so I can get the hell out of here. I just want to hold Emily in my arms. It's doubtful I'll ever feel like she's safe at school after this.

When the clock strikes three, I say bye to Harper and get the hell out of Dodge. Just like every other day, Damon is waiting outside to take me to get Emily.

"How'd it go this morning?" he asks. "Surely they understand what happened was completely ridiculous."

"They made excuses. Can you believe it?"

"Not surprised."

When we get to the school, I go in and get Emily from the office. At least they can listen to directions. If only they followed the rules last week, none of this chaos would have ever happened.

"Thanks for keeping my daughter safe," I said slyly, leaving the office.

How can I make sure this doesn't happen again to Emily or any other children? The news did a report on the abduction and people will be calling the school to complain and ask what they are doing to prevent this from ever happening again. Parents should be worried about sending their children to school there if they aren't going to follow the rules put in place to make sure our kids come home to us every day.

When we make it home, Emily heads straight to the kitchen for an after-school snack, while Damon and I talk about the next steps.

"So, Lex referred me to a lawyer." I hand him the card. "He's a friend of his and handles family cases. I really think even if I can't afford it upfront, talking to someone to see what can be done would help ease my anxiety when Emily is away from me. Today was awful, and I don't want that to be every day. You know?" I hold his hand. "I just want to be able to trust again, the school and myself."

He offers to help with the cost, but can I let him do that? This isn't his problem and his money shouldn't be spent on something like this. "No, I can't take your money. That doesn't feel right."

He moves closer to where he is practically inches away from my face. "Listen to me. It's my problem too. Emily became a part of my life the day of that fire. I want what's best for her, and that means getting a lawyer and making sure Chris can never do that again."

I cave, realizing he's right. There is only one other person besides my mother that I know has Emily's best interest at heart and that is him. With this help, I can secure a lawyer and get the ball rolling on some kind of action against Chris. *The sooner, the better.*

Damon calls the guy listed on the paper, Randall Richmond. He wants to talk to him about the cost and get everything on that side squared away before I get involved. I know how much lawyers cost, but he didn't want me to have to carry that burden. They stay on the phone for about twenty minutes, discussing pricing and all that jazz.

"Tessa?" Damon yells from the dining room. "He's ready to speak with you."

I take the phone and put it to my ear, "Hello, sir."

"Good afternoon. I just want to see when you're available to meet. I'd like to start getting everything together and organized for your case. Can you stop by today?"

"I'm free for the rest of the day, actually. Just tell me when."

"Okay, why don't you head over to my office. It's 5804 Bell Street."

"On my way," I say, hanging up the phone.

Damon drives me to his office. "I'll take Emily for ice cream and keep her busy while you get this handled. If you need anything, call me."

For the next few hours, the lawyer and I focus on getting information together. He asks me a million questions, and I answer honestly.

"Do you have anyone that would make a statement against Chris? Just simply to confirm that he abandoned you and didn't have contact for years? Do you have any proof of this?"

"My mother could, and maybe my old roommate. Would you like their numbers?"

"Yes, write them down on this paper, and I'll contact them."

If all goes well, we can file for an emergency temporary custody hearing that will put things in place until we actually go in front of a judge over permanent custody.

"If Chris contacts you, I wouldn't mention that you've talked to me yet. Or better yet, just don't answer the phone."

When our meeting is over, Damon picks me up, and we grab something to eat on the way back to his house. I'm not going to talk about the visit in front of Emily because there is no need for her to be in the middle of her father and me.

After we finish eating, I ask her to get a shower before bed so I can fill him in on what Randall told me. Things are going in the right direction, and hopefully we can get that emergency hearing approved.

"Time will tell. You just have to be patient and let him do his job," Damon replies with a smile and then pulls me into his lap. "Until then, try not to stress about Chris. Emily is safe with us now, and after everything that happened, he wouldn't be stupid enough to try that again."

His words make sense, but my mind just won't give in. I would worry no matter what until everything was finalized.

"But for now, Emily's in the shower and we get a couple minutes of alone time. Get over here." His lips land on mine for a sweet passionate kiss, before breaking it and looking into my eyes. "Remember, I'm always here for you two. Never be afraid to ask me for help because you two are my life now."

14

DAMON

A few days pass, and I can tell the meeting with the lawyer provided some reassurance for Tessa. She isn't completely back to her old self yet, but she's getting there. Every day, I can see the noticeable change as her anxiety goes down when dropping Emily off and picking her up. It is natural for her to feel this way after what Chris did, but soon, if everything goes right, he won't have the option to do anything like that again.

I want to do something different tonight, so Liam is coming over for dinner. At first, I thought about inviting Aiden too, but I didn't want to overwhelm her. He could be a bit much at times.

Plus, Thanksgiving is fast approaching in three days, and I think this will be a good test run. There are no qualms about Liam and Tessa getting along because he is thrilled I finally opened my heart to someone.

The doorbell sounds, and Emily races past me to answer the door.

"Hi there, little one. You must be Emily."

"That's me," she replies, giggling.

Here we go. One thing everyone worries about when bringing new people into your life is that your family incorporates them too. Not sure how to have a healthy relationship with someone if your family hates your partner. "Come on in, we have about ten minutes until dinner's ready."

He decides to join Emily in the living room and watch the latest Animal Planet special. One thing they will have in common is Liam is a huge animal lover. If he could have a tiger as a legitimate pet, he probably would. Honestly, I am still surprised he didn't go to veterinarian school and instead became a firefighter.

From the kitchen I can hear them talking about their favorite animals, and then Emily goes on to tell Liam all about our trip to the Dallas Zoo. I smile. That day was a great first adventure for all three of us, and it melts my heart to know she holds it in such high regard.

Tessa comes out of the bedroom and stares at me, wondering what the hell I'm doing. Eavesdropping, but trying not to make it obvious, thanks. I'm not sure why having them meet my brothers put me on edge, but it does. Especially Aiden. He can be an asshole sometimes and can't keep his personal opinions to himself. Perfect reason why he isn't here tonight. It's best to start slow, instead of bringing them both in and having a shitty night.

Once the food is complete, Tessa and I take it to the dining room, with Liam and Emily following suit. Most of the conversation is between those two and consists of a million and one questions about him. She really is a curious person, but that's good. It warms my heart to know they get along so well.

"So, now that you and Emily are best friends, I'd love to get to know more about you," Tessa says.

Liam isn't a shy person, but he isn't like Aiden who loves to talk about himself to others.

"I know being a firefighter runs in the family, but if you could have chosen a different profession, what would it have been?"

He scratches his chin. "Maybe a pilot. That's always interested me."

The questions continue, about him growing up and what sports he played, and then she tries to sneak in and get him to tell her all my embarrassing stories. Not going to happen.

"Nope. That's it. Enough with the questions. You don't need to hear those." I laugh.

"Okay, what about a girlfriend then?"

He blushes. "No. I work a lot so I don't seem to have much time for that. Although I'd love to find someone, it just seems like it's not the right time for me yet."

"Be patient. You'll find her."

Once dinner is done, Emily runs and jumps into Liam's arms to give him a hug before he leaves. It's so sweet to see how much they get along already. Liam has always talked about having kids someday, and hopefully he gets the chance to be a father.

After Liam departs, Tessa and I take a seat in the dining room and discuss Thanksgiving. It's coming up soon, and we need to have a game plan set. She has no problem with my brothers coming, which I didn't suspect she would, but there's one other surprise I have in store for her on that day.

"Oh, by the way, Harper asked if I wanted to get dinner and drinks tomorrow. Is that okay?"

He kisses me. "I already told you to go out and have some fun. You have me now. Go enjoy yourself without worrying about Emily. She's in good hands, promise."

Her phone rings and we both look at each other briefly before she answers.

"Hello?"

I can't hear what is being said on the other end, and it leaves me in suspense. From the slight smile on her face, it must at least be good news. My eyes are fixated on her, waiting for her to fill me in.

"Who is it?" I ask as she puts up a finger.

"All right, well, I appreciate you calling me. Yeah, I'll see you then. Have a good night," she replies and then hangs up.

"Okay, tell me already. What's the good news? I'm dying over here!"

She gets up from her chair and peeks in on Emily before coming back to sit next to me. "That was the lawyer. We were granted an emergency hearing in two days."

"How is that possible so fast?"

"They had someone cancel for whatever reason, so Randall took advantage. He contacted Chris's lawyer and let him know about the hearing. That's why I only got the call now."

I pick her up, and twirl her around, and then bring her down for a sweet kiss. That's the best news we've had all week. Finally, we can get some concrete answers on what Chris can do legally. Maybe this will help relieve some of that stress for Tessa. I try to be as supportive as I can, but in this case, there's nothing I can do.

"They are assigning a guardian ad litem to meet with each of us, inspect the homes, and then make a recommendation to the judge until the hearing for full custody is heard."

"Don't worry. They will find no reason to give him custody, Tess."

Her arms fold around my neck, and then she pecks me. "I know. I'm just ready for it to be over and finalized."

"I say you go put her to bed, and then we can have our fun." I wink at her, and she smiles in return, leaving me to go get Emily down.

With no time wasted, I lie on the fresh clean sheets, soft against my naked back, as I wait for her. Our relationship has only brightened my life, and I never want to go back to the depression. As long as we stay open and honest, there are no doubts we will make it.

About ten minutes go by, and then she crawls into bed with me, her cold feet touching me, and I shriek. "Goodness gracious, you need to warm those bad boys up."

Her head rests on my bare chest, and we relish in the quiet, not worried about anything else but spending whatever time we have next to each other. Most nights we are so tired by the time we make it in here, and we go straight to sleep, but not tonight.

Her hand sneaks downward, playing with the waistband of my boxers, lightly caressing my stomach. The soft touch brings goosebumps, and her emerald-green eyes peer at me; she doesn't say a word. Somehow, I know exactly what she wants, and I'm happy to oblige.

Tess wraps her hand around my hard cock and begins to stroke me, first slow, and then upping the tempo. My head flies back on my pillow as I try not to come too fast. A woman like her deserves immense pleasure, and that can't happen if I bow out early.

As much as I love feeling her mouth close around me, tonight is not just about me. She needs a release just as much as I do, if not more. I ease her off me and lay her back on the bed, her hair splayed out everywhere. Starting from her lips, I begin kissing, gently biting her lower lip. I continue my descent until her thighs are reached. A gentle bite ensues, and then I warm her up with two fingers. My baby needs to be ready for me, and I will make sure that happens, even with her body writhing around. As she gets wetter, another finger enters, and right before she is too close, I slip myself inside her.

"Oh," I say, groaning as her walls begin to constrict around me. My tempo is slow, trying to help us both reach the maximum intensity before speeding up. Sometimes I just want to savor the buildup instead of wham-bam-thank-you-ma'am. Although there is nothing wrong with a quickie as long as you both are up for it.

"Don't you dare make me come until you're ready too," she yells, but whimpers at the same time.

Oh, baby, tonight we are getting lost in each other.

I flip her around, with her ass up in the air, and ease myself back in, and I almost lose it. What is it about this position that just makes it that much better? The view? Tessa's ass is plump and wiggling upon every thrust, and I smack it to give her a little extra oomph.

We move in sync, trying to get there, moans and groans being heard from both of us. I speed up my pace, getting myself to the brink of no return, and we lose it, together.

I remove myself and scoot to the top of the bed, waiting for her to join me. The stress from Chris's out-of-the-blue visit, then the abduction, and now the court case has only made things better between us. It's given me the opportunity to show her the man I truly am. The person she can look forward to being with, possibly forever, and that will be by her side no matter what pops up.

Tess and Emily are my whole world now, and I won't dare do anything to mess that up. It's what I've always wanted—a family. I know some people don't want kids, and that's their own right, but for me, it's a fulfilling thing. Having a child directly depend on you and raising them to be a great person, it only makes your life better. Emily might not be my blood, but I love her as my own.

Tessa finally joins me at the head of the bed, placing her head on my bare chest, still trying to catch her breath. My fingers run through her hair, and we both stare off into space until the blackness takes over.

15

TESSA

The guardian ad litem shows up for her house check, and we both make sure everything is spotless. My hands are shaking, not knowing what kind of things they will be looking at or what questions they are going to ask.

"My name is Lindsey, and I'll be working with you today."

"Come on in," I say, opening the door all the way, trying not to make my nervousness obvious.

"Is Emily here? I'll need to talk to her as well. I'd like to do that first if you don't mind."

I call for her to come out of the bedroom, and we all go into the dining room and sit at the table.

"This part is just me and Emily. I'll let you know when we are done."

Why couldn't I be present for her questions? At first, I get upset but then realize it's probably normal protocol. For abused kids, they are more likely to tell the truth without their parents in the room, not that I'm worried.

"What do you think she's asking her?" Damon asks.

"Probably questions about me, her dad, and if she has any concerns about either. Who knows."

I try to stay far enough away to where she can't see me, but close enough to possibly be able to hear them. All I can make out is Emily laughing a couple times, and then my name. They stay in there for almost half an hour before Lindsey calls my name.

"You can go play now. I'm gonna talk to your mommy. It was nice to meet you, Emily."

She scampers off to the living room to watch TV, and I take a seat at the table.

She pulls out some papers from a manila envelope and starts writing some things down as she asks me questions.

"How long have you lived here with"—she flips over the paper and reads—"Damon Jackson?"

"Well, we have a duplex, but haven't been back to it since Chris showed up and threatened to take me to court."

"I see. So will you be staying here or there?"

"We will be staying here until I feel safe enough to take her back there. He knows that place now and I don't want something to happen again."

She nods and continues writing my response on her little paper like I'm in a therapy session. Oh goodness, I didn't even think about us staying at Damon's. Would they have a problem with that?

"How long have you known Mr. Jackson?"

"A couple of months, maybe. He was one of the responding fire-fighters."

"And are you guys seeing each other? Or just staying here?"

"We are seeing each other. Is that a problem?"

She doesn't respond, but just keeps writing, and it irritates me. Why should it matter who we live with? Emily is safer here than with Chris. End of story.

"I think I have all I need. Good luck with your hearing, ma'am," she says, getting up from the table and then shaking my hand.

Did it go well? I have no way to know until the hearing. She can't possibly think he's a better fit for her than me.

"I can tell you are freaking out already. Stop! Don't get yourself worked up. The hearing is tomorrow, and we will find out some more concrete answers then. For now, let's start dinner."

Damon and I pull out everything needed for spaghetti and begin prepping. Emily is enthralled with the special on sharks and doesn't want to help cook tonight.

Once dinner is finished and eaten, Emily goes to sleep early and we stay up talking. The hearing tomorrow is just to determine who will have custody of her until the final hearing. The woman that came today will give her recommendation to the judge and he will go from there. I'm not sure if our lawyers will speak on our behalf with evidence or if it will just be a simple hearing.

"Let's get some rest. No sense staying up worrying about something we can't control."

He's right, so I give him a kiss and sneak into the bedroom with Emily without waking her up. I don't know what I'd do if I lost her.

TODAY IS THE EMERGENCY HEARING, and after last night, I feel confident it will go my way today. It must. With Chris's history, there will be no way a judge will grant him even temporary custody. Not after hearing how he left, abandoned us, and then didn't reach out for at least three years. My lawyer is pretty confident. Especially after he swooped in and took her from school.

"Breakfast is ready!" I yell, alerting Emily and Damon.

"Smells delicious," Damon says, sneaking a kiss to my cheek before sitting down.

We enjoy our pancakes, eggs, and bacon in silence. Emily isn't aware of what today is, and I want to keep it that way. All this legal stuff doesn't need to impact her life. For her, she will go to school like normal and be none the wiser. Chris really screwed up his relationship with Emily by taking her. That's on him.

Afterward, Damon and I head to drop her off at school.

"Don't forget, we have our field trip today."

I completely forgot. "That's right. The Gardens, right? It's beautiful. You're going to love it," I reply, smoothing down her hair in the back.

With everything going on recently, I blanked on the field trip, but I am glad I didn't sign up to chaperone. There will be no way I can add that to my plate right now. The stress of this emergency hearing is already making my hair fall out, and for a short time, I consider picking up smoking to relieve some of the stress. "Make sure to listen to your teacher. Stay close to them, okay?"

"I will, Mama," she says, getting out of the car and running inside the school.

Damon takes today off and gets Liam to cover so he can come to court with me for moral support. His buddies at work are probably sick of him missing because of me, but I don't let it get to me. It is nice to have someone to support me during these times, especially with my mother being so far away. The outcome of today's hearing could change both mine and Emily's lives forever, and with everything inside me, I hope and pray that it goes our way.

"You ready?" he says, his hand landing back on my thigh. "Remember to take a deep breath and stay calm. Even if it doesn't go our way."

"What are we gonna do if they give it to him?" I ask, fighting back tears.

"We'll cross that bridge if so. Until then, don't stress yourself out."

We walk inside the courthouse, hands entwined, and find my lawyer who is standing outside the room in a suit. This man is going to fight for me and Emily. I have to keep my faith in him.

"Are you ready?" he asks, waiting for my signal, and then we walk inside together.

The hearing is over within ten minutes and leaves me happy. The guardian ad litem recommends that I retain temporary custody and the judge rules in the same favor. I almost jump for joy knowing that I get to keep my baby girl.

"See! No need to worry."

"We still have the hearing for permanent custody. Yet, after hearing him rule in my favor, I don't think I have anything to worry about. Randall has evidence and witnesses to prove Chris being unfit. I'm sure we will come up with even more by the time the hearing is here."

We enjoy the rest of the day before Emily gets out of school. Things have been nonstop hectic since Damon and I got together. Now, things can slow back down so we can enjoy our time together. Thanksgiving is tomorrow, and groceries have been acquired to cook an amazing meal for our guests. I've never been able to cook a full-fledged meal on a holiday so this will be new to Emily and me.

"You're not nervous about tomorrow, are you? Everything will go fine," Damon says, reading me like an open book.

"How do you do that? Know how I'm feeling. It's sort of creepy sometimes."

"You give it away with your facial expressions. You're not very good at hiding things."

After picking up Emily, we go home and plan out our meal for tomorrow. It will be the first holiday we spend together and his family will be here too. They seem to like us which is good, 'cause if they didn't, that could cause problems. Who wants to date someone their family hates?

I throw on some jeans and a t-shirt and get ready to meet Harper.

"Is that what you are wearing?" Damon asks.

"Yeah, what's wrong with it?"

"Nothing. Don't girls usually dress up for these sorts of things or is that just in movies?"

"Never really had a girlfriend to have dinner and drinks with, so I'll let you know when I get home." I laugh, making my way to give him a kiss and then slip out the door. Emily is already asleep in the bedroom.

I meet Harper at Dixie's Bar, which I have never been to before, but Damon and his brothers like to go here so it only seems fitting. As I walk in, the atmosphere seems less like a bar and more like a club tonight. There are people up dancing around; the music is really loud, and God forbid if someone actually wants to have a conversation in here.

"Over here!" Harper yells, her hands in the air. "So glad we could do this. I've been needing a girl to hang out with since I moved down here. Too many of them have a twig stuck up their ass or something."

"Agreed. Always thinking they are better than everyone else. What a shame."

The waitress comes over and takes our order of two glasses of red wine and a basket of wings and fries. I didn't eat dinner before coming because it was implied we would eat here, but a single order to share isn't going to be enough. So, I signal the waitress and hold two fingers up. *I'll need my own order, please and thank you.*

"So, how did the meeting go?" she says, then takes a sip of wine. "Please tell me they didn't give that asshole custody?"

"Hell no, I retain full custody. But we have a hearing to work out the rest. It's only temporary until then. But I'll take it. Chris is not going to take my daughter from me. Ever."

Things start to get a little heated when Chris comes up, and then I go on a tirade for almost twenty minutes about all the shit he did to me and how horrible of a person he is, or at least the man I knew for all those years before having Emily.

"Just remember, you have... What's his name again?"

"Damon."

"Yeah, you have him now. Who gives a shit about Chris? He should be so far gone from your mind. Don't let all this get to you. You're a good mom. Own it."

Where has Harper been all my life? I wish I had someone like her when I first moved here from Oregon. Things would have been less stressful if I had someone to talk to about things.

"You know, you haven't touched your glass of wine. Drink, girl. Drink."

I'm usually a beer girl but instead just for tonight, Harper gets me to drink some red wine, which isn't all that bad. Would I want to pay and drink it again? Probably not. I'll stick with my beer in the future, but that's what friends do. Try something new.

"Speaking of my man, it's been nice chatting with you, but I know he's lying in bed waiting on me."

"Go get it, girl," Harper says and then clicks her tongue.

I walk away with a huge smile on my face, knowing that Harper and I are going to be friends for a long time.

16

DAMON

*H*olidays always leave me getting up earlier, especially Thanksgiving. There are so many things to prepare and the turkey takes so many hours to be cooked to perfection. If something goes wrong with the turkey, then the whole meal would be subpar.

I don't disturb the girls at seven a.m. when I wake, but rather focus on getting the turkey basted and seasoned before sliding it into the oven to cook. I set the timer for four hours, and then I pour myself a cup of coffee and enjoy the view from the window. My neighbors across the street already have cars in their driveway. Our guests won't be showing up until around two or three, so we have plenty of time to get everything cooked.

About an hour later, Emily comes up and wishes me a happy Thanksgiving before going into the kitchen and pouring herself a bowl of cereal and then coming back to sit with me in the living room.

"Are you excited to see my brothers?"

"Yeah, are they bringing dessert?"

"Why does that matter?"

"We forgot to get a pie. Mama and I always have pumpkin pie for dessert."

Tessa didn't mention that to me, and I've never really been a big pie fan. Guess I'll text Liam and ask him to pick up a pumpkin pie before heading over later. I wouldn't want to break their tradition.

She fumbles out of the bedroom, straight into the kitchen. "Turkey's already in the oven? How long have you been awake?"

"About an hour or so. How'd you sleep?"

"Like a baby. Can't believe I slept in that long."

We spent the next couple of hours with the three of us on the couch watching *A Charlie Brown Thanksgiving*. It's another one of their traditions. I couldn't believe I have never seen it before now, but when I was younger, I spent most of my Thanksgiving in the kitchen helping my mom.

After the movie is over, we all three gather in the kitchen to start preparing the sides before our guests arrive. The turkey should be done just in time for their arrival. I prepare the mashed potatoes, corn, and stuffing while they focus their energy on the cranberry sauce and green bean casserole. I make everything without any mistakes, which is just how we want it.

"I just want to take a moment to say how thankful I am for you ladies. My Thanksgiving is going to be much more special with you around."

Emily comes in for a hug, and Tessa gives me a kiss. "We are happy to be here with you, too. Let's hope our first holiday goes smoothly."

The table is set, and the food is ready. All we are waiting on is Liam, Aiden, and a special surprise guest to arrive. When Tessa had suggested inviting my brothers over, my hesitancy showed. Aiden didn't like that she has so much baggage, but then again, he isn't the one dating her. Liam already met her and is thrilled I found someone. He won't be the problem.

My hope for today is that nothing gets out of hand and it goes smoothly.

The doorbell rings, and Emily runs to answer the door, only to find a surprise waiting for her.

"Hey... we made it. Sorry we are a little late," Aiden says.

"Grandma! You're here!" Emily yells.

Tessa looks at me and runs over to find her mom standing at the front door. Tears start falling, and they don't stop hugging for a good minute.

"How... are you? I... didn't know you were coming..." She is beside herself.

I wanted to surprise her. Leslie and I exchanged numbers when Emily went missing, and when I heard about her saving up to get out here for Thanksgiving, I had to help out. The fact that she hasn't seen her mom in three years killed me. What I wouldn't give to see my mom just one more time.

"Damon flew me in. You got yourself a great guy here," Leslie says.

Her eyes sparkle, and Emily won't let go of Leslie. I'm so glad she said something to me about it, or else this moment would've never happened.

"Well, let's get to the table and eat while the food is hot. Plenty for everyone." I say, ushering people into the dining room.

The entire table is covered in delectable dishes, and I stand up to start carving the turkey.

"Normally, we would go around and say what we are thankful for, but today I just want to say I'm thankful for each and every one of you for being here today, and hope we are all at this table for many more holidays to come."

Aiden and Liam whoop and holler while I carve the turkey into slithers.

"Well, dig in," Tessa says, glancing over at me.

It's crazy to think we are so cohesive. Our lives mesh perfectly together, and I wouldn't have it any other way. Since I met her, my life hasn't been the same, and every day I'm thankful to have worked that day. To have been the one to save them, or this never would have happened. I would still be stuck on the couch, alone, in a morbidly quiet house. Most likely feeling sorry for myself. But not now.

"I knew that Damon would find someone... and I'm glad it was someone as kind as you," Liam said between bites. "He really needed someone to swoop in and show him how to be happy again."

I take Tessa's hand in mine because she means so much to me. She literally pushes me out of depression and makes me realize what it's like to be happy.

"I'm the lucky one, that he opened up his heart to us," she replies.

Emily is chatting on the side with Aiden, and they are laughing up a storm. At least he is getting along with her. I don't think he would be rude to Tessa, but I hope he changed his mind about her. Most people at mine and Tessa's age have baggage. I mean look at me, late wife. That shouldn't be something that stops someone from being with another. Or else how would anyone in their thirties or older be in a relationship? They wouldn't. Baggage sometimes sucks, but it's pretty common. The real test is whether the other person can handle it and thinks it's worth it to deal with it. With Tessa, it doesn't bother me a bit. The only thing that concerns me is their safety.

Many conversations are going on and it's hard to keep up with what everyone is talking about among themselves. This is a good sign, and everyone is getting along. There is plenty of food on the table so I go in for seconds, which prompts my brothers to as well.

"Who made the green bean casserole? That's like the best I've ever had besides my mom's," Aiden says.

"That would be us," Tessa replies, pointing to herself and Emily.

"Dang, Damon. You lucked out again, landing a woman that can cook. I'll never be that lucky."

Leslie begins talking to my brothers, asking them where they work and other basic things when you first meet someone. I want to continue listening to make sure they don't drop anything bad, but I don't want to seem rude or give her the wrong impression. It's important that her mom likes us because I don't plan on going anywhere.

Aiden doesn't get out of line. In fact, he ends up having a conversation with Tessa. I stand outside the room, but eavesdrop just in case I need to drop-kick him for saying something. He's respectful, and it makes me think he might have gotten over his reservations from the past. That makes me happy. Tessa isn't going anywhere, and I really want us all to get along. She needs family in her life, and one day it will be official.

Aiden and Liam even take care of cleaning up and doing the dishes which surprised both of us because usually we did that together. But we aren't going to complain. We snuggle up on the couch and watch an episode of *Love It or List It* while her mom takes a shower. We have grown to love the show and look forward to seeing the transformations they did on the houses. It really makes me think about buying a house, one where it will be ours. Where we could make all new memories as a family one day. I haven't spoken to Tessa about it yet because we did agree to take things slow, and I don't want to scare her away. But truly, I don't think she will have a problem with it. She could have gone back to the duplex by now, but she decided not to.

"Dishes are done and the dining room is all clean. I never realized how many dishes could come out of a Thanksgiving dinner. Mom really must have hated having to do cleanup after cooking all day," Liam says.

I get my love of cooking from her, and if I was younger, you would find me in the kitchen with her preparing the sacred meal. My mom would have loved Tessa, and I really wish she could be here to meet her and Emily. She always used to tell me that I better give her grandkids, and it was sad to think she passed before she could experience it. Even if Emily wasn't biologically mine.

After my brothers leave, Emily crawls up into our laps and falls asleep. It's a perfect ending to a perfect day surrounded by those I love.

17

TESSA

*D*amon works today, so we get to spend the whole day with my mom. It has been too long since I've seen her, and she's aged. I can't believe Damon flew her out for Thanksgiving. Totally caught me off guard. These are examples why I'm falling head over heels for him. He cares and does things for those around him without any benefit to himself. So selfless.

Our morning routine is the same, except I sleep with Damon, and Emily with my mom. Yes, my mom might not be too happy about me sleeping in the same bed with him before we are married—she's old-school—but she'll get over it. I didn't want her to have to sleep on the couch. The pullout is not comfortable at all, and she already has back problems. There is no sense in making matters worse.

We sip on our coffee, snuggle up on the couch, and enjoy the quiet for a little while before they get up. Yesterday really showed me how much Damon cares. For our families to come together and get along means the world to the both of us.

"So, your mom will be here for a couple of days. Got any exciting plans?" he asks.

I haven't even thought that far ahead yet. She just got in last night. "I don't know. Maybe get out of the house and go do something. Too bad you have to work today."

"Um... it's a girls' day. I wasn't sure if you would freak out, but I booked something for you three. You've got appointments at Berlin Spa starting at ten."

"You did not?"

"I wanted you to be able to spend some time with her and vice versa. You never get to treat yourself and now's the time. It's all paid for. Just enjoy yourself."

This man is going to spoil me, and I'm not used to that. Being on my own for so long, I can't tell you the last time I even got my hair cut, let alone been to a spa. Actually, I don't think I've ever been in my life.

Emily comes out yawning and sits beside us.

"You sleep good?"

She nods, and my mom comes out right after her. "Morning, Mom. Coffee's made."

The one thing I know is my mom isn't a morning person, especially without coffee. My dad used to tell us not to speak to her until she finished with her first cup completely.

"Thanks, hon," she says from the kitchen.

Damon leaves me to get ready for work, and Emily snuggles up to me.

"I can't believe Grandma's here."

The hard part is going to be when she goes home. A couple of days just isn't long enough. *Ugh.* In the past, I've tried to talk my mom into moving down here, but she doesn't want to leave Oregon. Maybe I can talk her into it while she's visiting. Fingers crossed.

She always assumed after college that I'd come back and find a job in Oregon, but after dropping out of TSU, it made more sense to just stay in Texas. At that point, I had met Chris and moving away from him didn't seem like a viable option. She always brings up me moving back on every phone call, and I'm sure her being here will only warrant more conversations about it. Thankfully, she can see that Emily and I are doing great, and Damon is a wonderful man. She might not even ask about it, knowing I wouldn't just up and leave him behind. I'd be a fool.

Before Damon leaves for work, he gives me a kiss, Emily a hug, and bids us farewell.

"Well," my mom says, sitting down on the couch. "That's quite a man you found there."

"Tell me about it."

The thing that drives me nuts about us... we don't have sex a lot, but he doesn't complain. I don't feel comfortable while Emily is in the next room. I've given in a couple of times because sometimes he's too hard to resist. Liam has offered to watch her if we ever need some adult time, but we haven't taken him up on the offer yet. We just might soon though.

I watch her and Emily giggling and playing with a doll. Seeing them work on repairing their relationship makes me smile. After not seeing her for so long, I'm surprised she takes to her so fast. Emily isn't exactly shy, but it does take her a little bit to warm up to new people. Three years is a long time to go without seeing family, and I hope we never have to go that long again.

"So, Damon booked us appointments at the spa. Starts at ten."

"That boy spoils you, dear," she says, "but that's not necessarily a bad thing after you-know-who."

My mom loved Chris when we were together. She used to tell me I'd be crazy not to marry him. This was in our early twenties. We were young and in love, but thank God I didn't make that mistake. Back then, he was a decent guy. Something changed when I got pregnant, and everything went to hell. It was almost like it was just too much for him. I laugh, thinking back, because every man knows what happens when you have sex without protection. The chance of having a baby was pretty high, but whatever. Closer to the end of my pregnancy, he started drinking a lot. Of course, I confided in my mom but she said that was normal. Some men just need time to adjust and let their fate of becoming a father sink in. So I brushed it off, until it just kept getting worse.

"We don't say his name around here, Mom," I say. "Not after what he did."

My mom nods. "Understandable."

Something I never have to worry about with Damon, getting drunk and not coming home. Sure, he goes out and has a few beers with his brothers occasionally, but he's not an alcoholic. That's something I never want to deal with again. Total dealbreaker for me.

We all get ready for our spa day, wondering what even happens at spas. Hair? Makeup? Sauna? We can only go off what we've seen in movies.

My phone beeps with a message.

Harper: *What are you doing today?*

Me: *Spa day with my mom. Damon flew her in to surprise me for the holiday. Isn't that sweet?*

Harper: *Seriously though. Please tell me his brother is single!!!!*

Instead of answering, I smile and slip my phone back in my pocket and head to the car, wondering how this experience is going to go.

When we pull up and go inside, it's not what I'm expecting. There are women everywhere, some getting their hair done, some getting waxed, and others nails. They are in fluffy robes and slippers and look like they're having the time of their lives. *So, this must be what it feels like to be rich Stepford wives.*

"Can I help you?"

"Yes, we have appointments at ten. Tessa, Leslie, and Emily," I say, looking around the room.

Emily tugs on my shirt. "Do I get to do this too?"

I nod and a smile erupts across her face. She's so excited.

"It looks like we have you down for hair, nails, and massages. You ready?" he asks, waiting for us to respond.

"Oh yes... of course."

The three of us sit down on the salon chairs and look at each other like we don't belong here.

"So what are we doing with hair today?" a sweet middle-aged woman asks me.

"I would just like a cut for my daughter and me. Whatever my mom wants for herself is fine."

"Just a cut," she replies.

The stylist looks at us like we're insane. "Just a cut. No blowout or color... nothing? Looks like it's covered by a credit card. You can have more than just a cut, sweetie."

I think about how I always wanted to have blond highlights in my hair. Go big or go home, right? A little change won't hurt. "Blond high-lights for me. Just a cut for her."

The stylist smiles. "You only live once. Ever had your hair colored before?"

"Nope. Never."

"Then this should be a piece of cake. Sit back and relax."

These chairs have built-in foot massagers. It wouldn't be hard to take a good ole nap right here. The three of us sit back and let the ladies do their magic. Damon wants us to enjoy ourselves so I'm going to try my damndest to do so.

I'm enjoying my massage when my mom starts laughing. When I open my eyes to look at her, her hair is short. Now keep in mind that I haven't exactly been listening to their conversation, but I'm sure that's not what she asked for. It's like a pixie cut short. That's something my mother would have never asked for. She's freaking out. I try to hold my composure as I stare at the lack of hair on my mother's head and the glob of hair on the floor.

What if they mess up Emily's or my hair? Now I'm scared to close my eyes and relax after seeing what happened to my mom.

When the stylist walks away, my mom looks over to me. "What the hell did this lady just do to me? Why would she cut my hair so short? This is not what I asked for."

Her voice raises, and people around the spa start looking her way. "Mom, keep your voice down. Don't make a scene."

"Scene? Are you looking at the same haircut I am?" Her voice goes up another octave as the stylist walks back in, places a hair dryer on her station, and goes to the back.

So here we are at the beginning of our spa day, and already we've encountered an issue. Of course something like this would happen to us. It's not like we come here often so maybe she just didn't use the right words to describe what she wanted.

I look over at Emily and her hair has been cut to her shoulders which to me was shorter than I asked as well. What is wrong with this lady? How long has she been doing hair?

"Sorry. I didn't know it was going to go this bad. We can leave if you want..."

"No, I'd rather just go ahead and move on to something else. I can't stand to look at myself in this damn mirror."

When the stylist comes back, I try to come up with the nicest way to change my mind. There's no way I'm going home with a pixie cut.

"I've changed my mind. No cut or highlights for me. Maybe next time," I say, getting up out of the chair, heading for the hills.

"Would you like to go ahead and book an appointment?"

"No, not sure when I'll be back. But thank you." There is no way I'd ever get mine done here after watching the crap job done on Emily and my mom.

We move to getting our nails done, which thankfully is a better experience. Nothing goes wrong, and Emily makes my mom laugh the entire time.

The massages are the best. It's been so long since I've had one, like back when Chris and I first got together. The lady that did my massage is finding every single achy spot and fixing it for me. If I was ever rich, I'd come here like once a week just to relax. How much is this costing Damon anyway?

Once we leave the spa, we decide to go have lunch at a little diner off Ninth Terrace called Lucy's. My mom asks me all kinds of questions. Does Damon treat me well? Does he treat Emily like his own? Do I see a future for us?

And honestly I just want to tell her that I've never been treated better by a man in my life. He and Emily share a bond that I couldn't be happier with. As for the future, I hope I'm lucky enough to be married to him someday. And possibly have kids together. I can see a long and fruitful life with him and that scares me.

My mom knows how important having a loving husband and stepdad for Emily is and I know that she's being critical of Damon but there really is no reason. He's great to both of us and we are extremely lucky for him to come into our lives when he did.

Damon wants to have kids and it's a big deal for him. Before Carol passed away, his dream was to become a father and that was taken away from him. He still has a chance.

"How can you be so sure when you've only been together for such a short time?"

"The big difference in this scenario, Mom, is that we lived together. We haven't had a single fight besides the night that he told me he wanted to be with me. And only because I wanted to make sure he was one hundred percent ready for a relationship after losing his wife."

I guess my mom didn't know that his wife had passed or that he was married previously but being in his house made it obvious. He has pictures of them together everywhere and I won't dare ask him to take those down even if we get married. She is a big part of the person that he became and the person that he wants to be.

She is now directing her attention to Emily and wanting to know what Emily thinks of Damon. *News flash, Mom, she loves him.* Anyone that watches them together can tell. They are stuck at each other's hips. From the day they met they have been like best friends. He cares for her like his own and that speaks volumes for him as a man and as a future husband.

Emily smiles. "I love watching Animal Planet with him. Going to the zoo. Coloring. He plays with me, and sometimes even plays dolls with me. I hope he can be my dad someday."

At least we're both on the same page when it comes to Damon. It isn't like I want to get married next week or next month, maybe not even next year, but I couldn't be happier.

Once our food arrives, the conversation stops, and it gives me time to think about what the next step in our relationship will be. Since we already live together, does that mean that the next step is engagement? Is that something that I'm ready for? I mean it isn't like I wouldn't say yes if he asked me to marry him today because I would, but am I one of those crazy girls who got engaged after three to six months with someone?

I guess maybe I am, but not so much like the other girls. There is a big difference between a normal relationship and my relationship with Damon. The major one is that we lived together from day one of meeting each other and our happiness only grew more and more every passing day. We already know each other's schedule and what each other likes and dislikes. Normally you don't find that out until deciding to move in together and that's usually when most people have their problems. That's when most people begin to fight and realize that maybe that person is not who they are meant to be with.

But that isn't me and the person I'm meant to be with is most definitely Damon.

After I pay for lunch, we head to the fire station to pick Damon up. I wonder how long it'll take for my mom to say something about her fucked-up haircut. Or if Damon would be the first to say something?

When we pull up, Damon and Liam are waiting outside. *Please don't mention her hair or all hell will break loose.*

"Hey, girls, how'd your spa day go?" Liam asks.

Don't ask! Leave it to Liam to ask an open-ended question like that. My mom is not great about thinking before she speaks, and Damon did a nice thing for us. He didn't know our experience would be like that, and I don't want him to feel bad since he orchestrated the whole day for us.

My mom begins to answer but I cut her off. "It went great."

Liam walks around to the back seat and speaks with Emily as Damon gets in the car. I thought he'd want to drive, but instead he climbs in the passenger seat and gives me a kiss.

"Hopefully your day went way better than mine. We had two fires today, no casualties, but both homes were unsalvageable. We might have some new people moving into the duplexes. I gave them my phone number just in case."

"The duplexes?" my mom asks.

Here is something that will make my mother like him more. It will show her how caring and passionate he is toward helping others.

"Yeah, my two brothers and I bought three sets of duplexes, and we offer them out to people who lose their homes."

My mom is now looking at Damon like he's a complete saint. Maybe now she realizes why I'm falling in love with this man and how much he means to me and the community as well.

"Wow, that's really nice of you. How long have you been doing that?"

He looks at Liam and shrugs his shoulders. "I don't know. We closed on them about a week after Tessa and Emily moved in with me."

"So instead of moving into a duplex, she continued to live with you?"

Geez, Mom. I really want to give her the *what the hell* look but she is too busy staring out the window. There are reasons why we aren't living in that duplex, and frankly it's none of her business. Why is she being so judgy? I mean, can't she just be happy I found a man like him?

"Chris showed up the day after we moved into the duplex. Then the next day kidnapped Emily. So that's why we never went back. We would never feel safe there after that and Damon's house was our safe haven."

Damon looks over at me and I can tell he knows something is wrong. It isn't anything against him. My mom can be hard to deal with sometimes. She is stuck in her ways. Yet we are stuck with her; she is family after all.

Before the conversation can go on any longer, I thank Liam and head back to the house. Maybe she will chill out once we get there and stop being rude. It just seems like she's trying to find a reason not to like him, and that's not fair. He's done nothing but be kind to her, and even flew her out here to visit us. Why can't she just be thankful?

When we get there, I put my mom and Emily in the living room and Damon and I cook dinner.

"Your mom seems different today," Damon states.

I know he wants to say more, but he bites his tongue. "Yeah. She didn't exactly have a great experience at the spa today. I don't know why, but she seems kind of mad about me living with you. I'm not worried about it."

Damon just wants her to like him and there's no reason she shouldn't. Once she gets over her preconceived notions, she will see the man I'm falling in love with, and everything else will fade away.

"It's important that she like me. What can I do?" he asks, rubbing his forehead.

"That's not it. There's nothing wrong with you. She's just... her."

If things didn't start going better, I'll have to sit down and have a serious conversation with her about this. Damon doesn't deserve to feel the way he does right now, and all because she can't get past the fact that we are living with him. It's my life, not hers. *Get the hell over it.*

18

DAMON

*Y*esterday didn't go as expected. Her mom seems to be agitated with me. For the life of me, I don't understand why. Tessa says she is old-fashioned and didn't like the fact we are living together before being married, but what about Chris? Leslie liked him; that's the difference. But what have I done to warrant her not to like me? Things are different in this generation, and she is going to have to realize that eventually. Why couldn't she just see how happy we are together?

My feet drag as I walk into the kitchen to brew a pot of coffee, hoping I can sneak in a nap later. Leslie leaves today, and it's important that she understand how much I like her daughter and care for her granddaughter. I will protect them with my life.

Since it's her last day here, we should go out and do something together and let her see how invested I am in their lives already and the fact that I'm not going anywhere. Tessa means too much to me to give up, and even though she says it's okay, I know it means a lot to her for Leslie to like me, too.

"Morning, babe," she says, trotting into the kitchen and placing a kiss on my cheek. "You look rough. Feeling okay?"

"Couldn't sleep. I'll be fine. What about you?"

Leslie slept with Emily in the bedroom again, which means Tess slept in my room. Hopefully that didn't give her any more ammo not to like me.

"Good. Wish I was off today. But I think it's a good way for my mom to get to know you."

That's my fear. What if she gets to know more about me and doesn't like me, anyway? It's terrifying to think that everything else in our relationship is great, except her mother. It is a big deal for my family to like Tessa, and it's important that her mother likes me. If I want to someday marry her, then I want her blessing. That won't happen if Leslie still feels the way she did last night.

"I was thinking of taking them to the zoo. Let them have some time and get to know each other. Instead of just sitting at the house all day..."

As she pours her cup of coffee, she stops for a second. "I'd see if she would be interested. That would be a lot of walking, and she's not getting any younger. Although she'd kill me if she heard me say that."

Good point. I can always bring it up and see how she feels about it, and if not, there are other things we can do around Grapevine. This is my last chance to get through to Leslie, and I'm bound and determined to do just that.

Tessa and I snuggle up on the couch as we savor our second cup of coffee while watching the morning news. Over and over, I cringe, realizing there's nothing good being reported. It's all break-ins, murders, or stupid politics. Why do we continue to watch it? I get the remote from the table and switch it over to HGTV to view something else.

"Morning," Leslie says, strolling out of the bedroom, rubbing her eyes and searching for caffeine.

"Don't talk to her until after she finishes her first cup of coffee. Not a morning person, remember," she whispers to me.

Leslie comes and sits down in the living room, quiet as a mouse, drinking her coffee. I wait patiently for her to be finished, but gosh it takes forever. Like over an hour. As she takes her last sip, Tessa nods to me.

"So, what would you like to do today?" I ask.

Her eyes fix on mine. "I'm not really sure I'm up for an adventure after yesterday's disaster."

There's nothing I can do about what happened yesterday. *Let's move forward!*

"Well, I was thinking more like maybe the zoo. Let Emily get some sunshine. You should see the way she goes gaga over monkeys," I say.

The only response I get is a shrug.

Tessa comes out, dressed and ready for work. "Mom, you okay staying here while he takes me to work? Emily's still asleep."

"Of course, dear. Gonna have another cup of coffee, anyway."

I throw on my shoes and head out the door, waiting to speak until we are both inside the car. "What the hell happened since Thanksgiving? It's like your mom literally hates me."

"It bothers her that we lived together before we were actually dating, and that you've been married before."

"How does my being married before have anything to do with our relationship?"

"I told you, don't worry about it."

The conversation stops there. Once we pull up to the office, Tessa gives me a kiss and wishes me luck. Heading back to the house, I wonder if I should even worry about her mom not liking me anymore. It's going to give me a damn complex. And I'm not going to change who I am to appease someone else.

Heading up to my door, I can hear Emily inside laughing. When I open it, she runs and gives me a huge hug.

"Hey, sweetie," I say, taking my coat off. "How'd you sleep?"

"Good. Grandma made me cereal for breakfast."

My anxiety is high, not knowing how today is going to go. Oh, who cares. I'm not going to ruin my day. If she ends up hating me for something stupid, then so be it. At least I can say I tried.

"So guess what we are going to do today?" I say, smiling over at Emily.

"What? What?" She starts jumping up and down. "Tell me."

Leslie is staring at me, so I change course. "Well, what do you wanna do?"

I know her mom didn't want to go to the zoo, but I refuse to sit at the house all day. We should get out and have some fun.

"Could we take Grandma to the pizza arcade place? Have you ever been?"

Leslie smiles. "I haven't. That sounds like fun, baby girl."

It's decided. No zoo but at least we can do something that everyone could enjoy. Who doesn't like pizza?

"Well, you better go get dressed then. We're losing hours in the day..."

While Emily gets dressed, I talk to Leslie. As a man, I need her to know I'm serious about them.

"So, I know you have a problem with me... and I'm not sure why... but I love your daughter... Emily's like my own... I don't plan on going anywhere."

Her eyes narrow as she smirks, and then she responds, "The fact that you love her isn't the problem..."

"Then what is?"

"You guys are living together. Sleeping in the same bed. From what my daughter has told me, Emily got attached to you quickly, and I don't want her to get hurt in this. She already lost Chris..."

Well, there it is. Out in the open. Her problem with me. I get it. Chris ended up being a total douche, but I'm nothing like him. As far as living together, it's a mutual decision, and I don't see anything wrong with it. We are happy. What else does she want?

"I'm ready!" Emily says, running back into the living room to fill the awkward silence.

We head out the door toward Martin's. It's the best family-friendly, all ages, place around. They have a pizza bar, arcade games, miniature golf, and a couple lanes of bowling.

We spend the next few hours playing arcade games. Leslie seems to enjoy herself and isn't giving me as much side-eye as before. Emily holds my hand while walking around and pointing to each machine. We have plenty of time. There is no rush. I encourage her to play any game she wants.

While she is playing Hit the Otters, Leslie pulls me back a bit.

"I just want to say that I don't have a problem with you. I just don't agree with some of the things you two are doing. My daughter is smart and if she really likes you, then I'm happy for her." She smiles and pats me on the shoulder.

Maybe she is finally coming around to realize that I'm not a bad guy. That's all I want. Family is important to both of us, and even though she tells me not to worry about it, I know she cares. So I want to do everything I can to change her mind about me.

Once we get done playing the games, we hit up the pizza bar. Emily scarfs down four pieces of pizza before we leave.

I say today's outing has been a success and maybe Leslie is finally seeing how happy we all are together. She just needed a little push and some confirmation from me. Maybe today proved that to her.

19

TESSA

Why did I have to work today? It isn't very often I have to work on a Saturday, but we are behind, so everyone is here. I spend a few hours filing paperwork and getting things ready for Monday. Lex even bought us lunch for coming in today. After Kevin, I never thought good male bosses existed. One that isn't trying to sleep with me. But Lex is a good family man. I think I'm going to like it here.

"We might actually get out of here before five," Harper says, picking up another stack of papers to file. "Can we pick up the pace so we can get out of here at a decent time?"

"Why, you got some hot date I don't know about?" I ask.

"Maybe." She laughs. "No, I don't. But it's Saturday. We should be out enjoying ourselves. Not stuck in this damn office."

Lex is very particular about how things are filed, and I don't want to get yelled at if it isn't done right. "Hello, my mom is in town, remember? So I want to be anywhere but here as much as you do. Let's get this done. For both our sakes."

We each have four stacks to get to before we can leave. That's if they don't find something else for us to do after that. It's been dwindling down all day, and now it's only two stacks.

"You and Harper may leave for the day. I've got some things I need to handle," Lex says, coming out of his office.

She glances over at me and we both grab our stuff and get the heck out of there. It's Saturday. None of us should be in the office working on the weekends.

"You need a ride home?" Harper asks.

I nod and follow her and get in the passenger seat. She puts my address into her GPS and takes off, and it only takes about ten minutes to get there. Harper tells me about how hard it is to find a decent guy, and I tell her about NeverTooBusy. It's advertised on TV all the time. Maybe she should check it out and see if she can find anyone decent.

"Not sure I'm one to be on a dating app. Aren't they usually all pervs just looking to get laid?"

"Probably, but you never know," I reply as we pull into Damon's driveway. "Thanks for the ride. I'll text ya later."

The aroma of fresh pasta and vegetables is profound when I walk in the door.

"I'm home," I say loudly, setting my bag down by the door.

"Hey, didn't expect you home for another hour or so," Damon says. "Dinner is almost ready."

Emily surprises me from behind with a big hug. Maybe everything worked out today and my mom has finally decided to like Damon.

Conversation flows well during dinner, and the tension between the two of them is gone. It's nice to see them getting along. They even do dishes together afterward while Emily and I go to the living room to watch Animal Planet.

"Mom, have you checked my folder? There's a dance coming up," she asks, handing me the folder.

I open it. "What kind of dance?"

"A father-daughter dance."

My body freezes, knowing how horrible it was after my dad passed, not being able to go to these sorts of things. Is she going to ask if Chris can go with her? I can't allow that. "That sounds nice. Did you want to go?"

She's twiddling her thumbs. "Do you think Damon would go with me?"

Hearing that come out of her mouth makes my heart melt. She isn't even thinking about Chris, but Damon. He really is like her father in Emily's eyes and that means so much to me. "I think he would be honored to go with you. You should ask him."

He won't say no, but he might cry. The fact that Emily wants to go with him will mean the world to him.

When Leslie and Damon join us in the living room, Emily goes and sits on his lap. I can tell she is nervous. She doesn't need to be. Damon isn't the type of man to say no.

"So, Emily has a dance coming up."

"Oh, really. How exciting. Are you going to go?" Damon asks, tickling her.

"I want to, but it's the father-daughter dance," she says, briefly looking up at Damon. "Would you go with me?"

Damon sits still and his face softens, and then he smiles. "I would love nothing more than to accompany a princess to her ball."

Emily's eyes sparkle, and her arms squeeze his neck. "Thank you. Thank you."

Tomorrow, my mom will be flying back home. And it's nice to get to spend a couple days with her. Hopefully it won't be three years before we see her again. Emily has really enjoyed having her around. Eventually, I'd like to talk her into coming to live in Texas. Things would be so much easier if she would just move here. I hate that she's all alone, and what if something happened?

When we wake up bright and early at five a.m. to take her to the airport, Emily isn't happy. She begs her to stay. My mom's response is not what I expect. "Maybe I'll come back down here soon. I really hate going so long without seeing you girls."

Maybe she means she has given it some thought. I cross my fingers that she will come to her senses and just make the damn move.

The ride to the airport is short, but Emily doesn't want to let go of her hand when she tries to get out of the car.

"Please. Don't go. Stay with me." Tears fall from her eyes, leaving a pale streak down her face. "I'm going to miss you, Grandma."

She cups her face. "I'll be back soon, sweetie. Don't you worry."

I hug her tight. "Call me when you get home, please. Be careful."

Damon gets out and helps her take her bags inside to check in with the airline. Watching her leave is rough, for me as well as Emily, but we can't change her mind.

20

TESSA

The day is finally here for the judge to rule on who gets full custody, and if Chris gets visitation. Emily is now a little more aware of the situation because the ad litem asked her some questions about it. My goal has been to keep her out of it, don't let it affect her, but that's out the window now. She has expressed her disinterest to stay with her father again and would rather stay with us, which is expected after what he has done. Hopefully, the judge will rule in our favor, and we can move on with our lives with no say so from Chris.

I put on my black pencil skirt and cherry-red blouse in case I end up going into work after. My boss has been very understanding with this whole situation and just asked that if I get done at a decent time to come into work, if possible. That's all up to the judge. I'd imagine it would be at least a couple of hours for each lawyer to argue the case and bring up evidence, then the judge has to figure out his ruling.

My chest rises and falls. I'm ready to get this over with and stop worrying. Chris pulls up next to us, gives me the side-eye, and then heads inside the courthouse. *Fuck you, asshole. You only want to make it appear like you want full custody. If you got it, she'd end up at your parents' all the time. She's much better off with me.*

"You ready?" Damon says, his hand landing back on my thigh. "It's a big day."

Emily sits in the back seat with a new tablet Damon bought her and doesn't even pay attention to our conversation. The way she answers the questions from the judge will have an enormous impact on his decision, and as her mother, I'm scared. Not that I've done anything wrong, but even after he kidnapped her, she still loves him and wants a relationship with him. Like any little girl missing her father.

I go around to her door and open it. "Today is the day. Remember Mama told you the judge is going to ask you some questions, and all you have to do is tell the truth. That's today, sweetie. Randall is going to get you a juice box and a pack of peanut butter crackers to tide you over until you talk to him, okay?"

She runs off with him, leaving Damon and me on the steps. "What are we going to do if, by a miracle, this judge gives him visitation?" I say, walking into the courthouse. "I mean, to have to drop her off to him after he took her—how would I ever trust him to bring her back? Emily doesn't want to stay with him, but she does want to see him."

"Don't get yourself worked up over something that hasn't happened yet. Let's focus on today, and then after the outcome is decided, we can figure out what's next," Damon replies.

He has been by my side through all of this and very supportive. Damon didn't sign up for this when he met me, but the connection we have, the bond he shares with Emily has been real from the very start. There is no denying that. There will always be tough times, and it's the people that are there for you through those times that are worth keeping in your life. He proved to me that he is a loyal person and will be by my side every step of the way.

I take a breath before walking into the courtroom when my nerves attack me. My hands start to shake. In the back of my mind, the fear of him having her is terrifying. It keeps looming over me, and I can't make it go away. *Remember, trust the judge. He won't.*

The judge does the opening spiel, and our lawyers are told to plead their cases. My lawyer warned me that his lawyer would probably say many things that were false, and not to let them get to me. The fact that we have proof of his wrongdoings will overshadow anything "good" his lawyer might throw at the judge and to trust him.

"Your Honor, Chris is a parent that just wants to be around his child. He has made attempts to see her, but the mother has refused that right since she was three. He believes she still holds resentment for him leaving her and taking it out on their child by withholding visits. We are here before you today to ask that you grant joint custody."

You've got to be fucking kidding me. How can he lie like that? I start to speak, but my lawyer puts his hand on top of mine and shakes his head. He expects me to just sit here and let that imbecile lie about me and my intentions. I'm only doing what's best for our child, and he should see that, but he's too damn blind. Only thinking about himself and his image.

"No father should be kept from his child, especially one that wants to know their child. And that's exactly what the mother is doing."

I have to sit by while his lawyer keeps telling lies, to make Chris look good, but it won't stick. We have worked tirelessly getting all the evidence and proof we could get from the last few years from cell phone companies and testimonials. *He's going down.*

The judge calls for character witnesses and his lawyers bring up Chris's parents. Are they going to lie on the stand? They know exactly what happened all those years ago, and lying under oath is a federal offense, not even they would do that for their son.

"Can you tell me how long it's been since you've seen your grand-daughter, Mrs. Blakely?"

She takes the handkerchief and wipes her eyes. "Over three years."

"And have you witnessed your son trying to see Emily, only to get turned down by her?"

"Yes, many times. The holidays are about family, and she won't let us see Emily. The last time we saw her she was a toddler, and look at her now."

Emily has been brought into the courtroom and placed in the back by the doors, able to hear everything that is being said about both parents. Is she going to hate me for this when she gets older? Will she understand I only did it to protect her from getting hurt?

"No further questions for Mrs. Blakely, Your Honor."

Time is passed over to us, and Randall looks a little on edge, like something is wrong. I nudge him, but he just looks at me before standing up and beginning his argument.

"Your Honor, we are asking you to consider no visitation rights or joint custody for Chris today. If you look over the evidence, it's proven that he is unfit to take care of Emily full-time, and after the arrest for him taking Emily without permission from school, we believe it could happen again. The abuse Tessa endured while being with him leads us to believe he is a dangerous man who should not be left alone with Emily at any time."

The judge takes his argument into consideration and calls Emily up to the stand. He asks her some basic questions like who she would rather live with, does she get along with me, and is she getting good grades at school. The ad litem inspected both of our homes and even though I live with a man I'm not married to, it shouldn't make a difference. She can't live with him or be alone with him anymore. If the judge rules in his favor by some miracle, I'll stay broke fighting for what is right. End of story.

The judge instructs her to step down and thanks her for her honesty and talking with him today, and then Emily leaves the courtroom. Next, he opens the folder and starts reviewing the paperwork inside while he continues.

"He did not reach out to the plaintiff for three years. It says here he took Emily without the mother's permission, and she was later found alone in his apartment with no supervision while he was at work."

There is no denying what a shitty parent he has been. The judge is now seeing the whole picture. Chris isn't a father; he's a deadbeat who only wants his daughter around when it is convenient for him. It's a shame to think I actually loved that man once upon a time, and I'm damn happy I got away from him. Oh, what my life would be like now if I would have stayed with him all these years. *Hard to imagine.*

"Do you have any other information you would like to provide before we dismiss for recess so I can review and make a decision?" the judge asks both lawyers, who agree there is nothing further. "We will reconvene at two."

Randall packs up his stuff, and we follow him downstairs so we can talk. Did he still believe the judge wouldn't give him visitation?

"Well, his lawyer definitely tried to buy the sympathy card for the judge," Damon says, laughing. "Too bad you blew that up for him."

"Yeah, his lawyer lied through his teeth," I blurt out, frustrated about the things Chris's lawyer said. *Bullshit.*

Randall replies, "Right, but here's the thing. You were smart and brought evidence to back up your claims. He has no evidence that you were keeping him away from her, but the other way around. He didn't want anything to do with Emily. That's what the judge was able to see. Or at least I hope."

"You hope?" Why would he say it like that? I can't take bad news today. There's no way I'm going to explain to Emily that she won't have a choice but to stay with her father. No, as her mother, it is my job to protect her.

"The judge does have the final say, unfortunately. So, let's cross our fingers and hope he has some good sense," Randall replies.

We leave to grab something quick to eat across the street at a little bistro. Nothing sounds good, so Damon just orders me a burger and fries. The most I can do is pick at it.

"Come on, you need to eat something."

"I just can't. My stomach is in knots, and until I know what the judge rules, it won't stop. I'll eat after we get good news." There I go trying to push myself to be optimistic.

He runs his left hand up and down my back as he eats with the other hand until it's time to go back to hear the ruling.

"Alright, this is it. Whatever way the judge rules, we'll deal with it. I'm not going anywhere," Damon says, kissing me on top of my head and pushing the courtroom door open.

"After reviewing all information given to me at this time, my ruling is in favor of the plaintiff keeping the child and maintaining full custody." The judge pauses.

Damon and I both shriek, "Yes."

"I find that the defendant has neglected the minor child. His careless disregard for her safety when he left her alone while working makes him a danger to her. The father should adhere to the restraining order in place and not go within five hundred feet of Tessa. I order that the defendant receive supervised visitation every Wednesday at six p.m. for one hour at the Grapevine Police Department."

It's over! I can finally sleep peacefully knowing that he can't take her from me without going to jail. I wrap my arms around Damon and kiss him. "I couldn't have gotten through this without you."

21

DAMON

*I*t's been a couple days since the hearing, and things have gone back to normal around here. Emily was excited to see her father, but he never showed up to his first scheduled visit. No surprise there. All he's doing is letting her down once again and proving that Tessa is doing the right thing by keeping her away from him. Any judge will see that if he ever tries to go to court again. Emily doesn't understand why he didn't show up and blames herself, which breaks my heart.

Tessa and I have had little time alone lately, and that's going to change, at least for tonight.

I don't want her to know that all I want to do is shove her up against the wall and have my way with her. Would she like that? Since our last encounter, her moans have appeared in my dreams, begging her to ride me until I come and she does with no hesitation. Whatever I request, she gives me. Of course, it's only a dream, and women aren't like that in real life. I wish!

Carol was always super sexual, and I didn't mind it, but since getting together so young, we never really experimented. Not that I wanted to bondage her up and have her spank me or anything, but different positions every once in a while would've been nice. Regardless, she was my wife and I loved her all the same. The sex was still amazing! Feelings really make it ten times better. But with Tessa, the fact she lets me do those things to her, it was exhilarating. And then when she squatted down between my legs and took all of me, fuck, I thought I was going to blow right then, but I've been good about taking care of myself so that wouldn't happen. Coming too early can really put a damper on an evening. No one should ever leave a sexual encounter unsatisfied. And Tessa would never have to worry about that with me. I'd fuck, lick, and suck her anytime she commands, and not think twice.

It's been a couple of days and I'm craving her. I want to ravish her, but it's hard to do with Emily in the house. How can she let go and give all of herself to me if she has to focus on being quiet? Fuck that, I want to hear her scream! That gives me an idea and I pull out my phone.

"Sup?" Liam says suspiciously.

"Listen, you and Emily get along good. Any chance you could watch her while I take Tess out tonight?"

"Sure. It's not like I ever have plans of my own or anything."

"Did you?"

"No, but maybe soon." He laughs. "Anyway, I'm happy to watch her. Bring her over and I'll order in whatever she wants to eat. No biggie."

"You're the best. I'll drop her off in an hour. After Tessa says it's okay."

"See ya then."

Tessa and Emily are snuggled up on the couch watching Animal Planet as always. They look so comfortable, I almost don't want to disturb them.

"Hey, Em, you think your mama will mind if you go hang out with Liam and eat junk food?" I say, raising my eyebrow.

"Oh, come on! I never get to hang out with Uncle Liam. Please?" Emily jumps up and down in front of Tessa.

I get a sly look. "Okay, but you better mind. Or he won't let you go back."

She's funny. We both know she never causes a ruckus, but it makes Emily sit up straight on the couch.

"I will. Promise."

Tessa smiles and follows me into the kitchen. "So, why is she going over there?"

"'Cause me and you have a hot date. So you better go get ready." I smack her ass.

"Yes, sir."

I run after her, through the kitchen, down the hallway, and then we each go to our bedrooms. I'm not sure where I will take her, but a pair of dark jeans and a button-up will do.

After getting dressed, I go into the living room and sit down next to Emily, waiting for Tessa to be ready to go. Of course, it takes about thirty minutes, but well worth the wait.

"Mama, you look beautiful," Emily says, grabbing my attention.

Tessa is wearing a mid-thigh lavender dress and strappy black heels. I lick my lips. That's gonna look great on the floor later.

She twirls around. "Thanks, sweetie. Should we go? I packed a bag for you with pajamas in case you want to change before we pick you up."

Oh, so she plans for us to be late. I'm already loving the way she thinks. We are definitely fucking tonight.

Emily jumps up, and I put my hand on the small of Tessa's back, walking out of the house and to the car. Emily jumps in the back seat, and I open the door for Tessa, watching her slip inside, her dress rising up, showing off her thighs. I can't wait to spread those open after dinner and claim my dessert.

My head shakes, stopping a naughty daydream, and I get in, start the car, and head over to Liam's.

As we pull up, Emily unbuckles. "Woah, you have to wait for me to park first," I say, laughing but also being serious.

The car is put in park, and Emily jumps out and runs into Liam's arms who is waiting at his door.

"No need to come in. Go enjoy yourselves."

"Wait, here's her bag," Tessa says, getting out and walking up the driveway to hand it to him and give Emily a hug. "Love you, booger. I'll see you in a couple hours."

It takes me a minute to remember she usually doesn't get time alone without her. This might be a hard night for her, leaving her with someone.

She gets back in the car, shuts the door, and buckles. "Okay, let's go get food. I'm starving."

Shit. I haven't given the restaurant much thought. We could go to Simones. Although it might be packed. "We can try the new restaurant. The one off Red Haven."

She nods and crosses her legs.

"You keep making that dress go up farther and we might not make it to dinner," I say in a low growl as I put the car in reverse and pull out of his driveway.

She chuckles. "Is that a threat?"

"No, threats imply danger. It's more of a promise." I wink.

She uncrosses her legs, almost like she's inviting me in. Game on. I put my hand on her thigh to see what she does, and just ever so slightly they part wider, so I massage her, and start moving my hand up farther to see if she stops me. I can tell you it's hard to pay attention to the road and do this. Her breathing starts to waver, and then I hear a slight moan. That's my girl. There it is. Let me hear it again. My finger slides across her panties, and they are wet. Fuck. My dick starts to get hard. Maybe I didn't think this through. How am I supposed to get out and go into a restaurant with a hard-on? Nope. I flip a bitch and head to my house.

"Where are we going?"

"Fuck it. I want my dessert first."

Thank God we are only a couple blocks away, and I step on the gas, booking it home. We both get out of the car and run inside. I smack her ass, and she backs up against the wall. *Right where I want you.*

Her hands go around my neck, pulling me in closer. "Take me."

I hold her hands above her head as my tongue explores her mouth, and then I let go as I shift to my knees. There's my dessert, wet and begging for me to eat it. She wiggles her hips, helping me pull down her panties, and then her left leg is resting on my shoulder, giving me a great view.

"I've been dreaming of this for days. Tonight I'm gonna make you come at least three times. One from my tongue, and twice from my cock. And I promise on the last one you'll be screaming my name."

Without giving her a chance to respond, my tongue is circling her clit, ravishing her, and then the first finger eases inside and a moan erupts.

"Fuck."

"Not yet. Be patient." I chuckle.

My nails dig into her thigh, and she almost growls. *Fuck, that's sexy. Please do it again.*

Her leg begins to tremble on my shoulder, and that tells me she's getting close, which only means one thing. "Come for me. No holding back."

I want to feel her climax, her walls closing around my fingers and her body writhing from pure ecstasy. Please God, let her come so hard for me.

"Don't stop. I'm so close," she screams, running her fingers through his hair. "Right there. Yes. Yes. Yes!" And then her legs practically throw me backward against the floor.

God. She's the one. I've never been so fucking turned on in my life. The way her eyes sparkle while she's looking at me after she just came all over my hand.

I bounce up off the floor and spin her around, kissing her neck and unzipping her dress so it now sits around her waist. No bra or panties. Things just got ten times hotter. My left hand rests on her shoulder, bending her over slightly as my rock-hard cock slides into her, while she steadies herself against the wall with both of her hands.

"Now, remember what I promised you."

"Two more times. So fuck me already!"

And on that note, I thrust into her, and she moans. *Fuck, you feel so good. And I'll do whatever it takes to earn your heart.*

After ten minutes, and an orgasm later, she eases me out of her, and then walks me back to the couch and straddles me, her tits in my face in all their glory.

"I'm gonna ride you until you come for me." She takes my hands and puts them on her tits.

She eases up and onto my dick and then starts off slow. She runs her fingers through her hair, making all kinds of sexy noises, and then she bends back a little, making my dick hit a spot that clearly makes her come, but she doesn't stop. She rides through it and takes it like a champ.

As she eases back, riding me, I play with her clit to give her some extra pleasure and make her work harder so we can come together.

"Ride my dick, Tess. Show me I'm yours."

She picks up the pace, and my dick is as hard as it can get. I'm gonna come but I want it to be together so I hold out, rubbing her clit as fast I can, so we can be in sync as we come. Both of our heads fly back, and we bask in the glory of our dessert.

"I'm starving. But I think I'll always want dessert first from here on out," I say, giving her a kiss and pulling her on top of me.

"Same. Let's get dressed and actually grab something to eat. But honestly no more dress and heels. I just wanna put on some yoga pants and a t-shirt after that workout."

"Of course. Go get dressed and we'll grab some burgers or something before we pick up Emily from my brother's. It's already eleven."

I do a double take at my watch. The sex is so good, we've been going for almost two hours. How can any man give up a woman like Tess? They are crazy because now that I've had her, I'm never letting her go.

22

DAMON

*T*he father-daughter dance is tonight, and I've been looking forward to it since the day she asked me. Maybe this will put a little more pep in her step.

She's been talking about it for the last couple of days and coming out of the room wearing froufrou dresses and saying that she's a princess. And that's true. She's my princess and deserves to have someone who loves her, cherishes her, and wants what's best for her.

I take the entire day off so I can prepare while she's in school. The tuxedo shop calls and lets me know mine is ready. Tessa took her dress shopping yesterday, and I really can't wait to see what they picked out. No matter what it is, she will look gorgeous. I swing by the flower shop and pick up a corsage because what's a dance without a corsage? It makes me think back to my prom days with Carol when I put the corsage on her and ended up stabbing her.

The plan for today is to stay away from the house until it's time for me to pick her up. I'm taking her to dinner before the dance.

When it hits five o'clock, my nerves rattle. Not that I'm necessarily nervous about going to the dance with her, but with the issues with her actual father, I feel like this is an enormous step for our relationship. The night needs to be perfect.

As I head over to my house in the tuxedo, I think about what the night has in store for us. And a smile sweeps across my face, knowing that tonight is all about Emily and me.

Walking up to the door, carrying the corsage in my hand, I can hear them talking inside. The excitement was apparent in her voice.

As the gentleman I am, I ring the doorbell and wait for Emily to answer.

"He's here, Mama. He's here."

When the door opens, I fixate my eyes on her and her dress. They picked out a beautiful lilac princess gown and gave her ringlets. "Oh, my goodness. I get to go to the dance with a princess tonight. How did I get so lucky?"

I pin the corsage on her dress, and we are on our way. She does not know what I planned, and that is the best part. The surprise.

"Would you like to accompany me to dinner, my lady?"

She giggles. "Oh, good. My tummy is growling."

We get into my car and head toward the restaurant. Her smile doesn't waver for a single second on the ride over.

"Here we are, princess," I say, opening the door for her.

The inside of the restaurant is beautiful, but nothing compared to Emily. It's a nice restaurant, but not too nice where there isn't something that a kid would eat.

"Welcome to Robertson's. I'll be your server. What can I get you?"

I look over to Emily who is looking at the menu. "Do you know what you want, sweetie?"

She looks over to me and whispers, "Can you help me look at the menu?"

Of course, I forgot. She is still young and needs help reading a menu. Idiot. "Give us another few minutes."

I sit down next to her, reading her the menu. "You can have whatever you want."

After a couple of minutes, the waitress comes back and takes our order and compliments Emily on her dress.

"Thank you. We are going to the father-daughter dance."

It will never get old, seeing her smile so big. She is a big part of my life now, and her happiness means a lot to me. Her acceptance as her stepdad is huge.

"So, I wanted to talk to you about something. But it's a secret," I say, putting my finger over my lips. "Can you keep a secret from your mom?"

"Yeah."

"Okay, what do you think about your mom and I getting married someday? Would you be okay with that?" I ask, watching her face to gauge her reaction. Truth is, if I knew she would say yes, I'd ask her tomorrow.

"Married? So, you would be my dad?"

"Stepdad. But you can call me whatever you want. That's up to you."

"That would be awesome. We could finally be an actual family."

It means a lot that Emily is okay with the prospect of us getting married someday and having me as a father figure. I really try my best to do everything right by her and Tessa. My plan is to give them everything they want and more.

Once we are finished eating, I take her back to my house for a surprise. Tessa isn't even aware of my big plans tonight.

"What are you guys doing here?" she asks, stepping outside.

I can hear the trotting coming down the street and wait to see Emily's face.

"Woah. What is that?" she says, looking down the street.

A horse-drawn carriage pulls up to my house, and Emily starts crying which in turn makes me teary-eyed.

"Mama, look. Just like Cinderella! I'm a princess."

That's all I ever wanted is for her to feel as special as I know she is. This night means everything to me, and she deserves to go to that dance feeling like a complete princess.

"You didn't?" Tessa says, wiping the tears from her eyes. "How did we get so lucky to have found you?"

"Fate, babe. It brought us together."

Emily and I get into the carriage and wave goodbye to Tessa to make our way to the dance. She's so adorable, waving to all the people she could on the way. All I could do was sit back and watch her.

When we pull up to the school, everyone outside stops to watch us get out. A bunch of little girls come over and start talking to Emily.

"I love your dress."

It isn't long before she's pulling me inside to dance to some song about how a fox speaks. Weird.

The night is perfect, and we dance almost the whole time, except for when we have to take a break due to being out of breath. She introduces me to all her friends, and I truly get a look of what Emily is like outside of the house. The sparkle in her eye, and the kindness she shows others.

When we get home that night, I hate that it's over. Couldn't we go back and replay this whole day over again? Emily is exhausted, but she wants to tell her mom all about it.

I leave them alone and go into the bedroom to reminisce over all the amazing things that happened today. The future is looking promising for the three of us, and I'm overwhelmed with joy. The fact that someday I will be able to call Tessa my wife. To be able to be the husband and father I always dreamed of being. *Maybe you can have more than one true love.*

23

TESSA

*T*onight showed me the father he would be. The thought he put into things. It's magical to see everything he put together for the father-daughter dance and could really tell how much it meant to him.

After Emily finally falls asleep, I make my way into the bedroom. Damon is scrolling through his phone, looking at the pictures they took tonight. I snuggle and look them over. They seem so happy.

My lips land on his, and all I want is to show him how much he means to me. His hands curl around in my hair. This kiss feels different, hungry. I want him just as badly as he wants me.

My nightgown comes off over my head, and I want to feel his body against mine. It has been too long, and I can't wait another second.

"Are you sure?" he asks.

"Shut up and kiss me."

He grabs me by the hips and puts me on top of him. As I bend over to kiss his chest, a low moan erupts. The warmth from his skin feels great against my naked body. He pulls me down to kiss me and then rolls me over.

"I need you now."

He swipes his boxers off and kisses the inside of my thigh. The pleasure that this man gives me is earth-shattering, and I can't imagine getting to experience this with him all the time. His tongue is my weakness, and my body knows it. The powerful swirls of motion, sending shivers down my body, and then a finger enters me. They work in sync with each other to get right near the edge, and then he stops.

"Are you ready?"

I used my foot to inch him toward me, and he slides himself inside me. I sigh at the sensation. Our bodies move ceremoniously together, helping each other reach the ultimate climax. He goes deeper and deeper. *So good.*

"Let go... don't tense," Damon says, moving at a faster pace.

Not that I'm not comfortable with him, but before him, I never experienced an orgasm.

"Let go... I'm gonna..."

I do, and the passion writhes through both of us, and we know that this is the ultimate experience. Being able to make love and reach a release that's much needed for the both of us.

"That was the best sex I've ever had."

"No need to flatter me," he says, eyebrow raised.

"It makes a big difference when you love someone."

Wait, did I just tell him I love him for the first time right after sex? That's not how it's supposed to happen. My hand clasps over my eyes.

"You love me?" he asks, looking deeply into my eyes. "I love you, Tessa. More than I could ever truly show you."

It makes me feel better hearing him say those words. But it was not how I expected it to be said for the first time.

WHEN I WAKE up the next morning, I'm dreading going back to work.

"You guys ready?" Damon calls out from the front door.

He drops Emily off at school and then me at the office. "Love you. Have a good day."

Harper and I spend the morning finishing up the filing from the previous week and get done around lunchtime.

"Ready to go eat?" I ask, grabbing my lunch box that Damon made for me.

She follows me to the lunchroom, and she asks me about how the court hearing went, and I explain that it's finally over, and Chris can't just walk into our lives anymore. Supervised visitation is more than I think he should have gotten but I'm not the judge.

"Emily deserves so much better. So glad she has Damon. You make him seem like such a Prince Charming. I'm so jealous."

"Believe me, I'm lucky. I couldn't ask for a better man. Hopefully it continues to go this good. I've got no complaints."

My phone starts ringing, but it's a number I don't recognize so I decline. After the third call, I answer.

"Hello?"

"Tessa, what took you so long to answer?" It's Liam's voice on the other end of the phone.

"I'm at work. And I don't have your number saved. What's going on?" I can tell by his tone something is awry.

"Damon's hurt. At the hospital. Room 285."

I drop the phone, and Harper stares at me.

"What's wrong? Are you okay?"

"Damon. He's in the hospital. I have to go."

"Here." She hands me her keys. "Take my car. I'll tell Lex. Don't worry about it. Go."

I race to her car as fast as I can and drive like a bat out of hell all the way there and almost forget to put it in park before getting out. The automatic doors open, and I take the elevator to the second floor and approach his room. How badly has he been hurt? Mentally preparing myself for the worst, I take a breath before opening the door.

"Damon." I run to his bedside, trying to keep the tears at bay. "Oh... what happened?"

Liam tells me what happened. They were on a typical call, and the house was burning fast, but there was still a mother and child inside. "I told him not to go in, it was too dangerous, but he didn't listen. You know how stubborn he is."

As much as I told myself in the beginning not to get involved with a firefighter, Damon is my soulmate and that overrides my rule, but sitting here staring at him in this hospital bed only makes me feel like an idiot for getting so close. He could have died, and then I would have to go home and explain to Emily what happened, and it would ruin her just like it did me. Memories of the day the fire chief came to tell us my father would not be coming home flash into my mind.

As much as I hate to admit it, this day was bound to come. Damon is like my dad in that way, with a big heart, wanting to save people, but at some point he needs to recognize it's too dangerous. He should have listened to Liam, but he's stubborn.

The bleak, sterile room screams hospital, and sitting here in silence besides the beeping machines, causes me to wonder why they don't add at least a bit of color into their rooms. Being stuck in the hospital is bad enough, but with the all white walls and trimmings, it just feels like a prison. His hand is in mine, and my thumb is slightly rubbing his, as I try to stay positive and awake.

Liam is sitting on the opposite side of me, just reading a magazine. I didn't want to bombard him with questions when I first arrived because witnessing this tragedy is bad enough, but answers are needed. "So what did the doctor say?"

"He has lots of bruising on his body and cuts to his back from the falling debris. Damon will definitely be off duty for a while. Chief isn't too happy with him. Hope you are ready for him to be home for a while."

Emily wouldn't mind him being at home more, but if I know him at all, it will drive him crazy after the first couple days. He is such a productive man, and being subjected to staying inside for a long period of time is just going to get him upset. Maybe Emily and I can come up with fun ways to get him occupied like board games, charades, and maybe binge-watch some new show or something.

Speaking of Emily, she is going to have questions. Why Damon looks bruised. I don't have the heart to explain the consequences of trying to be a hero to her because she doesn't need to be worried every time he leaves the house that he might not come back. That's me, though. Especially now. He needs to understand that we are part of his life now, and even though getting people out is part of his job, he shouldn't be compromising his own life to do that. I know it's selfish, since if he didn't go the extra mile, I most likely wouldn't be alive today. No one else would have come inside and tried to find me with the way the building was collapsing. Yet, he didn't even think twice. That's just the kind of man he is—selfless.

Harper messages me to check on him and let me know she is going to come get her car, and she has a spare key so I don't have to leave his side. She really is a great friend, and I'm so glad I have her in my life.

For the next several hours Liam and I are silent, reading magazines and scrolling on our phones to help the time pass while the pain medications keep him knocked out. The clock is getting closer to three and Emily will be wondering where I am.

"I can pick Emily up from school and keep her so you can be here with him," Liam offers.

"Okay, I'll call the school and let them know you will be picking her up, and they will check your ID before releasing her."

"That's to be expected. I'll head on over in case I hit traffic. Call me after he wakes up or if you need anything."

He begins to walk out the door, but I stop him. "Don't mention this to Emily yet."

"Of course. Wasn't planning on it. See ya."

After calling the principal and telling her the situation, she agrees to let Emily leave with Liam and will personally check his ID. In reality, they should be doing this anyway if it's not the person who normally picks the child up. Too many child abduction cases happen every day and it's a good way to easily prevent that.

Right now isn't the best time to tell Emily about this. She will want to see him, and that's just not possible. I want to shelter her from the pain I endured from my father, and I never want her to experience it. She's already had such a rocky relationship with Chris, and now she found Damon who lights up her world, only to have to worry about him every day. No, thank you.

"Baby," he says, opening his eyes and blinking profusely. "You're here?"

My immediate reaction is to throw my hands over him, and he winces. "I'm so glad you're okay, but damn you. Why would you go and do that? You could've been killed."

Of course my voice did go up an octave, but he didn't seem to mind. He squints, trying to get used to bright lights right above his bed.

"I was just doing my job. There were people still inside... You know the person I am..."

I sigh, knowing full well. Selfless or not, I love this man, for everything he encompasses. That's why it's called unconditional love. You love every part of them, flaws and all. "I'm just glad you're going to be okay. I don't know what I'd do without you."

His left hand pats the bed, inviting me to come up and lie next to him. Although my butt hung off the side, it is still more comfortable than the hospital chairs. I try to be careful not to hurt him, and even though I have to keep inching closer to him to avoid dramatically falling off, he doesn't grimace once. "Please promise me you'll be more careful. I don't know what I'd do if I lost you..."

His face turns toward me, and his eyes bore into mine. "I wouldn't dream of leaving you, Tess."

My face smothers into his chest, the warmth seeping into my cheek as a couple tears escape. All my life I've dreamed of finding the perfect man, and here he is, lying next to me in a hospital room. A man that breaks the only rule I set for myself a long time ago. The day after agreeing to stay with him, things began to show. How selfless he is, what a great father he would be, and just amazingly passionate about everything he does. I never thought it would take me almost dying to find the man of my dreams, but it did. Fate pushed us together, and even though the circumstances were unorthodox, we have grown to love each other. Even after all my baggage has been exposed with Chris, my stubborn mother, and being a single mom. He never lets that falter him from wanting to be with me. Why should I let my rule, his career, jeopardize the love we share? Like everything else, sometimes you must compromise on things, and this is just that.

I pull out my phone from my back pocket and text Liam to let him know Damon's awake. His reply is a smiley face and a picture of him and Emily playing Candy Land. He's got this babysitting thing down pat. Emily loves Candy Land almost as much as Animal Planet specials. It's a close call.

Not wanting to miss a single moment, I slide the phone back into my pocket and go back to nuzzling into his chest while his eyes remain closed. The nurses come in about once an hour to check on him and ask him if he needs anything, but besides that he mostly naps.

Being this close to him only reminds me of all the precious moments we've shared. Scary things like this in movies always lead the two characters to get married quickly and pushes them to realize they are made for each other. I agree, the thought crossed my mind, but that's just not who I am. Of course I want to marry him someday and have the perfect house, with kids running around, and a marriage full of love and respect, but not just yet.

24

DAMON

Tessa stays nuzzled into me, and instead of letting her know I'm awake, my eyes remain closed as I just enjoy our time together. We don't get many moments of alone time with having a child in the house, not that I'm complaining, but this is nice. Hours upon hours of just cuddling and breathing in the lavender scent coming off her hair. Quite exquisite.

The doctor should come by to assess me and see how long until I can go home, but right now, I hope he takes his time so I can enjoy this a little longer.

Being a firefighter comes with its consequences, and both Tess and I are aware of them since losing our fathers to the job. The fear in her eyes, and the way her voice raised when I woke up, tells me she is not second-guessing being with me. I never want to put her in the position of losing me, but sometimes in the heat of the moment, I don't think properly, like today.

When pulling up to the fire, the first thing I notice is no one is outside but the cops and an ambulance, but no one else. My first thought is the people must still be inside. A flash of Tess takes over, and the only thing that crosses my mind is saving whoever is inside. The crumbling structure and cloud of smoke doesn't deter me from running inside without hesitation. I can hear Liam yelling at me, telling me to stop, but I block it out. Maybe I have a hero's complex where I feel the need to save everyone, even at my expense.

Inside, the roof is collapsing, and I can hear screams from inside the front door. There are people still in here, trapped somewhere. I do the only thing I know; I yell. "Grapevine Fire Department. Can you guide me to where you are?"

In response, all I can hear is a child sobbing, and my eyes close to block out all the other noise and focus on just her. Debris is falling all around me, and I try my damndest to follow the sound to a door. The smoke is roaring out of the crack at the bottom, and inside is where the sobbing is coming from. I touch the doorknob and the pinch of scalding hot metal hits me. Fuck. How am I going to get in there? I glance down at my suit and unzip it, taking my t-shirt I have on underneath and using it to protect my hand.

"I'm here. Everyone's going to be okay," I say, rushing over to the little girl hovering over her mother, who has clearly taken in too much smoke. "Take this shirt and put it over your nose and mouth. Run to the front door without stopping. Go!"

My eyes run over the woman's body, assessing for any injuries that could be worsened by moving her, but none appear. "I've got to get you outta here."

I scoop her up in my arms and cross the doorframe when the roof collapses right on top of me, but my body is used as a shield for the poor woman in my arms. The slicing of the debris hitting my back causes me to wince, but I know not to move until it's done. I glance toward the front door which is still flung open, leaving me a perfect view of Liam heading toward the house in full gear.

My hands grip the woman, and I try to make a break for it, but just as I get to the door, the entire roof collapses on top of me, and everything goes black.

Yes, it was stupid of me to go inside, but if I hadn't, both the little girl and the mother would have died from smoke inhalation or worse. Do I regret it? No. Sometimes as a trained first responder and firefighter we have to make a quick assessment of the situation and go with our gut. That's just what I did.

I can feel Tessa slightly sliding off the bed, and I place my hand on her butt to help hoist her back in place. "Where do you think you're going?"

She sits up and places her feet on the ground away from me. "This bed hates me, and my stomach is growling. Cafeteria food sucks, but it's my only option. Do you want anything?"

Now that she mentions it, a slice of pizza sounds pretty epic right now. So I tell her, and she goes on her merry way. I watch her as she leaves, and there's nothing better.

A couple minutes later, a knock sounds at my door, and then a man slips in wearing some scrubs and a white jacket. "Mr. Jackson, my name is Dr. Ward. I'm glad to see you're awake. How are you feeling?"

He doesn't even look up from the chart he's holding, so I give him a generic answer. "Fine. When can I go home?"

He takes a minute and writes something down and then finally makes eye contact. "Well, that depends. Do you feel dizzy or light-headed at all?"

"No, sir. Just sore."

"That's to be expected. The nurse will come and examine you and then after she writes her report, we will decide if you can go home today. For now, make sure you are drinking plenty of water and getting rest," he says before slipping back out of the room.

I never understood why doctors and nurses say that. Isn't sleeping about the only thing you can do while in the hospital? At some point, you sleep too much and then just lie awake for hours. It's not like they get any good channels on the TV for me to watch to pass the time.

"So, they didn't have pizza," Tess says, shutting the door behind her, "but they did have pasta. So I got you some spaghetti. Or do you want something else?"

"No, that's fine. Just something to put in my stomach," I say, waving my hand for her to come closer. "I'm glad you're here instead of Liam. I'm saving his lecture for when I get home."

"Oh, believe me, it's coming. Just you wait."

The last thing I remember is Liam coming toward the house before my blackout. I'm hoping the woman is okay and my body took the brunt of it.

A nurse walks in and begins to mess with the machines, and at first I think it will be weird for me to ask, but what the hell. "Ma'am. Can you tell me if there is a woman here from the same fire as me? I just want to know if she's okay. And the little girl."

She looks up from her writing and replies. "I'm sorry, the mother didn't make it. The little girl is waiting to be picked up by a social worker," she says before exiting the room.

My chest gets tight, and it feels like all my air has been sucked out of my body. *Didn't make it?* I didn't have time to fully examine her, but she seemed to be only unconscious when I picked her up. What happened?

"Baby, I'm so sorry. You did everything you could," Tess says, grabbing my hand. "Is there anything I can do?"

"Call Liam. I have to know what happened after the roof collapsed. She was still alive when I found her, I thought. Her chest was moving. It doesn't make any sense." My head falls into my hands, trying to replay the situation in my head. I remember seeing her chest rise and fall, although I didn't have time to check for a pulse with all the debris coming down. Our time was limited for an escape, and if I would have taken more time, we wouldn't have made it out at all.

The phone rings, and then his voice answers. "I need you to tell me what happened after the roof collapsed. Everything."

"Don't you think..."

"None of that you need to rest bullshit. Tell me. The woman didn't make it and the girl is going to be put in foster care most likely. I need to know what I did wrong."

"Nothing. You tried to save her. The smoke was just too much. The little girl told us when she got to the paramedics that her mom has a lung condition. I tried to get to you to help as fast I could, but not fast enough. I'm so sorry."

No, she can't be dead. That little girl can't be put into foster care. It just isn't right. Maybe she will have a family member that can take her in. No child deserves to go into foster care. Especially after losing a parent like this.

Like normal, my head starts running through our route to the fire. Could we have gone a different way to save a couple minutes? Did I hesitate when we arrived?

"I know what you are doing. Stop. You couldn't have changed the outcome, brother. This isn't your fault."

Liam knows me so well because this happens after every call. It's just how my brain works. Assess the route, the time to go inside, and if anything could have been done differently. I run back through everything, and he's right. No time could have been cut anywhere to have changed the outcome, but it doesn't make me feel any better.

Tessa gets back up on the bed with me and hangs up the phone without warning. "You are an incredible man, but this isn't your fault. You literally risked your life for her. You did all you could, baby."

Somehow hearing that doesn't make me feel any better. All I can think about is Tessa and Emily being trapped inside and wanting to save them. Is that why I almost gave up my life today?

The doctor comes back and hands me some paperwork to sign. "You are free to go, Mr. Jackson. Remember lots of fluids and rest. I've included a doctor's note that will take you off work for a minimum of one week. At your follow-up appointment, your primary physician will decide if you should be off for a longer period."

Tess jumps off the bed and begins to gather up our things. "Emily is going to be so happy to see you."

"Does she know what happened?"

"No, and thankfully none of your injuries or bruises are somewhere where she can see. So, let's keep this hospital visit between us."

I'm excited to get the heck out of here, but my mind keeps going back to the poor little girl, waiting for some stranger to take her away. It might sound stupid, but I feel connected to her, like I should at least go and check on her before I leave. "Listen, I have one thing I need to do before we leave."

"Okay?" she says questioningly.

I go to the bathroom and change into some jeans and a t-shirt that Liam left for me and head down the hallway to the waiting room. There she is, the young girl, at most age six, sitting with a backpack, staring at the doors.

"Hey, sweetie. You remember me?"

"You tried to help my mommy."

"Yes, and I'm so very sorry for what's happened. Are you okay?"

"My throat still burns, but they said that's normal."

"Yes, it is." I take a seat next to her. "Do you have any family that the social worker can call?"

"My aunt lives in Florida."

"Okay, make sure to tell them so they can get ahold of her to come get you. I know this all seems very scary, but you're going to be okay."

She leans in and gives me a big hug. Tessa is standing in the corner of the room, just watching us, with a single tear falling from her eye. "Babe, do you have a pen and paper in your purse?"

She reaches inside and pulls out a pen and a half blank receipt. "That's all I have."

"It'll work," I say, taking it and writing my number down for her. "Keep this and contact me once you get to where you are going so I know you made it okay. Can you do that for me?"

She nods and places the piece of paper in her backpack pocket.

Just as I walk outside the doors, a black van pulls up, and the social worker gets out to head inside. Her badge gives it away.

"Ma'am, my name is Damon Jackson. I helped get the little girl you are picking up out of the house. She says she has an aunt in Florida."

"We will reach out to the family once we have her in a safe place for the night," she responds without even really stopping.

Tessa tells me to wait here until she brings the car around. I know it's stupid, but she doesn't need to take care of me. I'll be okay; I just need to take it easy for a couple days, that's all. Christmas is coming up and I intend to fully enjoy it with both my girls.

The ride back to my place is silent, and it leaves me time to prepare myself for Emily. Every day when I get home, she usually runs up and engulfs me in a hug. With my bruises and pain, I have to try to hide it since Tessa doesn't want her to know what happened. It's completely her decision, and I don't want to step on her toes on this.

Pulling up in the driveway, Liam's truck is parked, and I'm sure he's waiting to give me some long lecture. Here we go.

"Do you need any help getting out?" she asks, reaching out.

"No, I told you I'm okay, just sore."

She straightens up and backs up as I walk up the driveway and to the door. I take a deep breath, knowing what's coming next as I turn the knob.

"Damon. Mommy," Emily yells, getting up from the floor and running over to us. "We got to play Candy Land."

"Oh, you did. Bet that was fun," I reply.

She hugs me, and then I take a seat on the couch to help my back from hurting. I haven't gotten a chance to look at my back, but that's where the majority of my pain is coming from, and I can guess how bad it is from that.

Tessa looks at me and then Liam. "Em, let's go figure out something for dinner."

Liam didn't even wait for them to be completely out of the room before starting. "What the hell were you thinking?"

"I wasn't. There were people inside and I didn't have time to. If it wasn't for me, they would both be dead right now. I will not feel bad for saving a life, even if it means giving up my own. I can't, brother. And I shouldn't have to."

Liam runs his fingers through his hair. "Do you remember how you felt when you lost Carol? Why would you ever want Tess to feel that? Or Emily? Next time you need to think before you act."

He acts like I do this on purpose. Of course, I would never want them to lose me, but sometimes you have to take a risk, especially with the job we have. It's literally in the handbook. How could I live with myself every day knowing I didn't do everything I could to save someone? Or someone died on my watch because I just stood by and didn't go inside. Hell no. If the fire chief has a problem, then he can take it up with me; otherwise, I will keep doing exactly this.

25

TESSA

*T*hings have been touchy since Damon came home from the hospital. Even though he has no broken bones, he still needs rest, and he refuses to take it easy—typical man. The doctor took him off work for at least a week, and he hasn't tried to go back yet, but I know it's only a matter of time before he does. Emily and I have loved having him home, and he's been watching her while I work since school is out until January 6. Christmas is tomorrow, and I'm beyond excited to share it with him. Lex let me take the entire week off, since it's usually slow around the holidays, anyway.

"You excited about our first Christmas together?" Damon says, slamming down his UNO card.

"Christmas is my favorite time of the year. My dad was a fanatic with decorating. We would cover the house in lights and decorations everywhere. It was a big deal to him."

Remembering Christmases with my dad is hard. Sometimes he got a call and had to rush out, but he still did everything he could to make me and my mom happy with the time he had with us.

"Well, you can go pick out some decorations and get them up before we go shopping. I'll have Aiden and Liam come over and help put them up."

"You don't have to do that."

"You're right. But I want to. I want our first Christmas to be perfect."

He hands me his debit card and throws me the keys. "Emily can stay here with me."

When I get to the department store, I'm overwhelmed. There are probably forty aisles of Christmas related decorations, but blowups are my first pick. Maybe I can find some that are like the ones my dad used to put up. My eyes land on a blow-up Santa with a sleigh. Emily will love this one, so I have to get it, and then before I know it, I have a snowman and a big north pole sign thrown into my cart as well. What fun is Christmas without some huge decorations. Next up, lights. They have every color imaginable in lights, and so instead of getting a box of some colors, I decide on the multicolored lights and put six boxes into the basket. My goal is only to spend around two hundred dollars so that way I can just pay with my debit card. Damon doesn't have to buy these things. I can chip in. On the way to the check out, an aisle is filled with inside decor and I pick up a few things for the living room mantle as well before finally getting into line for checkout. The basket is getting harder to push with the amount of weight inside, but I get to the lady in aisle eight and she scans all the stuff.

"Your total is four hundred twenty-three dollars and twenty-one cents."

My eyes go wide, not meaning to get that much stuff, and for a brief moment think about putting some stuff back, but then I would have to have her void the transaction and remember where I got everything. So, instead I just swipe his card. I will give him money back the next time I go to the bank.

I have a hard time getting the basket to the car, but we make it without running into anyone or anything. The lights are placed in the front floorboard, and the Santa box in the passenger seat. The other two boxes are put in the back seat along with the inside decor. I am glad I didn't get anything else or there wouldn't be room. Damon still has his trunk full of stuff.

When I get back to the house, Aiden and Liam are waiting outside for me.

"So, what'd you get?" Liam asks.

"All kinds of stuff. Here are the lights," I say, handing them the six boxes of lights to choose from. "I've never done lights before. So hopefully they work."

While they string the lights, I get the blowups situated. The three end up being big enough to see from the road which I love. The Christmas spirit is going to be big in this house and I can't wait for Emily to see.

I carry the other two bags inside to set up in the house.

"Looks like you had a blast. It's looking great out there," Damon says, sitting on the couch. "I really wish I could've helped you."

A kiss on the lips makes him shut up and follow me into the kitchen. "I got some little things for Christmas Day for the table."

He looks through the bags and appears happy with my purchases.

"It's going to be the perfect Christmas after all."

He helps me put some little things up on the mantle while his brothers continue putting lights up outside. I can't wait to see the finished look from the road. My dad would be so happy right now if he were here.

Emily is sitting on the floor, cross-legged, watching Animal Planet like usual, without a care in the world.

"Do you want to go see outside with us?"

She gets up and jets to the door. "Let's go."

We all walk to the road to see the finished product, and it's absolutely beautiful and will be around for many more Christmases to come.

"It looks like you guys are the only ones on the street prepared. Your neighbors are slacking," Aiden says, laughing.

"Liam, you think you could watch Emily for a couple of hours while me and Tessa go pick up some last-minute things?" he asks as I look at him in confusion.

"Uh, sure. I'll take her to my house."

Emily smiles and takes his hand and gets loaded up in his truck. "We'll see you later."

After they have left, I turn to Damon. "What do we need to get?"

"More presents. I haven't had a chance to grab anything, being on house arrest and all."

I know it's our first Christmas, but Emily doesn't need a million presents. Yet, who am I to tell him he can't buy her something for Christmas? Let him enjoy the little fun he's getting to have. It's the first time he's been excited since he got out of the hospital.

"Let me put on some jeans real quick, and then we'll go," he says, heading inside to change.

I get in the car and start it, so it'll be nice and warm by the time he gets in. The doctor didn't say he couldn't drive, but I figured it couldn't hurt for him to let me chauffeur him around a little bit. He gets inside and buckles up.

"Let's go get some Christmas presents."

"Where should we go?"

"Wherever you want. I've never gotten to buy presents for kids before. I'll need your help."

I take off toward Target and find the closest parking spot, so he won't have to walk a mile. He might not voice his pain, but his wincing tells me he's still in pain whether he wants to tell me or not.

The automatic doors open, and the store is filled with last-minute shoppers, so much so, people are elbow to elbow at the checkouts.

"So, what should we get her?" Damon asks.

"I've got a hundred bucks to spend."

"Baby, you have me. I want Emily to have a great Christmas and honestly, I'd like to buy her that dollhouse. She's been raving about one she saw on TV."

"I can't let you do that. It's like three hundred bucks. That's crazy."

I have to remember that every Christmas before this one, it was just me and Emily. Christmases have always been more about spending time together and not about the presents. Damon doesn't struggle and just wants to buy her something nice.

"I have put back money to get it. Don't worry. When you decided to date me, you knew that would come with added benefits. Well, one of them is having a man that wants to give Emily everything and more."

He's right. Although it's a bit of a difference from what I'm used to, he just wants to give Emily the best he can. Who am I to fault him for that?

"I really wish I could have met you sooner."

"Well, you have me now; you might as well use me to your advantage." His eyebrow wiggles. "Now, let's get to Christmas shopping."

The first thing we grab is the Victorian dollhouse that Emily has been raving about ever since she saw the commercial on TV. A girl her age should have a dollhouse but I've never been able to afford one. Damon just keeps finding more and more things he wants to get her, and about an hour later, we have two baskets filled to the brim with stuff. It's not all presents. We end up getting stocking stuffers, breakfast for tomorrow, and so much more.

"You excited to play Santa with me?"

"Extremely. Let the fun begin," he replies.

"We have to stay up late, so we can put the gifts under the tree. Eat the cookies..."

"I can't wait to see her face in the morning. This is so thrilling. She is going to be so surprised."

After paying the ridiculous amount, Damon and I head back to the house to take everything inside so we can go pick up Emily. Don't want to chance her seeing anything. I carry the majority of the stuff in, trying not to make it obvious that Damon didn't need to be carrying anything, but he notices.

"Listen, I know you think I can't. Let me help. It makes me feel worse when you treat me like I can't do anything."

"It's not that. I just don't want you to hurt yourself and have to spend Christmas in bed. No need to overexert yourself tonight."

After everything was hauled inside, we head to pick Emily up from Liam. It's around eight and we expect them to be awake, but we can see inside where they are both asleep.

"I didn't realize how late it was. Poor thing."

I knock on the door, and Liam jumps up, startled, and then sees us through the window in the door.

"Sorry, I guess we wore each other out playing board games," Liam says, opening the door to let us in.

"That's our fault. We didn't realize it was already so late," he says as I pick Emily up and load her in the car. "I'll see you tomorrow for dinner?"

"Of course. Six, right? I'll be there after my shift."

"Yup. See you tomorrow, bro."

Once home, we try to put the cookies on the sheet and into the oven the fastest we can because Emily can barely stay awake.

"Have you ever met the real Santa?" Emily asks Damon. "I haven't. But I really want to."

"When I was eight, I snuck out into the living room when I heard a noise and saw him by our tree. Without turning around, he told me to go back to bed."

"He did? Was he mad?"

"Not mad. He just wanted to make sure I got good sleep so I could be wide awake to open all my presents the next day."

The oven beeps as Emily says, "Makes sense."

We take the cookies out and let Emily go and put her pajamas on while they cool. It's so wonderful to see how imaginative kids are, and how faithfully they believe in things that have been around for generations.

"All right, same as every year. Let's put six on a plate with a glass of milk. And you, little girl, need to get some shut-eye," Tess tells her, rustling cookies on a plate and setting them on the table by the tree.

Emily runs over to Damon, gives him a hug, and then follows me into the bedroom.

"Good night, sweetie," I say, knowing it won't be long until she's passed out.

"All right, let's get started."

We sit and start wrapping the final presents and put them under the tree, admiring the Christmas tree strung with blue, white, and gold lights.

"So, what are we doing from Santa?" I ask. "She's never got a big gift from Santa... never could afford anything extravagant. And kids discuss what they get... I've always felt anything big should come from the parents, so if talked about with other kids, it doesn't make them think that they are liked less for just getting a basketball or a teddy bear from Santa. Is that ridiculous?"

Damon fiddles with his jaw. "The karaoke machine then? It's not small, but not extravagant either."

"Perfect. That's what I was thinking."

After situating all the presents under the tree, we take a break on the couch. "Man, being Santa is rough. I think I'll have a cookie and some milk before I head to bed."

I laugh. "Be careful or you'll get a dad bod. Not that I'd complain either way."

We relax and watch our favorite show until about eleven. I'm not sure what time Emily will wake up, so I don't want to stay up too late.

"Alright, I'm heading to bed. Are we forgetting to do anything?" Damon asks.

"Actually," I say, pulling him close. "You're forgetting about me."

My lips are on his, and a goodnight kiss is just what is needed.

"I'll sleep with Emily tonight. See you in the morning. Bright and early probably."

26

DAMON

It's officially Christmas morning, and the clock shows six. I want to wait for Emily to get up, but I can't lie in bed any longer. Coffee is calling my name, and I figure Tessa will be up soon, too.

I trek quietly to the kitchen to start the pot of coffee, and Tessa is already sitting at the table.

"Good morning, handsome. Merry Christmas."

She startles me. "How long have you been up?"

"About an hour. Normally Emily is up by now; guess not this year."

I make my cup of coffee and sit down next to her. It has been so long since I had experienced the real joy of Christmas. I can't wait to see Emily's face when she walks out of the bedroom, knowing that I'm lucky enough to be a part of that joy.

The first sip goes down my throat, and I get up and walk into the living room. Christmas is going to be different this year. Last year, Liam and Aiden came for dinner, but there were no presents or happy times. There is something about having kids around during the holidays that makes it that much better.

"So, I feel like I'm not getting the full experience. In the movies, the kids are always up at the crack of dawn, shaking their parents awake, telling them to get up and come look under the tree."

"Believe me, you are lucky. Last year, she was up at like three in the morning, wanting to open what little we had under the tree. So for me, this is nice to enjoy a cup of coffee before the craziness begins."

Okay, maybe three in the morning is a little early, but I can't wait to see her reaction to everything. It fills my heart to know I could buy her some nice presents, and not have to worry about the cost. Tessa seemed to freak out about the prices, but she's with me now. Emily will never want for anything. And if one day, after we get married, we have another child, it'll be the same thing. Sure, I have money put away for early retirement, but it can be used on my kids too.

We both hear the bedroom open and a gasp. She's finally up.

"Mommy... Damon... Santa came!" she screams from the living room. "Come look..."

We both run and try to play as shocked as we can.

"Wow, look at all this stuff. Someone has been a real good girl this year," Tessa says, glancing over at me with a smile.

"I can't believe it. All this is for me?" she says, her hands to her chest. "Where should I start?"

Her eyes glance around the floor, trying to pick a present to open first. She runs straight to the karaoke machine unwrapped.

"Can we sing Christmas Carols on this? Can we, Mama?"

"Of course, but let's open the rest of the presents first..."

"Can you open my gift first?" she asks, handing both Tessa and me a card.

The emotions start taking over, knowing that she took the time to make me a gift. She's the sweetest little girl. Tessa looks at me, waiting for me to open it.

I open the card, and inside is writing from her.

Damon,
Thank you so much for being my hero. For keeping me safe. And for making my mommy happy. You are the best ever. I love you.
Love,
Emily

.   .   .

I WILL CHERISH it as long as I can. She deserves to have someone like me in her life. A man that is there for her, no matter what.

"Thank you, sweetie. This means so much," I tell her, wrapping my arms around her.

Tessa opens hers and immediately starts crying. So I peek over to read it too.

Mom,
I love you. I couldn't imagine life without you. If I could have picked the perfect
mom, you would be it.
Love,
Emily

BOTH OF US are emotional at this point, staring at this wonderful little girl who loves us both. We just want to give Emily the world.

Emily sits back down on the floor and eyes the remaining stuff under the tree. Her smile has still not wavered.

"What's next?" I ask.

She picks up a smaller present, shakes it by her ear, and then begins to tear the wrapping paper. "I wonder what it is." She struggles toward the end. I guess I used too much tape on that one.

"Let me help you," I say, reaching out my hand and tugging it open slightly. "Here, now try."

The paper slides off and she screeches. "Are you serious? I've been wanting one of these. Thank you. Thank you."

I watch as she plugs the earbuds into the mini iPod and starts listening to music. Tessa downloaded a bunch of her favorite songs on it already, knowing she would want to listen immediately once she opened it. Smart mama.

Next is something I know she will love and get used often. Plus, it's something we can do together as a family.

"Hmm. I wonder what this is. No sound," she says, shaking it next to her ear again before she tears the paper. "What is it?"

I take the plastic card from her. "It's a year pass to the Dallas Zoo. So me and your mom can take you anytime you want. Isn't that amazing?"

"Thank you. Can we go this weekend?"

"Maybe. Let's get through today first." Tessa laughs.

For the final big reveal, she walks over to the huge wrapped present and just stares. Emily begins slowly taking paper off it, but it looks like she has no clue what could be inside. This is the reaction I've been waiting for, hoping she likes it. Tessa goes over and helps her unwrap it faster since it's a lot of paper.

Emily's eyes get big, and without speaking, she turns toward me, tears making an appearance. "This is... the dollhouse I begged for. Mommy, how did you do this?"

"It's from both of us. We love you, sweetie. You deserve to have something like this to play with..."

Emily runs up and gives us the biggest hugs and then goes to play with the dollhouse. She will play with it on a regular basis, and it is well worth the money spent. Hell, just to see her reaction is worth it.

"While you play, we'll cook breakfast. What would you like this morning?" Tessa asks.

Emily thinks hard. "Omelets. We all like those."

Great choice. We migrate to the kitchen to get everything together for the omelets while she plays. I take bell peppers, red onions, and bacon out of the fridge. Just how we all like them.

"So, you sick of us yet?" Tessa asks, bumping her hip into mine. "Holidays are usually stressful."

"Never. You're everything to me. Literally the reason why I look forward to coming home every day."

She smiles and begins cooking the omelets.

I watch her, wondering when I should give them my gift. Hopefully she doesn't feel like it's too soon. Hell, we are already living together anyway.

We gather around the table to eat our omelets and talk about things we will do today. Emily is set on singing Christmas carols on the machine, which I am totally for. Believe me, I can't sing, but that doesn't bother me.

"We've got one thing I would like to do after we clean up breakfast."

"Really? What?"

"It's a surprise. Let's clean up."

After getting the dishes washed, Tessa turns to me. "A surprise, huh? Should I be worried?"

"Not at all."

We grab our coats and head to the car. We pull onto Sycamore Street, and I park.

"What are we doing here? Visiting someone?"

"Stop asking questions. Follow me."

They both get out of the car, hold hands, and walk up to the front steps with me. I knock on the door jokingly. Nobody is home.

I turn around to them with a key in my hand. "This might seem sudden or maybe just the right time, but I'd like to ask you to both officially move in with me?"

Emily answers yes right away, but Tessa wavers. "What do you mean? We already live with you... but of course the answer is yes."

"Not in that house. This one," he says, putting the key into the door and opening it.

With our relationship moving forward, Tessa deserves to have a home that she can call hers too.

"You... bought a house? But what about..."

I take her hand in mine. "I know I will marry you someday. We deserve a fresh start. Somewhere we can build new memories from the three of us."

She kisses me, and I begin giving them the tour. This house is much bigger than the other one. At almost three thousand square feet, it's almost twice the size.

The thing I love most about this house is the potential to grow. It has three bedrooms, two bathrooms, and a huge fenced-in backyard for Emily to be able to play in.

"Look at this kitchen. The countertops. The island," Tessa says, running her fingers along it.

"I figured we like to cook, so we should have a good-size kitchen.

Plus, I plan on having lots of holiday dinners here in the future with you."

The next thing is the bedrooms. We walk up the staircase to the second floor, and I open the first door on the right. "This will be our bedroom."

It's a big master bedroom with a walk-in closet and jacuzzi tub, his and her sinks, and a stand-up shower.

"Let's go see your bedroom." I take Emily's hand.

"I get my own bedroom?"

I nod my head, opening the last door in the hall. "This is all yours, sweetheart."

Emily has never had her own room before, but she will here. And it's big enough to fit plenty of dollhouses and toys. Whatever she desires. This is now going to be her safe place. One just for her to enjoy.

"So now that you have seen it and agreed to move in with me..." I get down on one knee. "I figured I'd take it a step further. Tessa, you have completely changed my life for the better. Will you marry me?"

Tessa wraps her arms around me, and Emily hugs my waist. "Of course I'll marry you."

27

TESSA

y heart nearly jumps out of my chest hearing him say those four words. Sure, it's not like we've been together very long, but we love each other, and I couldn't imagine my life without him in it. *How did I end up so lucky?*

I'm entangled in his arms as he dips me and then plants a kiss.

"See, Mama. I knew you would marry Damon." Emily smiles. "Now, we never have to leave."

The last few months have been a whirlwind since he came into my life, and I couldn't ask for a better man to have by my side or for Emily to look up to. He is going to be an amazing stepdad and husband.

The entire ride back over to our old house, all I can do is stare at the ring; it's gorgeous and fits perfectly. A flawless diamond with a solitaire silhouette and an eternity band. Nothing over the top, but simple and elegant.

I snap a quick picture and send it over to Harper. We haven't spoken since the start of Christmas break, but I know she will be happy for me.

"I can't wait to tell my mom and show it off."

He looks over and smiles at me. "Your mom knows. I had to ask someone for their permission."

That makes sense now why she has been rushing off the phone with me since she came on Thanksgiving. My mom's never been good at keeping a secret.

Once we get back, it's already after one and his brothers will be here in a bit for an early dinner and we haven't even started cooking. They will understand once they find out about the engagement. *I'm freaking engaged!* It's crazy to say that, because for a long while I thought I didn't deserve someone, and then Damon walked into my life like a knight in shining armor.

The ham is already in the oven, since we put it in before we left, but nothing else is ready. We better get to work. Emily and I prepare the sides, like mashed potatoes, green bean casserole, and stuffing. This Christmas dinner might be smaller than usual, but next year we will do a big spread at the new house.

Speaking of that, Damon really outdid himself. Emily is going to have her own bedroom down the hall, and there is an extra bedroom between us, which means we will have all the privacy we need to make use of that extra bedroom and big backyard. And let's talk about the kitchen. It's like my dream setup with double ovens and a granite island with bar stools. Hosting dinner parties is going to be so much fun once we move in, with plenty of room to entertain the guests while preparing the meal and even being able to see out to the backyard to watch the kids. *Perfect.*

"What are you thinking about?" Damon asks, coming up behind me and placing a kiss on my head. "You sure do have a big smile on that beautiful face."

"Just how lucky we are to have found you. Who knows where we would be. Wanna hear something funny?"

"Hit me."

"I actually noticed you before the fire. The grocery store I used to work at."

"Damn it. Oh well, fate brought us together."

I punch his shoulder and laugh. Crazy how things work out sometimes, without you even realizing it. We both just needed that extra push and that's what we got.

The doorbell rings, and I wipe my hands off with a washcloth and stop Damon. "No, let me answer it," I say, flashing my ring. "I want to tell them."

The door opens, and Liam and Aiden are standing outside with a box of store-bought rolls. "You know we don't cook, so here's our offering to the cause. Merry Christmas."

I go to grab the box and let my ring catch their eye.

"Wait, is that what I think it is?" Aiden asks, shoving Liam aside.

"Just happened this morning. You're looking at your new sister-in-law."

Aiden comes in for a hug. "That's great. So glad he's finally found happiness again."

Liam comes in for a hug afterward. "Me too. You guys are perfect for each other and we are excited to have a niece to spoil."

Emily runs into the living room and practically pushes Liam over to hug him. "I got my own room."

Liam looks at me. "Something else you want to share?"

Damon walks in and tells them about the house he purchased just a couple blocks over from Liam's house and that we will be moving in tomorrow.

Some people might find it crazy for us to be engaged and buying a house together already, but I think it's the perfect time. From the first night at his place, I hoped that he would open his heart to me, and he did. Damon is someone who deserves everything and more. He's handsome, thoughtful, caring, and loves Emily like his own. Plus, let me not forget to mention the mind-blowing sex. It's like the icing on the cake to prove that we can make each other happy.

As we all sit down and dig into the heaping dishes, the conversations branch out and it's hard to keep track of who is talking about what, but that's the fun of having family over. You never know what's going to come up.

A knock on the door sounds. We aren't expecting anyone else.

Damon gets up from the table to answer it and in comes my mother. "Surprise."

Two visits within a few months. Something must be going on.

"What are you doing here?"

"You think I'm going to miss my daughter getting engaged and moving into her first home? Not a chance," she says, pulling me in. "Now, let me see that ring."

She twists it around on my finger, not verbally saying anything, but the smile says it all.

"Enough staring. Let's eat. I'm starving," I tell her, walking into the dining room and pulling out a chair for her next to me.

If someone would have told me just four months ago that I would be engaged before the new year, I'd have laughed in their faces, but fate intervened and pushed me and Damon together. Sure, there are things that could have kept us apart, but we fought through them and preserved.

No matter what house we live in, Carol will have a presence, and that's okay with me. Damon trusts me with his heart, and who am I to tell him he can't love her? It speaks wonders for his character that he still thinks about her every day, and we talk about her often. I want to know the woman that I am sharing his heart with, so that I can help him stay true to the man she helped him become.

The dinner table is surrounded by our family to celebrate yet another holiday, but also something special. Damon has finally accepted the fact he's ready to move on and chose to let me in completely. I will not let him down and plan to never break his heart.

This is it for me. My heart belongs to Damon. Not only has he stood by my side when he had every opportunity to run for the hills, but he has embraced Emily into his life as his own since the night we showed up at his house. I couldn't ask for a better man to share the rest of my life with or to help me raise my daughter.

I stare into his eyes, brown and bold, and then lean in to whisper in his ear, "I'll love you for eternity."

Things have been intense to say the least, like we have been on a roller-coaster ride with our hands up for months, and now we are finally at the end. I plan on taking full advantage of this high feeling and use it to push forward toward the new year. *I get to plan my freaking wedding.*

That gets me thinking who I will choose to be my maid of honor. I really only have one person and that's Harper. Do I really have to have bridesmaids too? It's my wedding and I'm just going to have a maid of honor instead. She has been there for me repeatedly since starting the high school. I hope we continue to build that friendship even when she takes over as a chemistry teacher next month.

Then I think about what the perfect date would be. How about August 31? Eight letters, three words, one meaning. *I love you.*

After his brothers leave, we start packing up things we want to take to the new house. The movers will be here around noon tomorrow to load it all up and take it over for us.

"When do I get to see the house?" Leslie asks, her hands on her hips. "If you are going over there, do you mind if I tag along?"

"Mom, you are gonna see it. Calm down," I say, laughing.

The last time Leslie was here, things didn't start off great, and it took many attempts for her to finally see how great of a guy Damon is. By the time she left, we had her support.

"I bet the kitchen is amazing. Both of you love to cook. It's got to be the best room in the house," she says, now sitting on the couch, flipping through a *Homes & Gardens* magazine.

I stare at the clock; it's almost one in the morning. "It's time for us to go to bed. We don't need to be exhausted on moving day."

"Alright. I can take a hint. Good night, sweetie," Mom says, giving me a slight kiss on the cheek as she passes to the bedroom.

As my mind starts to wind down, the magic of today still hasn't faded. I'm going to marry Damon Jackson.

"So future Mrs. Jackson, what is your final consensus on our new home?" he asks, pulling me close.

"It's the perfect start to our happily ever after."

ADMIRE ME

BOOK 2

1

LIAM

I type in *NeverTooBusy* and click search on the app store. *Am I going to do this?* Once the download finishes, an exhale escapes before I tap the open button. The screen has a 'welcome' home page and wants to know everything about me and what I'm looking for, and it sinks in how long it might take to set up this profile. This could be all for nothing. *Will I find anyone on here worth a damn?*

The guys are hovering over me, encouraging me to at least try it out a couple times and see what I find. See, some of them have used it for the wrong reasons—you know, booty calls. Men like that only cloud the waters for those of us looking for something substantial. I might be damaged goods, but even I deserve to be happy, right? Shooting blanks isn't something anyone knows except Larissa, and she didn't even wait twenty-four hours before leaving me after hearing the news. Is this going to be the issue that ruins all my future relationships?

All the guys are huddled around me at the station, trying to talk me into using this new app. For the life of me, I don't know if it's worth my time.

"My cousin met his wife on there. Just give it a shot," Pedro says, slapping me on the shoulder.

"Don't think of her," Damon says, placing his hand on my shoulder. "You deserve happiness. Get out there and find it."

I've thought about telling him, but being sterile isn't something that just comes up in casual conversation. Damon already worries about Aiden and me enough, and he has plenty on his plate without adding to it.

"You still coming over tomorrow for dinner?" Damon asks.

"Free food? I'd never miss it," I reply, walking out of the station.

I get into my brand-new Jeep and head home to answer the bazillion questions to finish my profile. I'll try it for the guys, but if it doesn't work out, then I don't want to hear them say another word. The ride is smooth from the fire station toward my house, until my stomach starts to growl, and I call in a to-go order. There's probably nothing in my fridge at home besides a six-pack since I haven't been grocery shopping this week. *Maybe tomorrow.*

I stop my Jeep in front of the diner, and the bells rings, alerting the staff to my arrival.

"Hey, darlin'. Your order is almost ready."

This place has been around forever and as teenagers, my brothers and I spent a bunch of time here. The waitresses usually recognize us as soon as we walk in. I don't eat here often, but when I do, it's always good.

She comes back with a bag and tells me to have a good night, then I get back in the Jeep and leave. The grilled onions are all I can smell now. Probably should have thought that through, but oh well. After hitting every red light back to my house, I slide the key into the door and then use my foot to close it behind me. Finally fucking home. My boots come off at the door, and I set the food on the coffee table before changing into some sweatpants. I snatch a cold beer out of the fridge and then return to the living room and sit on the couch, bracing my feet on the table and phone in hand. Let's see what they want to know about me.

The first couple of screens are basic. I'm looking for a female, but then it asks about an age range. Okay, that one might be a little harder. Not sure. I'll say twenty-eight to thirty-four. I don't have the energy to keep up with girls in their early twenties that want to drink and party every weekend.

Nice to meet you, Liam. Let's dig a little deeper so you can be on your way to better matches and better dates. Ready?

I take another sip of my beer and slide left. *What is your height?* Six foot. *How would you describe your body type?* They've got to be fucking kidding me. What kind of question is that? The options crack me up. *Slim/Slender, Athletic/Fit, Muscular, About Average, Curvy, A Few Extra Pounds, Big and Beautiful, or Heavyset.* My first pick is muscular, but then I'm pretty fit, too. What do they consider muscular? I don't body build or anything. I choose athletic and move on to the next stupid question.

What is your relationship status? Definitely Single, Separated, Divorced, or Widowed. This presents some deeper thoughts from me. So many divorcees come on this app looking for love. Am I okay with being matched up with someone who's already been married? I guess so, but sometimes that comes with a problem. Did they initiate the divorce or did the ex-husband? It can get messy if they still love their ex-husband and are not over them. Yet answering for myself is easy. Definitely single.

Do you have kids? Now, isn't this a big question. I click the *No*, but talking about kids always messes with me. Oh wait, and there's the next one. *Do you want kids?* Fuck, how can I answer this? Of course I do, but the chances of me having them are slim to none. Only a five percent chance. The options are only, *Yes, Someday, and No Way.* So I click *Yes*, since that's honest. I quickly get through the next questions about my education and where I grew up and currently live, but they just keep coming. *Do you smoke?* No. *Do you drink?* I start to laugh reading the options on this one. *No, In moderation, Sometimes—it depends on the day, and when is happy hour.* Since I do enjoy a beer or two after work, the only option that seems fitting is in moderation.

Do they really need to know all this stuff about me just to agree to a date? Jesus. Oh, then there's the next one. *What is your religion?* There are like twenty-two options listed and I decide to go with not religious. I think the last one is bad, but then here's a doozy. *What makes you the happiest?* It lists almost fifty options to choose from like cycling, basketball, fishing, stand-up comedy, playing cards, and so much more. I don't get out much so I hesitate to pick any, but it won't let me move on without selecting at least five. Playing cards, movies, stand-up comedy, travel, and working out.

Tell us about your partner in crime. It wants me to select what I want based on those same questions, but for her. So I elect for her not to be a smoker, occasional drinker, and at least five foot three. The thought of her having kids is fine because then maybe it will alleviate some pressure for me. If she already has kids, maybe the subject of having more won't ever come up. I didn't care if she had kids already. Some men might see little squirts as a deal breaker but not me. I welcome it. Especially, if she is a good mom who takes care of her kids and puts them first like they all should.

Interests to show the real you. I laugh and type: Learning to cook without the microwave. And finally, the last damn step is to upload four to six pictures of myself. I click on the camera icon to pull up my library and notice I'm not really a selfie taker. I went to my Instagram which I haven't updated in probably a year or two and pulled some photos off there.

Right after submitting, a page comes up with some profiles that match what I'm looking for and I start scrolling through them.

The first girl is blond, curvy, and her bio screams only wanting sex. It literally says, *Don't DM before 1 a.m. because I'm not looking for someone to buy me dinner.* Next! This one looks promising. Long dark hair, beautiful blue eyes, and almost a perfect smile. I scroll down to read her profile. She seems like she is well educated since she graduated from Penn State and she works in a law firm. At the same time, I'm about to hit the message button, one comes through from her.

Leslie: *I know it's already eight, but would you like to meet up for a drink?*

I take a look at myself and decide why the hell not. The guys want me to try this out, then so be it. They can hear all about it when I go back to work.

I change my clothes, tracing a finger up my shirt to the last button, which I left open. Then I run a comb through my dark-brown hair, praying that tonight goes well. Are there any good women left around Grapevine? We'll see.

Once inside my car, I give myself a pep talk to get through the nerves and prepare myself for what might happen. *Just go in with an open mind. Stay positive, damn it.*

I arrive at Dixie's bar and sit in a booth toward the back, hoping that she at least looks like her picture and this isn't a total waste of my time. I scour my surroundings, looking for her, but she's nowhere to be found. I've been told that it's normal for women to be late on dates because they obsess over their outfits and such. But twenty minutes? If she's not here in the next ten, then it'll be time for me to leave and call it a day. Punctuality is something I look for in a woman, and I hate when people are late. I'm always early to everything, and I don't want to be sitting around waiting for her forever. It looks pathetic.

The server comes over and sets a menu down on the table, but I come here often so I know exactly what I want. "Buffalo wings and a Bud Light please."

A woman resembling Leslie's picture is standing behind the waitress as she leaves. "Liam, right?"

I nod, taking in her appearance.

"Leslie. Nice to meet you."

My first concern of the night is the very short dark-red dress and heels that are easily five inches. Why do women feel the need to wear something so skimpy? It's not a turn-on for me. I try to overlook it and get to know her while enjoying my wings and a beer.

"So, what do you do?" I ask, hoping to start off the conversation so we aren't just sitting here staring off into space. An easy way to see if you are compatible with someone is to see how the conversation flows. If there is constant dead air, then it's probably time to find someone else.

"Accountant. Boring job. Can't do it without a calculator though. Gotta triple-check everything. You?"

Her profile says she works at a law firm, so did she lie? "Firefighter."

She shoots me a seductive smile, almost undressing me with it. "Oh really? Can I see you in uniform? Or better yet, help you out of it sometime?"

Really? A sex joke? I barely even know her, but that's what people expect nowadays with all these apps that make it easier to just get laid instead of getting to know someone on a personal level. Not that I don't enjoy sex. I do, but it's not something I enjoy with just anyone who throws themselves at me. In fact, it turns me the fuck off.

"I don't let women see the uniform. I'm saving that for my wife," I reply, jokingly at first.

She looks at me. "You're married?"

"No, my future wife. You seriously think if I was married, I'd bring her up on a date?"

Already she doesn't seem to be highly intelligent and a part of me wants to go home, but I let her continue her story. "So, tell me about yourself."

Instead of telling me about her career or her children, she talks all about her ex-boyfriend who screwed her over, and even I know you aren't supposed to bring up exes on a first date. Let alone bitch about them. It's a telltale sign you aren't over them.

"My boyfriend cheated on me with some skanky hoe, and he wanted me back. I can do better than him. I've been screwed over so many times, I lost track."

It's strike after strike; first the outfit and now the language. This goes on for about another half hour; my food is gone, and my beer is warm. It's not that I don't cuss, but most people on a first date are on their best behavior, and if this is her best, then I'm out. Not interested. "Listen, I think I'm gonna head home. It was nice to meet you."

I flag down the server for the check and drop twenty bucks on the table for her.

"Are you serious?" Leslie grabs her purse and gets up, pulling down her dress. "Let's go."

I cringe at the thought of her accompanying me home. She seems a little crazy, and I don't need any more of that in my life. "I meant alone."

She grabs my arm. "I'd like to go back to your place."

"I'm not interested in sleeping with you, Leslie," I say bluntly.

It might be normal, sleeping on a first date, but that's not me. Hell, even in my younger years, there had to be feelings there. Sex isn't meaningless pleasure for me. That doesn't mean I haven't had one-night stands before, but Leslie is not my type. Plus, I doubt she really has a degree from Penn State.

"And why the fuck not, you pompous prick?" Her hands land on her hips, and she's looking at me through her fake lashes.

"For that right there. I'm looking for someone who doesn't talk or act like that. Have a good night."

She follows me at first, and I worry it might escalate, but she must have found someone else to prey on inside the bar, because once outside, I look back and she's nowhere to be seen.

What a fucking nightmare that was. These guys are insane if they think this app is going to help me find my future wife. It's probably like all the other dating apps that only have tinder mindsets and it's all about sex.

Driving home, the Bluetooth alerts me that Aiden's calling, so I press the answer button on the dash. "Hello?"

"Already done with your date? That bad, huh?" He laughs, and I can feel the judgment through the phone. "Why don't you just give in? It's been too long, and you are pent up, bro. Get some and maybe it'll help."

My brother is the womanizer and I swear, I don't understand how he can sleep with a different girl all the time. I'd be worried about catching something. Hazel fucked him up in the head, and until he finally gets over her, looks like it's one-night stands.

"You don't even know half of it. She's still there if you need someone. Not my type, but definitely yours," I tell him.

"No, thanks. Heading to the airport. Think you can cover for me next week on Tuesday?"

My brother isn't one to take vacation days—hell, I can't remember the last time he even called in sick.

"Sure, where you going?"

"Don't know yet. Spontaneously going to the airport, and wherever the next flight takes off to, that's where I'm going."

"You might end up in Michigan or worse." I laugh out loud.

"I'm hoping for somewhere warm. Since when did Texas get ice and snow like this?"

Aiden isn't great about communication, and even more so about saving his inheritance. There's no telling how much he has left with the way he spends it. The only good purchase he's made is the duplexes. Other than that, it's luxurious and extravagant spending for no reason other than he's bored.

"Whatever. Be careful. Call me from wherever you end up."

I press the end button and get out of the car. The wind is howling, and the temperature has dropped drastically in the last couple of hours.

A chill takes over my body as I unlock the front door and slip inside. Thankfully, I remembered to turn the heat up before I left.

I grab a beer and sit down on the couch. So much for finding anything on that app.

My phone dings, and a part of me thinks it's Leslie bitching about me leaving her there alone. Honestly, I think her profile is made up and the only thing true is the pictures. I open the notification from *NeverTooBusy*. My eyes swivel over the woman's profile that just started viewing mine. She's beautiful with long black hair and blue eyes. Her name's Harper. I patiently wait to see if she likes my profile instead of sending her a message first, and then another notification pops up. *Harper has liked your profile. Send her a message now.* I contemplate whether I should say anything. *But look at her, she's gorgeous. Looks really sweet.*

I click the send message button, and my finger hovers over the keyboard on my phone, trying to think of something to say. *Your eyes are so beautiful.* No, that's probably something she gets all the time. I look at her profile, trying to find something that might give me an indication of something she likes, and notice she teaches chemistry. Well, I bet her mailbox gets flooded with puns and pickup lines, and I'm definitely not going to be that guy. *Ugh, come on, just ask her out.* It's not that hard. I send something basic, just to see if she's interested, and if so, we can get to know each other better.

Criminal Minds is playing on the TV, and I almost doze off when my phone dings with a message back. My chest rises and falls before opening it.

Harper: *I'd love to. What about tomorrow night?*

Tomorrow is New Year's Eve. Everywhere is going to be packed, but I agree anyway. I can go after dinner at my brother's house. He won't mind if I leave a little early.

Me: *I'm free if you are. Around 7?*

After Leslie, I'm not sure if it's a good idea, but then the guys come to mind, telling me I won't ever find someone if I don't take risks, so here I am.

Harper: *Sure, drinks? Dixie's?*

She must live close to me if she knows about that place. It's the same bar my brothers and I go to when we want a good beer every now and again.

Me: *Perfect. Looking forward to it.*

2

HARPER

I stare at my phone, seeing his last message. His profile tells me he wants kids, likes to travel, and apparently can't cook. I shake my head, thinking of him burning something on the stove after his comment, *learning to cook without a microwave*. At least he's honest. That's hard to find from anyone. His hair reminds me of the CEO-type, but the muscles seen through his uniform make me hot.

About a month ago, Tessa talked me into downloading this app and trying it. I just want to find someone to share my life with, you know, an honest person who wants an actual partner.

When I first see Liam's profile and click on the pictures to scroll through, the uniform gives me bad vibes. He probably doesn't even have to work for it. Ladies are lining up outside his door right now, just to have a shot with him, and he probably has a wall of trophy underwear. He is definitely pretty-boy-esque, and usually I steer clear of them, but after reading his profile, he makes me laugh. Ugh, maybe I shouldn't have looked or messaged him, but I can't take it back now. Please God, don't let him be a douche. I can't take any more of those.

The pretty boy types are the ones who always think about themselves first and us later. They never want to engage in foreplay and it's always about their pleasure. I stay away from those guys. Of course, I have a list, but doesn't every woman who is looking for their Mr. Right? He needs to be attractive, but in a plain sort of way. I'm not looking for someone with a six-pack, perfect teeth, and looks that make me want to grab their shirt and rush to the bedroom, but someone who can make me laugh long after his looks depreciate. If there's one thing I know, when I'm old and saggy, the man sitting next to me is going to be the same, and things that once made him seem perfect like being great in bed and being easy on the eyes, aren't going to matter. It's what he stands for, how he treats me, and that's it.

Agreeing to the date, I fear the worst. My luck with dating apps has turned out to be a monumental mistake, so much so, I promise tomorrow will be my last one. I can't handle sitting through an hour of horrible conversation with guys who do nothing but stare at my breasts and talk about themselves. It's a waste of time, and I'm not getting any younger.

I've been on five dates since joining, and they have all been terrible. Although Jamie had to be the worst. His profile showed him in Abercrombie & Fitch clothes, which I didn't even realize was still a brand. So, I guessed he would be preppy, but I was wrong. When I showed up at the bar to have a drink with him, the man who sat down across from me was anything but what the profile depicted. He had a long beard with matching hair, biker clothes on, and tattoos everywhere. Now, this might be some women's type, just not mine. I like my man to be clean-shaven or maybe a bit of a five o'clock shadow and I've never been one to like tattoos.

So, one thing I really should have put on my profile is that I hate body hair. It's called trichophobia. I don't like excessive hair on the face, like Jamie. Hell, sometimes, I can't even look people in the eye because of their nose hairs or their ears have hair sticking out. *Gross*. And don't even get me started on loose hairs all over shirts and clothing. Don't people lint roll their clothes before leaving the house, or is that just me?

When I asked him why his profile was so different, he said the pictures were from ten years ago, and he saw nothing wrong with it. I'm not one to judge someone purely on their looks; however, so much differs from the profile that I was hesitant to even continue the date, but I did anyway to give him the benefit of the doubt. He could be a really sweet guy and surprise me.

We ordered some wings and beers while he asked me some basic questions that were answered on my profile. Clearly, he didn't actually read it and just sent me a message based on my picture. So, he can judge me based on my looks, but it's wrong for me to? Kind of a double standard.

For about an hour, he mostly talked about himself, telling me about his job and things he wanted to do in life. It's great to have aspirations, but he barely let me talk, and when I tried, he would cut me off and finish his sentence. *Rude!*

I finally decided I was done and let him know I was ready to head out and that's when he asked if I wanted to go back to his place. My firm answer was no, and so he slid me the check and said, "Why don't we split it then."

"So, because I don't agree to go home with you, you want me to pay for my half?" Fine. So I did, and I let him know I was not interested in seeing him again before hustling out to my car to get the hell out of there.

Some men just really appall me. The way they think that just because we don't sleep with them, we should have to pay for our own dinner? Now, do I think it's always the man's responsibility to pay for the ticket? No, but he made it clear the only reason I was paying was because I said no to his offer. Jamie was a perv, and I never wanted to see him again or that ridiculous beard.

When Tessa asked about the date, after I filled her in, she laughed hysterically for like ten minutes. I don't know why it's so funny. We've been texting each other every day, and when I found out she got engaged, she asked me to be her maid of honor. Of course, I said yes, because she's a wonderful woman and has my back. That's what friends do.

I commend her for all she does. Being a single mom for almost six years takes a lot out of someone, and she is still caring and willing to help others. I haven't met her fiancé yet, but the way she talks about him makes my heart melt. They seem so perfect for each other, and they found each other when neither of them were looking.

I pick up my phone and shoot her a text.

Me: *I have a date tomorrow night. I'll text you 911 if I need you to call and give me an excuse to leave. You know the drill.*

I haven't used her for that yet, but the day is bound to come eventually. Hopefully Liam turns out to be a good guy and his profile rings true.

Kids have always been a big part of my future, and to do that, a husband is required. Although, I guess I could go to a sperm bank, but I want my child to have a loving mother and father, just like I did.

Thinking about that makes me tear up, reminding myself that I'll never get to see my parents again. Yet, I don't let myself get caught up in it, and instead, I start surfing more of Liam's profile.

He doesn't smoke, thank God. The lingering smell on smokers is overwhelming. I briefly dated one, and it just didn't work out. He drinks. Well, good because I sure do enjoy my wine at night. There is wrong with that.

Although when school gets back in session, I take over as the chemistry teacher and it's a little overwhelming. Most of the break has consisted of me coming up with my lesson plans. After I graduated with my degree and moved to Grapevine, the receptionist position put me in the position to take over once their current teacher was set to retire. So, all I had to do was bide my time for a little while. It's what I enjoy doing, helping students learn a subject, especially if they think they won't do well and end up acing my class. That's my goal in my first year—to help students find a love for chemistry and get an A at the end.

I've always been an ambitious person at everything in my life, and that's what my parents were most proud of. They knew I would work hard to achieve my dreams no matter what was put in front of me. They believed in me, and I wish they were still alive to see how well I'm doing.

My phone vibrates.

Tessa: *Good luck. Hope it goes well. Have you picked an outfit yet?*

She has a good point. What the hell am I going to wear? I'm not exactly a big shopper, and most of my clothing has been with me for years. I dig through my closet to the back where all my nicer dresses are.

Me: *It is New Year's Eve. So should I dress up a little more? What do you think?*

I snap a photo of a maroon dress.

Tessa: *No, something more... glittery.*

Okay, something that has that New Year's vibe. I get all the way to the back and my eyes land on a silver strapless dress, not too short but just long enough, and I snap another picture.

Tessa: *Perfect! That's the one with your black pumps. He won't know what hit him.*

I glance at the clock. Holy crap, it's one in the morning. I hang up the silver dress at the front of my closet, and then I get in bed, smothering myself with the covers. School is back in session in just a few days, and I need to show the principal that I'm ready with a kick-ass learning plan and that means being prepared on day one. *Like a boss.*

3

LIAM

*B*efore I even step outside, the frost covering my windshield gives me insight that it's going to be a slick drive. As I run to my truck, the cold air is nipping and biting me. I hope the temperature rises soon. Switching on the defroster, I run back inside, waiting for the frozen portion to disappear before beginning my drive over to my brother's new house. It's a couple blocks away, but it's only a high of thirty-four degrees today, which is abnormal for Texas. Mother Nature is giving us a beating. What the hell did we do to piss her off? I can't remember the last time snow was on the ground here. At least a decade.

My relationship with Damon hasn't always been the best, especially after his wife passed years ago and he hit rock bottom. There was nothing Aiden and I could do to bring him out of it for the longest time. That is, until he found Tessa and Emily. They have played a huge part in helping him recover and open his heart again. If they didn't come along, his depressive state would've gotten worse. *Thank God for them.*

Their story is unique—and one day—I want to find my happily ever after. Yet, finding someone who will accept me has been rough. Not being able to have kids is hard for me, let alone asking someone else to share that fate. Since finding out, I have been hesitant after Larissa.

For a while, I didn't think I should date because subjecting someone else to not being able to have kids of their own is awful. Who wants to be that person?

The windshield is now clear of ice, so I run out to the car and get inside before the cold air cuts through me. The roads are slick, and my tires go sideways a couple times, reminding me it's also time for new ones. We get little ice and snow in Texas, but this year must be the exception. Most of us aren't used to driving in this type of weather, which only makes matters worse. You end up with people going either twenty miles per hour or sixty. There's no in between.

As I pull onto his street, I'm flabbergasted. *Holy crap!* These houses are gigantic and look like they cost a pretty penny. Damon must have gone all out, but that's just what I expect. He's always wanted someone to share his life with, even from a young age. Like me, he wants someone he can give everything to, and when Carol passed, he lost faith that he could be happy until he found Tessa.

My eyes land on a two-story house and I start muttering to myself how rich those people must be when I see the address on the mailbox. *This is his house?* Damon is pretty tight with his money, but it's obvious he didn't spare any expense when buying this. *Maybe he can loan me some money and I can upgrade, too.*

The porch is held up by pillars, and the front door is bright red, which only adds a little pop to the grayish color of the house, but the snow on the ground almost makes it sparkle in the little bit of sunlight left.

"Hello? I'm here," I say, opening the front door and walking inside, instead of waiting for them to answer.

"We're in the kitchen," Tessa yells out.

There is a staircase leading up to the second floor on my right, and the living room is in front of me. I cross through that, which has to be eight hundred square feet by itself, with a built-in entertainment center. My eyes widen, taking in the size of it. *Who needs a living room this big?*

"You want a tour?" Damon calls. "Did you get lost?"

Hell, I can get lost in this house. "No, but how big of a house did you need? It's only the three of you, right?"

The kitchen is the biggest room so far with granite countertops, two islands, and double ovens. We spend most holidays at Damon's house because Aiden and I can't cook for nothing. Maybe I should be happier, because that only means more ways for them to cook their delicious food on Thanksgiving and Christmas next year.

"I'm just saying, this house is bigger than I expected," I say, looking around the kitchen, which has a door leading to the backyard. Outside, there is about an acre and a playset.

Damon leads me outside. "This is Emily's favorite area, well, except for her bedroom. Wait until you see those."

Yes, the shock still hasn't worn off, but I'm happy for him. If his dream of having kids comes true, this backyard will be perfect for little ones to run around and play in.

We go back inside, and he hands me a beer before questioning me about how last night went. Apparently, Aiden has already told him it was a disaster.

"Oh, don't even get me started. The guys are insane for even making me sign up for that online crap. It's useless."

Tessa laughs at me. "I could've told you that. You have to be super picky on those. But there are good ones. Don't give up just because of one shitty date. Hell, I can't tell you how many horrible dates I've been on."

She's right. The women are good-looking, but it's not all about looks. Someone can be gorgeous on the outside and completely crazy on the inside. The woman I'm looking for is wife material. And yes, I know it's not possible for me to know on the first date if they are without asking some off-the-wall questions. The point is, whoever I end up with should be good with kids because even though I can't impregnate someone, that doesn't mean later down the line we might not adopt a child. There are plenty of kids who need good parents, and so many poor children are struggling to get out of the foster care system.

"Look at how Damon and I met. It was the craziest of situations. You need to stop looking. That's when she will fall into your lap," Tessa tells me, patting me on the shoulder. "The best things happen when you least expect them to."

The problem is, I don't want to stop looking. If I did, it's plausible that I'll be fifty and single. *Dear Lord, don't let that happen.* "I've got a date tonight. Might be my last one for a while if it goes bad. Crossing my fingers that this one goes well."

Tessa calls Emily down for dinner. The table always looks like it's a holiday covered in serving dishes filled to the brim with something warm and delicious. Maybe I'll get lucky and find someone who can cook. That is a major plus. No one wants to rely on me for the cooking or else someone will end up sick. Hell, I tried to cook Raviolis last week in a pot. I thought I did good, but then I tasted them and spit them right out into the garbage. So, me and the stove don't mix well.

"Uncle Liam," Emily says, running into the kitchen and engulfing me in a hug. "I'm sitting next to you."

"It's been a while, kiddo. Like six whole days!"

The conversation over dinner is about the duplexes and how many people we've been able to help since buying the properties. Most only stay a week which works since there is always another fire popping up to claim someone's home. It's the best investment we ever made. We don't only use them for victims of fires, but anyone who might need a place to stay until they get back on their feet after something awful. Last week, I let a guy move in whom I've known for a couple years and his house got foreclosed on because he lost his job and once he got a new one, he just couldn't catch up. We are nice people, and helping the community is something we will always want to do, but having a caring heart is important. Everyone needs help at some point in their life.

"Has Aiden been over to see the house yet?" I ask.

"I believe his words were, what are you trying to do, one-up me?" He laughs.

Damon's house is bigger than Aiden's by a long shot. Hopefully, he didn't go out and try to buy a new house just to prove a point. Sounds like something he would do.

We move on to small talk about Emily going back to school, Tessa updating us on her new ideas for the wedding, and even listening to her talk about it is raising my blood pressure. She talks a hundred words per minute, and trying to follow her train of thought is practically impossible.

Damon hasn't been kidding. I thought he had been exaggerating, but listening to her firsthand, I feel sorry for him. Apparently, she is making a running list of things that are my job for the wedding. Not that I mind. It will keep me occupied. Wedding planning isn't really my strong suit but if it helps her and Damon out, then so be it.

Once dinner is over, Emily gives me a tour, mostly wanting to show me her bedroom. We make it up the staircase and into the master bedroom. *Jesus, they are living like kings and queens.* The bedroom and en suite are the size of a presidential hotel room. Not kidding. And don't even get me started on the size of the walk-in closet that could fit all my clothes times four. Why do they need all this? I know we have money but it could be better spent somewhere else. Damon's never going to have enough clothes to fit in that damn closet.

"There's more. Come check out mine." She pulls on my hand. "It's the best room in the house."

The door opens to a giant bedroom painted a soft pink with built-in bookshelves and two massive dollhouses. I can see why she is so giddy about it. Coming from a single parent home, she never had a bedroom of her own, and likely didn't have many things to play with since Tessa lived paycheck to paycheck most of the time. That isn't a dig, but Damon has explained to me before how they lived.

"Wow, you have two now?" I ask, knowing she obsesses over them. "You are the luckiest girl in the world."

We sit on the ground playing, something I hope to do with my own daughter someday.

"So, I take it you like your room, huh?"

"It's the best. I've never had my own room before. I can be as loud as I want and never wake them up."

Emily always makes me laugh. She is very honest, as are most kids her age. They don't have a filter. You can always count on them to give it to you straight.

Damon texts me to come downstairs instead of just coming up to get me. *Lazy bum.*

"What, you couldn't just come get me?"

"I yelled, but you obviously didn't hear me," he replies.

"Ahh… probably because you live in a damn mansion and I was three miles away."

He shakes his head and rolls his eyes, then gestures toward the living room where Tessa is sitting on the couch. When he starts talking, it sounds like he's giving me a lecture, but toward the end, I can tell he's just worried. Damon doesn't want me to look for love in all the wrong places or end up dating someone just because I want to settle down. That isn't me. I won't do something like that, because I have a relationship to look at and see what I want. Their relationship is as close to perfect as you can get, and yes, I'm jealous. Not that I want Tessa at all, but just the bond and intimacy they share with each other. You can see how compatible they are, how good they work together, and just the overall love they share.

My watch beeps, informing me it is time to head to my date. "Wish me luck. Maybe this will be a good one, and it'll start my new year off right."

Harper and I are going to a mutual destination, Dixie's. The bar will have enough bodies around to give her a secure feeling. I wonder if her profile is authentic. It's not like there's a fact-checker option. I cross my fingers, praying that this is it.

Entering the bar, I snatch a booth near the back and patiently await Harper's arrival. I hope she looks like her picture. Sometimes they don't, especially with all the filters and stuff available nowadays.

There she is, standing by the front door in a silver strapless dress, her left hand across her torso, holding on to her right. Harper glances around the place until her eyes land on mine. A smile takes over her face as she walks toward me. Her long legs catch my eye and I try not to drool. Those would look great around my shoulders, hips, or anywhere really.

"It's jam-packed in here tonight. Maybe we should've chosen somewhere else," Harper declares, slipping into the booth and setting her handbag down. "Although, I should've expected as much with the holiday."

We survey each other, while the painful first date silence comes into effect. She looks precisely like her picture, with modest makeup, which is how I favor my women. "You're very beautiful. The picture doesn't do you justice."

A blush comes over her face. "You're not so bad yourself."

Harper is gorgeous with long dark hair, inviting blue eyes, and lips that I'd love to sink my teeth into later. If the date goes well, of course.

"So, you're a teacher, right?" I confirm, recalling her profile didn't distinguish what level. "What grade?"

"Tenth. Chemistry."

I have so many questions. Why did she want to become a teacher? She must have a lot of patience to deal with a revolving door of teenagers. There is no way I can ever do that job.

"Do you love it? Or was there something else you dreamed of becoming?"

She tucks her hair behind her ear. "I've always wanted to be my own boss, although I guess that's like the most basic answer. Doesn't everyone?"

The problem to that is the income. It would be based on how hard you work. Sometimes I find that thought more stressful than just holding down a regular job. "I'm not sure I'd want all that pressure on my shoulders. Running a business from scratch could be very difficult, but invigorating if it went well."

The discussion is progressing and doesn't seem awkward like other dates. It is an appreciable change of pace to not have to force it, and it just comes naturally between the two of us.

We obtain our drinks and chat about our jobs a bit more. There is no need to dive into the deep stuff just yet. It isn't like I can just come out and ask her if she wants kids. I need to play it cool, be myself, and see where the night takes us.

One thing I know for certain, she is one hundred percent more my type than Leslie.

"So, not to be too forward, but why is a guy like you on an online dating website? It doesn't seem like you would have an issue getting girls," she says, peering around at the prying eyes.

"I'd suggest the same. Every man turned their head when you strolled through the bar."

If this date results in anything, honesty plays a vast part. Harper is a down-to-earth girl, and from what I know about her so far, I can see us getting along very well. There are many things I note about her just from observing, like her tell is tucking her hair behind her ear, and she isn't high-maintenance. Even though the dress she's wearing probably cost a pretty penny, her hair is natural, nails aren't fake, and again, minimal makeup. That says a lot about a woman.

"The genuine answer is the women in Grapevine don't seem to want something real. Just sex."

"And you thought you'd find something real on the app?" She chuckles and tells me about a couple of disastrous dates she has been on recently.

"Well, it looks like we've both had the same luck. Maybe tonight's our night," I suggest, lifting my bottle to hers. "Here's to discovering something real."

4

HARPER

So far, with Liam, the conversation has flowed naturally, and he has expressed his interest in finding a real relationship like me. I'm almost thirty-one, and at this rate, my eggs are going to dry up before I find a man to marry, let alone have kids with.

He's the first guy in a while, to be honest, every time I ask a question, there is no sly redirecting or evading without an answer. Who the hell would have known I would find someone like him in a sea of jellyfish?

"Would you like another one?" he asks, pointing to my beer.

"Yes, please," I respond, taking the last swig into my mouth, my lips around the rim of the bottle. "I didn't expect this date to go well, and I figured I'd be home before nine, in my pajamas and watching some drama show."

He holds his finger up to get the bartender's attention and asks for two more beers. "I didn't know what to expect. I'm glad I came, though. I had second thoughts on the way here."

See what I mean? He's so forthcoming and honest. That's hard to find in a man, let alone a person anymore. The only thing that is a deal breaker for me is if he didn't want kids. All my life I have dreamed about being a mom someday and that's one dream I will never give up, not for anyone.

"Do you live in Grapevine? I haven't seen you around, and it's sort of a small town," he asks eagerly with an eyebrow heightened.

"Yeah, I live in the new housing development off Heather Court. I'm only subletting though. I don't plan to buy until I find the perfect home, and that's slow going."

"I own my house, but I don't plan on staying there forever. In a couple years, I plan on selling it and finding my forever home to grow old and senile in." A laugh erupts from my throat, and his eyes dart over to me, and then a grin appears.

"What? We all become at least a little senile in old age. Nothing to be ashamed about."

He's a jokester, and I like it.

We sip on our beers and keep the conversation going. I tell him about the three states I've ever been to, and I don't count in airports or if I stopped in to get gas on a road trip. It only counts if you are in that state for more than half a day. Liam has been a couple places, but nowhere iconic. There's something we share—wanting to travel, but not having someone to do it with. Seriously though, who wants to go to somewhere amazing by themselves? No, you want friends or a partner to share the experience with or it's just boring and lackluster. Somehow we glaze over our love of music and jump straight to current show binges. He laughs when I mention my current watch.

"I'll never understand the hype behind vampires and such. Do women really want to be with someone like that? I mean, from my perspective, Edward from *Twilight* was a stalker. Yet, women just think he is amazing. I'll never understand it. Now, Jacob wasn't a bad dude; he liked her before he knew what he was, and he just wanted to keep her safe."

"Wait, are we really about to get into a deep conversation about *Twilight* right now? 'Cause I'm down if you are."

"Let's not. I'm more into things like *Law and Order* and cop shows. Or like unsolved mysteries."

I watch them, too, but only when I'm really bored and can't find anything else.

He looks down at his watch and sighs. "I really would love to stay, but my shift starts early and my boss will kill me if I'm late."

He catches me off guard because I thought we were both enjoying the night. Is he trying to let me down easy? "No worries," I say, picking up my purse and slinging it across my body. "My best friend will be calling to check in shortly, and if I don't answer, she'll probably report me missing or something."

"We don't want that. I really enjoyed tonight. I'd love to take you out again," he says, his hand on the small of my back as we walk out of the bar and into the quiet, cold night with only the sound of crickets as music.

"Just call me when you're free," I say, standing by my car, awkwardly waiting for the goodnight kiss. After the nice date, I am expecting him to lean over and make his move, but he just stands there with his hands in his pockets, almost like he's too scared to do it. *Just kiss me, dammit.*

"Have a good night. Get home safe. I'll call you soon," Liam replies, giving me a quick peck on the cheek like I'm his damn sister or something, then opens my door for me. I wait for him to get into his vehicle before my hands hit the steering wheel. *What the hell is that about?* Is my Batman signal on the fritz? Because I practically begged. The first guy I find attractive in a while who isn't a complete douchebag and he doesn't even kiss me? Instead of harping on it, I put the car in drive and head home.

Tessa will be dying to hear about it. Maybe she can help provide some insight on why the hell he didn't kiss me on the lips. A kiss on the cheek isn't how you end a date. Or maybe he couldn't read my body language and didn't want to overstep. My mind goes through many scenarios. Yet none of them seem plausible in the least.

Tessa has been there for me, and after doubting myself, I need to talk to someone.

Me: *Details on date over coffee tomorrow?*

I slip my silver dress to the floor and ease on a t-shirt to replace it. The couch looks like a comfy place to be for a couple hours until I'm tired enough to sleep. I might as well enjoy my last couple of days before school is back in session and most of my free time is gone. I turn the TV on. *Real Housewives of Atlanta* is playing, but I use the remote to flip through the channels until I come across *Chicago Fire*. It only seems fitting to watch a bunch of sexy firefighters, living vicariously through them until I know if Liam is going to call or not. *Fuck, I hope he looks like they do with his shirt off.*

THE NEXT MORNING, I'm lying on the couch in my pajamas with my phone next to me, going over our date last night and wondering if he will call me. Honestly, I've been out of the actual dating game for far too long and have no idea what the proper etiquette is. Are you supposed to wait a certain period of time before texting someone? *Ugh.* Whatever, I will just wait patiently until his name shows up on my notification bar. Until then, I'll watch some of the *True Blood* TV series. I'm not really sure what attracted me to start it, but I'm glad I did. One thing that caught me off guard is how much sex is in it. Is there an episode without it? Nope. Not so far, and I have three seasons to go.

Now that I've met Liam, he reminds me a little of Alcide from the show. He's not as tall but has the scruffiness. And then my mind takes over, and I imagine him as an alpha werewolf. Why do we crush on men who are vampires and werewolves? I think it's being drawn to something unknown. If these things were real, it wouldn't be this way. Yet I let my mind wander anyway.

After watching four episodes back-to-back, I contemplate calling Liam myself, but what do I say? Or will he even answer? The more I think about it, the more I talk myself out of it. I should just wait for him to call.

Fuck it... the line starts trilling and with each passing ring, my anxiety rises. Three... four... voicemail. *Are you serious?* Now he is going to see that I called and didn't leave a message.

I need to get out and clear my head, so I text Tessa.

Me: *Wanna meet up at the café?*

I head straight to the bedroom and open the closet to rummage through until I find a t-shirt and some leggings. I've got to get out of here. Maybe I can wrap my head around this while eating a quiche and sipping on a mocha.

Tessa: *Be there in 5.*

The walk is short to the café, and after ordering, I find a table toward the back so everyone doesn't overhear me talking about my date. The mocha latte is the perfect temperature, just how I love it, and I set my phone on the wooden table so I can hear it vibrate if he calls. *God, I hope he does.*

I barely slept last night. Sometimes, I hate being a woman because you never know what the men are thinking, and it drives me nuts. Did he enjoy our date? He did say he would love to take me out again, so I would assume. Or did he just say that to make me feel better?

"Hey, girl, what crisis are we in today?" Tessa says, setting her bag down next to the table. "I take it the date went bad?"

I wrinkle my nose. "No, actually it went great, or so I thought, but he kissed me on the damn cheek like we are twelve. Weird, right?"

She nods, taking a sip of her Frappuccino with extra whipped cream. "What did you wear? Something not too revealing, but just enough, right?"

"I wore my silver dress. The one you helped pick out."

"Okay, so it wasn't the clothing. It could've been something you said, or he's just one who likes to move slow. Why are you stressing yourself out already? It hasn't even been twenty-four hours yet."

"He hasn't text or called."

"Again, it's not even been a whole day. If it went as good as you say, then he'll reach out. Give him time. Men aren't like us. Chill."

She has a valid point. Maybe he's busy at work or doing something else and he plans on calling me tomorrow or something. "That's why I have you to keep me sane. I love you."

Instead of making this coffee date all about me, I inquire about the wedding, and I should've known better. She whips out this binder filled to the brim with her ideas and layouts. Tessa has really been obsessing over this, and if she continues down this path, she might not make it to the wedding.

"I don't know which one to pick. This venue allows outside vendors, whereas this one requires you to use their list. They are around the same price, but they are both so beautiful. I can't decide anything else until this is set in stone."

"Is it still August thirty-first?" I ask.

She nods, still flipping through the photos of the venues.

"I say go with this one. It's got more of an elegant look to it, unless you want to go more rustic, then this one is perfect."

"See, it's hard, right? If I don't make a decision by the end of next week, I might just have you close your eyes and point. Damon says he doesn't care which one it is, as long as I'm standing at the altar next to him on the wedding day."

"You truly found a wonderful man. Hopefully, I'll find mine. I can feel my eggs drying up as we speak," I say.

"Oh, stop being ridiculous, you're like thirty. You've got plenty of time to make babies. Enjoy life before you jump into baby making."

Tessa knows about being a mom, especially at an early age. She has a seven-year-old daughter whom she has raised for the last four years by herself. I truly am lucky to have met her when I did. Good friends are hard to come by.

"I'm gonna head home. Damon and I are making homemade Chinese food tonight. Call me tomorrow," Tessa says.

I thought Liam would've called by now, but the fact he still hasn't left me wondering if Tessa is right. Did I say something to him that could've offended or changed his mind about me? Up until the kiss on the cheek, I thought we were having a great time. However, I do usually overthink things, so maybe I'm just blowing this all out of proportion and everything is fine. Time will tell.

I pick up my phone and purse, then head back to my house to work on my lesson plans to keep myself busy instead of obsessing over what could've gone wrong with Liam. *Stop freaking out.*

Once home, I gather my papers, turn on *True Blood*, and remain on the couch. It was meant to be background noise, but soon I find myself sucked into the show when Eric's character is introduced and it starts showing his slight obsession over the main girl character. I keep watching, barely able to look away from the TV, until my eye catches the time —it's 12:05 a.m.

This show might not be good for me to watch when I have things to do. I have a feeling that this is going to be a binge-worthy show.

I grab my phone to check it. Still no missed calls or text messages. *Why hasn't he called me?*

5

LIAM

Since I left Dixie's that night, it's been bothering me that I didn't kiss her. Why the hell did I kiss her on the cheek? She has to be wondering why. Hell, even I am. It's almost like I chickened out and instead of kissing her on the lips, I panicked. I'm not like my younger brother, Aiden. He has no problem talking to girls. For me, I get inside my head and start to overthink things, especially since everything happened with Larissa, and once that happens, it tends to go downhill fast. It's not usually about why the girl isn't right for me, but why I'm not the right guy for them. The children issue is a hard truth and I have to face that. Yet, it's not something you could come out to tell someone on the first date. I would sound like a lunatic. Yesterday, I thought about calling her a couple of times, but I quickly talked myself out of it because it felt too soon. Also, there's the idiot feeling that I'm a grown-ass man, and I kissed a hot-as-fuck girl on the cheek. I mean, who the fuck does that? She is probably laughing with her friends about me and telling them how I pecked her on the cheek like a scared twelve-year-old boy who has never kissed a girl before. *Pathetic.*

The one person I want to talk to today, Damon, is off and so Pedro is the only other person I can trust to not go around telling everyone in the station. He has already asked if I found anyone on the app, so I can just ease into the conversation while we are playing some poker as we wait around for a call. He is usually good about keeping things private, unlike some of the others who are like the girls from high school. You tell them something and the whole station knows within an hour. I won't make that mistake again.

"So, that app sent me a crazy girl."

"Oh really. Tell me more," Pedro says, laying down his cards and giving me his full attention.

"Well, her profile looked decent and said she had a degree from Penn State. We went out for drinks and let's just say, she was still not over her ex and just wanted to go back to my place."

"Maybe she just needed someone to get over him with." He laughs.

He knows I'm looking for someone real, and not just to get laid. So his comment makes me chuckle, but then my serious face takes over again. "Yeah, well, it won't be me. I'm not looking to be someone's rebound. Been there, done that."

Pedro is a good guy, but he's been happily married since his early twenties and wouldn't dare cheat on his wife. Is it bad that I'm jealous? If I could just find my partner, then all will be good in the world.

"Just remember, you have to dig through some weeds before you find the sunflower. Keep trying and don't give up."

He always has sound advice, and I feel like I can trust his since he has been happily married for many years. I've never heard him say anything negative about his wife, and he is always in such a great mood. If that is what finding a good woman does, then I need one ASAP.

The date with Harper comes out, and he doesn't say much, just continues to play and nods a lot.

"You gonna go out again?" Pedro asks.

"See, that's the thing, I don't know. I want to, but I'm scared she won't want to go out with me again. I kissed her on the damn cheek. Why? I honestly have no fucking clue."

A part of me doesn't want to admit how nervous I was that night. The date was going so well, and I didn't want to mess it up and just assume she wanted to kiss me, so I went for the cheek. In reality, I should have just gone for it. Women like men who take charge.

"Listen, man up. It's just a kiss on the cheek. It's not like you insulted her wardrobe or anything. Either call her and ask her out or give up and be single forever. Good things aren't easy to come by, so you need to fight for them."

He has a valid point. I can't give up on her so easily. But then my mind goes back to the five percent. No matter what, it always creeps up on me and makes me doubt myself. Sometimes I just ignore it, but maybe this time I shouldn't. Harper is a wonderful woman, but what if she wants kids? Sure, I have a five percent chance of ever having kids, so that's more like a miracle. Should I even get my hopes up with her yet? The subject is going to come up eventually and maybe if I walk away now, my heart won't get torn apart again.

No, don't run away just because you're afraid to get hurt. I have to break the cycle and believe that even if Harper isn't the one for me, eventually I will find someone who can accept the fact of my fate and still want to be with me for the long haul. If I keep myself from pursuing happiness, then I'll never achieve it. All the heartbreak will be worth it when I find my partner. Until then, I have to keep chugging along and hoping for the best.

After my shift finally ends, I head home and decide to turn on *True Blood*. After Harper mentioned it on our date, I think maybe I should see what she is obsessed about and get a feel for what women are falling head over heels for now. The first episode is weird, with lots of nudity and sex scenes. Oh, now I get it; it's like porn. They say women get hot and bothered by seeing the acts, but also just hearing the sounds. Men are more turned on when they can touch.

I keep watching until after four episodes, and then it starts to get a little better. It starts to delve into the characters more, instead of just focusing on the vampire aspect. One thing I'll never understand is the fact they treat the women like property, and this turns women on? Men would never get away with this in real life and they know it. But that's just it—it's a fantasy.

Too many things nowadays portray dark relationships, and even though women find them sexy, in the real world they are not. Stalking is not sexy, and neither is being controlling. Yet there are movies and books out there that sold millions of copies based on that factor. It makes for men like me to have a harder time finding women. We can't act like those men and still live with ourselves. There are still some of us who like to treat women with respect, and not like we own them.

I pick up my phone and start drafting a text to Harper, but delete it. This internal back and forth is not helping, but I need to make a decision. If I wait too long to reach out, she will think I'm not interested.

Why are men expected to be the ones to reach out after a date? Can't it be a two-way street? It would help a lot if I knew she's still interested in seeing me. I put the possible rejection out of my mind and make a decision.

It's settled. I'll call her tomorrow and ask her out. This will never go anywhere if I don't at least give it a shot. Am I scared? Yes, but I deserve to be happy, and maybe she won't freak out about the five percent. Obviously, I am not going to bring it up, but I plan to be honest if it does come up. She deserves to know, especially if we choose to be exclusive later on down the road.

THE NEXT DAY, I don't allow time to second-guess myself before I call Harper. It won't do me any good, and waiting another day to reach out is asinine. The line trills as I eagerly wait to hear her voice on the other end. After eight rings, I go to hang up, but right before I hit the end button, I hear her voice.

"Hello?"

"It's Liam. How are you?"

I hear some shuffling of papers and then a slight squeal. "Oh, I'm doing great. What's up?"

"Well, I get off in about an hour. Interested in going to dinner?" I ask, my voice slightly faltering.

"I'd love to."

See, she is interested, and I should have just called her yesterday, idiot. My mind mulls over where we should go, and a restaurant comes to mind.

"Okay, do you want me to come pick you up or meet you there?" I ask because I want her to be able to decide. She might feel more comfortable driving herself for an easy exit.

"No, I'll text you my address. I'll see you in about two hours?"

"Yeah, about sevenish. Bye," I say, before hanging up.

Pedro looks over at me and smiles. "See. Just do it. You're a good guy and deserve someone."

We spend the next hour playing poker, and Pedro is whooping my ass. I don't know why I keep agreeing to play when I don't think I've won a single hand. He tells me about his kid fixing to graduate high school and how stressful it is. Apparently, they are short of his tuition for the college he wants to go to, and he'll have to pick up a second job to make ends meet. This guy already works his ass off, and so does his wife. I hate to see people having to work two jobs and never get to enjoy their lives.

This is the main reason why I have been frugal with my money. The inheritance I received from my mom and dad is sitting in an interest building account and won't be touched until I decide to retire. Technically, with the money I have saved, I can retire by the time I'm fifty and pay myself $25,000 a year and have enough to sustain me until I'm seventy and still have some left over. It's easier when you have a house that is paid off and no car note.

Pedro deserves to enjoy his life and not struggle at every corner. "Listen, have you had him look into scholarships? They have scholarships for almost everything nowadays. That's something I would have him look into before you take a second job. You need time to decompress, man."

Not everyone is as fortunate as me and my brothers, but I don't take it for granted. Some people will go out and blow their money away like Aiden, but Damon and I are doing things right. We know that eventually we are going to want to retire and be able to travel and enjoy life. So instead of buying a million-dollar home or a fancy car that doesn't really matter, we put money into accounts that build it up over time.

It's three minutes until six and a shower is calling my name. We didn't receive any calls today, but I'm not one to go out with someone without showering.

"Enjoy your date tonight. Let me know how it goes," Pedro says, walking past me and my truck.

I jump in and head to my house, take a quick shower, and then pick out something decent to wear. Tonight, I'm going to kiss her good night like a real fucking man.

6

HARPER

I throw my latte into the trash can, while rushing to gather my things. He didn't give me much time to get ready, and I still need to take a shower. A sigh escapes my throat as I leave the café. I clutch my jacket, regretting walking here in these temperatures, and try to pick up the pace before I get sick. This jacket is barely helping, and the wind is cutting through me like a knife.

The sight of cookie-cutter homes graces my presence, letting me know I have officially reached my street, and I pick up the pace. My hands are like pins and needles, and snot is dripping out of my nose. Did I mention I despise cold weather? When I reach my door, I glance down at my phone. *Well, there goes almost fifteen minutes.* There is no time to waste if I want to be ready on time, and I use my foot to close the door behind me as I start taking my clothes off on the way to the bedroom. Thank God for heat and a great thermostat. I put my hair up in a messy bun after turning on the shower, because I won't have time to wash it and let it dry before he gets here. I stick my hand inside to feel the temperature of the water, which is not quite warm enough, but I jump in anyway. My feet hit the arctic bottom, and I start to dance around waiting for it to warm up enough to where I don't feel like an icicle. Once it does, I lather soap against my skin fast and wash it off in record time. I turn off the shower and grab the towel off the bar. I wrap it around me as I stand at the mirror, trying to figure out what the hell I'm going to do with my hair. There is no time to curl it, so I take out my volumizer and weave it through my hair, giving it a little extra oomph, and then I dart to my closet.

How am I supposed to pick an outfit if I don't know where we are going? Hopefully, it won't be anywhere too fancy. Maybe this red knee-length dress and a cardigan with some wedges? It needs to be something that can easily be dressed down or up.

I slip the dress over my head, slide the black cardigan up each arm, then I button it. I choose black wedges and slip them on my feet before I venture back to the bathroom to line my eyes and throw on some light-red lipstick. After glimpsing the time, I realize he should be here any minute if he's punctual. I do a quick once-over of my outfit before going into the living room.

As if on cue, the doorbell rings. *He's here.* My eyes get big; I'm getting nervous about tonight. Why? There is no need to be nervous, especially after how we hit it off. But tonight, I'll get my kiss.

I open the door. He stands there in a soft-blue button-down hugging his broad shoulders, surveying me, as I ask him to come in. "Let me just grab my purse."

He glances around the living room, probably seeing the mess I left. "Looks like you've been busy. We can go out another night if you need to?"

See, there's that gentleman quality I like about him so much. "No, that's okay," I reply before walking back into the room with my clutch. "I'm ready."

He opens the door and I whisk past him, his hand landing on the small of my back as he walks me to his Jeep and ushers me inside. Hell, when's the last time a guy opened the car door for me? I could get used to this chivalry. He comes around to his side, slips in, and we are on our way.

"I wasn't sure where we were going... so hopefully what I'm wearing is okay," I say, pulling my dress down a bit.

"You look gorgeous. Don't worry about that," he says, glancing at me, trying to keep his eyes on the road. "What do you feel like? Italian? French? I'm not a picky eater, so tonight you get to choose."

There are so many restaurants between Grapevine and Dallas. How the hell will I choose? What if he doesn't like my choice? "Pick a French restaurant. Do you know of a good one?"

"Sure do. I've heard L'Astrance is wonderful. Ever been?"

"I haven't. Let's go there. First for both of us. Only fitting." I smile.

The vehicle vibrates as we drive over some loose gravel, and when I look up, we are on a back road. He must want to take the long way instead of getting stuck in downtown traffic. Smart man.

"So, are you bummed about break being almost over?" he asks.

I shrug. "Not really. Just nervous."

He looks over at me. "What do you have to be nervous about?"

"I'm taking over for a teacher who retired. Kids usually give new teachers a hard time, so I'm trying to prepare myself for that."

The Jeep pulls up in front of the restaurant, and there is valet parking. Fancy. Liam hands over his keys, and then his hand falls back on the small of my back. Sometimes when a man does this, it feels uncomfortable, but not with him. It's like his hand belongs there.

He opens the door for me, and that's when I see the crowd of individuals waiting to get a table. "We should probably find somewhere else. It's packed."

"I'll go talk to the host. Be right back," he says, his hand slowly slipping off my back.

I watch him talking with the man; they seem to know each other. He points to the back of the restaurant and then smiles. The host goes to the kitchen and then nods at Liam.

"Come on," he says, waving me over to get seated.

"How did you get in without a reservation? Look at this place."

"I'll explain in a minute. Trust me."

When he says that, my heart drops. Can I trust him? Is he going to turn out to be just another player trying to take me home? My heart can't handle any more of that, and I'm beginning to really like Liam. *Please don't be the case.*

We sit down, and he starts laughing. "So, to answer your question. I know the owner."

"How?"

"About a year ago, this place went up in flames, I helped put the fire out, and he offered to let me to come in anytime. I've never taken him up on it 'cause I've never really had anyone to bring here. It's not like I could bring my brothers here. That would be awkward."

Oh, thank God. That puts my mind at ease. "You do a lot for the community, huh? You really enjoy your job."

"I do. Firefighting has been the career in my family for three generations, and it's something that has always been near and dear to me. Think about it. Fires pop up every day, and every minute counts when our sirens go off and we are on our way to a call. It could literally mean the difference between life and death, and we have seen lots of the latter."

Witnessing tragedy every day isn't something I would sign up for, but to each their own. Who wants to be around that? The grief alone would consume me and spit me out.

"Sorry, didn't mean to go all dark there. Let's change the subject," he says, the regret showing on his face.

"No, it just shows how committed you are to your job and what you do. Grapevine is lucky to have someone like you fighting to protect it. Don't diminish that."

His eyes lock with mine, and a smile takes over. "I just don't want to scare you away. You're the first girl I could see myself actually dating. My job can sometimes be morbid. I see a lot of awful things, and some still haunt me and my brothers to this day."

So, his brothers are also on the squad. Interesting. I wonder what it's like working so closely with them. I don't have any siblings, so I wouldn't ever be able to comprehend. Being an only child growing up sucked, even though most people think it's better that way.

"Anyway, where are you from? Grapevine, originally?" he asks me, changing the subject.

"No, Los Angeles, actually."

"Why on earth did you move here? Isn't the weather there like damn near perfect all the time?"

"Yes, most of the time. If you want me to be honest, I needed a fresh start. My parents were murdered and they never found the person responsible." Wow, I didn't mean to blurt that out, so I cover my mouth. "Sorry, talk about morbid."

He takes my hand from my mouth and lays it on the table. "Don't apologize. I like the honesty. Continue."

"After a year of therapy to help me grieve and process what happened, I got offered a teaching job here. Instead of waiting for the start date until the position was available, I worked in the office."

It's very personal telling Liam this, but I want this to work, and if I'm keeping secrets, it won't. Losing my parents has been rough, and I still think about them every day, but they would want me to go on and pursue my dreams. If it wasn't for therapy, I'd still be staying at their house in Los Angeles, curled up on the couch.

"I'm so sorry to hear about your parents. Mine are both gone also. It's hard to go on after losing them, but we must. If you ever need to talk, I'm here."

The conversation continues, and I fill him in on my move down to Grapevine, finding my house to rent, and how I like the small feel of the town. It's not too small, but not big either. I didn't really want to live in a big city again, so this is a nice compromise.

A chilled bottle of wine sits on the table, untouched. For a while, I try hard to resist, but a big glass of wine is exactly what I need right now to take off the edge. I reach for the bottle and pour the wine up almost to the rim.

"You okay? Am I stressing you out that much?" he asks, running his fingers through his hair.

"No, I just really love wine, that's all."

He probably thinks I'm an alcoholic, but stress makes me drink. There's nothing wrong with enjoying alcohol as an adult.

I change the subject and he tells me about his childhood, losing his parents both before turning eighteen. His older brother, Damon, ended up taking care of them until they turned eighteen. Is his whole family a bunch of saints or something? I haven't heard a bad word about anyone since meeting Liam, and that seems odd. Or maybe, he really is just a good guy who doesn't get enough credit.

"So, tell me more," I say, wanting to see what else he would offer up.

"It's just me and my two brothers. We own some property together to help aid those who lose their homes."

"You're kidding me? Are all the Jacksons perfect?"

"Far from it. We've just seen a lot of tragedy and wanted to do something good for the community."

Who is this guy? Who knew men like this even existed anymore?

Dinner is placed in front of us, and we take a break from conversation to enjoy the amazing French cuisine. I bask in the aroma of the fresh garlic breadsticks placed in front of us, which I would expect at an Italian restaurant, but who am I to judge? I cut a piece of my steak and slid it into my mouth, salivating at the seasoning of perfection gracing my taste buds. Whoever the chef is can cook for me anytime.

Everything seems so simple with Liam, and maybe that's the weirdest part of all of this. A part of me wants to take some of my guards down, but it's only our second date, and he could still turn out to be a complete ass. *Remember, Alec?* Ugh, why did he even have to come to mind?

Alec is my ex-boyfriend of not that long. We did meet outside of the movies while I was waiting on a friend. He struck up a conversation, asked me out, and I said yes. He seemed genuine and kept that charade going for about two months until the realization hit that he's just playing games until he can get in my pants. That was when I told myself not to fall for pretty-boy types. Alec is the reason I don't trust men who should be on the cover of a magazine. Yet, Liam might be hot as fuck, but he's nothing like Alec. He's been honest every step of the way and has told me stuff about himself without me having to drag it out of him.

Romantic comedies have girls in a daze to find their perfect man, and some of them even show a couple falling in love over the course of two or three days, but that's not reality. Especially with my history, I need to be careful. *Even with Liam.*

My eyes wander, drinking him in as he eats without a care in the world. Is it weird that I find him more attractive because he doesn't shovel food into his mouth? I can't stand people who eat that way. One of the worst things about eating in public is having to see everyone else eat, and even worse when you can hear that. Smacking is a no for me. I can't be with someone that does that.

"What?" he says, lifting his fork in the air. "Something on my face or…?"

I laugh and shove a piece of steak in my mouth before he's onto me. *Stop watching him eat, creep.* He goes back to eating and I try to check him out without drawing his attention. And believe me, it's hard. His eyes keep locking with me.

"Okay, seriously, why do you keep staring at me?" he asks, dropping his fork down on his plate, causing a bang.

I look around and lean in. "You really want to know?"

He nods.

"You look sexy as fuck when you eat. There I said it." I throw my hands up in the air with no shame, because what do I have to lose? One thing I know is, be yourself from the get-go, because falling in love with someone who is pretending is worse than being dumped via email.

"You should see me eat dessert," he says, picking up the menu to gaze at the options. "I'm thinking chocolate cake, you?"

I laugh awkwardly because all I can think about is him, drizzled in chocolate, and me having the pleasure of licking it off.

"I had something else in mind, but not tonight."

Yes, I'm old-fashioned when it comes to sex, and it can ruin a good thing if done too soon, and with the way things are going, there was no need to rush into that.

He winks at me and then orders the cake anyway.

My hands are in my lap, fingers fidgeting, wondering if he thinks I'm a total loser now. Do I regret tonight? Hell, no. I'll never find someone if I hide out in my house all the time.

"So, what are you doing tomorrow?" he asks, taking a sip of his wine and then setting it back on the table in front of him.

"Well, I don't know yet. Depends."

I'm trying to see if he is going to ask me out again. Sure, I might have made some off-the-wall comments tonight, but it's been wonderful. It let me see the humorous side of him, which is just my type. *Please ask me out again.*

The waitress brings the chocolate cake with two forks, and his eyes lock on mine again. This time there's a smile on his face as he takes the fork, cuts a piece, and so sexily puts it in his mouth. *Ignore the inappropriate feelings. You are not going to sleep with him tonight.*

"So, what do you think? Eating cake is much hotter right?"

I laugh, nod, and then pick up the other fork and we devour the piece of cake without much hesitation. It is the moistest piece I've had in a long time, so compliments to the chef or baker. After it's gone, my hands fall back in my lap as I wait to see what he says. He might want to do something else after this, or he might just want to take me home. Hell, at this point, I'm okay with either. *No, you're not. Go home alone. Don't sleep with him yet.*

The voice inside my head is agonizing, and I wish I could just shut it off, but it's the better version of myself, trying to keep me from doing something I'll regret. Sure, he might fuck my brains out tonight, but what if he didn't call me tomorrow? Then I'd feel like shit, dumb for sleeping with him, and back to square one. Inner me is right.

He examines the check, slips a hundred dollar bill into the billfold, and stands up. I follow his lead, and his hand falls to the small of my back again before we pass the host stand, then go out the front door, and wait for the valet.

"I had a wonderful time tonight. Work comes fast, so I gotta get home, but would you still be interested in going out with me again?"

Is he crazy? Who in their right mind would say no? Liam is the closest thing to perfect I'm going to find, and on top of that, he wants to date me. I'm keeping him close, because if he's good in bed, too, it seals the deal.

His Jeep pulls up in front of us, and we get inside, his right hand resting on my thigh. It only makes me think of everything I'd love for us to do to each other all the way home. Like straddle him in the driver seat and take exactly what I so desperately need, or him throwing me up against my door and screwing my brains out, making me come multiple times. He clears his throat which brings me back to reality and I realize he can feel my thigh trembling. Crap.

"Everything okay?" he asks, lightly brushing his fingers over my inner thigh.

"Yeah, perfect."

This is usually when things get awkward. The end of the date, when we walk up to the front doorstep, and neither knows whether the other wants to kiss. *I do, damn it. Kiss me.*

"So, I had a great time tonight," he says, standing with his hands in his pockets.

Listen, it's cold. I'm not going to stand around and do the dance.

"Just kiss me already," I say out loud, instead of to myself.

His hands come out of his pockets, touch my cheeks, and he brings me into a mind-blowing, intense first kiss. His tongue explores mine, and boy, is the wait worth it, but then he stops and leaves me wanting more.

"I'll call you tomorrow." He smiles awkwardly. "Have a good night."

Is he serious? My mouth is gaping open, wondering why the hell we couldn't enjoy that for a bit longer. Liam is one hell of a man and I'm glad that I decided to give him a chance. Yet, I find myself entertaining the idea that maybe it's all a show and after a couple months I'll get to see the real him. Not "be on your best behavior" him.

The door shuts and my back is against it, my head hitting it repeatedly. What the hell was that? Is he trying to make me crave him? Because if so, it's totally working. My fingers touch my lips, wondering if he's that good at kissing, then how amazing is he in bed? Okay, so I know the saying size doesn't matter, and personally I think that's true. I think about it this way. Even if it's nine inches, if they can't hit the stop, then it doesn't matter. They can be five inches, hit the spot every time, and be amazing in bed. The stigma around penis size is just ridiculous and men need to worry more about their skills rather than how well they are hung.

I stop relishing in our kiss and pass through the living room to grab a bottle of water, kick off my wedges, and take a seat on the couch. Tonight did go fantastic, but why am I always waiting for the shoe to drop? For something to go wrong? I pick up my phone to update Tessa because she's probably dying to hear about it.

Me: *Home from dinner.*

A quick sip of water wets my throat, and the condensation comes off on my hand from the bottle.

Tessa: *So, did you get your damn kiss? Have to beg for it?*

Me: *Oh, I straight-up said kiss me. Wasn't taking the chance. I had to know if he was a good kisser before going any further.*

Tessa: *Of course you did.* 🙃 *So does that mean there's a next date?*

Me: *Yes!!! More details later.*

My eyes start to burn, and it's as good a time as any to get all this makeup off my face and get some pj's on before Liam takes over my dreams tonight.

7

LIAM

The guys have been bugging me about details on how it's going on with matches, and I'm honestly not sure if I want them to know. They are so immature sometimes, and one of them literally only asks if I've gotten laid yet. Jeff's only twenty-one and a total whore, but Pedro is more interested how it's been going.

After taking a short nap, we play a round or two of poker to pass the time. Of course, he kicks my ass because I suck at this game, but really, I use it to tell him about Harper. When I tell him about our second date, he is laughing.

"Please tell me you're kidding. She actually told you that?"

"Apparently, women think not shoveling food into your mouth is sexy. Who knew!"

My phone buzzes against the card table inside the station as I wait for my shift to be over. *Just ten more minutes.* It always seems like when it comes to that last ten minutes of a work shift, time seems to slow, and that block of time takes three to four times the normal to pass. Story of my life when we don't get any calls, but at least no one loses their homes.

Damon: *So... details on the dates? Tessa won't stop bugging me for an update.*

Crap. I forgot to call. It's actually nice to see my brother taking an interest in my dating life, but mostly because it proves that we've gotten closer recently. He just wants me to be happy and now that he has Tessa, it's become more forefront in his mind. Being with someone does make a huge difference in your mental state and how you go through life. They can tear you down or build you up. Tessa and Emily have shown him how important family is for a support system.

Me: *How about I come over? See you in 20?*

Damon: *Cool. Any idea when Aiden comes back?*

Our little brother decided to travel to Europe. Weirdly enough, he's always wanted to go, but the last-minute trip calls into question what exactly he is running from. Did he catch a category five clinger at a bar and now she won't leave him alone? Does he have a crazy stalker? I can't wait to question him on that when he gets back. I'll save all the questions for a later date.

Me: *Supposed to be next week. I guess we will see.*

Finally, the clock shows four, and I'm out of here, jumping into my vehicle and heading down Main Street toward Damon's house. I have so much to fill him in on. I can hear him now. "You've only been on two dates… slow your roll, brother."

He should understand better than anyone that people show up in your life when you least expect it. If he hadn't been one of the responding firefighters the day Tessa's complex burned down, they would have never crossed paths. It's funny how things work out sometimes, and how fate brings people together. Lame, I know.

My Jeep screeches to a stop in his driveway, and I run inside to get out of the cold. They are all sitting in the living room watching Animal Planet because Emily can't go a day without watching a special. It's actually cute. Most kids are obsessed with animated shows but not her. Her love for animals might play a huge part in her career choices later on.

"What's the special on now?" I ask, plopping down on the couch next to Emily. "Tigers? Sharks?"

Her eyes roll. "Seriously? No. It's koalas today."

She never ceases to amaze me how she can be so sweet one minute and have a total attitude the next. I will pray for them when she hits her teenage years. Those are going to be rough. They say girls are worse at that age than boys. Obviously, I don't have any kids, so I have to go off others that do. Pedro talks about his children all the time, and sometimes he makes me rethink the desire to have kids. The dude is always stressed to the max, taking up extra work to pay for birthdays, Christmas presents, and all the sports, and that doesn't even include saving up for their college funds. If he isn't careful, his health will deteriorate. Yet, it proves another side of the coin—parents will do anything for their children.

Tessa locks eyes with me, like a death stare. "So I'm sick of waiting. You ghosted us on New Year's Eve after you left."

Well, shit. I didn't realize my dating life is something that needs to be a public matter. Why is she so interested in this? I want to ask, but it might come off as rude.

"I was on a date, then another one, and then work."

"No excuses, now dish!" she says, sitting cross-legged on the couch and facing me so she can really focus.

I go over our first date with her, constantly being interrupted with questions. The main points are made like she is easy to talk to, and she's well educated and well mannered.

"And at the end of the night? Please tell me you didn't sleep with her on the first date? I always hated men who did that."

Wow, that's one hell of a question to ask. Is that really any of her business?

"No, I was a gentleman. We didn't even kiss."

Tessa looks at me, then over to Damon.

"What?" I ask.

"What is this girl's name?"

Why does it matter? Her name is irrelevant to the story.

"Harper."

She smiles, then puts her hands up. "Well, it seems you're dating my friend. So I can't ask any more questions because I already know the answers."

Out of all the women in Grapevine, my date has to be with one of her friends? What did Harper tell her about the date? Maybe I can use this to my advantage. Although I don't like the thought of Tessa being friends with her. Not because of anything against Tessa, but I like to keep my business private. We all know how girls are, they gossip, and I don't want anything said out of context. Hopefully, they aren't close.

"Well, what did she say?"

"Nope, not my business to tell. I'm officially out of this. You'll have to talk to Damon only,"

My text notification tone goes off. *That must be her.*

Harper: *Had a good time last night.*

I smile as I look down at my phone.

Me: *So did I. When are you free to go out again?*

My attention is now placed elsewhere, and hearing from her is just what I need. I don't know why I keep doubting myself, especially when we had an amazing dinner.

Harper: *Maybe this time, I could cook dinner for you. Stay in.*

I like the sound of that. Did I just find a good-looking, intelligent woman who can cook? Jackpot.

Me: *Sounds fantastic. When?*

When I look up, they are both staring at me, eyebrows raised. It's not like they don't get texts while having company. Chill.

"Aren't you here to visit?" Tessa asks.

Harper: *How about now?*

Me: *See you in 20 or so.*

"Well, time for me to head out. Supposed to be at Harper's."

"Already? Wow! It must be going well for you guys to be seeing each other every night. That's great. Have fun," Tessa says, watching me walk to the door.

"Oh, I will," I respond, closing the door behind me.

Things are obviously looking up for me in the dating game, and hopefully it continues upward. Harper is a blessing in disguise. It almost seems too good to be true, for us to hit it off this well.

I put the Jeep in reverse and look over my right shoulder to make sure I am clear of traffic, before backing out and heading over to her place. Harper is an amazing woman, and she seems genuine which only heightens my desire to get to know her better. Hell, I'll see her every day if she wants.

I pass through Main Street with barely any traffic and head down Heather Court, and park in the street. I take three deep breaths to calm my nerves before walking up her steps and knocking on the door.

When Harper opens the door, I take in the leggings and t-shirt she has on and revel in the fact she still looks gorgeous. I'm glad I didn't get dressed up, because it must be a low-key night, which are my favorite. She shuts the door behind me, and I follow her into the kitchen. I lean my shoulder against the entryway and watch her whip around the area, preparing everything.

"Have a seat. You don't have to stand while I cook." Harper laughs.

"Oh, of course." I take a seat at the kitchen table, watching her make her way around the kitchen, prepping the food, and dancing around a bit. She is so full of energy.

"Wanna have a glass of wine until dinner's done?" she asks, opening the cabinet and peering over at me. "I've got white and red."

"I'll take red."

I'm trying to concentrate, but my thoughts are getting to me and psyching me out.

She joins me at the table, taking a seat and looking at me. "So, Tessa texted me. Apparently, you're her brother-in-law."

Will she have a problem with that?

"Yeah, small world, huh?"

Seriously though, out of all the girls, how did I end up finding Tessa's only friend?

"Is that a problem?" she asks, looking at me while taking a sip. "It's not for me."

"No, of course not. I just won't talk about us in front of her."

It shouldn't matter if she's friends with Tessa. Only that she and I are hitting it off and we like each other. It's actually kind of nice that she knows someone in my family already. It will make introducing her less nerve-racking.

Harper pulls dinner out of the oven and dishes it onto two plates.

"One thing you don't have to worry about is cooking when I'm around. My dad loved to whip things up with random items in the pantry. He could've been a great chef, but never pursued it. He was more worried about making money and supporting my mom and me."

This is an area I am familiar with, talking about my parents after their deaths and knowing it only shifts my mood for most of the day afterward. Sadness isn't something I want her to feel on any of our dates, but it is one of the things we have in common. It's nice to have someone who can relate.

"I'd love to hear more about your parents sometime. I miss mine every day."

"Yeah, I moved here after they passed. Home just didn't feel the same without them, and I don't think I could've stayed in their house so it ended up being the perfect time for a new start in Grapevine."

"Let's have some more wine," she says, filling both glasses.

Harper is opening up to me in a way no woman ever has, and it shows that she trusts me to an extent. I want to get to know her better and see what kind of woman she is and what her ambitions are.

Once we finish dinner, I gather the two plates and take them to the sink and begin washing them.

"What are you doing?" Harper asks.

"You cooked, so I'm cleaning."

She sits back down and finishes her wine, her eyes locked on me. I get the feeling she is thinking very dirty things right now.

"Do you leave them wet?" I ask.

She snaps out of her daydream and raises her eyebrows. "What?"

"The dishes. Leave them wet to air dry or...?"

She laughs. "Yeah, put them on the rack and let them air dry so we can go into the living room and sit."

Once we migrate to the couch, the realness of this dating game comes to fruition. Is she expecting us to have sex tonight? I mean it is our third date. She moves closer to me. Instead of initiating that, I think it's better if we get to know each other first. Although, if her hand comes any farther up my leg, I'm going to get hard and it will be noticeable.

"So, what do you want out of life? A relationship?" I ask.

She bites her lip. "Let me think about that. What about you?"

"I like the idea of having someone to come home to. Sharing things with someone is important to me. Life isn't the same without having someone to enjoy things with, even the ups and downs. My future wife should be someone I can lean on, count on, and talk to about anything."

Her hand moves to caress my cheek. "That sounds amazing. I've always been envious of my parents' marriage. They were married for over twenty-five years and hardly ever fought. They didn't let anyone else into their marriage, no social media, and no talking about each other to friends. That's how a marriage fails fast. If you can't speak about it honestly with your significant other, then why are you with them in the first place? It's all about communication and trust."

Harper is one hundred percent correct.

"So, do you want kids someday?" she asks.

At first, I'm not sure how to respond, and I decide telling her I want kids isn't a lie.

"I want my kids to have the world, and that means both me and my husband will need to be prepared. Sorry, is that weird?" she asks.

"Not at all. It proves how mature you are and that you want nothing short of great things. We are on the same page."

This isn't something I want to discuss tonight, but I will tell her. Before I completely ruin my chances with her, I at least want to see if we can make this work.

"My father once told me that all the bullshit you go through in life is made up for when you have a child of your own. It makes things worth it and changes your whole outlook on life," I say.

"He sounds like he was a great father." Her hands fall on mine. "My only regret is that my future kids won't get to meet their grandparents. It kills me."

My mother, if still alive, would have been over at my house every day to see the kids and spoil them rotten. When Damon almost got Carol pregnant in high school, Mom freaked, but I knew that just meant she would be alive long enough to spoil them. It was a false alarm, and from that point on, she always talked about how excited she was to be a grandma someday.

"Let's change the subject because it feels like the mood is shifting. If you could travel anywhere without worrying about money, where would it be?" Harper asks.

"Hands down, Italy. There's something about the Roman Empire that has always intrigued me. I mean, who doesn't want to go and see the Colosseum?"

She smiles big. "How did you know that is my dream vacation? I've been saving up to go on my thirty-fifth birthday for years. It's so expensive. The Florence Duomo Santa Maria del Fiore is supposed to be one of the best cathedrals in the world."

This is probably the weirdest thing ever, but if we get married, I have the perfect honeymoon destination. It's somewhere we both truly want to see, and what better way to start a marriage than to visit one of the most romantic places in the world?

The night continues to get better with each passing topic, and I am getting to know her on a better level. For three to four hours, we talk about our childhoods, our fears, and so many other things, while our glasses kept being filled with wine. After the sixth glass, it's all a blur.

8

HARPER

*M*y eyes open and Liam's face isn't even two inches from mine. What the hell? When did we fall asleep? The last time I checked my watch, it was one. I guess we can blame it on all the wine.

His eyes ease open, looking into mine. "Good morning, beautiful. How'd you sleep?"

I shrug my shoulders, even though I slept like a baby. Normally, my night consists of lots of tossing and turning, but it's different having someone with you. It just seems more comfortable and safe. It helps scare the nightmares away and inputs blissful unicorn dreams into the mind.

"We should probably get up. It's already almost six thirty." My feet hit the hardwood floor immediately, feeling like I stepped onto an iceberg.

I walk to my room to grab a pair of socks and then make a pot of coffee. My usual is two cups before heading into work, and believe me, I need it to deal with moody teenagers today. Hell, I might even chug down a third one for the hell of it.

I pour three scoops into the pot, then add water. I've had an obsession with coffee since high school. My junior year was the bane of my existence with the SATs and even though my parents weren't pour, I wouldn't consider them rich either. I needed to get a good score to be able to receive scholarships to attend college without putting them in a bind. In the months leading up to it, I studied like a maniac late into the night, and sometimes staying up for two days trying to cram. The local coffee shop became my go-to place and coffee was the only thing that kept me going.

I go to the living room to turn the news on, and Liam sits up, joining me with his hair all messed up, but somehow he looks even hotter this way.

"I didn't mean to stay over. Guess we both fell asleep."

Things happen. I didn't anticipate him staying over so early in our relationship, but I am kind of glad he did. The sleep I did get last night is going to help me through my hectic day at work. I'm still not positive I'm ready for it, but it's not like there's an option to stay home. This is something I've been looking forward to since moving here, and I just have to embrace it.

The brewing has stopped so we make our way to the kitchen, each grabbing a mug and filling it up with the yummy hot beverage and then sit at the kitchen table, watching the sun creep in. Sometimes I like to just sit here and enjoy the sunrise, and it's even better with Liam sitting across from me. He looks like he's doing some heavy thinking. "What's going on in your head? Talk to me."

"I know it's totally high school behavior, but I am just wondering if I should be calling you my girlfriend?"

I laugh and nod. Things aren't so black and white when you are an adult, and most just assume they are in an exclusive relationship. I'm glad he is taking the initiative to ask. I don't want him seeing anyone else.

His chest rises and falls, and his nervousness goes away as we hold hands. I could get used to my morning being like this, with him here.

"Just think about how beautiful the sunrise will be in Italy when we go one day. I'll get up early just to see it," Liam says, staring out the windowpane.

Normally, you don't hear a guy talking about your future so early in the game, but it doesn't bother me. Things seem to be progressing nicely between us, and hopefully it continues that way.

I set my mug down and leave him to bask in the morning glory while

I decide what to wear today. My closet is a disaster which I'll need to fix later, but for now I grab a pair of black pants, a red blouse, and pair it with some black wedges. Simple, yet professional. My hair is down to the middle of my back with a mixture between curls and waves, but it's actually chic, so I leave it but run the comb through it a couple times to take out any tangles from sleeping on the couch. I decide not to put on any makeup today because wearing it too often really screws up my skin.

When I get back to the kitchen, Liam looks at me with one eyebrow raised. "You can be my teacher anytime."

I laugh, make another cup, and sit across from him again, and we sit in silence just enjoying the beauty of Mother Nature. Sunrises are interesting because it almost makes me feel like it's a complete reset from the previous day and it helps you enjoy the little things.

"You getting ready to leave?" Liam asks, standing up from the table and heading to the living room to grab his boots.

"Yeah, I've gotta head out of here. Long day ahead and I don't want to be late."

He grabs my keys and heads outside, and I watch from the window as he starts my car, and then he comes back in.

"You didn't have to do that."

"I should do that. It's called being a gentleman," he says, smiling.

"Okay. I'll see you later?"

We both finish the last of our coffee and then head toward the door.

"Just call me later. I'm not sure what time I'll be heading home," I say, both of us walking out the door. I close it behind us.

I get inside my toasty warm car and head to the school. Last night was amazing and Liam really has thrown me for a loop. His pictures might have made me second-guess my decision to go on that initial date, but every evening with him has proven he is not the typical pretty-boy type. *Thank God.*

After hitting plenty of morning traffic, I park my car in a parking spot and proceed inside to my classroom to get everything ready before the bell rings. This is it. I'm officially a teacher at Grapevine High School and my parents would have been so proud if they were still alive. Being a teacher wasn't for everyone, but some have a true passion for it. Going into college, there are plenty of required courses you have to take, and one of them was chemistry. I didn't expect to enjoy it as much as I did. By the end of the semester, I made a decision to major in education with a minor in chemistry. Many of the other students struggled with it, so I organized a study group that met twice a week and I worked with them to understand the material as well as I did. That's when my passion for teaching began.

After getting everything ready in the classroom, such as my computer and the handouts for today's work, I pass through the hall of students and drift into the teacher's lounge to grab another cup of coffee. The math teacher, Ms. Kennedy, is talking about how much she dreads today. I try not to make it obvious, but I keep my ears open while putting in my creamer.

"The students are always grouchy and it's like a transition for them back to school. They have to get back to learning again," she explains.

I chuckle silently because that's the truth. How can she expect anything different? We get kids on a pattern of coming and learning every day and then let them leave for two weeks? I would need an adjustment period too.

The lounge's door shuts behind me, and I wrestle through the crowd with my coffee, barely making it inside before the first bell rings. Kids start filing into my classroom. The chattering starts and it doesn't bother me.

"Welcome back. Most of you might already know me from the office. I'm Ms. Davis. Hopefully, all of you had a good break. I'll be passing out your exam grades from the test you took before break."

The previous teacher left me to grade them over the break, which is fine, but really, she should have done it. Yet, nothing is worse than starting out your career by bitching about the person before you. So, I kept my mouth shut and just did it.

As I walk around the classroom, the students continue to talk to one another about what they did over their breaks. Most of them stayed home and played video games or binged the latest *To All The Boys I've Loved Before* movie.

After handing them all out, there's still about forty minutes left of class time. Since this is my first day, I decide to just have a classroom discussion about what we did over our break. It's all volunteer; I'm not that teacher who makes every single student stand up and tell us about themselves because I hated that.

It goes over pretty well, and over half of the students have volunteered so far, but then my phones buzzes against my desk.

Liam: *Have a good first day back, Ms. Davis.*

I smile and hope he comes over later tonight again, even if he doesn't stay. It's nice to have someone to talk to besides Tessa.

Me: *All I can think about is having you next to me tonight. =)*

The bell rings, and I remind the students to read over Chapter 1 of the textbook and we will discuss it tomorrow in class. I might be the only teacher here who doesn't believe in exams or pop quizzes in the first week of school.

Class after class files in, receiving their exams, and then giving us a short glimpse of the fun they had over break. I would say doing this instead of jumping right into reading Chapter 1 in class has gone over well, and I might continue to do this. Another thing is with this being my first year, I would like my students to have high grades, and with that comes expectation. If I need time to adjust, then so do they, and pushing them before they are ready is not going to help with scores.

When the bell rings, excusing my final period, it means my day has ended. Usually, teachers don't actually get out like students do at three fifteen because we have to look over our lessons for tomorrow, or sometimes I try to get a jumpstart on grading if necessary before I head home to relax. The plan is to get out of here and enjoy a glass of wine at home, until Tessa walks in and sits on my desk, crossing her legs, waiting for information.

"So, I know he's my brother-in-law, but I know you're dying to talk to someone. So just no sex details," Tessa says.

"It's been a whirlwind. He ended up staying over last night."

"You little vixen. Thought you wanted to take things slow? Seems like you're doing the opposite!"

"It's just, we click. We've talked about things that normally wouldn't be discussed until further down the line, but getting it out of the way early, and knowing we want the same things, only makes me like him even more."

"Must run in the family because that's exactly how I felt with Damon," Tessa says.

Maybe the Jackson brothers are the exception to the rule of being dangerously sexy, but also with the temperament of a teddy bear.

"I think he's coming over again tonight. I'll talk to you tomorrow."

The hallway is quiet, as most of the teachers are already gone, and the parking lot is dark with only two overhead lights shining on the entire employee parking. I rush to my car, get inside, and lock the doors. As I pull out onto the road, the car picks up Liam's incoming call.

"Hey, babe," I answer.

"Are you headed home?"

"Yes, just left work. You coming over?"

"With food in hand. See you in ten."

You never realize something's missing in your life until it's in front of you. I've gotten so used to being alone over the years, having someone is a nice change of pace. Not only for the intimacy, but to have an emotional and intellectual connection with another person. I could get used to having someone to talk to, wake up next to, and just enjoy life with every day. I guess until now, I never realized how lonely I've been.

The drive seems to take way too long after getting stuck in backed-up traffic, and Liam has to be at my house by now. I'm still a couple blocks away, and it seems like I've been sitting at this light for five minutes or more. Why don't they stagger work schedules to alleviate traffic? Just a thought. The light turns green and I put my foot on the gas, hoping I can make it through this light. *Come on!* The car in front of me isn't paying attention and my hand slams on the horn. The driver starts to go and the light turns yellow, but I buckle through right before it turns red. No way am I going to wait for that to turn green again. The damn food will be cold. After three right turns, I pull up in my driveway and see Liam waiting at my door.

"What did ya bring?" I ask, getting out of the car.

"Chinese takeout. Can't ever go wrong with that, right?" he says, two bags in hand.

He makes way for me to unlock the door, and I hold it open while he sets the bags on the kitchen table. The aroma causes my stomach to growl as I realize I never ate lunch today because I let myself get too busy worrying about my lesson plan.

My purse lands on the table, and I kick off my wedges before I head to the fridge to pour myself a glass of wine.

"Would you like some?"

He nods and starts to take out the food.

"What did you get? One of everything?"

"Pretty much. I wasn't sure exactly what you would want."

"We are going to have leftovers for days. Not that I'm complaining."

Some girls won't be themselves in the first month of seeing someone, but not me. If I'm hungry, then I eat. If he didn't like me because of the way I eat, then he isn't the right guy for me, anyway. I never understood the point of acting like someone else, or as many people say, let them see the crazy side before things are serious. How can someone fall in love with you, if you aren't being yourself? Then that contradicts everything, and they fall in love with someone else.

We both dig in, starving after a long day at work. His will always be worse than mine. Poor guy has to deal with burning buildings, rescuing people, and sometimes the fact that he can't save them.

"Any calls today?"

"Yeah, a couple fires," Liam responds.

"Lose anyone?"

"Not today, thankfully. You'd be able to tell. It really screws up my whole day, and I can't help but run through and think if I could've done something different."

He didn't lose anyone today, but a family lost their house and everything in it. When he talks about it, I can feel the pain through his voice and how much he wants to be able to change the outcome, but he can't. That's when he tells me more about why they acquired the duplexes and that he offers them to move in until they can get back on their feet. Another thing that just amazes me about him is how kind he is. He is dedicated to helping the community in multiple ways. This is a man I could be proud of.

After dinner is consumed, and two glasses of wine later, we move to the couch and continue talking about things he wants to do for the community and some programs he hopes to implement one day. Our fingers are interlocked and I'm lying back against his chest, feeling his hot breath on my neck.

"Do you think it's weird that I already can see a future with you?" I ask.

"No, because I can, too. I've been waiting for a woman like you to come into my life and I have no plans on letting you go," he says, running his fingers down my arm.

A real relationship is what I've been craving, someone to share my life with, and at this point, it's only fitting that I give Liam all of me to make sure that we can make it. Sometimes, I want to hold back, guard myself so I won't get hurt, but it won't do any good. Keeping walls up only hurts the relationship.

"I think fate brought us together after seeing how much we wanted something real," he says, brushing a strand of hair out of my eyes. "I was about to give up, and then you walked into my life and showed me that it really does exist."

He really knows all the right things to say, and it terrifies me. How do I know he won't completely shatter my heart with a hammer? My heart beats faster when I'm around him, and as cliché as it sounds, I get this feeling in my stomach, and nervousness sets in.

"You mean a lot to me. Finding you after searching for someone for years is just what I needed. I'm happy, and even my family can see it."

When you are falling head over heels for someone, it's quick like a roller coaster, and most of the time you don't even realize it until you reach the end.

I move to sit on top of his lap, gazing into his beautiful eyes, and just smile. I did want to take things slow, and maybe we should talk about it. Is he freaking out, too?

"Listen, I don't mean to sound like I'm not enjoying my time with you, but do you think we are moving too fast? I mean, both of us had bad luck trying to find someone, and then bam, we found each other and have been seeing each other every day."

"Are you wanting to slow things down?" Liam asks.

"It's just you slept over on our third date. Normally, that wouldn't happen with me. But I find myself wanting to break all my rules for you, and I don't know if that's healthy."

"If you want to slow down, let's do it. No pressure."

Why does he have to be so understanding about everything? Hell, I don't even know what I want. Speed up or slow down?

Sitting on his lap, my hands around his neck, gazing into his eyes, makes me want to go faster and feel him inside me, but I know it's too soon. "Let's just play it by ear."

He nods, and his soft lips embrace mine. His tongue explores my mouth, and I could kiss him for hours and be perfectly fine and content, and that's just what we will do.

We both enjoy getting a feel for each other's bodies with our clothes on, me squeezing his biceps and admiring his broad shoulders through his shirt. He wastes no time, slowly running his hands up my back, and then moving them back down to my butt. That's one thing men have always complimented me on is the shape of my ass. *I'm blessed, I guess.*

His hands fall on my ass, and he lightly takes me off his lap and gets up.

"It's getting late, so it's time for me to go. I'm not staying over tonight," Liam says.

"Oh, okay," I respond, wondering what the hell just happened. "Are you sure you don't want to stay?"

"As much as I'd love waking up next to you, I think it's better for me to go home tonight." He kisses me and then heads out the door.

So badly, I want to run and stop him, tell him to come back in, but I don't. *Protect your heart, Harper. Always.*

9

LIAM

Something has changed between us, and I don't know if I should worry or not. Harper mentioned us moving too fast, but I thought we were moving at a great pace. I might not have slept with her and that's where it was leading last night, but things seem great. We've had four dates now, over the course of a week, and each interaction has shown me the kind of woman she is, what she wants, and future aspirations. Things have just been clicking between us, and I would hate to do anything to jeopardize that. Some might find it weird how close to her I already feel, but it's not about the length of time we have been dating, but the amount of time spent with each other. Some people only go out once a week and fall in love over the course of a couple months. Another big component is we don't just sit around and watch movies. We discuss the things that are important to us. In hindsight, this might be why I'm so attracted to her. My aspirations to be a father one day might not happen, but if there's even a chance, then the person I end up with needs to be maternal. Harper is funny, kind, intuitive, and most of all understanding. If I have learned anything from being around Tessa's kid, Emily, it's the older they get, the more patience you must have to deal with them. Harper will make a wonderful mother someday.

Is it possible I'm putting too much pressure on her? After mentioning slowing down last night, she did end up on my lap and if I wouldn't have stopped it, we most likely would have made love, and that's the opposite of what she expressed. So, I couldn't in good conscience go through with it. Instead, we should take the time apart to evaluate where we want to go from here with a clear mind.

Damon is the only brother I will talk to about this because Aiden wouldn't even begin to understand. He hasn't been on a real date since his high school sweetheart dumped him on graduation day. He has been womanizing ever since. I keep telling him that he better stop or he is going to end up with a sexually transmitted disease or something since he doesn't know half the girls he takes home. Why does he find random girls wanting to bone him attractive? I think a woman wanting to settle down and give her all to another person is infinitely sexier.

He's here today and I'm sure he will bring her up, but can I trust him not to discuss what I tell him with Tessa? Or is Harper discussing us with her too? It's a fine line and we haven't really discussed that aspect of our relationship yet.

"Hey, the family in 2604 just called. Apparently, the plumbing is acting up, and they had to turn off the water. You know anyone who can go assess it without charging us an arm and a leg?" Damon asks.

My lips scrunch to the left as I think of someone who could help. What's the guy's name we went to high school with? Jack? No, I pull up my profile and search.

"Yeah, I'll call Joseph. You know, the one we went to school with. He owns a plumbing business. I'm sure he can give us a good deal."

Clicking on the message button, I send him my number and ask him to reach out to me for a quote.

"Let me know what he says so I can tell them. I don't want them to have to go without water overnight."

The duplexes are full right now with families who have been displaced by recent fires. They are all very grateful to us for letting them stay there without paying a dime of rent. I always tell them to thank Damon because it was his idea. Aiden and I just helped him bring it to fruition.

Joseph: *It'd be fifty bucks for the tech to go look at it and see what's wrong. Once he knows, I can give you a quote on fixing it. Sound good?*

I let Damon know that Joseph is going to send someone out immediately.

The duplexes have proven to be a good investment, just to help the community, but the upkeep on them is going to be more than we realized. Some of the appliances that came over with the sale have stopped working, and the electrical in one of them looked to be done by someone unlicensed who didn't know what they were doing. So in the last two months, we have poured another twenty grand into upgrading all the electrical within the duplexes and replacing appliances. I'm not at all complaining because giving needy families a place to safely sleep with their kids is worth every penny.

"Listen, we've got to come up with a better system for maintenance on these duplexes. Do you think we should contract someone to work on them? Like someone we can call when we need something worked on at a fixed price?" Damon asks.

"Actually, that sounds like a good idea, but I wouldn't know where to start," I reply.

"I'll research it tonight when I get home. It could save us so much money in the long run. As much as things keep going wrong."

He calls the tenants and lets them know a technician will be there shortly, and then we go back to our poker game.

"Dare I ask how the wedding planning is going? Have you guys picked a venue yet? Or is it still undecided?" I ask.

Tessa is scary when it comes to the wedding. The only thing she has decided is the color scheme; the rest is yet to be determined. I've offered to help, but she wants to make these decisions with Damon. I respect that, but it needs to be made soon if she wants to get everything together in time. Hell, she hasn't even picked the venue. In my opinion, that's the first thing she needs to work on. It determines how many people can attend.

"Listen, you don't understand. I have told her that I'm happy with whatever she decides, and her response was, 'it's important where we get married, and it's the memories we will have for the rest of our lives so we need to make it together.' As long as she's standing next to me, I couldn't care less where we are."

Poor Damon. Things are only going to get worse the closer we get to the wedding day. Has Harper tried to help? It might be better coming from her than us anyway. Wait, no. We should keep our relationship separate from theirs. Even though I'm dating Tessa's best friend, that doesn't mean I need to tell her things, does it? Isn't that crossing a line?

"Isn't Harper her maid of honor? Why doesn't she ask for her help?" I ask.

"She's offered, but right now Tess is stuck in this phase where it should be me and her making the decisions."

"Are you guys fighting over the wedding?"

"I wouldn't call it fighting, but we do make up afterward." He laughs.

I have never even seen them argue before. Sure, even happily married couples fight, it's inevitable, but it's what you do to resolve it that makes a difference. Some couples say things they don't mean, and once it leaves your mouth, you can't take it back. Marriages are ruined because of fights all the time, but they are not going to break up. They are just too perfect for each other.

On that note, I decide to change the topic of conversation.

"So, Harper and I are still doing well. We've been out four times now, but something weird happened last night and I don't know if I should be concerned."

"Okay, talk to me. What's going on?" He lays his cards down and gives me his full attention.

"Well, obviously you're aware we've been seeing each other practically every day since we met. But yesterday, she mentioned we might be moving too fast. She said she wants to play it by ear. What does that even mean?" I shake my head. Trying to decipher what women say can sometimes be impossible.

"Honestly, maybe she is just feeling a little overwhelmed. I know when Tessa showed up in my life, it terrified me. I didn't think I was ready to open up to her, and things started to escalate. Before I knew it, she was a part of my life whether I wanted her to be or not. Sometimes we don't get to choose who we fall in love with, and that's the best part."

So maybe Harper is just as scared as I am. Neither of us wants to get our hearts broken, but I don't plan on hurting or breaking up with her.

"Just let her express her fears and acknowledge them. Do whatever she needs," Damon says.

I take out my phone and text her.

Me: *Let's go out to dinner tonight. Pick you up at 7?*

There are some things that we should discuss and it will be easier for both of us if we aren't at her house. After drinking some wine, and getting cozy on the couch, I don't want to fall asleep again and overstep. She did bring up me staying over already, and so I need to be diligent about not staying over.

Harper: *I'll see you then.* =)

The rest of my shift flies by, and then I'm at my house, showering and getting ready to take her to dinner. Tonight will be more about getting to know where she's at and what she wants going forward. I want to get a handle on how she is feeling and make sure she knows I'm not pressuring her into anything.

After my shower, I grab a plain blue button-down and dark jeans and decide to throw on my dress shoes, too. You can never look too good for a date. I run a comb through my hair, then take a couple minutes to blow-dry it so I don't drip everywhere.

Let's go get the girl.

On the drive over, I remind myself of what tonight is supposed to accomplish and when I pull up, it's like she's been watching for me as she is already coming out of her house wearing a red dress and black pumps. *The things you do to me.*

I get out and open the door for her, like every man should. "That dress is wonderful."

It's hard to keep my eyes on the road when her thighs are exposed and just begging me to kiss them. I shake my head, trying to get the dirty thoughts out of my mind for now because tonight is not about sex.

"So, this was last minute. Just couldn't resist seeing me tonight, huh?" Harper asks, smiling.

Okay, so maybe she's right. "Why you gotta call me out like that? Can't a guy just have dinner with a beautiful woman?"

"Of course. I'm not complaining. Plus, I love to see you dressed up. It's sexy." She smiles and winks at me.

Once we get to Rolando's Cuisine and get a table, she just sits there and stares at me, but not in a creepy way. In more of a loving way.

"So, I figured we should talk about yesterday. You mentioned us going too fast and I just don't want you to feel pressured by me. Are there rules you want to follow?" I ask.

She laughs and takes my hand in hers. "Listen. It's more scary to me that we are progressing fast, and I'm already breaking my rules for you. We've been on five dates now, counting this one, and my feelings are..."

"Are what?" I ask.

"Let's just say we might have only known each other for a week, but it feels like months. And I know that sounds childish." She continues to talk, but I stop her.

"Same. I think it's because we talked about things upfront, instead of waiting. Knowing things about you makes me feel closer to you."

She leans in and kisses me.

"If we ever need to slow down, don't be scared to voice it. There is no pressure to hang out with me or for sex. I just want to get to know you and go out to nice dinners like this as often as possible."

"Perfect."

Harper spends the night making me laugh and telling me about the kids in her class bitching and moaning about having to speak in class or being called on to read from the textbook. I know she just started, but she shows such a passion for the subject itself. I failed chemistry in high school, so I can promise I know nothing about it, and I hope to God I never have to worry about it ever again. Yet, I will listen to her talk about it because that's what I'm supposed to do, be encouraging and supportive.

Tessa somehow gets brought up, and then the wedding. We both express how stressed out she seems and that someone needs to step in and help her move forward. The venue needs to be decided so all of us can get started on our duties.

"I'll talk to her tomorrow. We're having lunch. Maybe I can work some magic and get her to finally come to a conclusion."

I sigh. "It's just a standstill. I've got my list of things to do, but until I know the venue, there's not much I can do. And if it takes too long, she will probably be upset with me even though it's not my fault. And because I'm a nice guy, I'd just take it."

"Tessa has expressed her dream for a perfect marriage, and unfortunately it doesn't exist. People fight and have differences, but the main importance behind these is that their partners accept them for who they are and don't harp on them."

"Is she having doubts about my brother?"

"Oh no, nothing like that. She is scared. Not of him, but of messing things up. Hell, she has even called your brother her Prince Charming on at least five occasions."

Tessa and my brother are made for each other, and whether they have differences or not, I know they will be together for the rest of their lives.

"Come on, babe. I've got to get home and grade some quizzes before school tomorrow. It's already ten," Harper says, standing up from the table, staring at the check.

I slip cash into the black booklet and walk her to my truck.

The ride to her house is mostly filled with silence. If we didn't just have a great night full of conversation, then I would be nervous, but she assured me that we are doing great and nothing is wrong.

As I pull up to her house, she takes her seat belt off, leans over, and kisses me.

"Just so you know, I'll be thinking about you. Are you sure you don't want to come in for some wine and watch me grade?"

I open my mouth to answer, but she beats me.

"Just kidding. It's not fun, plus I'll have *True Blood* on in the background and I know how you despise it. See you tomorrow."

The door shuts behind her, and I watch her walk up the driveway, unlock the door, and slip inside before I take off.

Is Harper the girl I've been waiting for my whole life? Can I be her Prince Charming?

10

HARPER

*T*he chemistry test today will provide some quiet time, so I can start putting together our labs for next week. I like to make learning fun, so we are going to work with some common chemicals to make some nice colored vapors. We did this in college and everyone loved it, so I hope the kids do too.

The first couple periods go smooth, no one is trying to cheat, and Liam sends me a picture of him at the station playing poker with Damon. It really gets me thinking about how my feelings are bursting at the seams already. My phone vibrates.

Tessa: *Still on for lunch?*

Me: *Yes! Wanna go to that Mexican restaurant down the street?*

The bell rings, and students come to the front to turn in their test, then file out of the classroom.

Tessa: *Yes, meet me out front and I'll drive us over.*

After the last student leaves, I grab my purse, lock the door, and head out. Tessa is waiting in front of the school for me.

"I could've walked."

"Nonsense. It gives us more time there if we drive."

When I get inside, I notice the wedding binder in the back seat and think about what Liam mentioned yesterday. This would be a good chance to bring it up nonchalantly and offer some help. I hate seeing her so stressed out about something that is supposed to make her happy.

When we pull up to the restaurant and get out, I grab the binder. "Let's look over wedding plans at lunch. Maybe we can knock some out."

After getting our table and drinks, I open up the binder to see everything in order. She is meticulous about having each part of the planning color coded.

"So, first decision is venue." I flip through the pictures, getting a feel for each of them and pointing out what I like about each of them. "In my opinion, I think it's better to use this one. It's more elegant, and it comes with a list of vendors you can use that are vetted by the venue itself."

She nods. "Okay, that's the one I like, too. Damon doesn't seem to care either way. So let's go ahead and mark that one."

"I can take some of this off your hands and call and set it up. Just give me a list of things I need to do, and I can take care of it this weekend. Less stress on you."

She closes the binder and changes the subject.

"So, how are things going with you and Liam?"

I push my hair behind my ear. "Almost too good to be true. Now I know how you felt when you found Damon."

One thing I can say is that their parents raised them right, and the community is lucky to have them watching their backs.

"Liam is a good guy. Obviously, I haven't known him too long, but he wants to settle down. He reminds me a lot of Damon in the sense, it's almost like he doesn't feel like he deserves happiness. They don't want to burden anyone with their demons," Tessa says.

I might be falling in love with him. Deep down, I know it's too soon, but I can't help it.

We end the conversation and try to eat our food before heading back to the school to finish out the rest of our workday. Mine goes by fairly fast since it's just testing, and I ask Liam to come over for a home-cooked meal tonight.

Before I know it, the final bell rings and school is over. I pack up my things and head to the market to pick up some vegetables and pork chops. Liam should be over shortly, and I want to make sure I beat him to my house. That will give me some time to clean it up a bit and get a load of laundry started.

Is it weird I'm okay with wearing leggings and a t-shirt around him? Normally, ladies want to dress up for dates and look their best, but he doesn't seem to mind. I'd rather be comfortable, especially after walking in heels all day at work.

I throw my hair up in a bun, load the washer, empty the dryer, and then fold the clothes before my doorbell rings promptly at seven.

"Come in," I yell from the kitchen, folding the last pair of pants.

He walks in, wearing gym shorts and a white t-shirt. "Hey, gorgeous."

I lean over to kiss him before taking the basket of folded clothes to my bedroom, and he follows along.

"Hope this is okay. Just threw something on after my shower."

I look down at myself. "It's great. No need to dress up. I feel the same."

He watches me as I put away my clothes, and he even attempts to help me, but he doesn't know where anything goes. Points for trying, though.

As he sits on the edge of the bed, I let him know that we finally decided on the venue. He seems pleased by this and pulls me close, his arms going around my waist. A passionate kiss leads me to being on top of him. It's like he could hear my thoughts because he pushes me off him.

"Listen, let's eat first. I need energy for what I wanna do to you," he says with a straight face.

"Promise?" I ask with a smile.

Seeing his broad shoulders in his t-shirt and the shorts barely holding on to his hips, just makes me want him so fucking bad. It's not like it's our first date and we barely know each other. And even if it was, we are both grown adults. This is the second time he has rejected me. What is going on? Of course, my insecurities start up, wondering if something has changed, or if he doesn't actually like me as much as he says.

The oven beeps, and he smiles. "Time to build our energy. Let's go eat."

I follow him into the kitchen, then I take the pork chops out of the oven and dish them onto two plates. The pork chops were baked with mushrooms, tomatoes, bell peppers, and onions on top. Something my father used to make for us all the time. This isn't quite his recipe, but it'll do.

"So, did anything interesting happen at work today?" I ask, just trying to keep the conversation flowing.

"Not really. We didn't have a single call so we just played a lot of poker. The duplexes are having problems with plumbing, so we had to reach out to someone to go over and assess it."

Even though he has told me about them, I forgot he owns the property until he mentions it. "It's so refreshing to see how much you care for Grapevine."

We don't waste any time eating our dinner so we can get right to dessert. Once we are both done, I gather the plates and put them in the sink and grab a bottle of wine and two glasses.

"Let's go to the couch and enjoy some wine. Maybe watch some *True Blood*," I say, joking around.

"It's not that bad, I guess. I still don't get the hype around wanting to be a vampire or werewolf, but whatever."

So he's been watching it in his spare time? *Interesting*. It just shows how much he actually cares to watch something I like.

We sit on the couch and clank our glasses together before I turn on the TV.

"What season is this?" he asks.

"Four."

I enjoy the wine and try to finish the episode, but it's gotten even weirder. Now they are witches, and Jason has somehow gotten involved with a coyote, and things are just all over the place. Eric has lost some of his memory and is now nice and has a crush on the main girl. Jesus, can't they just stick to one type of weird and let it be? No, now they are fairies, werewolves, witches, and who knows what else running around in this fictional world.

"So, what do you think?" I ask, pausing it and turning to him after the season finale is over.

"Why so many different paranormal creatures? Couldn't they have just stuck with vampires and werewolves? I only watched the first four episodes, so I apparently missed a lot," Liam says.

Instead of watching any more, I have something else in mind that he will enjoy more. I climb on top of him and start kissing his neck, while his hands wander up to unhook my bra. He flips me over, leaving me on my back, and lies down almost on top of me, taking my shirt and bra off, then nips at my breasts. The electricity shooting around in my body makes me feel like a teenager again, and I wonder how he's going to feel inside me, but at the same time, I want him to take his time. It's our first time, and I want to savor it.

I push him off and slide down his shorts, which doesn't take much, and his erection is eagerly waiting for some attention. I get on the ground and take it into my mouth, looking up at him through my lashes, wanting to watch him enjoy the pleasure that is going to be coursing through his body in just a second.

He takes the back of my head in his hands and flings his head backward as I work my way up and down. It's a definite turn-on when I can see his enjoyment.

"Okay, it's my turn. Lie down," he says, raising his voice just a little bit.

I follow his command and lie down, and then he's on me, kissing me down to my belly button and then sliding off my leggings and underwear. He nips my inner thigh, and then his mouth is on me, and the fire starts to build. The circles he places cause me to moan and writhe under him. *Fuck, it feels so damn good.* My hands run through my hair and wrestle with my breasts, trying to keep myself from giving in too soon. I want to enjoy this for as long as possible. He's not like most men who just want to hurry up and get to the penetration. No, he is taking his precious time, enjoying me as if I came to him wrapped in nothing but a bow.

"You taste sweet, but now I want to feel you," Liam says, wiping his mouth and positioning himself on the couch above me. He looks into my eyes, smiles, and then eases himself into me, causing both of us to moan at the same time. Liam kisses my neck and continues pumping inside me until we both can't control it any longer, and we give in to utter bliss.

Liam lies down on the couch, covering his eyes with his hand, panting.

"Best damn dessert I've ever had," I tell him.

He moves his hand and looks at me. "I normally last longer than that. Don't think that's typical."

Maybe I'm the weird one, but I couldn't care less how long it takes for us to get off as long as we do. Hell, I've been with guys who took half an hour to get off and didn't even help me finish. Now that's the selfish prick type.

We spend the next twenty minutes lying there, savoring our releases, until I turn over and lie on his chest, playing with his little bit of chest hair. Normally hair grosses me out, but I'm not vomiting yet.

Liam is a great man, and I wish Tessa would have introduced us earlier on. It still cracks me up that he ended up being Damon's brother, and I asked many times for her to introduce me.

"So, it's already two. You mind if I crash here?" he asks, his arm around me.

"Of course you can, but let's move to the bedroom. The bed is more comfortable."

We pick up our clothes and move in there, and it only takes five minutes for both of us to fall fast asleep in each other's arms.

11

LIAM

*E*choes off the walls are making me wince from not getting enough sleep last night. There are four tables in the break room at the station, and poker has become popular with the other guys. It's six hours into my shift, and we've responded to one fire. Thankfully, no one was hurt when we arrived on scene.

"You've been too quiet today," Damon says, walking up behind me and sitting down at the poker table. "Something on your mind?"

Harper. The baby thing.

"Just thinking about some things that I need to discuss with Harper, that's all."

He scratches his chin. "Everything okay?"

"Yeah, great actually. I'm happier with her than I ever was with Larissa."

"So, I'm sure I'm not the only one thinking about it, but don't you think you are moving too fast? It's been like a week and already you feel this strongly about her. Next thing you are going to ask her to marry you."

"Don't forget, you and Tessa only dated for two months or something like that before you proposed. Hypocrite."

He nods. "True, but I just don't want you to get hurt. I like Harper, but sometimes things just don't work out. Guard your heart, brother."

"Right." It's all I could respond with because he's right.

"Don't forget Aiden got home this morning. Dinner at my house."

It completely slips my mind and I'm not even sure Aiden will show up. He bails on us a lot and it pisses me off. "I sort of have plans with Harper."

"Invite her. Tessa already knows her; it's not like it's that big of a deal."

I pull out my phone and text her, hoping she wants to go.

Me: *So short notice—but my younger brother gets back into town today and Damon is having a dinner at his house.*

Harper: *What time should I be ready? Assuming you want me to tag along?*

The fact that she isn't even fazed by it makes me smile.

Me: *I'll pick you up at six. Don't have to wear anything fancy.*

"Alright, she's coming. Hopefully, Aiden isn't drunk off his ass tonight."

"He's not going to hit on her. That was one time. Get over it."

Damon has always taken his side, but drunk or not, it wasn't right. I mean, who hits on their brother's girlfriend in front of everyone?

"Time to get out of here. See you in a bit," Damon says, parting ways at our vehicles.

The nervousness begins to set in when my truck grinds to a halt, and I rush inside to the bathroom. A quick shower is necessary before picking her up. I don't want to smell like smoke, even though my brothers will be used to it. Using my time wisely, I grab a pair of jeans, a blue button-down, socks, and my shoes and set them on the sink before popping into the shower. The hot water hits my skin and almost feels like it's washing away all the bullshit from today. It clears my mind and helps me see that this is good for our relationship, even if it is early. My loofah is saturated with body wash and it runs up and down my body, removing the dirt and ash. Now I'm clean and smell good for Harper. After turning off the water, I grab the towel and begin drying off my hair first and then my body. Hopefully everything goes smoothly tonight. You just never know with Aiden around.

The jeans go on seamlessly, but the button-down is a different story. I keep missing buttons. *Calm down. There's no need to stir yourself up.* As the last button is threaded through, my chest rises and falls.

Me: *You ready?*

I take a moment to have a look at my appearance before walking out the door to head to Harper's.

Harper: *Waiting for you.*

When I arrive, she is wearing a simple emerald-green sweater dress, black boots, and her hair is in curls. Cute but comfortable. She didn't have to go through all that trouble just for dinner. "You look amazing," I tell her as she gets in my Jeep.

"So do you." She places her hand on my chest and slides a quick kiss on my lips before I take off toward Damon's.

On the ride over, I tell her a little bit about my brother Aiden since she doesn't know much. He is the one I have to worry about tonight, since he likes to make a fool of himself sometimes. My hope is that he won't get hammered at dinner. One thing about him; he really likes alcohol.

"Why did he go to Europe for so long?"

"He says he just needed some time away, but I think he got his heart broken and he just doesn't want to tell us."

Aiden isn't one known to date, but usually we hear about a different woman every week, and a couple days before he left for Europe, he just stopped filling us in.

After pulling into their driveway and parking, my heart starts hammering. "Thank you for agreeing to come tonight. You didn't have to."

"Are you nervous your brother isn't going to like me?" she asks, her eyebrow raised.

"Quite the opposite actually."

My feet scurry to the passenger side to help her and then up the foyer to ring the doorbell beside the big red door. Tessa opens the door and greets us.

"Hey, girl! So glad you finally get to see the new house. Come in," Tessa says, going in for a hug with Harper.

"Where's Aiden? I thought the whole reason we were having this dinner was for him?" I ask, noticing he isn't anywhere in sight.

"He'll be here shortly. You know him. He's always late."

I let out a deep sigh, and Harper whispers to me, "You okay?"

"Fine. Just typical of him."

We make our way into the kitchen while they finish preparing for dinner, and I pour some wine. The fact that Tessa already knows her makes it a little less awkward and eases the tension. They sit down and start talking about the wedding.

"I still think we should do navy blue and maroon. They look great together and give you a rustic but elegant look to the room," Harper says.

"Give it up. One thing she won't budge on is the colors. Believe me, I've tried," Damon says, laughing.

Tessa has been stressing out over planning the wedding, but she has eight months. Plus, she has Harper to help alleviate some of the stress. The last thing we need is for her to snap.

"Maybe, instead of you worrying, assign Harper some things to do, or even me. We don't mind helping. Best man and maid of honor have that role for a reason, right?"

Damon and I sit at the island while the girls talk.

"Tessa thinks you guys are gonna work out. She's secretly rooting for you guys," Damon says, taking a sip of his beer.

"Well, cheers to that."

The room appears to go silent, and that's when the subject of kids comes up. I cringe, waiting to see what is said. Tessa has already made it clear to Damon that she wants at least one more, and he's fine with that.

"I've always wanted kids. It'll happen when it's right," Harper replies.

I slouch, and my hand goes to my forehead. *Fuck, maybe I should just go ahead and tell her.*

"Looks like another one I'm gonna lose," I say, not loud enough for her to hear.

"What are you talking about?" Damon asks.

See, I haven't told my brothers about my inadequacy, but I didn't really have a choice but to explain to Damon now. I have no idea how he is going to react so I brace myself but keep my voice low.

"I can't have kids—well, my chances are slim to none is more what the doctor told me."

"Fuck, brother, when did you find this out?"

"About five years ago, when I was dating Larissa. We were getting serious and talking about having kids. We tried, but she never got pregnant. So she asked me to go see a doctor, and as soon as she found out, she left me."

"What an asshole," Damon says, the girls looking over at us.

"Now, I'm gonna lose Harper, too. Why the hell did this have to happen to me? I mean, I want kids badly. And to tell a woman who is desperately wanting to be a mother that I can't give them that, it's heartbreaking. I'm broken."

The front door opens and we all look to the hallway to see who it is.

"Long time no see," Aiden says, walking into the house.

"Can you arrive for anything on time, brother?" I ask. "Ten minutes is excusable, but almost an hour?"

He sits down next to me in the kitchen, and his eyes set on Harper. *Don't you fucking dare.*

"Harper, this is Aiden," Tessa says.

"Nice to meet you. How was Europe?"

Aiden moves and takes the seat next to Harper and starts telling us all about it; however, his eyes are fixed on her. He tells us how life there is so different from the states, and there is a bistro on every corner. At least he isn't talking about all the women he probably slept with while being over there. It makes me a little uncomfortable for him to be that close to Harper. Damon catches my eyes and tries to get everyone to head to the table.

"Alright, it's ready. Who's hungry?"

We all take our seats, and Aiden is on one side of Harper and me on the other. *Seriously, there are four other seats at this table you could've chosen.* The stench of his breath is hitting me from here, and I know at that moment, he's plastered. Why can't he show up to a family dinner without being drunk? Is that all he does in his free time? Drink and have sex?

"So, Harper, what made you agree to a second date with Liam?" Aiden asks, passing around the salad bowl.

She turns and looks at me. "He was honest and upfront about what he was looking for. You don't find men like that nowadays."

Aiden eyes me and smiles. "Good answer. Damon and I have been hoping he could find someone to put up with him. Want the best for his family, you know."

Harper blushes. "I know. My intentions are good, I promise."

Everyone goes back to eating, and the conversation lags.

I reach my hand over to Harper's lap, taking her left hand in mine, to show her some support. Aiden is being abnormally weird tonight. What is going on with him?

"Do you want kids?" Aiden asks.

Damon looks over at me apologetically and my salad flies out of my mouth all over my plate.

"Are you serious?"

Why is that any of his fucking business? It's like he knows my secret and wants to taunt me.

"It's okay. Of course, I want kids. I'd like two, maybe three," Harper replies.

A bit of frustration washes over me.

"Can't wait to have more kiddos in the family. Right?" Tessa replies, trying to keep Aiden from chiming in more.

The table is silent for the rest of our time. I think Aiden can tell I'm unhappy and doesn't want to press his luck. After we finish eating, I take Harper's hand in mine and stand up.

"Thanks for dinner, but I think we're going to head out for the night," I say, trying to get out of here.

"Oh, come on. We haven't even had dessert yet," Tessa replies.

"That's okay, maybe another time," I say, ushering Harper out the door. "Have a good night."

I slam the door behind me. "I'm so sorry, Harper. I had no clue he was going to ask you such personal questions."

"Really? I thought it would be worse. If my father were alive and meeting you for the first time, it would be intense. That was nothing."

"Still. Personal questions like that should be between us, not them. He had no right."

"It's fine, really. I like your family," she says, taking my hand. "Let's go back to my place, snuggle up on the couch, and watch some TV."

"Sounds like a perfect night."

On the way to her house, I try to simmer down, but Aiden is going to feel the wrath when I see him next. What the hell is wrong with him?

12

HARPER

*L*iam spent most of the night apologizing for Aiden. I understand where he is coming from with his agitation, but it's done. He knows my answer and I know his. Harping on it will not make things better. It didn't offend me, and I don't understand why he's so mad about it. His brother isn't allowed to ask me a question? Something just doesn't seem right, and he's been acting strange ever since dinner last night. Like he's stuck in his head and just not present. Something is bothering him and tonight I will figure out what it is.

I'm almost done with my second cup of coffee. Seven is approaching and another day of school is ahead of me. Today is exam day, which means I'll mostly spend it in silence and trying to keep students from cheating.

"I'll see you later." I give him a kiss and head out the door.

On the drive, I go over last night, trying to figure out if I said or did something wrong, but nothing is sticking out to me. The only thing I can think of is Aiden. I knew they didn't get along that well, but the animosity between them is borderline hostile.

I pull into the faculty parking lot, and students are mingling outside the school, waiting for the bell to ring.

"Good morning, Ms. Davis," Shelby, one of my favorite students, says.

"Ready for that exam today?" I respond.

"I was up until two studying."

"No need. You're going to ace it. Believe in yourself. Good luck," I say, walking past her and into the building.

Tessa catches up to me and walks with me to my classroom. She's apologizing for last night, even though she did nothing wrong.

"Liam and Aiden... well, they are fickle. Aiden once slept with one of Liam's girlfriends, so let's just say he doesn't trust his girlfriends around him."

"Like I would ever cheat on Liam with his brother. Surely, he doesn't actually think I'd do that."

"No, it's an insecurity thing. He didn't think she would do it either. Cut him slack, but seriously, next time you come to dinner, it won't be that eventful and we can all enjoy ourselves without the bickering."

"I'll bring two bottles of wine next time," I reply, laughing as some of my students begin to come in before the bell rings.

"I'll talk to you later," Tessa says, strolling out of my classroom.

Surely, he trusts me and knows I would never sleep with his brother. I'm not that kind of girl and I've been cheated on before. Why would I ever want to make someone else feel that hurt? Could it just be that? Or is something else bothering him too?

The bell rings, letting the students know they are now tardy for class, and they start filing into the classroom with nothing but pencils.

"Glad you all came prepared. Let's see who studied last night," I say, walking around and handing each of them their test. "And don't try to cheat. The questions are numbered differently on each test. So, looking at someone else's paper isn't going to help you."

I make my way back to my desk and take the time to pull out my phone and draft a text to Liam.

Me: *Listen, you have nothing to worry about with me and Aiden. I would never cheat on you. I'm not your ex. Is that really what is bothering you so much? Do you not trust me?*

I hit send and set it back on my desk.

Waiting for the period to be over, I find myself daydreaming about what my life will be like if Liam and I work out. Tessa will be my actual family. She would be a best friend and a sister. I smile at the thought of marrying Liam someday, having the perfect house, and children running around, playing in the backyard.

The bell rings.

"Alright, pencils down. We will see which of you studied. Place your test in the box on your way out."

Students file out of my classroom, and I'm trying to decide if I want to stay and grade some exams tonight or just wait and do it all tomorrow. It would work out better if I did half tonight. So I take the exams out of the box and begin grading. Next thing I know, it's already six. My phone vibrates on my desk.

Tessa: *Remember to cut him some slack. He really likes you, girl. Don't let this ruin that.*

Me: *There may be more to it than just his ex. I'm starting to think he is keeping something from me. It all started when the topic of kids came up.*

I grab my stuff and head to my car. The rest can be graded tomorrow. The school doors close behind me, and for a moment it's silent except for the sounds of crickets chirping in the distance and the sound of my heels against the pavement as I rush to my car, get inside, and lock the doors behind me. It's eerie at night. I start the engine and take off toward home.

I call Liam through Bluetooth.

"Hey, you coming over after work?"

"Of course. I'm about to get off now, and then I'll be heading that way. Do you want me to pick up something for dinner?" he asks.

"Yeah, don't care whatcha get. I'll be fine with whatever. See you soon."

Pulling up in my driveway, all I want to do is get inside. Being a young woman living alone, things can get weird sometimes, but now I have Liam.

After turning off my car, I grab my bag and head up to the door, but I notice it's slightly ajar. That overwhelming creepy feeling is back, and even more so now that it's clear someone has been in my house. This can't be a coincidence, right? I back away to the sidewalk and dial 911. My heart is racing a mile a minute, and this only confirms that I'm not crazy. Someone has been watching me.

"9-1-1. What's your emergency?"

I tried to calm my breathing. "Someone broke into my house. I haven't been inside yet. My front door was open when I got home."

It's not like they can really expect someone to go inside. Sure as hell not me.

"1305 Grand Avenue, right?"

"Yes, that's my address."

"Okay, stay outside until the cops arrive. They're on their way."

I pull the phone away from my ear to text Liam and then get back into my car and lock the doors. The person might still be inside.

Me: *I need you. Please hurry.*

My mind starts running, thinking about how unsafe I feel now. My lease is up in a couple months, and then I can just find a new house. After this, I can't stay here.

That's when I thought about what could have happened if I had been home when they broke in. I shudder at the thought.

Blue lights flash as the cop car comes down my street and parks in front of me. The officer approaches. "Good evening, ma'am. I got a call about a break-in."

I nod as I roll down my window, not wanting to get out. "Yes, they might still be inside."

He walks up to the doorstep and takes a look inside without going in.

"Stay in there while I inspect the house," he says, walking inside, gun drawn.

My nerves are shot, and all I want to do is cry. Why me? Who would want to break into my house? Besides my TV, there is nothing of any significant value. It seems pointless.

"Harper!" Liam yells, running from across the street. "Why are the police here? Are you okay?"

I open my car door, and his arms are instantly around me, pulling me close, and the tears let go. "I came home and my door was open."

He pushes me away to look at me. "You didn't go inside, did you?"

"No, I called the police and then texted you right away."

He stands there, his arms wrapped around me, consoling me. I know he is the only person who is going to make me feel safe again. "I won't let anything happen to you. It's gonna be okay, baby."

We wait for the officer to come out, which seems to take forever.

Those ten minutes feel like an hour, and my anxiety is just continuing to build.

"There's no one inside, ma'am," the officer says, stepping back onto the porch. "You might want to come in and let me know if anything was taken."

He notices Liam. "You live here, too?"

"Nope, this is my girlfriend's house, Scott. Thanks for responding to her call. It makes me feel better knowing you are here."

They must have worked together on a fire or something before. Whatever. All I want to do is find the person responsible for this.

I look at Liam and grab his hand before stepping inside. Things are strewn all over the living room, every drawer opened, and everything pulled out onto the floor. The TV is left on the wall, which I find odd.

"Who would go through so much trouble and not take anything?" I ask.

"That's what I'm trying to figure out, ma'am."

Liam walks with me to the back of the house to my bedroom, which is even worse. My clothes are all off their hangers and on the floor.

I drop to my knees, bawling, knowing someone has come into my house and gone through all my things. There is a purpose to all this and I just need to figure out what that is.

"It appears they were looking for something. This wasn't a typical burglary. Do you notice anything missing?"

"I'm honestly not sure, sir," I reply, my mind not working properly right now.

"Well, we'll taken some fingerprint samples, and maybe that will point us in the direction of the person. We'll be in touch."

The officer goes outside when another car pulls up. For the next hour, they take samples and do their thing until the house is quiet again. Liam remains by my side. I stand in disbelief at the shape of my house, knowing how long it is going to take to get everything organized again.

Why would anyone break into my house? I try to think of anything of value they could've taken but there's nothing. I don't have any expensive jewelry. What could they have been looking for? This unsettles me even more.

I begin picking up clothes off my closet floor and putting them back on their respective hangers. I'm not going to be able to sleep tonight, so I might as well start picking up. It's going to take forever to clean all this mess up. Liam stands there and watches me for a moment before he starts to put things back into my dresser.

"You know, you don't have to do this tonight."

"Gotta do something to keep my mind occupied. Or else I'm gonna break down. I feel violated. None of this makes sense."

"Are you sure there's no one you can think of who would want to hurt you? Nothing they could have been after? I agree with Scott; it's abnormal for someone to break in and not take anything."

I slump down onto the bottom of my closet and close my eyes. Does he think I'm keeping something from him? Why would I not help the cops find the person responsible?

"No, no one. Maybe they came to the wrong house? Maybe it was supposed to be my neighbor's house or something? I don't know what to tell you."

My agitation is getting worse, and all I want to do is curl up into a ball and cry. How am I ever going to feel safe in my home again? One thing's for certain, I won't be able to sleep tonight, even with Liam here.

We continue hanging everything back up until the closet is done.

"I'll take care of the living room."

This man has only known me for two weeks, yet he is already so invested in my life. Not that I'm complaining. I could truly see a future with Liam, and that scared me shitless.

He ushers me into the kitchen, which remains untouched, and pours a glass of wine. "Drink this. I'll work on the living room. Try to calm your nerves."

After tonight, I'll be looking for a new place. It doesn't even feel like home anymore, and there is no way I will be able to keep sleeping in that bed or coming home to this house after what just happened.

"You wouldn't happen to have a duplex open right now, would you?" I ask.

"I wish we did. You could always come stay at my place. It's up to you."

I sip on my wine, trying to forget and basking in the glory of Liam Jackson in a pair of gray sweatpants hanging off his hips perfectly.

13

LIAM

*A*round midnight, Harper falls asleep in my arms. I move her off me and make my way to finish tidying up the house. At least she won't be constantly reminded of the incident. The question Scott posed is still haunting me. Why would someone break in and not take anything? It just doesn't make any sense, and she mentioned that they could have come to the wrong house, but that's unlikely, too. Whoever did this, they were looking for something, and I'm damn glad that Harper wasn't home.

As I clean up, I take notice of the ransacked items, trying to put together a scenario of what they were after, but the pattern isn't clear. It seems like they just went into every room and threw everything on the ground. Wait, maybe this wasn't a burglary and it's just staged that way to throw us off. It would make sense why nothing is taken.

The lack of sleep might just be messing with my head. I'll go through this again once I've had some sleep and see if it's something we should make the police aware of.

I try not to let my mind wander while she sleeps, but then a gut-wrenching scream comes from the bedroom, and I rush in to find her curled up in a ball, tears streaming down her face.

"Are you okay?" I ask, looking around the room. "What happened?"

"I keep having nightmares, vivid ones, that someone is trying to kill me."

Why would someone be trying to kill her? Her mind is probably playing tricks on her, and because of the break-in and the stress, it's making her dream about even more horrible things that could happen.

"No one is getting you while I'm around. I can promise you that," I say, bringing her closer to me and wrapping my arms around her.

I lie down in bed, trying to console her back to sleep and it works, but not for very long. Around one thirty, she wakes up screaming again and then can't go back to sleep. I can't blame her for not feeling safe anymore. Poor thing.

Neither of us are getting any sleep tonight, and that's okay. Maybe I'll get lucky and can take a nap when I get into work tomorrow before a call comes in. One thing is for certain; I have to be alert for my job.

At about three a.m. Harper decides to turn on something to watch. She tries to play it cool, like she doesn't want me to know it's bothering her, but it's obvious.

I continue to clean until the sun comes up, and then I make a pot of coffee to help keep me awake. It's always when you can't sleep that your body and mind finally get tired. Go figure.

I make both of us a cup and go to the bedroom to join her.

"Here, baby. You're going to need it," I say, placing it on the nightstand next to her side of the bed.

She takes a sip and continues to watch her TV show, and then she leans over and snuggles against me. It's nice to know I help her feel protected, but the nightmares prove something is still bothering her, and even with me here, it's not enough.

The incident has changed her a little, and she's more jumpy than normal. Around seven, the trash truck came down the street and she squirms at the sound of a trash can hitting the pavement. It's going to be harder to get over than she thinks.

"How the hell am I supposed to live like this? They could come back, and this time I might be home. How am I ever supposed to sleep?"

We can solve that problem by going to my house, but if they are targeting her specifically, then they will find her eventually. Yet, she seems certain there isn't anyone after her and no reason for there to be.

I crinkle my nose, trying to believe her, knowing I need to be able to trust her, but something just doesn't add up and it's really making me second-guess everything.

My mind goes back to our second date. They never caught who killed her parents. Maybe we should bring this up to the police and let them at least be aware of that fact. I highly doubt it's the same person, especially since that was many years ago, but better to be safe than sorry.

How do I bring this up to Harper without sounding insensitive? I don't want to drudge up the horrific actions, but it might be something the detective could at least look into. Aren't they still working the case in California? Surely, they didn't just give up on a double homicide. I'll bring it up later, after we are off work so it doesn't ruin her day at work. She has enough going on in her mind right now.

I finally get out of bed to make another cup of coffee before I leave for my house and find her in the kitchen. She is standing there, in a black pencil skirt, red silk top, and black pumps. I don't think I'll ever get over how beautiful she is.

"Sorry you didn't get any sleep," she says. "I don't know why this is happening to me. The dreams were so vivid. They felt so real."

"Baby, you don't have to apologize. I just want to make sure you are okay. Other than that, I couldn't care less about no sleep," I say, then take a sip of the hot coffee. After last night, I'm going to need about twenty of these to keep me awake at work today. Although maybe I'll get lucky and catch a nap in between calls today.

Dark circles are already starting to form under her eyes and it's time to talk about us going to my house for at least tonight. She will sleep much better there.

"So, what are your plans for today?" I ask, sitting down at the table. "After work, I mean."

"I'm not really sure yet. All I know is I don't wanna be here."

I can understand her wanting to be around people today, and at the school no one can get in without showing ID. I hate that she is scared and hurting, but there's not much I can do to make it better.

"Okay. I've got my shift today, but I'll be off around six or seven. Calls depending, of course. Would you feel safer if we stayed at my house?"

Her eyebrows raise, and she puts her coffee on the counter. "Are you sure that's a good idea? It might be a while before they find anything out."

"Why wouldn't it be? I've stayed here two nights in a row—not that I'm complaining at all. My house isn't too far from here, and you could get some actual sleep there."

"I'll think about it." She gives me a quick kiss, then prances to the door. "I'll see you later. Make sure to lock the door when you leave."

I stay to finish my coffee and walk around the house. The guest bedroom isn't really touched, which is weird. Things aren't thrown around like the other rooms, but some things look like they were gone through. Paperwork mostly and old newspaper clippings. Why go through these?

My watch alerts me it's time to head into work, and I still have to stop at my house and grab a change of clothes. Fuck. I grab my keys and lock her door behind me.

I end up being about ten minutes late, and Damon is waiting for me in our normal spot at the makeshift poker table.

"Dude, you keep ghosting us, and we're going to stop inviting you over. I'm starting to feel used."

"Shut up. Her house got broken into last night. I slept over there."

I set my things down and try to keep my cool.

"Oh, Tessa didn't say anything. They know who did it?"

They did get fingerprint samples, but who knows if it will even point to anyone. They could just be mine or Harper's. I try to stay positive that they will find the person responsible, but there really isn't that much to go on.

"Not a clue yet. We're probably gonna stay at my house tonight."

Honestly, I think that's the best idea. If we stay at my house, we can both get some sleep, and after last night, it's needed. My eyes are burning, and as much as I want to stay and chat with Damon, the bunks are calling my name.

"I'm gonna take a nap. The alarms will wake me if we get a call. Otherwise, just let me sleep."

If she doesn't end up going to my house tonight, then it'll be another sleepless night, yet I want to be supportive so at least if I get a nap while here, I can focus on her.

Last night, I planned on talking to her about my five percent chance, but then the break-in happened, and she is already stressed over that. I don't need to add something to her plate. Deep down, I hope she won't leave me once she finds out, but who knows, maybe with the right person that small chance will be enough to have a child. Yet, I'm not sure if Harper will be okay with chancing it, especially with how badly she wants to be a mom. And I don't feel right keeping this from her, but just a couple more days, and then I'll come clean.

14

HARPER

On the way to work, I catch myself watching out the rearview mirror of the car, seeing if anyone is following me. This break-in has really messed with my head. Why would anyone be after me? *Stop being paranoid.* It's easy to say, not so much to do. I wonder if this is how others have felt after something like this happened. Is it normal to want to move?

I walk past the students with a smile on my face, trying not to let anyone know anything is wrong. When I'm here, I need to be on my game, it's my job, but I'm still freaking out inside. Something just doesn't feel right, and until they find the person responsible, it's not going to go away.

Once I get into my classroom and set my things down, I get out my syllabus and look over what is being taught today. The only thing I can do is keep my mind busy so it doesn't go haywire.

My phone vibrates against the desk.

Liam: *Hope your day goes well. Can't wait to see you tonight. Let me know if you need anything.*

He really is a sweet man and takes great care of me when he doesn't have to. It shows his character and proves he is someone I can spend the rest of my life with someday. I find myself falling more in love with him with each passing day, him comforting me and being there through these tough times. Isn't that the best part about having a partner? Having someone to share the hard times with and get through them together? My hope is my life can go back to normal and the nightmares will stop once I leave that house. The thought of staying there after someone has violated my privacy scares the everliving shit out of me.

I thought about reaching out to my therapist, the one I saw after my parents' deaths. We have a session twice a year through video chat, just to make sure I'm doing okay. She might be able to help me with a way to cope with what happened. I don't want to constantly be looking over my shoulder, wondering if someone is coming after me.

I send her an email letting her know what happened and to see if she has time to chat with me later. Liam knows about my therapy after my parents' deaths, and this isn't something I'll keep from him. Every step of the way, he's been supportive. Hiding things from the person you're with only hurts the relationship in the long run.

A knock sounds on my door, which I find odd because no one comes to see me before class starts. I start to freak out, but then I remember no one can get this far into the school without showing ID and checking in with the front desk.

"Come in," I say, peering over at the door, seeing who it is.

Tessa storms in, arms crossed. "Why didn't you call me? I had to hear from Damon that my best friend got burglarized. What the hell, Harper?"

Honestly, I didn't even think about that. I've been kind of dealing with my own shit here. She needs to calm down. "I'm sorry. I'll be sure to call you next time," I respond sarcastically.

She just stands there and stares. "Okay, whatever. Are you okay? You don't seem like yourself. Is there anything I can do?"

"I got no damn sleep last night, and I don't know if I will ever feel safe going home. So, no, I'm not fucking okay, Tess."

After saying it, regret washes over me. It's not her fault this happened and here I am taking it out on her when she is just trying to help. *Stop being such a bitch.* "Sorry, I just... really need some sleep."

Liam is right. I am not going to be able to sleep at that house anymore, and right now my only options are staying with him or shelling out a lot of money to stay in a hotel until my lease is up. The only thing hindering me from saying yes to going to his house is I don't want it to affect our relationship. Moving in with each other is a big deal, especially when you have only known the other person for two weeks. What if we fall apart?

"What is going on? Talk to me."

"Liam has offered to let me to stay with him, but it seems too soon. Things are going so great between us, and I don't wanna ruin them. Maybe I should just go stay at a hotel. No pressure."

She scoffs, "I thought you knew Liam better. He's offering because you need somewhere to stay. He isn't asking you to move in with him, girl. Stop overthinking things, and just go with the flow. I'm telling you, y'all are the end game."

I try to take my mind off the incident and onto something else. "You make your decision on the vendors yet? I called and booked the venue. The deposit needs to be made by Sunday, so don't forget."

"I've got two picked. The others I will work on this weekend. It's harder than you think. Seriously, all I can think about is what if I choose the wrong one and everything goes wrong the day of the wedding. I'll have a freaking heart attack."

"Stop being so crazy. Everything will go perfectly. I'll make sure of that. Don't you worry."

Tessa put her trust in me to make sure everything goes smoothly, and I haven't skimped on my duties as maid of honor. I've planned an awesome bachelorette party for just the two of us in July. We will both be off for the summer and can take a weekend away.

"You know, you truly are the best friend I've ever had. I love you, girl."

I shoo her off to the office as the bell starts to ring. Students will be filing in here at any moment.

Maybe I should just go stay with Liam and if anything weird starts happening, then I can go to a hotel. With everything that happened, being next to him will make me feel safe, and that's something I need right now. It's settled. I'll pack a bag for his house after work.

The rest of my day flies by between teaching the newest chapter out of the textbook and just daydreaming in between periods about what living with Liam will be like. Is he messy? Does he leave dishes in the sink overnight? All things a girl needs to know.

Before leaving the classroom, I shoot him a text.

Me: *I'm gonna go home and pack a bag. I'll be ready when you get off.*

Going home by myself is a little nerve-racking, but I can't go through life being scared. Things happen to innocent people all the time, and I just have to deal with it.

I grab my stuff and head out to the parking lot, the sun already almost gone, and head home.

When I get on my street, I peer around, looking for anything suspicious before I pull into my driveway. I take a deep breath. It'll be okay. *Liam will be here in an hour, and then we will go to his house.*

I grab my purse, head to the door, and go inside. Usually, the first thing I do when I get home is pour a glass of wine, take off my heels, and sit on the couch, but not tonight. All I'm worried about is getting the hell out of here.

My closet is all picked up and I grab the small suitcase from the back and open it up on my bed. I start throwing stuff inside, and after about ten minutes, I've gotten everything packed for the next week.

I pull out my phone and text him.

Me: *I'm all packed and ready to go. Still getting off soon?*

I set my phone down on the bed and go to the kitchen to get a glass of wine to ease the tension in my body. *Just a little while longer, and then you won't have to be here.*

I take a sip, then a hand comes around and covers my mouth, blocking the gut-wrenching scream coming from me. *They're here.*

15

LIAM

The blaring alarm wakes me up out of dead sleep, and I rush to the truck. Every minute matters. Damon takes off, and when he pulls onto the street, my heart drops. This is Harper's street. *That's her house.* My stomach drops when we get farther on the street, and I see it. The smoke rising from the house, flames out of control, and the structure falling. *Please don't let her be hurt.* Approaching the house in the fire truck, I gaze around to the bystanders lurking on the crosswalk across from the house to see if Harper is there. *Nope. Where is she?*

"That's..." I can't even finish the sentence before the truck stops.

"What the hell are you doing?" Damon yells, grabbing me by the arm of the protective suit.

"It's her house!" I jerk out of his grasp and take off, not worried about anyone else but her. She must still be inside.

The black smoke has taken over the sky, and the creaking of the structure is just waiting to give out more.

My feet carry me fast, up the street and steps and to her front door. "Harper!" I yell, opening it and rushing into the living room, covering my face because I forgot my headgear. "Harper! Are you here?"

The far side of the living room is in bad shape, and the roof could collapse at any moment, but Harper might be in here somewhere, and I'm not leaving until she's safe. When I pass through the hallway and into the bedroom, I find her.

"Oh my God, Harper. Are you okay?" I ask, untying the rope holding her to the chair. There is blood everywhere, and bruises cover her entire face. She's almost unrecognizable. Who the hell did this to her? The same person who broke in last night?

"Can you hear me? Baby, please. Answer me." Tears are leaving streaks on my face through the black soot accumulating, and my index finger lands on her neck to check for a pulse. It's faint, but it's there. *Please don't leave me.*

Her limp body slumps against mine, and the flames have reached her bedroom. How the hell are we going to get out of here? I search for a way out, and that's when I notice the window. I wrap one of her shirts around my elbow and slam it into the glass, shattering it everywhere. I clutch her body to mine. Maneuvering out the window with an extra hundred and forty pounds isn't easy, but I do it.

After escaping through the window, I double back to the front of the house and hand Harper over to the paramedic. "She's not responding. Pulse faint. She needs a hospital now."

The EMT observes the amount of damage to her body and straps her onto the gurney to take off. "Liam!" Damon yells. "What the hell happened?"

"I don't know. Found her like that. Tied to fucking chair. Whoever did this didn't expect her to make it out alive."

I begin to get into the ambulance, and Damon stops me. "You can't go with her. You know that. Let's put out the fire, and then I'll drive you to the hospital myself."

We exchange some foul language and the ambulance takes off. "What the hell is wrong with you? If that was Tessa, you wouldn't think twice."

"Fine, go," Damon says, understanding my reasoning and not wanting to argue with me right now.

My mind keeps going through the motions, like I could have prevented this if we both had stayed home today. She would have never ended up like this. My hands run through my hair, tears streaming down my face, hoping that she's okay.

Please be okay. I just found you. I can't lose you already.

I take off, and everything else is background noise to the sound of my feet hitting the pavement. I can't wait any longer, and Damon understands even if the chief doesn't. I'll take disciplinary action over not being there for her any day.

I approach the hospital and then the front desk, taking a second to catch my breath. "I'm here for Harper Davis. She was brought by ambulance from a house fire."

The nurse comes around and puts her hand on my shoulder. "Sir, I can't give out any information just yet. Are you a relative?"

"She doesn't have any relatives. I'm her boyfriend."

"I'll let you know as soon as I can."

I canvass the hospital, knowing the police have to be here somewhere. With the way she was found, they would've received a call.

The elevator takes me up until I reach the fourth floor. This has to be where she is. I peek inside every little window, and nothing. That's when I noticed Officer Scott from yesterday.

"Have you guys figured anything out?" I ask. "This had to be the same person."

"No. The fingerprints didn't come up with any hits. We need to know what they are after."

Harper seemed pretty diligent that she doesn't have a clue who would do something like this. "Listen, I know I'm not family, but I really just need to know how she's doing. Harper doesn't have any family. No siblings and her parents passed years ago. Please."

"She's in surgery."

I fall to the floor next to him, my head in my hands, wondering how this could possibly be happening. Harper didn't seem like she could hurt a fly, so why her? None of this makes any sense, and my head aches trying to figure it out.

Damon rushes out of the elevator and crouches down next to me. "How is she? I called Tessa, and she's on her way."

"They won't tell me a goddamn thing besides she's in surgery. I can't see her, only family. Do you know how fucked up that is?"

A doctor comes out and begins talking to Scott. I pretend not to listen.

"She's out of surgery, but there might be complications. She had a brain bleed and will be kept in a coma to allow time for it to heal."

A freaking coma? Brain bleed? Oh, Harper. I was supposed to protect you and I failed.

Damon is speaking to Scott, and I try to calm myself down.

"Listen, they are going to talk to the hospital and explain the situation. Since you were with her yesterday, they might be able to get a little leniency on the rule."

My head flies back as I thank God. Surely, they'll understand. What if it were one of their girlfriends?

Tessa steps off the elevator frantically, not able to stop crying.

"Where is she? What happened?"

I pull her in close, wrapping my arms around her. "We don't know anything except she's in a coma."

"When can we see her?"

"They won't let anyone see her unless they are family. We both know she has none."

"Oh, I'm seeing her, whether they like it or not. My girl isn't going to be posted up in some hospital bed, possibly dying alone."

Let's not even go there. She's not going to die. Not on my watch.

Damon and Tessa sit with me on the floor, waiting for the other cop to come back and let us know if we can see her. Honestly, I don't know what I will do if they say no. I can go in any way and maybe get arrested, but will they really arrest me for trying to see my comatose girlfriend?

It's not like I can possibly be a suspect.

"So, we have to go through some channels before we can allow you in. The detective is reaching out to verify your whereabouts for today, and once they can confirm you have a solid alibi, then we can rule you out."

"You think I fucking did this to her?" I yell, my knuckles white. "What kind of monster do you think I am?"

Damon tugs on my arm. "Chill. Once they rule you out, you can see her. Stop acting like an idiot."

Scott flinches like he expected me to hit him. "I'm sorry, but I have to go through the procedure. I can't risk my job. I have kids at home to feed."

"However, the chief of staff agreed to let me supervise you in the room for her protection, until they can rule you out."

"I don't give a shit. Just take me to see her."

Tessa jumps in. "Can I see her, too?"

Scott says no, only one visitor at a time right now. She will have to get cleared as well.

He makes a good point, because the asshole who did this could be trying to get in to see her right now. "Nobody sees her but me and Tessa."

"The exception is just for you. Until alibis are sorted and you surrender your fingerprints."

Tessa has Damon take her down to the station to provide them with whatever they need to clear her name.

I follow Scott, trying to prepare myself to see her all beaten and bruised again. It's etched into my brain, and I don't know if I'll ever be able to get it out.

The door begins to open, and he puts something underneath it to hold it that way and stands in the hallway. "It stays open."

The room's dim, and the only thing I could hear were the machines doing their best to keep her stable. Seeing her like this, hooked up to all kinds of machines, only makes my anger grow. The way I found her, all beaten and bloody—the officers are right. Whoever it is, is targeting her. Why didn't she tell me? Tell the cops, at least. There's something she is holding back, and it might just cost her her life.

My fingers run through my hair as I go through all kinds of scenarios in my head. Going back through every conversation we've had since our first date, trying to find something that might give me a clue as to what it could have possibly been about.

"So, how long have you two been together?" Scott asks. "Must be a while. You being here and all."

"Actually, we just had our first date on New Year's Eve."

"Wow, she must be a fantastic girl, then. Glad she has someone with her during these times. My mom was a surgeon and always said a support system helped with recovery."

"Oh, I don't plan on leaving her side unless you make me," I respond, looking over my shoulder at him. "You sure there's no way to let Tessa in here?"

"Yeah, as soon as her fingerprints and alibi are sorted out."

All I can do is make sure to keep her company, so I slide the chair from across the room next to her bed so I can hold her hand.

Please come back to me. I need you.

How could I feel this way after only this short amount of time? It makes no sense logically. My heart knows tragedy, time after time, and I pray that this would not end in more. Not after I finally found the woman of my dreams. How cruel could this world be?

IT'S BEEN thirteen days and the doctors still appear every hour to monitor her vitals and medication levels. They have pulled her off the medicine inducing the coma and now we are just waiting for her to wake up. The stories of people waking up years later are rare. If God grants a miracle for Harper, I'll take it. My eyes are crimson and puffy but that's what anybody would foresee, being at the hospital for the last two weeks.

Tessa has been able to come in and see her, but it took a couple of days for them to verify she was working all day.

The police searched her home for evidence, but the fingerprints found did not match anyone in their system. The fire left the second bedroom unscathed, but there is still yellow tape surrounding the home.

I did inform the detective about her parents' homicides, and they have taken that into consideration in looking for suspects, but apparently there have been no leads on that case in years.

Her room is filled with vibrant flowers and cards from coworkers. I'm not thrilled with the local news after they played a story on the fire, and now the person responsible will know she's still alive. What if they decide to complete the job? She's safe here, but what about when she leaves?

Scott and I are well acquainted now since he's been defending her door and has kept me updated on their search for the individual who did this. Right now, there is no progress. It forces me to conclude there's more to this than anybody realizes, and the key everyone needs to solve the case is in Harper's mind. We need to be patient until she wakes.

"What is next? I mean, we can't sit here and wait," I say, my head in my hands. "How does someone not leave any kind of evidence behind in two different crimes? It makes little sense. We are missing something."

Scott shakes his head. "They're going through the house a second time, to see if they missed anything."

It's been thirteen days. Any evidence is ruined due to the fire or soot left behind.

"How much do you know about Harper? Whoever did this, it's personal. The detective mentioned her parents' homicides. They are working to try and get some leads on that case and it might point us to solving this one as well."

Before this transpired, we had only been dating a little over two weeks. Shivers run down my spine, thinking about what they could bring to light. Everybody has skeletons in their closet, stupid things, but maybe Harper doesn't.

"Excuse me," Tessa says, shoving past Scott on her way into the room.

He gives her a *don't push it* look.

"No progress still?" she asks, peering at Harper. "Do they have any idea when she might wake? Should I worry? It's been a while."

I wiggle my shoulders. "They said it's normal. The brain is working to heal. She should wake up on her own when she's ready. Until then, all we can do is sit and ride it out."

She doesn't move, only stares at Harper. "I'm here. I love you."

The doctor tells me that chatting with her while she's unconscious can help her. Some patients said they could understand their loved ones speaking to them while being under, and it encouraged them to fight harder. So, most of the day, I am telling her a story about me, something from my childhood, or listening to music, and periodically I read a novel to her.

One thing I picked up on when I spent the night with her that first time was her assortment of Nicholas Sparks books, so I went to the local bookstore and grabbed a couple different ones to read to her.

"Call me if anything changes. I'm gonna go get out of my work clothes and shower," Tessa says.

She comes by every day to check on her, and when it came time to ask her questions about Harper, she really couldn't give Scott or the detective much, which is peculiar, because you would think a best friend would know more than someone who had only known her for two weeks.

I once again sit next to Harper and I take her hand in mine. "Please wake up. It's been rough, keeping my cool around everyone checking in on you and not really knowing what to tell them. I can't wait to see your beautiful eyes again and hear that obnoxious laugh of yours. Just don't leave me, okay?"

The worst part of this situation is getting no privacy. Scott refuses to let me close the door, which means he can hear everything I say or do. He knows I'm not the one who did this to her, and a bit of trust couldn't hurt. I'm not a suspect and don't like being treated like one.

My phone rings, and a name pops up on my screen. Just what I need right now.

"Hey, Chief."

"Listen, we need you to come back to work. Being short-staffed this time of year is killing us."

"I can't until Harper has recovered. I thought I made that clear."

How am I supposed to go on living my life when she's fighting for hers? What if she wakes up and I'm not here? And she's all alone? Hell no. This is where I belong until she is better, and if I lose my job, well, so be it.

"Listen, I can't hold your job forever. Once your vacation time runs out, I'll have no choice but to fill your position."

"If you feel the need to replace me, do it. Bye, Chief."

A knock sounds on the open door, and a nurse is standing there with another vase of flowers.

"Sorry to interrupt. Just putting these up," she says.

I take notice of the shift in the room since everyone saw the report on Harper's house. It moved from sterile and white to vibrant. The fresh flowers produce a fragrance in the air. Most of them appeared after her story went live, and I didn't mess with them, because they're not mine.

Once she wakes up, I'll read the cards to her and let her enjoy their smell, but one in particular catches my eye. It's a vase of tulips, her favorite, with a rosy-red card inserted into a bow. I can see from my seat the words *Secret Admirer*. How didn't I catch that?

"Scott, come here," I say, raising my voice to get his attention. "Look at this."

"What is it?"

I point my index finger at the vase. "Who brought those in? Were they delivered?"

"No one but the nurse can get past me," he replies, taking the card out of the bow and coming to stand next to me so we can both read it.

I'm sorry that they saved you, but next time you won't be that lucky.

"They've been here!" I holler.

"Now calm down. Maybe they were delivered. I'll check with her nurse."

Scott takes the card, thrusts the blossoms in the trash, and exits the room, leaving the door open. They could be anywhere in this hospital— any staff member, visitor, or even patient. Not knowing is killing me, and she'll want answers when she wakes.

I cross my arms and begin to pace in front of the door, waiting for him to come back.

After half an hour, Scott returns and doesn't appear happy.

"Whoever this is, he's good. He avoided looking at the cameras, but he gave them to Harper's nurse. She says he's a white male, five-eleven, around midforties."

"So what do we do now?"

"I called the detective, and without more, there's nothing he can do."

Is this how our police departments runs? It's been two weeks and nothing to show for it. I'm not blaming Scott because he has barely left since they brought her in. The guy is dedicated, but his partner is on vacation, and so he decided he could use extra money. His back must hurt from standing all day and sleeping in a freaking chair.

One machine goes haywire with loud annoying beeping. *What the hell is happening?*

"Doctor, something's wrong!" I scream, and Scott yells, echoing me.

I rush to her side, and her face is redder than normal, flushed.

My hand falls to her cheek. "You're going to be okay, and I'm not going anywhere."

I want to keep her calm until the doctor arrives. Sure, she's unconscious, but for a minute there I swear I see her eyelid twitch like she's trying to open her eyes, but it's probably just me seeing things.

16

HARPER

*P*eople are talking around me, and someone is lightly caressing my hand in theirs. The machine begins going haywire, alerting everyone that my heart rate is elevating. *Calm down.*

Do I even want to be able to open my eyes being surrounded by strangers in a foreign place?

"Doctor!" a man yells. "What's going on?"

I hear someone else come into the room. "It's just her heart rate. Nothing to be alarmed about. Just keep talking to her. Believe it or not, I've had patients tell me it's helped them."

The voice sounds vaguely familiar, but I can't put my finger on it. I try to speak, but something is in my throat, making it impossible. *Who are you? Where am I?* Those are the questions I beg to ask and get answers to, but it's pointless. Without being able to speak, I'll never get answers. I'll just be trapped inside my own mind forever.

His hand is back on mine. "I remember our first date... how nervous we both were... online dating, right? Who knew we would find each other—on there of all places—it truly is a miracle."

First date? I haven't been on a date since my junior year of college. He obviously is delusional.

One thing's clear from the noises and him calling the doctor, I must be in a hospital. With the many hospital dramas I've seen, it's possible I've been in an accident, the thing in my throat a ventilator, and on a vast amount of pain medication to keep me sedated. But it still remains unclear. What put me in here? Who is this man?

"I'm hoping for another miracle. Harper, you need to get better. Come back to me."

His sobs echo around the room. This man knows my name and feels so deeply for me, yet I have no recollection of who he could be. Hell, why I am even here? I truly hope I recognize him once I open my eyes so I can extend that same care. Maybe something will shift and I'll know him.

With my eyes shut, I try to think back to the last thing I remember. *Think hard.* That only makes me wince. I've got to be missing something. Where are my parents? Why aren't they here? Everything about this situation seems weird, and it makes my stomach tense. Did something happen to them too?

"Did you just squeeze my hand?" he asks. "If so, squeeze it again."

I focus on it and use all my energy to do it again.

"Doctor! Come quick!"

"What is it, Liam?"

"She squeezed my hand. I even asked her to do it again," he tells her, the excitement in his voice apparent.

Another set of footsteps comes in. "I'll lower her dose so that she can wake up as naturally as possible. But you need to be prepared, we're not sure yet what complications the swelling could have on her."

Complications? Swelling? What the hell are they going on about?

The weights on my eyelids are wavering, and before I know it, I can see. My eyes dart around the room, to the doctor, to the man named Liam, and then to the police officer standing in the doorway. What the hell happened to me? I try to talk, but it gags me.

"Can't we take that out?" Liam asks the doctor. "It seems like it might be hurting her."

I'm not sure who this guy is, but he can read my mind.

Before they take the tube out, they instruct me not to fight. "Your throat will be very sore for the next couple of days. So take it easy."

When I can finally breathe on my own, it's the best feeling in the world. Everyone has their eyes on me, waiting for me to say or do something. I have no clue who any of them are, and there must be a reason a police officer is guarding my door. Something bad happened, I can feel it.

"Not to be rude—but could you stop staring at me," I say, my voice raspy. "It's really starting to freak me out."

His arms close around me, and I recoil from his touch. "Do I know you?"

At that moment, the despair in his eyes breaks my heart. He's hurt by my words and stands up and moves away just a bit from my bed.

"Liam," he answers, pointing to his chest and looking over at the doctor, completely shattered. "You don't remember me?"

The doctor comes over to me. "How are you feeling? Any pain? Nausea?"

"A headache," I reply, touching my head, feeling the surrounding bandage. "What happened? Where are my parents?"

They would never let me sit in the hospital without them. Something is wrong.

"You were assaulted, Harper. Beaten and bruised very badly with a major concussion and contusions that required multiple surgeries."

Assaulted? By who? What the hell was she talking about? "What hospital am I in? I want to call my parents."

"Grapevine Medical. And of course." The doctor hands me the landline next to her bed. "Call anyone you would like."

Liam keeps looking at me, almost like he can't believe what I'm saying.

"Grapevine Medical? Never heard of it. Where exactly am I?"

"Texas."

What? How did I get here from California? No wonder my parents aren't here. They probably have no idea and are worried sick. "How long have I been here?"

"Two weeks," Liam responds, his eyes boring into me. "Harper— you're scaring me. You know why your parents aren't here."

No, I don't. My agitation is only growing fiercer at this man trying to tell me what he feels I should already know. Why wouldn't my parents be here? He acts like he knows me, but if he does, then he would know my parents would never leave me in a hospital alone. Ever.

The doctor pulls him away and closes the door behind them. I grab my head as it starts pulsing repeatedly. *Ow. Make it stop.*

I dial my parents' home number, but all I get is three beeps and "we're sorry, the number you dialed is no longer in service. Please check the number and dial again."

That's weird. No way my mom forgot to pay the bill. What am I missing? I try both their cells and get same thing: disconnected. I slam the phone down, and tears begin to fall.

A wave of craziness comes over me, and all I want to do is scream. Nothing makes sense. How the hell did I get to Texas? Most of all, who is this Liam guy? Nothing is adding up.

"I need to talk to the doctor now."

The officer nods and steps outside, returning with only her.

"I'm not sure what's going on here, but I'm from California. I don't live in Texas, and I just graduated from college. Who is that man?"

The police officer responds, "Ma'am, that was the man who saved you after the assault. And he was with you when we were called about your break-in. He's your boyfriend."

Boyfriend? No, I don't have one. Plus, we have at least a ten-year difference between us. "There must be some mistake. I don't understand..."

The doctor comes over and puts her hand on my shoulder. "Listen, Harper. I know this is going to shock you, but your memories seem to be gone from the last few years."

"What the hell do you mean? How old am I?"

"We have your medical file. You're thirty-one."

Okay, seriously, this must be a dream or a prank. There is no way. I shake my head and close my eyes, trying to make sense of it all.

She opens her phone and turns the camera on me. The woman in the camera is me, but older. My heart starts racing. How is this possible?

"You're suffering from memory loss. It's common with the amount of trauma that occurred to the brain. But some of it should come back over time."

Nine years of my life have been ripped away, and the fear of not getting those memories back is frightening. To go from being twenty-two to in my thirties is ridiculous. Although, it does make sense why that guy is claiming to be my boyfriend.

There are so many questions running through my head, but no one to ask. Who can I even trust? I'm surrounded by strangers.

A knock on the door sounds, and a woman pokes her head inside. "May I come in?"

I nod, and the officer follows her inside.

"I just wanted to see how you're doing. Not being able to see you has been killing me."

"And you are?"

"Liam told me you were having trouble remembering. I'm Tessa. We've been friends since September, and you are my maid of honor."

So not only do I have a boyfriend, but a best friend whom I can't recognize. I feel as if I have woken up in someone else's body. "I don't know you. Sorry."

Tessa pulls out her phone and hands it to me. "Maybe this will help."

I start scrolling through her social media account to see tons of pictures of us together, smiling and laughing. Pictures don't lie. She obviously knows me and we're close, but I'm not that girl.

"I see you with me, but that doesn't change the fact I don't recognize you. There are no memories."

A single tear sheds, leaving a wet streak down her face, and she retreats from the room.

"Can you please tell me about the break-in and the assault? I need to know," I ask the police officer standing next to my door.

"My name's Scott, ma'am. I can only tell you what I personally know. Other than that, Liam might be able to answer more questions. He was the one who you called to be with you when we were searching your house, and he was the one to get you out of your house alive after the assault."

The police have seen him with me, so him being my boyfriend can't be a total lie. *Confirmed.* "My house was broken into... did you catch them?"

"No, ma'am. From what you told us, nothing was taken. The house was just ransacked. We ran fingerprints but got no hits."

"And this Liam guy. How do you know he's not responsible?"

"We ran his fingerprints and blood, and it came back negative. He's just a good guy who stayed by your side every day for the past two weeks."

Okay, that clears him off the list of potential suspects. "And the assault?"

He explains the police were alerted by a neighbor about a fire inside my house, and Liam found me tied to a chair, beaten and unconscious. What the hell have I done over the last nine years to warrant someone wanting to do that to me? They have no suspects for either crime, and I'm sitting in this hospital bed, my memory wiped.

"Was I raped?" I ask, staring at the wall, not knowing if I even want to know the answer.

"No. Thank God. No sign of that."

A sigh escapes my throat, just trying to cover all my bases before Liam comes back so I can ask him a few questions. If we have been spending a lot of time together, he must know me the best. And if so, then he would be able to give me more answers than the officer could.

Still, how could I trust him fully without knowing him? He could be some crazy stalker guy pretending to be my boyfriend.

17

LIAM

She doesn't remember me...

When she recoils from my touch, my heart drops. Her eyes run over me like I'm a stranger. And to her I am. All of our memories have been wiped away. I'm trying so hard to keep it together, but the thought of her not knowing who I am breaks my damn heart.

I pace outside her room, wondering if she will even want me to go back in. How am I supposed to just go home and not worry? Even if she doesn't want me in the room, I can sit outside until she's ready. Harper deserves to have someone who knows her here.

Her door opens, and the doctor steps outside.

"What's going on? How is this possible?" My fingers run through my hair as I pace the hallway, trying to understand.

"Memory loss is common. We just need to give her some time, let her work through it. No pressure. It will only make matters worse. Only answer questions she asks you. This recovery will be very overwhelming, and at times she may become irritable. Stay focused on the woman you knew before..."

The only problem is, she is missing nine years of memories. The knowledge of her parents' homicides, moving from California to take the teaching job, and even where she lives. It's all just gone, wiped away by the bastard who did this to her. How is she going to know who to trust?

I need to clear my head. Not knowing what the outcome is going to be is the hardest part. What will I do if she never regains her memory? I'll lose her, and that can't happen. Harper is the woman I'm falling in love with, and for this to happen is just absurd. Whoever is responsible for her accident not only took something away from her, but me, too.

I dial Damon's number, and after three rings, he picks up.

"How is she doing?"

"She's awake. But..." I try to hide the pain in my voice, but I can't. He is the only one I want to talk to right now.

"But what? What's wrong? You don't sound good."

"She thinks she's twenty-two."

"I'm not following..."

"She has no memory of the last nine years, Damon. No memory of me. Of any of our time together." I try so hard to keep it together, but my emotions due to lack of sleep are all out of whack.

"But that doesn't mean she won't get the memories back, right?"

"That's the thing. There's no guarantee. That scares the living hell out of me."

"Don't stress yourself out about it just yet. Give it a couple of days. She's been through a lot and her body needs to heal. Remember that."

"I know, but she doesn't know me. What if she doesn't even want me around? Damon, I don't know what to do."

My brother has always been the best at calming me down. That's exactly what I need right now, because my head is being overwhelmed with the doubt that we might never be the same after this.

"Think about it this way. She's alive. Focus on that."

I think of all the things I'd be missing if I lost nine years of my life. All the bad relationships would be erased, and they couldn't hinder my future relationships anymore. That is the only thing that I would want to forget. But Harper, she's had so much happen to her that it must be devastating. To have to relive some of those moments over again, go through all the pain and grief. Someone must tell her about her parents.

The doctor finally leaves, and I pop my head inside. "Do you mind if I come back in?"

"Sure," she answers, looking at me and then the floor.

Instead of sitting next to her, I pull the chair back over to the side of the room and take a seat. The doctor told me to remember my version of Harper and that's what I'm going to hold on to for now. The girl who swept me off my feet and made me believe in happily ever after.

"So, what did you mean, I know why my parents aren't here? Do you know where they are?"

I don't want to be the one to break the news to her because it will devastate her. If it were me, I'd never want to relive hearing that news. Even so, it's the right thing to do. Getting answers to her questions could very well help bring back memories, which is exactly what we both want. "Harper, your parents passed."

Her hands fly to her mouth. "No, that can't be true. I just saw them last week. They were healthy. How could they possibly be gone?"

It's a rhetorical question, so I don't answer. She needs to be able to process and understand the reason why she can't get ahold of her parents. It isn't that they aren't here; it's that they can't be. "But from what you have told me about them, I bet they are sitting in this hospital room right now, watching over you."

Tears spring from her eyes, and I want so badly to console her, but I don't. She doesn't know me. I'm not her boyfriend right now, but solely a stranger who can answer her questions. That hurts most of all.

Tessa shows up. As her friend, I know she must be hurting knowing Harper can't remember her, but we will get through this together. We just need to be there for her and answer her questions as best we can.

"Hey, sweetie. How you doin'?"

She eyes her. "Wishing I could remember. I just feel like a stranger in my own body. Like I'm in a sci-fi movie and been abducted by aliens and came back with my brain wiped."

She rubs Harper's shoulder. "I know, but we are here to help. What can we do?"

Most of the day is spent with Tessa and me answering questions for her. We are the only two people who are close to her, and even we don't know all the answers. We explained what we know, that she came to Texas after her parents' deaths and got a job at the high school, waiting for a teacher position to come open. It seems like she doesn't want to believe us. I can understand her hesitancy. Hell, if the roles were reversed, I probably wouldn't be very receptive either, having some strangers tell me all these things about my supposed life.

"How long have we been dating?" she asks.

From the outside, it sounds ridiculous. "Well, technically a little over a month. But two of those weeks, you were unconscious."

Her head turns. "Are you serious? You must really like me."

"I do." If only she could remember the first week we met. Then she would understand the connection I feel, even more so after being by her side for the last two weeks. How a week feels like a year to me.

"Have we..."

"Yes."

The questions finally cease and she continues looking around the room.

"I think I'm done for the day. I can't handle much more right now. You can come back tomorrow, but right now, I'd like to get some sleep."

That's her nice way of asking us to leave. I hesitate because I don't want her to be left alone, but Scott isn't going anywhere. "Okay, I'll see you tomorrow, Harper. Call me if you need anything at all."

I look back at her before I shut the door behind me, leaving her overnight for the first time in two weeks. My hair is a mess and sleep deprivation is starting to set in. Yet, I don't know if I will even be able to fall asleep at this point. My mind is going over everything, trying to piece together a way to help her memory come back faster. I send a quick text to Damon.

Me: Are you up?

I keep looking back up at the hospital, wondering if Harper will ever look at me the same way. Would she ever remember how that first week completely changed our lives for the better? Or would all those lost memories remain just that, lost?

As I jump in my truck and turn the engine on, my phone begins to ring.

"What do you want?"

"Damn, what a way to answer the phone. I'm at Damon's and we were wondering if you want to meet up and grab a beer? You're going through a lot and we just figured you could use one."

Aiden and I aren't close, but we're brothers and try to be there for each other nonetheless. He has called to check in a couple times while Harper was unconscious, but not much. To be fair, he has been covering all my shifts for me, and I need to be thankful for that. There's still no word if I have a job to go back to. "Why not. Meet you at Dixie's in ten."

The last two weeks have been hell, and to know that she might never get our memories back scares the living shit out of me. Can this version of Harper fall in love with me? Will she even want anything to do with me once she gets out of the hospital? These are things I can't stop contemplating, and it's going to drive me insane.

I pull my truck to a stop and park, jumping out to go inside Dixie's. It's a Thursday night, so the bar has some bodies inside but not too many. I take our usual booth and put my hand up for the bartender who knows my favorite beer by now. She just nods and continues working without skipping a beat.

"You look rough, brother," Aiden says, sliding in across from me.

"I take it today didn't get any better?" Damon asks, sitting next to me.

My hands slide down my face. "It did not, but maybe tomorrow. I'm trying to stay positive because I can't imagine what I'll do if she doesn't want anything to do with me."

"She'll get them back; you just have to give her time. Be patient. Stressing yourself out over it isn't going to help the situation," Damon says, his hand on my shoulder. "I can tell from dinner with her that she cares about you. Things like that don't just go away. If she cared for you before, then you can make her care for you again."

He says it like it's so simple, but without any of her memories, she sees herself as a twenty-two-year-old college graduate, not a thirty-one-year-old chemistry teacher. The woman who fell for me and the Harper who woke up are not the same person. So, I'm asking a new person to fall in love with me. Would the new Harper and I even be compatible? At twenty-two, I don't think my need for a relationship or settling down was even understood.

"I can hear the wheel in your head catching fire. Down that beer, go home, and get some sleep. Wake up tomorrow refreshed and ready to go," Aiden says.

I do just that, the beer bottle barely making a sound as it hits the table. My eyes are red, and my mind is mush, just ready to be in my own bed again.

"Talk to ya tomorrow or something," I say, walking toward the exit, ready for my head to hit the pillow.

Thankfully, home is only about five minutes away, and the thought of sleeping in my bed, with the covers wrapped around me, almost puts me to sleep while driving.

When I get home and lie in bed, I feel the need to check on Tessa. This isn't just impacting my relationship, but hers as well. She was Tessa's only friend and now she has no one.

Me: *How are you holding up with all this?*

I lay on my back with my phone above my face, waiting for her to text back, when it falls and thud. *Fuck!* I rub my forehead and roll over on my stomach.

Tessa: *Not gonna lie. I'm ready to have my Harper back. It's hard not being able to talk to her about stuff because she doesn't even know me. Our friendship doesn't exist to her. You think she will remember us?*

Me: *I hope so. All we can do is be there. See ya tomorrow. Get some rest.*

18

LIAM

*M*y worry for Harper has increased since hearing about the nightmares because they appear too coincidental for them not to be pulling from a memory, especially since it matches her injuries.

The nightmare explains that she knows this man from a previous encounter, and somehow she could identify him in a crime, which is the reason behind the assault and fire in the first place.

The man in her nightmare must be the man who killed her parents'. There's no way it's not connected. Someone like that will never give up until the person is silenced. Something has to be done—whether it's her telling the cops about the nightmare—or the police finding a way to ID the guy. What faith are we supposed to have in the system if they can't even get the identity of a guy who broke into a house, started a house fire, and tried to murder an innocent woman plus committed a double homicide? Let's just say that mine is dwindling every day when they have no news to share. No new suspects or leads.

If this nightmare is a memory, then someone is out to get Harper, but for what? Even more so now, she can't tell us with all her memories wiped away. I understand the reasoning around not wanting to believe it's real, but if it somehow helps the police find the person who is responsible for this and puts him away, then so be it. Harper just needs to be safe, and with the culprit still out there, she's far from it.

I pull up to her house, and it looks like so many homes I have seen before, mostly grayish black from the soot, with some parts completely sunk in from the devastation of the fire. There is no desire to come back here. The nightmares have been taking over my sleep too, seeing Harper in that position, tied to a chair, almost every night. I couldn't imagine how horrible it was for her when she slept every night.

The intact front door opens, and I step inside to where the bright-blue walls were previously, and now they were just dark gray and covered in ash. The one good memory I have in this room was on the couch on our third date. How could I ever forget that? Could the new Harper fall for me like the old one did, so quickly? With everything that happened to her, it would be unlikely, not knowing what's truth or fiction. I shudder to even remind myself of that statement.

I open the spare bedroom door, and nothing is in there. The only things left are some ungraded random papers strewn about the floor. This can't be right. Scott seemed sure there were salvaged items in this room, and now they are gone. My hesitancy takes over, and I dial Harper's hospital room to speak to him.

"Hello?" Harper answers.

"It's Liam. Can you put Scott on the phone for a second?"

"Why? What's wrong?"

I can hear the worry in her voice. "It's okay. Just put him on the phone, please." The phone thuds as it hits the table while Harper gets Scott's attention. The footsteps can be heard from the door to the phone.

"Hello?"

"Listen, I don't want to freak her out, but there is nothing in this room. Only a few papers on the floor and that's it. Can you call and check with the station?"

"Got it. Call back in five," he says, hanging up.

Harper worries, and that is normal in her condition, but I do not need to alarm her unless we have to. Maybe Scott understood them wrong, and that is all there is left. Nevertheless, confirmation will make me feel better.

"It's me," Scott answers. "The paperwork shows there were a couple boxes of things left in there. An officer is on his way. Stay put."

If there were boxes here when the last officer left, then that means someone has been in her home again after the assault and fire. This man keeps coming back for more and more, and it terrifies me. How are they ever supposed to ID this guy if there aren't any fingerprints or anything to go off of. He might just get away with it and never be found. That can't happen. Harper will never feel safe without him behind bars.

My phone rings.

"I wanted to check in," Aiden says.

"We're working through it. Listen, can I call you back later?" I ask, a police car coming down the road toward me. "I'm trying to get some things done."

"Yeah, talk to you later."

The officer steps out of the vehicle and begins asking me questions as we make our way inside the house. He's positive there were four boxes of items in this room when he filed the report. Someone has been here. I gulp, knowing that he will be coming after Harper again, but how can we stop it if none of us have any clue who the man is?

"I'll get someone down here to see if we can recover any fingerprints of who got in here."

"Please keep us updated," I say, getting into my truck. "Harper is going to freak when I tell her."

The truck starts and I head back to the hospital to break the news. How is she ever supposed to feel safe anywhere if things like that keep happening? We need to figure out who this guy is and fast, because if it continues, I worry about where it might be headed.

I want to protect her from whoever the evil man is, but it's hard to do that when I don't even know what to look for. He could be anyone. There are hundreds of hospital employees, officers, and even visitors of other patients coming in and out of this hospital.

I walk past Scott and open the door. "I'm back."

"What did you find?" she asks, smiling.

"There wasn't anything." I grab the chair from the other side of the room and drag it back to her bedside. Her eyes study me.

"Well, what was there?" Her hands go up in the air. "I thought there was stuff after the fire? Now it's just gone? That doesn't make any sense."

"Just a couple of papers, that's all."

"But Scott said there were boxes. What was in those?"

"They are gone, Harper." I close my eyes, trying to find the right words to tell her that he went to her house since she's been here, and he took everything.

"Okay, go to the station and get them. Maybe they took them into evidence or something."

"No—they were taken by someone else. They are *gone*."

I could see the wheels turning in her mind as she processes what I'm telling her. Why won't this person leave her alone? Without anything from her past, how is she supposed to get her memories back?

"They are going to see if they can find any fingerprints to ID the guy. But no luck so far, as usual," I tell her, eyeing Scott.

The fact remains that they haven't even been able to partially identify the person who is doing this to Harper. Where are all our taxpayer dollars going? It's been over two weeks and still nothing?

"You should tell Scott about your nightmare. I really think they need to at least hear about it."

I continue to beg and plead. Sure, she never saw his face, but it's something. Right now, the cops don't have anything, so what can it hurt?

"Please, if it doesn't amount to anything, then fine—but what if it does?"

She calls Scott over and starts explaining the nightmare, but he keeps interrupting her, asking questions. What did he look like? Any tattoos? Scars?

"Just let me talk!" Harper screams at the top of her lungs. "I can't do this anymore!"

A nurse comes in and asks Scott to step outside. "She can't think at the capacity you are asking her to. You're putting her brain into overdrive."

Harper presses her hands to her forehead, tears leaving a streak on her face.

"Would you like me to go?" I ask as her head hits the pillow. "I shouldn't have pushed you."

Her hand grabs mine. "No. Please stay for a little while."

Harper holds my hand as she drifts off to sleep, and for the first time since she woke, I feel like maybe she could fall in love with me again. There is hope for us yet, and that makes my day. This whole time I've been terrified that because of the beating, I lost her. My chance to be with her was gone, but maybe not.

I sit still while she gets a nap in, which she deserves after the day we've had. She should be able to get discharged soon which I think will make a big difference for her, not being stuck in a hospital all the time.

Although, that just makes me think about all the things that could happen once she leaves here. Where will she go? I'd offer to let her stay with me, but with the way things are, she might not consider it. The house is not livable—not that she would even want to go back there after the horrible things that happened. I couldn't walk into that house every day and feel safe even if they catch the suspect, and I'm not even the victim. I wish one of the duplexes were empty.

"Good afternoon, sleepyhead. How's your headache?" I ask, brushing the hair out of her face. This time she doesn't recoil from my touch which is a step in the right direction.

Her arms stretch, and then she sits up. "It's finally gone. How long was I asleep?"

"Just over an hour. Not long."

"You didn't have to stay with me."

"I wanted to."

Our eyes lock on each other, and the essence of a smile appears on her face as she realizes we are still holding hands. "So, I want to know more about us. It's crazy to think you are this way after a week of knowing me. We must have one hell of an epic love story."

Indeed, we do. I can't imagine life without her, and everything will be done in my power to get her to reciprocate those feelings again.

The rest of the afternoon is spent telling her about our first and second date, then the two nights we spent together following them. She seems intrigued by the story like I'm reading it straight from an epic romance novel written by one of the greats.

"You seem like a really good guy, and I'm glad that I met you when I did."

I smile, because at some point maybe the memories will come flooding back. Even in bits and pieces.

"I'm gonna go to the cafeteria and get something to eat and possibly some coffee. Would you like anything?"

"A cheeseburger would be amazing right now. A coffee too, please." She winks back at me.

Shutting the door behind me, I let Scott know I'll be back, and I make the long walk to the cafeteria. It gives me time to think about everything, and something comes to mind. If they found fingerprints in her house, besides the ones they couldn't identify through the database, whose were they? If watching cold case files has taught me anything, sometimes the person responsible can be right in front of our face and we don't even realize that. Her boss or a colleague even. But that wouldn't explain the insight from her nightmare where she obviously knew him before, because she would have recognized him before the break-in. My mind is going over all kinds of different scenarios while I pick out two cheeseburgers, coffees, and then pay for them and head back to Harper. The tray of food they brought her in her room looked god-awful.

The elevator takes me back up to the fourth floor and it opens to chaos. Nurses are running around, and then I see her doctor running into Harper's room, and the food and coffee fall to the floor.

"What's going on?" I rush over to Scott.

"It's been two minutes. I literally stepped away to go to the bathroom and when I came back, the nurses were already in there."

I shove past him and go into the room. Nurses are trying to wake her.

"Harper, can you hear us?" the nurse keeps asking, trying to get her to wake up.

The monitors are beeping rapidly, and that's when the nurse yells, "Ten cc's of naloxone. Someone increased her morphine drip."

My eyes fill, and I don't know how much more of this I can take right now. "What's going on?"

The nurses do their job, and then one pulls me outside the room. "Someone upped her morphine which caused an overdose. Too much, too quickly. The naloxone should help alleviate it and bring her back to normal."

That's it. I'm never leaving her alone again. "Why the hell did you leave her alone? You know he's still out there, and you still left. This is your fault!"

I run to her bedside. "You're going to be okay. I'm never leaving you for a second until we get out of this godforsaken place."

And I don't.

Scott hasn't been in to check on her in hours, and honestly, I don't care. My anger toward him right now is through the roof, and I'm not sure what else I would say to him at this point.

A knock sounds at the door, and the doctor checks Harper and then stands next to me.

"So, Scott has decided to share some information with you."

"And?"

Scott walks into the room, his head down. "We pulled security footage and got a still image of a man coming into her room."

"That's great. We can finally get this guy's ass in the electric chair."

"It's not that simple. He was very careful at not letting himself be exposed to the cameras. There are no clear shots of his face, but maybe she will see something else that can help once she's awake."

He shows me the man in the photo and Scott is right. It is blurry and very poor placement. It doesn't show any distinguishing factors, just his back, which means he probably can't be identified. "Why does this keep happening? At some point, we need to get this guy put away. Harper can't keep living her life in fear of this guy coming after her."

"Understood and agreed."

They leave me alone with Harper, who should be waking up sometime soon. Whatever they are giving her is bringing her vitals back down to normal.

Please just come back to me, baby. I'll never leave you again.

19

HARPER

*M*y eyes start to flutter, able to see bits and pieces of light and surroundings, but my lids still feel like concrete blocks, not wanting to open fully. I start to panic, my brain showing images of the last thing I remember—the man walking into my room. Scott wasn't at the door or else he wouldn't have been able to just stroll in here. A scream erupts from my throat as my eyes finally pop open, and I see Liam at my side.

"L-Liam?" My hand clenches down on his. "It was him. He did it."

Scott comes running inside. "What the heck is going on in here?"

"It was him. He was here."

"Did you see him, Harper?" Scott asks.

"Yes, brown hair and blue eyes. White."

My heart is racing, having just woke up from a horrible dream that just keeps replaying in my head over and over while I'm asleep. One thing is for certain; I have most definitely seen this man before. My eyes clench as I try to make my mind work. I need to remember and fast. If I can figure out where I've seen him, then it will help the police track him down. "I need to see everyone that I would have seen in the last two weeks before the fire."

"On it," he says, pulling out his phone to call the station to alert them of the necessary photos.

For the next several hours, I go through every photo of every person they believe I've come in contact with including students, colleagues, and café workers. None of them are him. "This can't be it. We are missing an important piece of the puzzle."

"How are we supposed to know what the piece is without you being able to tell us?"

Change of plans. "Can you get me photos of any law enforcement or hospital workers I've come in contact with since the break-in?"

"Really?" Scott questions me.

"I don't want to leave any stone unturned. This man has proven that he wants me dead."

The longer I'm stuck in this bed, the easier it will be for him to get to me.

"You really think it could be a worker?"

"Think about it. The nurses and doctors would know how much morphine would kill me, right? Or someone with any kind of medical school basic training, I guess. Something just doesn't feel right, like it's right in front of me and I'm too stupid to see it."

"Well, in that case, we need to get you the hell out of here. You're not safe here anymore," Liam says, walking outside to talk to a doctor.

The door is left open and I can hear Scott on the phone with the station, explaining my request. Honestly, he should have been the one to think about this. If I didn't hear the man's voice, I would think maybe Scott is behind this.

"Okay, you're being discharged in an hour," Liam says. "The only question is—where are you staying? I have an extra bedroom if you would like to stay with me, no pressure though."

Where else will I go? The only person who makes me feel safe is Liam, so I'll go wherever he does. It's not like I can go stay by myself somewhere, Well, I guess I could but what kind of sense does that make? Especially, while all this is going on.

The next hour passes by in milliseconds, yet seems to go on forever until they finally bring me my discharge paperwork and ask Liam to bring his truck around to the front. Scott will bring the photos by the house once they are retrieved and put together for me to look over.

"Are you ready to get out of here?"

"Never been more ready for anything," I reply, heading toward the elevator.

Thank goodness the hospital has some scrubs or I'd be stuck going home in a hospital gown. I will need to go to a bank to get money out—but which bank? Now that I'm out, clothes and toiletries are needed. Yet, I don't even know where my bank account is located here to be able to get money out. So many things were lost in that fire, and things will be hard until I start remembering my life.

Of course, I have visited Texas a few times, but I never thought about moving here. The weather is warm, and the sun is out in full force, making me squint my eyes, watching for Liam to pull up.

He helps me in the truck and shuts the door behind me. "So, off to my house we go. Is there anything you need while we're out?"

"I really need some clothes and a pair of tennis shoes, but I can't go out looking like this." I peer down at myself in light-blue scrubs.

"Here's my phone. Call Tessa and she can pick you up some things and bring them over to the house."

At some point, I am going to need to figure out things between her and me. If I am supposed to be her maid of honor, then that means we were close.

"That's Damon and Tessa's house," he says, pointing to a bright-red door. "I'm just a couple blocks over."

His brother must be pretty well off considering the home he lives in. Of course, the cost of living is probably significantly lower than California, but still. A house like his would cost over two million there.

"And here's mine," he says, turning off the truck, getting out, and then opening my door. "Let's get you inside and settled in."

His house isn't as fancy as Damon's, that's for sure, but it's still nice. He gives me a tour and shows me the bedroom where I'll be staying that has an attached bathroom.

"Of course, Tessa is going to pick up some things for you, so you can take a shower and get normal clothes on, but do you need anything until then?" he asks, standing awkwardly in the bedroom doorway.

"No, I think I'm okay. Actually, something to eat that's not hospital food."

He smiles and gestures for me to follow him as we wander into the kitchen to pull out a bunch of take-out menus from a drawer. "You pick whatever you want, and I'll have it delivered."

There are so many things to choose from, but what I'm really craving is a big juicy cheeseburger with grilled onions and fresh tomatoes. "In-N-Out. Double-double with cheese and grilled onions, please."

Surprised at my request, his eyes widen. "Dang, you really are starving. That's what I usually get too. And a chocolate shake."

"I'll take one of those, too." My eyebrow slightly lifts, thinking about how good a shake sounds right now. The food was horrendous at the hospital and now it's time for my taste buds to have something magical again. In-N-Out is huge in California and I am happy to see they have a location close.

Liam steps outside to place the order, and I take a seat on the couch and surf the TV until he comes back inside with Tessa carrying a couple bags.

I smile. "I'll take those to my room. Wow, how much stuff did you get?"

"A couple pairs of jeggings, tops, and some comfy shorts for bed," she says, pointing to the bags now in my hands and following me to my room. "Oh, and a pair of tennis shoes. I didn't know what you would prefer, so I just got you some Converses. Everyone seems to love them."

"That's perfect, thank you," I say, setting the bags down on my bed. "I'll pay you back as soon as I figure out where my bank is and such. There's still nothing working up here." I indicate my head.

"Don't you worry about it. You've been through enough. Is there anything else I can get you?" she asks, standing in the doorway.

"Nope, that's it. I appreciate it. I'm gonna take a shower real quick, and then I'll be out," I say, and she takes off toward the living room.

After hearing her voice in the kitchen, I shut the bedroom door so I can jump in the shower. I empty the bags to get my toiletries and find a pair of underwear, leggings, and a simple black t-shirt to put on after I'm clean. I traipse into the bathroom to start the shower. The running hot water and steam fills the bathroom, fogging up the mirror, as I remove the scrubs I'm wearing, wanting to get the hell out of anything that will remind me of the time I spent in the hospital. I throw them into the hamper behind the door, and I step into the hot water, letting it run down my back, warming me up instantly.

Out of the shower and dressed, I open my door to the overwhelming smell of onions. In-N-Out is in the house. I practically run to the kitchen, which surprises Liam.

"Slow down there. You don't wanna end up back in the hospital."

"Haha. Very Funny. I'm here for my burger. I'm frothing at the mouth," I say, playfully grabbing mine. "You don't want me to get hangry over here."

Tessa laughs, watching us play fight over food. "You guys are a hoot. I'll leave you to it. See you tomorrow for dinner, Harper."

It's nice to see Liam interact with his family, since really I've only seen him around me so far. You can tell a lot about a person by the way they interact and treat their family. Sometimes it can give you an inside look on how they will treat you.

I snuggle up on the couch under a Sherpa blanket and probably shouldn't have, considering the sauce and innards are spilling out onto my hands. That's exactly what I love about their burgers; they are so jam-packed with ingredients. They aren't stingy like other chain places.

"You lost some there," he says, laughing and pointing down to the blanket. "Saving some for later?"

It's nice to be able to joke around and laugh with him. A different atmosphere provides a comfortable place for us and for me to be able to see him in a new light. I've seen him under crisis, but what is the normal down-to-earth Liam like?

20

LIAM

Screams can be heard from my bedroom and wake me out of a dead sleep. I look around my room, not exactly awake yet, then rush into hers. Harper is still asleep, but thrashing around in the bed, screaming. I want to hold and console her, but right now she isn't my girlfriend. In her mind, she's twenty-two and doesn't really know me.

"Stop. Please don't hurt me!"

Instead of shaking her awake, I call out her name, trying to get her attention that way, but it doesn't work. "Harper. Wake up. It's just a dream."

Since we came to my house, I'm surprised none of my neighbors have called the cops at night. I know if I heard anything like this coming from somewhere, that's the first thing I'd do.

As she continues her nightmare, I sit on the bed next to her and take one of her hands in mine. It helps ease her a bit, and she stops thrashing. How the hell is she ever going to get over this? I can't imagine what all is going through her head. Waking up missing nine years of memories, finding out your parents were murdered, and not having any recollection of it. At the bare minimum, it's fucking with her head. Maybe she should go see and talk to someone. It might help her get to the bottom of these nightmares.

I continue to hold her hand, and I lie down next to her. The screaming has stopped, and my mind begins to wander. Should I look into the murder of her parents myself? What if the police overlooked something that a fresh pair of eyes could catch? It happens in cold cases all the time, so why not this one? He's got to be the culprit, but without an ID, how the hell will we ever find him? He didn't leave anything behind at the break-in, nothing at the fire, and when he showed up twice at the hospital, we couldn't even get a picture of his face. Whoever it is, this can't be the first time he's committed a crime, which only means there are more cases out there connected to him. Possibly cold cases, gone years without being solved.

I grab my phone and text Scott.

Me: *Is there any way we could look at the case files on her parents? Maybe we can find something they missed.*

I press send even though it's three in the morning. He might be asleep, but he'll respond when he wakes up. Something has to be done to push this investigation forward, and right now, it's at a standstill. He's already shown he's ballsy, coming to the hospital twice, so what is going to stop him from coming to my house? Although, he would have to find out where Harper is first, and it's not like we are forwarding her mail here or anything. So she's safe for the time being.

Around five, she wakes herself up screaming, then snuggles up to me.

"When did you come in here?"

"A couple hours ago. You were screaming and I thought you needed some company. Just wanted to keep an eye on you." I smile.

"Did I keep you up all night?" She sits up, looking at me.

"Only since midnight. I'll be fine. I'm more worried about you."

She doesn't seem repulsed by my touch like at the hospital, and all I want to do right now is have her snuggled up against my chest like before. What if I never get that again and she never ends up getting the rest of her memories back? This Harper isn't the same woman I fell in love with, but I still love her. The hopefulness has to shine bright and giving up isn't an option.

I think it's been an adjustment being here. Even though she's safer, it's a strange place.

"Is it bad that I want to go back to California? Everything just seems so foreign here," Harper says.

She wants to go back? Does that mean she's leaving me? My heart sinks, because if she goes back, I can't. My whole life is here, including my brothers and my job. "I think it might be best to wait. Where would you stay?"

"My parents' house. I do remember in their will, the last time they went over it with me, the house was coming to me. So it should still be in my name."

She makes her way into the living room and grabs my laptop off the coffee table.

"How do you know you didn't sell it?" I ask.

"I would never do that. That's my childhood home. All my memories are in that house."

"But they were also killed there. I'm not sure you would want to hold on to those memories," I say. Yes, it was an asshole move, but it needed to be said. It's not like they passed of old age. No, they were brutally murdered.

She doesn't respond; she just opens up the laptop and starts typing.

"Anything I can help with?" I ask, sitting down next to her.

It looks like she is looking at houses. Why would she be doing that? I look at the top and she is looking at the sales on a particular property in California. "Is this your parents' house?"

"Yes, housing sales are public record. So, if I did sell it, then it would be on here." She continues to scroll down the page. "There isn't any record of sale on the property since 1975 which is when my parents got it."

For a minute, I feel like a selfish ass, because if she did sell it, then my chances of her staying around are better. Now I imagine she will be on the first plane back. I can't stop her from leaving, and as much as I love her, she's not in love with me. All I can do is let her go and hope maybe someday she will regain her memory and come back to me.

"I'm sorry for keeping you up all night," she says, closing the laptop. "I'll make it up to you by cooking breakfast."

"So, how does it feel being here? Do you feel comfortable?" I only ask because that is my goal. Maybe one day she will officially move in with me and this will be her home too. If she doesn't end up back in California.

"With you here, yes."

"Well, that's something we need to discuss," I say, walking down the hallway and leaning against the kitchen counter. "The guys have been covering me for weeks."

"I'll be fine. Go back to work. You have a gun?"

My head cocks. "Actually, no. Never really been a fan of them."

"Well, what do you do if someone breaks in?"

"Hope my baseball bat or knife take them out."

"You've got to be kidding me. Well, if I am going to be staying here, something needs to be in place, especially if I'll be alone."

"Understood. We'll figure something out before I go back to work. I promise," I reply, grabbing my coffee cup and filling it.

Harper works around the kitchen like a breeze and makes us French toast and sausage for breakfast. This woman is amazing, and even with everything that happened to her, she still has the best little sly sense of humor around.

"Let's go look at some security equipment. I've been wanting to get some anyway," I say, trying to be supportive and wanting her to feel completely safe here. I can't expect her to stay here alone while I'm at work without something in place. Hell, look at what happened at the hospital with all those people around.

After breakfast, we get dressed and head out. Traffic is light since it's only about seven thirty in the morning, and barely anyone is in the store. We check out every piece of equipment and decide on cameras for inside and outside.

"What about this?" she says, holding up a package with a woman screaming on it.

I take it from her and read the box. You install it and program it so if you need help, you say help me three times, and it will alert the police and ambulance. It's mostly used for the elderly but could work in this situation too and it's never bad to be extra careful.

"Can we stop over at the mall? If I'm going to be meeting your family tonight, the least I can do is look nice. I'm not sure jeans and a t-shirt is the best outfit."

I smile and oblige. At the second store we visit, she finds a dress that suits her, as she says. Honestly, she could wear anything and look gorgeous.

"Let's head home. They will be over shortly, and we still have to get stuff prepared," I tell her, paying for the dress and then heading to the car.

Once we arrive at my house, I change into my blue button-down and watch Harper cook until my brother arrives for dinner.

"Good to see you out of the hospital, Harper. You're looking much better. Finally healing up okay?"

"Yes, thank you." She continues to work with the bread. "If y'all want to have a seat in the living room, I just have to get this in the oven, and then I'll join you."

They follow me into the living room, and Tessa starts asking how it went her first night here and if there's anything she can do to help. I know she just wants her friend back, but pushing her to remember things isn't going to help in the long run. The doctor said to let her stumble upon them herself.

I snuggle up with Emily under my arm. "How are you doing, kiddo? Haven't seen ya in a while."

Emily tells me about the new dollhouse Damon got her, and it's just like Cinderella's castle. She explains it to me in great detail, and I can literally picture it in my head.

I slip into the kitchen to check on Harper, who is grabbing a bottle of wine. "Do they drink?"

"Yes, I'll pour it. Go mingle, pretty lady." I sigh, placing a kiss on her cheek as it reddens. She looks up at me through her lashes and smiles.

When she leaves, I grab four wineglasses, and as I'm pouring, I listen to see how she interacts with them without me in the room.

"I know a little bit about how you got together. Fate works in mysterious ways."

At first, I laugh, and then my eyes widen. The wine bottle falls to the floor and shatters, sending wine everywhere.

"Everything okay?" Tessa says as I'm walking into the room.

"Harper, how do you know about their story?"

"You told me... duh."

"No, I didn't," I respond and look over at Tessa. "Do you say something to her in the hospital?"

"No."

She looks around the room and then starts to shake. "Okay, so maybe it's a memory. I don't know, but can we not make such a big deal about it? I feel like a freak show over here now with everyone staring at me."

She's starting to get her memory back—at least one so far. This gives me hope that she will regain the rest.

Harper rearranges herself on the couch and finishes what she was saying before I interrupted her. "Okay—so I somehow remember a bit of your story—it's a beautiful one. You guys look so happy."

Tessa and Harper pretty much talk about their epic love story for the next hour, while Damon and I sit back and listen. To watch their faces and expressions as the story unfolds is sweet.

The oven beeps and dinner is done. Harper runs off to the kitchen, while we take our places at the dining room table, waiting to see what she has made.

She comes in with honey mustard baked chicken, mashed potatoes, fresh green beans, and rolls. "Dig in, guys."

One thing about us Jacksons, we don't have to be told twice, especially about a home-cooked meal.

"Glad to see he found someone who can cook. He needs that. Liam could burn water if that was possible."

The atmosphere is perfect, and the conversation flows without hesitation all throughout dinner. Before we know it, the night is over, and they are heading out the door. "Thank you for coming."

"It was really nice to see you again, Harper. You'll make a great addition to the family," Damon says.

Jeez. Slow down. Don't scare her away.

As the door shuts behind them, I apologize. We've got a long way to go. If she can remember their story, then maybe she will remember other things like the night we met.

21

HARPER

After they leave, I change into leggings and a t-shirt. Tonight went well, but I still feel like a stranger. Tessa seems like a great friend and wants to continue, but how do I? Is it easier to push them away and move forward? I shake my head, not knowing what the answer is, but maybe it's time I start thinking about that. What am I going to do if I don't get any of my memories back? I can't stay with Liam forever, and somehow, I have to continue living life without any knowledge of the last nine years. How the hell am I supposed to do that? There must be a way I can speed up the process.

Every time he looks at me, I can see how much he cares about me, but I'm not the same Harper. He's in love with the old me, and I'm not even close to the same person. Tessa says I drink, but my grandparents were alcoholics and my parents made me make a vow to never drink. Why would I do that? It doesn't make any sense to break it. There are so many questions that I need answers to, and the only thing that will do that is to gain my memories back. Why the hell, out of all the places I could have moved, did I pick Texas? What the hell happened in California that made me want to up and move?

It's like an instant thought, and Dr. Newman comes to mind. She could help me. My parents used to make me see her at least once a year, not that anything was wrong with me, but because they wanted me to have someone to talk to about things I didn't feel comfortable talking to them about. Dr. Newman. I could call her and see if she can video chat with me. Honestly, with all these years gone, who knows if I've even talked to her since being here.

I go out to the living room and open the laptop again, searching for a way to contact her online. There can't be that many Dr. Newmans in Covina, California. I am sadly mistaken. The search results come up with seventeen pages and as I start going to each one, Liam joins me.

"Whatcha doin'?"

"Well, I used to see this therapist, and I thought maybe I could reach out to her. Surely, I've talked to her since my parents' deaths. In fact, I think she is the first person I would go to."

After ten pages, I finally pull up her website and find a contact number for her. I dial it on his home phone and it just rings before going to voicemail.

"Hi, this is Harper Davis. I'm not sure how long it's been since we had an appointment, but I really need to talk to you. Please call me back 986-856-8548."

Since the police never recovered my phone or any of my personal things, I can't really do anything without proper identification, and unfortunately, that means I have to wait until I get my new birth certificate so I can get a new driver's license.

Liam picks up the remote and starts scrolling through Netflix, and I tell him to stop. "That one."

"Okay, if you say so."

It looks like something I would watch, and honestly, I just want something to escape into that isn't reality. Not that Liam isn't great, but how do I know if I actually like him or if my feelings are there because he's been by my side in all this? Without my memories, he's basically just a stranger whom I'm living with.

After the first episode, he stops it and asks me, "What did you think of the first episode?"

"It's a little sexual if you ask me. But hell, you can't find anything on TV anymore that isn't. Hopefully the storyline gets better as it goes on. If not, I might fall asleep."

He presses play and I curl into him on the couch, and for a second, it's awkward but then it just feels like home. Like I belong here, with his arms around me. Yet should I be doing this? Isn't this leading him on? Feelings are there, but are they real? How will I ever know? This is why I need Dr. Newman. I've been seeing her since I was a teenager, and she knows more about me than I do myself.

This is why things are so up in the air for us, and it's not because he isn't a great guy—he is—but my feelings before my accident aren't known. All I can do is get to know him now and see if those feelings hold up. Yet, I don't want to hurt him after everything he's done for me.

Tessa might be someone I can talk to about this, but the fact she's his sister-in-law can make things a little complicated. Can I trust her not to say anything?

Everyone just needs to let me move on and figure out how I am going to move forward. Right now, the only way to do that is to talk to Dr. Newman. At least she can give me some insight on my parents' deaths, and maybe tell me why I decided to go to Texas. Until then, all I can do is be thankful to Liam and Tessa for standing by my side through all this, and hope they understand if I don't stick around.

How do you willingly leave behind a guy like Liam? Someone who stays by your side not only during one attack, but two?

22

LIAM

*A*fter the conversation with Harper last night, my nervousness about her leaving me only gets worse. It's not like I blame her, and she has every right to be cautious about being with me. I might not be a man she thought she would end up with and that's okay. I just have to deal with it, but no matter what she decides, she will need someone in her corner and I plan on being that person whether she stays with me or not.

Some might think I'm crazy to be in love with her after such a short amount of time, but when you know, you know. When I almost lost her, twice, the sorrow my heart felt and the thought of not having her by my side to laugh, play fight, and watch bad TV shows struck me. It helped me realize that it doesn't matter how long it's been. The search for my partner has been ongoing a long time and I finally found her. Sure, she might not remember me from before, but if given the chance, I have faith that if she gets to know me, those feelings will emerge once again.

"Back to work today. You ready?" Harper asks.

The nightmares don't help, constantly dreaming of someone attacking her, but with the security systems now set up, if anyone gets in the house, all she has to do is say help me and the cops will be called without alerting whoever else is inside. She is trying to play it cool and not show how much of a nervous wreck she is, but she doesn't have to pretend with me. I'm the one person she can be completely honest with, and I hope she knows that.

"I'd feel better if someone was here with you, but that's beside the point."

We migrate to the couch, watching the morning news and trying to ease the thought of her being alone all day. One thing to remember is there is nothing that ties us together so the chances of him finding out she's at my house and where I live are slim. My address isn't listed on anything of hers, and besides police files, there is nothing on social media or anywhere else. *Shake it off; she's going to be fine.*

Over the next hour, I can feel the hesitancy beaming off her with a jump at every sound outside. "Are you sure you are going to be okay today?"

"I just feel like I need a babysitter, and that's ridiculous to say at my age. What am I, five?" She laughs at herself.

"It's perfectly normal for someone who has gone through as many traumatic events as you have in the past few weeks. No one thinks less of you," I say.

She looks down at the floor and fiddles with her thumbs. "I wish you didn't have to go to work, but life keeps going. The whole world can't stop just because I got attacked."

I sigh and take her hands in mine, staring into her eyes. "I would stop my world for you, Harper. That's how much you mean to me. Say the word, and I will."

She pulls her hands away from me, gets up, and starts pacing.

"What?"

"This is what I was afraid of. What's going to happen if I never get my memories back? Are you going to be able to love this me? Not the Harper you knew? How would that even work?"

"The fact of the matter is, I love you. The old you and the new you. I'm not going anywhere."

She seems very confused and it's better if I stop complicating things. Maybe we need to start over from the beginning, like it's our first date. "I would like to take you out on a date. A real one. To get to know this version of you."

Her eyes meet mine, almost scared. "You sure? Hell, you might not even like this me."

"When are you going to get it through your head? I'm not going anywhere. Stop trying to push me away. If you really don't want to be with me, then say so. Don't tell yourself it's because I don't want you, because that's the furthest thing from the truth."

I walk away and let her think on it, because pressuring anyone isn't me. Hopefully, she will come to her senses and realize how much I care for her. If I was going to leave, then it would have been when she was in the hospital. Not after I moved her into my house.

I get ready for work, and before I leave, I write down Tessa's number in case she needs anything before I get home and stick it to the fridge. My chest is getting tight because I'm not ready to leave her alone yet, but it's not by choice. If I don't go back to work, I'll lose my job, my livelihood, my passion.

"Please don't open the door for anyone unless it's Scott. He should be bringing the pictures." I get close enough to kiss her, but then back away. "Sorry, habit."

She pulls me in and kisses me anyway. "You can kiss me, silly. I like you, too. But really, you need to get going. You don't wanna be late on your first day back."

A smile takes over, and I nod. This is going to be an anxiety-inducing day, but we have to take that first step. We can't always live in fear, or he wins.

"Seriously, call me or Tessa if you need anything. I'm only about fifteen minutes away," I say, opening the door.

"Go. I'll be fine," she says, but not very convincingly. "Maybe I'll hang out with Tessa and Emily today. I really should be trying to mend our friendship and get to know her more. Plus, we can work on wedding stuff. What better way to keep me occupied?"

I laugh. "Okay. See you later."

The door closes behind me and when I'm about to get in my truck, Scott pulls in. I wonder if he has had a chance to get the files for me yet. Or maybe he looked through them and didn't find anything.

"I'm heading to work, but she's inside," I say, rolling down my window as he approaches carrying a box.

"I didn't know if Harper knew, so here. The detective said I could take a look at them today. If he knew I was letting you go through them he'd kill me, so this has to be between us."

Inside is all the information I need about her parents' deaths and anyone they looked at in connection with it. Hopefully something inside will point us in the direction of their killer and her attacker.

"I'll call you later after I take a look at it. Did you already?" I motion to the box.

"Nope. I just got them and came over here. Maybe I can come to the station and we can go through it together after my meeting with Harper?"

"Alright, just call me. But go easy on her. She might seem like she's fine, but she's far from it. She's still having nightmares."

"Can't say I blame her with all that happened. Hopefully, we won't even need that box, and she can identify him in this array of photos I gathered."

"Let's hope. Maybe her life can go back to whatever her normal is going to be now."

He nods and heads back to his car, getting a huge manila envelope. Let's cross our fingers the man responsible is inside, and all this can go the fuck away.

23

HARPER

*T*he phone rings and it makes me jump. No matter how I feel, I need to be strong today, because Liam needs to feel okay with me being home, and showing him how nervous I am will only make things worse for him. So, I try to bury it deep down and not let anyone know how scared I am.

"Hello?"

"It's me. I see Liam's leaving, but I'm here. I didn't know if you wanted me to knock or not."

I open the door and usher him inside. "Don't be silly."

He smiles and looks around for a place to sit. A practically bulging manilla envelope is in his hand. Those must be all the pictures of the employees and officers. Honestly, I didn't think it would take this long to get it put together, but once I look through them, I will feel better.

"Well—let's cut to the chase—you know why I'm here."

"You want some coffee or something while I look through them? I just made a new pot."

"Sure, that would be great."

Sitting back down at the table, I open the envelope and pull the gigantic stack of photos out. There has to be at least three hundred here. The man behind all this drama could be in here, and if he is, then I can finally breathe, knowing we at least have a suspect for the cops to go after.

As I go through picture after picture, I'm getting discouraged. Maybe he isn't in here. Maybe these nightmares are just that and I've blown things way out of proportion. But that still doesn't discount the fact that a man came in and tried to kill me.

"Anything yet?"

I shake my head, trying to hide the disappointment. When I come to the last picture, I scoff and push them off the table. "I don't understand. This doesn't make any sense. I'm not crazy. Am I?" I pace around the kitchen, my palm against my forehead, trying to piece together everything I know so far. "He had to be in there. It's the only thing that makes sense."

Sooner or later, he will come for me again, and eventually he'll succeed at trying to kill me. They need to catch him before he has the chance to. That's why this is so important, to get ahead of him and figure out who he is.

"Calm down. We are going to find this guy. In the meantime, we need to keep you as safe as possible. Liam told me about the security measures he bought, and we have increased patrol around the neighborhood."

I know he wants me to feel safe, but it feels like no matter what, while this guy is still out there, danger is coming. He won't stop until I'm dead, and if my nightmare is true, he has a good reason behind it. If I could just remember what that reason is, all of this would be much easier, and the cops would have more information to go off, but my brain has been anything but helpful at this point.

Scott gets up from the table and collects the pictures as he says, "I've got to head back to the station, but don't let this deter you from your progress. Liam said you uncovered a memory yesterday. Keep working hard, and before you know it, everything will come back to you."

Honestly, he's right. I should be focusing on the good things, like Liam and how our relationship is progressing naturally. I'd love to make him a special Italian dinner tonight. After Scott leaves, I peer at the refrigerator, seeing Tessa's number, and I dial it.

"Everything okay?" she says as she picks up.

"I'm alright. I just wondered if you could take me to the grocery store to pick up stuff for dinner, and whatever is closest to pick up something to wear tonight."

"On my way," she squeals.

As I slip on the Converses, the bedroom door shuts behind me, which makes me jump. Heading to the front door, I see she's already in the driveway waiting. A key is left on the counter for me, so I grab it, lock the door, and sprint to her car.

"What's so special about tonight?" she pries. "I'm really glad to see you guys so happy. It means the world to us."

"Well, if I'm doing my math right, then we didn't celebrate our one-month anniversary. I know it sounds silly, but I honestly just want to do something for him."

Once inside the grocery store, I explain that I want to do something nice for him after everything he has done for me in the last month and a half and during my recovery. Never in a million years did I think I would ever find a guy like him, let alone someone who would stick around after what I went through, and still going strong. Wouldn't most men have run by now? Yes, but Liam is different.

Once the dinner ingredients are bought, we walk next door to a local Ross discount store, which Tessa recommends for something that isn't too pricey but nice. I didn't want to go full gown or anything, but something that looks elegant and sexy. We both want each other, but neither have acted on it yet. It's sweet of him to do that for me, but him being a gentleman only makes me fall for him faster.

His hesitancy to be intimate with me scares me, like he thinks I'm some broken girl, that if he touches me, I'll break. I really want to change that perception of me because even though I don't have our memories, I chose to be with him and stand by the guy who stood by me through some of the toughest times that I knew of in my life. He has been nothing but patient throughout this whole adjustment period, and I wish he would just hold me and kiss me passionately. My body craves it.

After finding the perfect dress, Tessa takes me home, and I start to prepare dinner. I never cooked chicken tortellini before, but a recipe I found online walks me through the preparation so I don't screw anything up. Tonight needs to go perfect.

The alarm I set on my phone goes off, which means he will be home soon, so I rush to the bedroom to get my dress and heels on. My hair has been in waves since I left it in braids after showering, but I put a little bit of eyeliner on my eyes and slap some mauve lipstick on my lips for the finishing touches.

"Harper—I'm home," he says, trailing off toward the kitchen, probably because of the delicious smell. I had left two glasses of wine on the table, along with rose petals. I know, cliché, but whatever. It will get my point across to him hopefully. "What's all this for?"

I scurry out of the bedroom to meet him in the living room. "I just wanted to do something nice for you."

His eyes survey me, and I can tell he likes my dress. "You look gorgeous. But you didn't have to do all this."

Without responding, my face is inches from his. "But I wanted to." My lips are on his, and at first, he doesn't kiss me back, and it's not because he doesn't want to. From other body parts, I can tell that isn't the problem. "I'm not broken or fragile. You can kiss me." I take his hand and start at my shoulder and bring it down my arm. "You can touch me."

His hands envelop me, and his tongue wrestles with mine. This is how I pictured our night going, engrossed in each other, getting to know each other in a different way. The timer goes off, but my lips don't want to leave his, my body wanting him to continue, but then he backs away.

"You should probably get that, and I'll go get showered and changed," he says, smiling and looking back at me while walking to the bedroom.

Finally, we can start acting like a real couple, because that's exactly what I want. I know he wants me to be able to remember, but at some point, we have to start making new memories. I don't want to stay stagnant until I remember. Moving forward is the right direction. Tonight is all about doing that. I'm home alone with a handsome man who adores me, takes care of me, and he deserves to be rewarded for being a great boyfriend.

While he showers, I pull out some candles and place them on the table to set the mood, and then I dish two plates and arrange them nice and pretty. The lighting is turned down, and it's just how I want it to be— romantic. Now our night can officially begin.

"This is the only shirt I could find that was clean and seemed dressy enough." He looks down at his chest, buttoning the shirt.

I stop him mid-button. "That's okay. I don't plan on you keeping it on long, anyway."

My fingers work his top three buttons undone, and then my hands are on his chest. How am I lucky enough to have this man? It's time to show him how grateful I am for him to stay by my side through my recovery and letting me stay with him until I can get back on my feet.

Our lips touch, and electricity shoots through my veins, among other sensations, and he still doesn't put his hands on me, so I pull away.

I take his hand and place it on the small of my back.

He hesitates for a second, but then he starts to move his hands to caress my back as he brings his lips back to mine and the rest of the night is history.

24

LIAM

The case files are still in my truck, locked up, because I couldn't leave them at the station. Scott never came by to go through them yesterday. He is going out on a limb for me, but he believes something in those files might help us catch him. It's the only thing that makes sense. Why else would someone come after her?

Will Harper get upset with me for going through the files? Honestly, at this point, I don't know, but I am trying to keep her out of it. She doesn't need to be reminded of that day or see the crime scene photos which are inside the files. It would break her.

Sleep hasn't really been in the cards for me much lately, between her nightmares and my worry. It's starting to get to me, not being able to concentrate, daydreaming, and never-ending terror that something very bad is going to happen to Harper. If I can prevent it by going through these files, then what's the harm? She will forgive me for lying to her, right?

"I'll be off around seven. Come home, shower, and then we will go to dinner, okay?" I say, gauging if she still feels up to it.

"I've been looking forward to it," she replies. "I'm just going to do some cleaning around the house. Keep myself busy."

"Okay, just call me or Tessa if you need anything," I say before dipping out the door to head to the station.

Surely, Scott will stop by today since it's his day off and we can finally dive into the files. He has to give them back to the detective, and I want enough time to go through them with a fine-toothed comb before that happens.

On the drive over, I contemplate why anyone would want to kill her parents. They seemed like average people, hardworking folks, paying their daughter's way through college. However, that's just what Harper has told me, and we all know there are always two sides to every story.

I must prepare myself that there is a chance something in these case files could change my perception of her, and not for the better. *Let's hope there are no skeletons in her closet.*

Damon is waiting for me as I walk inside, ready to jump on me.

"What are you doing?"

"I'm here to work. Why else would I be here?"

"Don't lie to me. Why is Scott here? Tell me what's going on," Damon says.

Will he understand or throw me under the bus to Tessa?

My hand on my hips, I contemplate whether I should tell him. My brother has always had my back, and he might tell me I'm being an idiot, but at least that would be honest. I feel like one, going behind Harper's back, and who knows if she would tell me not to look into it, but I won't have peace of mind until I do.

"We are looking into her parents' murder."

"What good is that going to do?"

"That's the only person who might have a reason to hurt her, and that's good enough for me. I'll do anything to protect her. I have to."

Damon runs his fingers through his hair and starts to say something, but then he puts his hand up. "Just remember, if she finds out, she won't be happy you are keeping it a secret. Tread lightly."

I don't have a chance to respond before he walks away and Scott is approaching me.

"We need to go through these files today. The detective called and wants them back by tomorrow afternoon."

Fuck, that doesn't give us adequate time. How the hell are we going to be able to go through all of this before I get off work?

"Well then, we better get started and stop wasting time."

I get them out of my truck and we go into one of the rooms where we usually take naps and lock the door, opening the box and pulling out a stack of papers combined together.

"Where should we even start?" I ask.

"Let's go through it together, it's all marked so let's start with the crime scene."

Scott opens the folder of the crime scene and starts laying photos out on the table. As a firefighter, I've seen dead bodies before, burned to a crisp, but this is different. I try not to look at them, to save myself from seeing the gruesome work of their killer, but I have to. This could help Harper's case. I take a deep breath and start looking at the photos. Her parents are on the floor, bludgeoned to death, blood everywhere. A part of me wonders if looking at the photos is necessary, but I can't overlook anything within this file. Someone missed something.

After Scott puts the array of photos on the table, he starts to read the initial report from the scene, including that her mother and father were stabbed over thirty times.

"Whoever did this—it was personal. It takes rage to continuously stab two people that many times."

I don't want to think about that, because Harper might know the person responsible for her attack and not even realize it.

"Here are some footprints they found tracked through the blood, but the report shows blood only matched the victims and it appears they found the murder weapon."

I take the report out of his hand, going over it myself too. A knife from their own kitchen was found on the ground covered in blood. He didn't even think to take it with him? Yet, no prints were found on the weapon. How is this guy so damn smart at covering his tracks?

We banter over the details of the crime scene and spout off reasons why the person would come after them. Gambling debt? Scorned lover? Money motive? Neither of us have ever investigated a murder before, and we come up with nothing that isn't already theorized in the report and from the detective who worked the case.

There are never-ending notes from the detective in here; he was meticulous. In the box is a series of recordings; these are interviews with witnesses and neighbors on the night of the murder. I pull the one with Harper's name written in bold black ink and pop it into the tape player Scott brought.

At first it is staticky, and then I hear a man ask her to state her name for the record.

"Harper Davis."

Her voice is shaky, and there is a sense of fear in her voice.

"Ms. Davis, can you tell me what made you visit your parents this evening?"

For a moment, it was silent, and Scott and I just looked at each other.

"I was supposed to have dinner with them."

Hearing her voice, shaky and terrified, kills me.

"And I'm told you are the one who found them and called 9-1-1, is that correct?"

"Yes."

The interview is basic questions I assume a detective would ask, but knowing Harper it made it feel like they were treating her as a suspect. I get it, she's first to the scene, calls 911, and no one saw anyone else go in or out. Of course, it makes her look suspicious. About halfway through the interview, a woman comes in and introduces herself as Detective Westfield and asks if Harper knows of anyone who would want to hurt her or her parents. The answer makes Scott and me stare at each other.

"A couple of months ago, there was a guy stalking me and my parents told him to leave me alone. He would watch me from outside my window at night."

They ask Harper for his name. *Keith Standridge.*

I press pause. "So before we move on, let's figure out what they found out about that guy."

It takes about twenty minutes of going through all the damn papers before we find anything about him in the file. The only thing that is really said is his alibi checked out for the night of the murders, so he was not named a suspect.

Harper never mentioned any of this to me, but it could just be because of her memory being wiped. I have to stop thinking she's hiding something from me and letting this come between us. It's not like I can come out and ask her about it now, or she will want to know how I found out in the first place. All that will cause is more pain and confusion for her.

"I find it odd there is no picture of this guy. Every other person they interviewed has a corresponding picture in here, except for this Keith guy. Although, it does give us his address at the time of the murders, which isn't helpful."

Scott presses play to listen to the rest of her questioning, but I try to block it out and go over the report of the crime scene again, looking for anything we might have missed. The house showed signs of forced entry at the front door, almost like someone tried to pick the lock, and then once they gave up, they busted out a bedroom window and climbed in through there.

So, we know how the perp got inside, but now we need to find a motive. Even if this Keith guy was stalking Harper, why would he kill her parents?

We spend most of the morning and afternoon combing through each page and interview, trying to come up with something to investigate further that could help us solve who is behind Harper's attack, but we come up nothing. The only person who stands out is her stalker. Even though he had an alibi for their murder, he could still be coming after her now.

Scott leaves to talk to the detective about it, and Damon is sitting at the poker table, trying not to make it obvious that he's pissed at me.

"You can't blame me. I'm doing everything I can to find who did this to her," I say, pulling a chair out from the table.

"But you're going about it the wrong way, behind her back."

"Am I supposed to tell her I'm looking into her parents' murders, and then let her join in because she will be curious on what happened, and then watch her go through all that pain and misery again? No fucking thank you."

Damon throws his hands up in the air and gets up from the table. "We are the good guys, remember. Once you start hiding things, it only goes downhill from there. Think about what you're doing. How can anyone trust you if you are keeping secrets from them? What if the roles were reversed?"

Instead of letting me respond, he walks out of the room and leaves me pondering his question. If my memory was gone and I had been attacked, I would want everyone to do anything they could to help me find my attacker.

Yet, if I didn't see anything wrong with it, then there would be no need to hide it from Harper. Damon's right. I'll let Scott handle that side of it from now on. I don't want anything to ruin my chances with her.

I just can't help but think that maybe there's a reason she never mentioned Keith before, and it's not like stalkers are first date conversation. It's been years and maybe she just forgot all about him and never thought to mention it. Either way, the benefit of the doubt is given as I try to get the image of their dead bodies surrounded by a pool of blood out of my head.

My phone vibrates.

Harper: *Excited for tonight. Getting ready now.*

I didn't forget about our first date tonight, but I'm not sure how I'm supposed to act like everyone is fine and dandy when there is a killer out there trying to get to her. Maybe we shouldn't be going anywhere in case he sees us and finds out where I live.

No, fuck that. We can't live in bubbles for the rest of our lives. She's been afraid and stuck in the house long enough.

I'm going to take her out and show her a good time and make her forget all about this fucking mess.

25

HARPER

Since the other night, I've noticed that the intimacy we shared has improved our relationship. Sex isn't something that should be used to keep someone with you, but I wanted to sleep with Liam. Something about him draws me, and the way he continues to keep me safe only heightens that. If this man loves me, then I need to do whatever I can to get to know him and try to get my feelings back. Sure, I'm not the same Harper he fell in love with, but there's a chance our feelings can still be real. That's my plan over the next few days, to find out if the feelings we are both having are real or because of the tragedy of my accident.

Everyone knows when two people go through a tragedy together, it either brings them closer together or tears them apart. I'm not saying he doesn't love me, just that it might be more so because of the fact I needed saving, and many men have a hero complex. I'm not a damsel in distress waiting around for someone to save me.

Tonight is our first official date, and all day I've been looking forward to it, wondering what we are going to do and how the night will end.

A knock on the door startles me as I glance over at the clock. He shouldn't be off yet. Instead of letting my head get the best of me, I peek through the hole to see Tessa on the other end.

"It's me. I come bearing gifts."

I unlock the door and gesture her inside, a bag in her hand. "What is that?"

"Girl, Damon told me you guys have a first date tonight and I figured you could use something to wear. I was already out and saw this and thought it was perfect," she says, handing me the bag and gesturing for me to go try it on.

"Okay, but I won't lie if I hate it," I reply, arching my brow.

As I turn around, without her seeing me, I smile. Inside is an emerald-green dress and black strappy heels. Maybe we really were best friends before my accident because it's one of my favorite colors.

"So, what do you think?" she says, raising her voice.

I come out of my room and prance around for her, feeling the silk against my fingertips. "It's fucking beautiful."

"A little gift, hoping tonight goes great. Nervous?" she asks, folding her hands in her lap on the couch.

"Eh, not really. He has been great to me, and this is a formality. He already loves me; he just want us to get to know each other now, know the new me. It's crazy that I'm living with a guy I barely know," I say, pushing my black hoops into my ears and then latching on a basic black necklace to match.

"It's Liam, though. Believe me, he isn't going anywhere. He cares about you too much. Just enjoy your date."

She takes some of the nervous energy away by making me realize she's right. It's Liam. It's not like it's someone going out with me for the first time; that's only me because I can't freaking remember. He's a guy I can see myself falling head over heels for and having babies with one day. We sure would make some cute ones.

The front door opens and shuts before I hear his voice call my name, alerting me he's home.

"That's my cue to leave. Let me know how it goes," Tessa says, smiling on her way out past Liam.

He sets his keys down on the coffee table and smiles. "You look gorgeous. Were you two having a girls' day or something?"

"Or something." I laugh. "Go get showered. I'm ready to go."

Thank God for Tessa because I had no clue what I was going to wear until she brought this over, so she saved my ass a lot of time from digging through the bare minimum closet of mine.

I take a seat on the couch and turn on HGTV to pass the time until he walks out with his shirt half-buttoned.

"You're not supposed to be half-dressed until the end of the night."

He smiles and continues to button it up. "Save that for later."

He grabs his keys, and I take his arm on our way to... where are we going? Oh, who cares. I'm up for the surprise.

When we pull up to a bar, I'm a little taken aback. He chooses to bring me to a bar for our first date? It's a little odd, if you ask me. I thought we would go to a fancy restaurant or something.

"Recognize this place?" he asks before unbuckling.

I shake my head.

"This is where we had our other first date. You picked it."

As much as I didn't want to repeat what the old Harper did, it's not really my choice now. He drove us here, so I have to shut up and pretend to enjoy it. As we walk in, it's not as bad as the outside portrays, and it's pretty roomy. Why would I have picked this place to meet him?

He takes me to a booth in the back corner away from everyone and orders two beers as we take our coats off.

"So, tonight is all about getting to know each other. What do you want to know about me?" I ask.

The first question is about college and my experience. It's a weird question, but I answer it. College is something I will always remember because I made some very good friends there, none of which I apparently talk to anymore, but things aren't at all what I would have expected at thirty-one either.

"Okay, so where did you think you would be at your age? I know you mentioned in the hospital this isn't where you saw yourself. What did you mean?"

Isn't that a loaded question? Texas has never been in the cards for me as far as moving away. Honestly, I planned on staying in California and teaching up to the point where I could become a professor and get offered tenure. To realize I just started utilizing my teaching skills a couple months ago is sad. Why did I waste so much time? I could have taught anywhere, so why did I come to Texas and wait for a job to open up instead of going somewhere where there was one already available?

"Married, kids, hanging out at the beach on the weekends. Successful."

"And how do you know you aren't successful? Isn't success defined by the person trying to acquire it?"

"I guess I'm just not where I saw myself being. Sounds stupid, I know."

He takes my hand. "No, it's not, but don't count yourself short. You are a wonderful woman and Tessa tells me how much your students like you. You did something right. You are a success in my book."

The waitress comes over and asks if we would like anything else, and he smiles. "Want anything to eat? The wings are delicious."

"Sure, do you have honey BBQ?"

"Yes, ma'am. Coming right up."

The conversation changes subjects after the wings arrive, and we cover things from favorite foods to dream vacations. It's nice to just sit and talk with him, outside of the house, and find out new things I didn't know, like he owns duplexes with his brothers. That's an interesting tidbit he kept from me. Is he a saint or what?

It's getting late, around eleven, and he pays the check.

"It really is time for us to get home."

When we get in the door, I want him to rip my clothes off, but sadly he just offers for me to sleep in his bed tonight. I get it, early morning and all, but that's not how I wanted our date to end.

Instead of complaining, I go to the bedroom, throw on a nightgown, and crawl into bed next to him, warm and safe.

26

HARPER

*W*hen the house is quiet, my imagination runs and never does me any good. It only takes me to places that lead me to bawling on the couch for the rest of the day. I try to keep music or the TV going at all times, so there isn't a single moment of complete silence in the house.

For the first few hours, I just clean up the bedroom, do a couple loads of laundry, and sweep the floors. I want to go back to work, but the school district wants me to take a minimum of three months leave to make sure I'm mentally ready to come back and not jumping the gun.

My phone beeps, and I have a few missed texts from Liam.

Liam: Just checking in.

Liam: What are you up to?

Liam: You asleep in the middle of the day?

He must be worrying about me, texting me that many times in succession.

Me: I'm fine. Listening to music and cleaning the house to keep myself busy. Can't wait to see you later.

I slip the phone back in my pocket and start dancing around the living room, mopping, when a hand comes around and covers my mouth.

"We gotta stop meeting like this, Harper." The sinister voice makes my stomach turn. "You know... you made this too easy with that music blaring like you're at a rock concert."

I'm screaming, but his hand muffles the sound. Struggling isn't going to help. Why am I so stupid? Blaring this so loud no one is going to hear my cries for help, and this might just be my last breath. He's here to finish the job, and there is no one coming to save me. Maybe I can keep him talking, buy some time when his hand comes off my mouth. "Why do you keep coming after me? What the hell did I ever do to you, huh?"

When he comes around for me to see his face, I go ghost white, finding myself standing in my parents' house in California, surrounded by cops asking me a million questions. "Stop. Leave me alone... please."

There is blood on my hands, spread all over my clothes, and my parents are lying dead on the floor. "It was you," I yell, coming back to reality and seeing his face in front of me. "You... you killed them."

His fingers slowly make their way up my arm. "Did you really think I'd let you live after everything you did?"

It's all coming back to me, how I know him, and the awful things he has done. "Why did you kill my parents? They did nothing to you. They were innocent."

"Far from it. They took you away, told you not to go near me, and then had the audacity to go to the school administration," he says, whispering in my ear from behind with a knife grazing my throat, leaving behind a trickle of blood. "They ruined my life... got me kicked out of college... and all because you thought you were too good for me, when in fact, you were just a slutty whore."

I slam my foot backward into his kneecap to get free. In an attempt to get my cell phone out of my pocket, it falls when he knocks me down. "Help me."

"No one can hear you with the music. Although, you were never that intelligent, were you?"

"Help me. Help me, please." In the back of my mind, Liam reminds me all I have to do is say it three times, and the police will be on their way. However, I didn't think about that when turning the music up so loud. Did it even pick up my screams? The realization that my stupidity might be the reason I die today hits me. Why did I have to turn it up so damn loud?

His hands are on my wrists, pushing down hard, while he sits with his knees on each side of my body. "You ruined my life and could send me to prison. I can't let that happen; you screwed enough things up for me. Now it's your turn."

This man is out of his fucking mind. He brought all this on himself. He took my parents' lives because he's a psychopath who can't handle consequences for his actions.

"I've dreamed of this day since slicing up your parents. Tell me, where would you like to be cut first?" The knife spins around in his hand, a sick smile on his face that makes me want to vomit.

"What made you this way? Did someone hurt you as a child? Beat you? Something had to turn you dark. Tell me. What was it?"

Honestly, I didn't give a shit, but if my calling out worked, then the police would be on their way and I just have to stall until they get here. Just keep him talking and not hurting me for as long as I can.

"Maybe I'm the one who's normal, and you're the fucked-up one. Ever thought of that? Flaunting yourself, teasing me, and then making it seem like I'm crazy."

"You're pathetic."

"You're just begging me to put this knife in your heart, aren't ya? Were you planning on dying today, Harper? I've been waiting for my moment ever since I followed you here from California. I joined the force and bided my time until we could meet again. Today is the day I get to slice into you and hear your bloodcurdling screams until the light goes out in your eyes."

Just as he raises the knife over his head, the front door flies open, and a shot goes off. Instead of looking at who has come to my rescue, my eyes slam shut, hoping this isn't going to be my death. A familiar voice is barely sinking into my brain, and the shock begins to take over. *I almost died.*

"Are you okay?" Scott asks. "I got the call when I was already patrolling the area."

When my eyes finally open, I sweep my hands over my body, checking for any wounds, but I'm fine. The only blood is coming from the knife wound on my neck. He stares at me, not looking at the body, until he checks me out first.

"Let's get you off the floor," he says, pointing to the blood pooling around the body.

That's when he gets a better look. His audible gasp makes me turn, and I see his eyebrows rise. "How do you know him?"

"That's my partner... Larry," he says, shaking his head, probably feeling like a damn idiot for not putting two and two together. "It all makes sense now. He probably took his picture out of the envelope, and that's why he took that leave right when all this stuff happened to you. God, I'm such a damn idiot."

"His real name is Keith. You couldn't have known. He's done hurting me now."

"But how many others have been hurt? It's not like you can be the only one he's done something like this, too."

"I wouldn't be alive right now if it weren't for you." As inappropriate as it is, my hands fly around Scott's neck. "You saved my life."

Paramedics rush inside, heading straight for the body as I wave them off. The first one checks Keith's pulse and pronounces him dead on scene. The blood is now creeping its way toward me, so I back away further and stare at the man who can no longer hurt me. A sigh of relief washes over me, knowing I won't have to watch over my shoulder anymore or worry every time I hear a noise. My life can go back to normal.

27

LIAM

*S*itting at the table with Aiden, playing poker, my phone starts ringing. I wonder why Scott is calling me. Maybe Harper is able to pick someone out of the photos and all this will end today. It's already gone on too long, and something needs to happen.

"Hey, what's going on? You take Harper those pictures?" I say, throwing down my full house on the table for the win.

"He's dead," Scott stutters.

"Wait—who's dead? What are you talking about?" I jump up from the table, and fear washes over me. "Is she okay?"

"He got into the house, but she'll be fine. She's headed to the hospital just to get checked out."

"I'm on my way."

I look at Aiden, my phone still up to my ear. "I've got to go. Harper is headed to the hospital."

Instead of waiting for a response, I run out the door to my truck and skid out of the parking lot, speeding all the way to the hospital. How did he know where I lived? None of this is making any sense.

I call Tessa on my way over, just to update her.

"Liam..."

"Listen, he found her. She's okay but at the hospital. I'll update you once I get there," I say fast, not having time to really explain before walking through the automatic doors of the hospital.

"Harper Davis?" I say, walking up to the front desk when I see Scott waving me over.

"Where is she?" I ask, looking around.

"She's in there," he says, pointing to the door. "She'll be out in..."

"Are you okay? Did he hurt you?" I run my hands over her body, checking for any injuries or wounds. "Your neck!"

"It just barely cut through skin. It'll heal quickly."

My arms surge around her. A huge weight has been lifted off our shoulders knowing we can finally live in peace. No more hospitals, police presence, or trying to find the man who is responsible. He's dead.

"I have questions, but right now I want to get you clothes and to a hotel," I tell her, kissing her on the forehead. "What do ya say?"

"Nothing sounds better."

We walk out of the room, hand in hand, ready to take on the world together. Things can be different for us now.

As we pull up to my house, there are about four police cars parked in front with their lights going, and yellow tape surrounds the house. My neighbors are outside, gawking at me, probably thinking I'm a serial killer or something.

"Stay here. I'll go grab some stuff for us," I say, stepping out of my truck and approaching an officer.

"Sir, this is an active crime scene."

"This is my house." I show him my driver's license. "Can we just get inside to get some clothes? We are gonna stay at a hotel while you guys finish."

"Yes, of course. Penny will escort you inside."

She follows me as I open the front door, and I immediately see a river of blood on the floor. That must have been where he died. Is it weird that I don't have an inkling of remorse for his life being taken? Someone who would go through all this trouble to hurt Harper... he deserved just what he got. The only thing different I could've wished for is that it wasn't quick and that he suffered in those last moments, thinking about everything he has done in his life to end up lying on this dining room floor, bleeding out.

I step carefully around all the yellow marker cards and head straight to the bedroom. A suitcase sits on the bed while I throw some of our things inside.

Would she ever feel safe in my home again after today? Even though he's dead, the memory of almost dying here could impact her wanting to stay. Maybe it's time to put this one up for sale and upgrade to my forever home. I've been thinking about it a lot, wanting a home where I could retire. Harper is the end for me, and I don't want anyone else. She needs to feel safe wherever we are staying, and it won't be here.

"Alright, I'm done," I say, picking up the suitcase and heading back to the truck.

I put it in drive and head for the Eldridge Hotel where we will stay until everything at my house settles down. "We don't have to talk about it now, but I would really like to know who it was."

"His name was Keith... and it's a long story."

28

HARPER

When I was a senior in college, things were hectic like for every student, trying to make sure I graduated on time and focusing on my studies. My roommate, Darcy, and I had known each other for the last four years and she recommended that I go out and blow off some steam with her. Initially, I was against it, since I had so much left to do with finals only being a month away.

"Come on, you've been stuck in classrooms and this room all year. You deserve to get out and have some fun, even if it's just a couple of hours. Please?" Darcy begged, sitting on my bed, glaring at me while I was typing away on my computer, trying to get my notes in order to study.

"I really can't..." I held up a stack of papers that included my notes for the entire week. "I've got to get these typed up and added to my document."

"You can do that later. It's just a couple of hours. Live a little." Her head cocked, and whining ensued.

"Ugh, fine. I'll give you three hours, but that's it." I wanted to make it abundantly clear that I wasn't going to stay out with things that needed to get done. My future depended on acing these finals and graduating with a 4.0 GPA. No one worked their ass off for four years with straight A's to end up ruining it in the final weeks. At least, not me.

"Okay, so we are going to a little celebration party. It's at Matt's house."

"You never said a party... not really my thing..."

"Shut up and get dressed. You're going." She walked to my closet and pulled out a summer dress and some heels. "This is perfect."

Instead of arguing, I slipped it on and headed out with Darcy.

Some people think of college as the time to party and be stupid, but I was the complete opposite. For the last four years, I had focused on my studies and never once been to a party. Drinking wasn't really my thing, and headaches appeared when music was played too loud.

Approaching Matt's house, I knew I was in for a rude awakening with the speakers blaring, and people outside on the porch drinking from red solo cups. This was not my scene. "This is a mistake. I'm going back."

She grabbed my arm. "Too late to turn back now."

We entered the front door, and that's the moment I knew these three hours were going to leave me with a migraine. She tugged on my hand while we squeezed by people to get to the kitchen.

"Darcy, you made it," Matt said, looking over at me. "Who is this?"

"This is my roommate, Harper."

"Where have you been hiding?" a guy said, walking into the kitchen behind me. "I've never seen you around before."

"Focusing on my studies... parties aren't my thing."

His hand extended to me. "My name's Keith. It's nice to meet you."

Sure, maybe I didn't want to be here, but that didn't mean I was going to be rude. "Same."

After Matt poured us drinks, we went and sat in the living room, where Darcy sat on Matt's lap so Keith could sit next to me.

"So, what are your plans after graduation?"

He was asking me questions like he was interested in actually getting to know me. "Teaching. I'm not sure where yet."

Keith surveyed my body. "I could see you as a sexy teacher."

This was exactly why I never went to parties or even really dated anyone in college. Everyone was so focused on the booze and getting laid. I was surprised to see how many girls ended up pregnant in college, and from attending this party, I could see why. The girls were all wearing short skirts and rubbing all over the guys. I wasn't a prude, but I wasn't one to sleep with guys just to get a release. Sex should mean something and be shared between two people who plan on committing to each other, and not just for one night.

Darcy and Matt were making out, and it was getting intense, which meant they would probably be heading upstairs any moment to find a bedroom. I wasn't going to stay down here by myself. Hell, I didn't even want to come in the first place.

"I'm gonna head out. You two need to find a bedroom and I've got studying to do."

"Why don't you stay here with Keith? We'll back in a bit. Enjoy yourself." *Her hand flapped at me to stay seated.*

"I'll walk you back, if you want some company," Keith offered.

The naïve part of me thought it was no big deal, just walking me home. *"That's fine. Have you been drinking?"*

He gets up and does the sobriety test. "Nope, sober as a clam."

The red solo cup full of whatever concoction they made me was still sitting on the table, and I had no intention on drinking it. "Alright then, but straight back to my dorm."

On the walk back to the dorm, he asked me questions about myself. Where are you from? Are you single? Even though I thought that answer was obvious, but I guess not.

"Would you be interested in going out with me? Just like dinner." He slyly drops that into the conversation.

Keith was cute, but I didn't have time right now to start dating anyone. My whole future was dependent on passing these finals, and nothing was going to screw that up. "I don't really have time for that right now; plus, we graduate soon."

"It's just dinner. We could go tomorrow after you get some studying done. You seem like a really sweet girl."

"Let me think about it," I said, standing at my door with my hand on the handle.

I thought that was the end of Keith, but it wasn't.

The next day, my phone rang with an unknown number.

"Hello?" I said, holding it with my ear and shoulder.

"It's Keith. Give any more thought to our dinner plans?"

"I just don't have time. I'm still so behind."

"Come on—what if I promise it would only be an hour."

"Sorry, I can't," I replied and hung up the phone.

Why was Darcy giving out my phone number? I'd talk to her about that when she got home.

That's when it began. Texts started rolling in, and I received calls begging me to go out with him over the course of the next week. Not once did I reply or answer. He would get the point. Yet, he was relentless and just kept on contacting me.

Darcy felt horrible for giving him my phone number. She thought Matt knew him, but apparently not.

I started having these dreams that someone was watching me. No longer feeling comfortable at the dorm, I went home to my parents' house.

At first, they questioned why I wanted to stay there instead of the dorm. Besides dreams, I had no proof anyone was watching me. I'd just sound crazy.

"Who keeps calling you? I swear, your phone has gone off seven times in the last couple minutes," my mom asked, sitting at the table.

"It's a boy from school. He wants to take me to dinner, but told him no. He's been calling and texting me ever since."

"And you've made it clear you're not interested?" my mom asked, her eyebrows raised.

"Of course."

That's when a call came in from Darcy. "Sorry, I forgot."

"What happened to our dorm room?"

"What are you talking about?"

"It's trashed. Clothes and books everywhere. Beds unmade."

"I haven't been there in a couple of days and it wasn't like that when I left." *It scared me to think about who would do something like that, but it my mind went back to Keith.*

"I'll call you back."

That's when I worked up enough courage to explain to my mom what was going on. I could talk to her about anything, and she would always give me sound advice.

"It sounds like this boy won't leave you alone. But do you really think he's capable of doing that to your dorm?"

"I don't know. I only knew him for less than an hour; plus, no one knew him from the party Darcy took me to. Doesn't it seem odd?"

My mom shook her head and got on the phone with the school. I didn't want her to make a big deal out of this; school was already hard enough.

"They want us to come down and talk to the dean. They consider the excessive calling harassment and will send officers over to your dorm also."

After our meeting, we found out he was a repeat offender and transferred here from a different school. Apparently, the school administration warned him that if there was one more incident, then he would be kicked out.

"Mom, I don't want to get the kid expelled. We're seniors. Can't I just stay with you instead of the dorm and let this all blow over?"

My mom agreed and took me back home, where I spent the rest of the week studying for finals since there were no actual classes. As time passed, the calls and texts dwindled down. Maybe he was finally getting the hint that I wasn't going to answer.

That's when the doorbell rang, and I could hear my father talking to someone.

"Don't show up here again. You are not welcome here or anywhere near our daughter."

"Sir, I think there's been a misunderstanding."

"No, Keith. There hasn't been. Please stop contacting our daughter."

The door slammed, and I hid like I had no idea what was going on. He showed up at my parents' house? How did he even know where they lived?

My memory of Keith is back, and explaining to Liam is becoming overwhelming. It is like as I am telling the story, things are flooding my mind. The fear I felt when he showed up on my parents' doorstep and the anxiousness I felt every time his number popped up on my phone.

When finals week started, every time I would go to campus, I looked over my shoulder, wondering if he was there. What would I do if I ran into him?

Darcy and I tried to stay together when walking to and from classes. She was aware of the situation and didn't want me to be left alone.

"I don't understand why he won't just leave you alone... it's all very creepy..."

"Tell me about it..." I said, standing outside the hall where I would take my last final. "Good luck."

Once finals were over, there was no reason for me to go back to campus except to pack up my dorm and then graduation. My parents accompanied me to both, knowing that I was still frightened. Everything went smoothly.

Everything seemed to go back to normal after that, and Keith didn't show up at the house anymore.

Until that night, six years ago, when I went to visit my parents. When I knocked on the door and neither answered, I took the spare key hidden under the mat and let myself in.

"Mom! Dad! I'm home!" I yelled, shutting the front door.

The house was eerily quiet, which struck me as odd right off the bat, because normally a TV was going or a radio somewhere in the house.

That's when I found them, in a pool of blood, dead.

My heart sank, and I dropped to my knees. "No—how could this happen?" I pulled my mother into my arms, begging for her to wake up, but the number of stab wounds told me that would never happen. Her pulse is faint at first, then slowly slipped away, and so did she. I pulled my cell phone out of my back pocket and dialed 911.

"9-1-1. What's your emergency?"

"My parents have been stabbed..."

"Did you say stabbed, ma'am?"

"Yes, repeatedly. Neither has a pulse."

"We are sending an ambulance and officers to you now. Is anyone else inside the house with you?"

As the operator asked me that question, I realized I had no clue. Once finding my parents lying in a pool of blood, I didn't even think to check the house to see if the person responsible was still inside. If they were, then they would know by now that the police have been contacted. "I'm not sure. I haven't checked." My head swayed around the room, wondering if I was being watched right now.

"I'm gonna have to ask you to step outside the home until the officers arrive."

"I can't leave them here..."

"It's for your own safety, ma'am. Please go outside by the street until officers arrive. ETA is three minutes."

I ran out the front door and to the street. Our next-door neighbor rushed over and began asking if I was okay.

"You've got blood on your clothes." She yelled to her husband to call the cops.

"They should be here any minute..." I said, trying to calm down and pull myself remotely together. Well, as much as I could after finding my parents brutally murdered.

More neighbors began coming outside and staring. My shirt and pants had blood all over them, and as bystanders, they probably thought I had killed someone.

The sirens were getting closer, and when the cops and ambulance finally got on scene, I couldn't breathe. One officer approached me cautiously and asked if I was the one who called 911.

"Yes. I found them."

"Okay, is anyone else inside the house?"

"I didn't check."

Another squad car pulled up. "You will need to stay with them until we clear the house. They will have questions for you."

LIAM'S ARMS were around me, trying to keep me calm. Once I started explaining, my mind wouldn't stop. It filled in the blanks as I was speaking.

"So, you never thought it was Keith? Didn't tell the cops about him?" Liam asked.

"I did, but he ended up having an alibi."

Alright, he knew the story, and right now, that was as much as I wanted to talk about him. Keith is gone and there is no need to mention his name ever again.

29

LIAM

When we arrive at the hotel and get to our room, Harper immediately wants to take a shower. It gives me time to process how she knew Keith.

My phone starts to go off, and it's Aiden.

"What's going on? Is she okay? There are cops at your house."

"We are at a hotel. They found him, and he's dead."

The line is silent for a second. "Who was it?"

It's not my place to tell Harper's business, especially since it directly links to her parents' deaths. "A man named Keith. Scott's partner, no less."

Even that leaves me with questions, but answers some at the same time. Scott has been a great ally during this whole investigation, so I doubt he had any idea that Keith was behind this. Did Keith ever show any special interest around him? How long was he on the force? Has he been planning this all along?

"Tell Harper I'm glad she's okay. We are here for her if she needs anything. Damon said to call him tomorrow. Tessa is worried sick, but I'll update him," Aiden says, then hangs up.

It's amazing how much my family has come together in the last six months, and it really shows in times like these when my brothers are there for me.

"Who was that?" Harper asks, a towel wrapped around her midsection, using another to dry off her hair.

"Just Aiden. Checking in."

She still seems jumpy, but there is no need for that anymore. "Why don't you hurry up so you can get some rest. It's been a traumatic day for you."

Her eyes pierce through me. "Please don't treat me like a victim. It's over and that's all I care about. Things can finally go back to normal and hopefully they will let me go back to work. All this unnecessary sitting around is going to drive me nuts."

Things haven't been easy for her since coming home from the hospital, the constant watching over her shoulder and being stuck in the house. Maybe she is right. Work can be a good outlet for her and help her get back into a routine for more memories to start coming back.

"Sorry, I don't mean to raise my voice; it's just too much. I don't deserve to be stuck in the house anymore. He's dead. I just wanna get my life back."

I get up from the bed and throw my arms around her, bringing her close to my body. "Baby, I want nothing more than to help you. Tell me what I can do."

My shoulder gets wet and I try to console her but it's no use. All the emotions have been building up, and it's finally come to a head. So, I just remain there for her, for as long as she needs.

I can understand her frustration. Why the school won't let her come back is beyond me. It's only adding to the stress at this point, and working can be a stress reliever for her. Plus, it would help to get back to her full normal routine.

Her head lands on my chest, and my fingers stroke her hair. "It's going to get easier. Better even."

"How do they expect me to sit around and do nothing for months? I'll see a therapist if I need to, but work is what I need right now."

Tomorrow we will tackle the school situation, but her breathing has shifted, and that means she has drifted off to dreamland which is where I'm headed.

"I love you, Harper," I say, kissing her head before my eyes close too.

FIRST THING IN THE MORNING, before I've even had coffee, Harper is up and on the phone with the school administration to see what she can do about coming back early. This seems very important to her, which means I'll support her.

It's not even been a full twenty-four hours since Keith's death and she is like a new person. It makes sense since she doesn't need to be afraid anymore. She can put all of this behind her and get a fresh start. No matter if she gets the memories back or not, I still love her.

She doesn't seem happy as she storms back in. "They won't let me back until I get signed off by a therapist saying it's okay for me to go back to work due to the severity of the trauma. This is ridiculous."

"You gonna reach out to Dr. Newman again? Or my brother might know one. Let me ask."

I text him and ask for his therapist's name. He started seeing her a couple times a year after Carol passed away from cancer.

"Okay, he sent me her number. Might as well call her and schedule an appointment. The earlier, the better. You can be a working woman again."

She smiles and plants a kiss on my lips. "You really have been great throughout all this. Who knows what would have happened if you didn't let me stay with you. Or you weren't there with me in the hospital."

She seems to need reassurance, and so I give it to her, letting her know Tessa and I aren't going anywhere. I can imagine with everything she has gone through in the last month, her mind is probably spiraling out of control, trying to find some sort of pattern or routine to hold on to, but there is none. There is only one constant from the moment she woke up, and that's us.

I hold her hand while she calls and schedules an appointment for the end of this week. It might not be today, but it's better than having to wait a month or two.

"I'm going with Tessa to do some wedding stuff. She's on her way."

I didn't want to say she's been waiting for Harper to come around, because then it might make her feel guilty. What are you supposed to do when your maid of honor gets her memory wiped and can't help you plan your wedding? Tessa has been a trooper through all this, but I know deep down she is scared as hell that their relationship will never get back to normal. "She'll love that. That wedding is really driving her crazy."

"I've gotta step up my game as her maid of honor. Starting today, I want to work on mending our friendship."

I love hearing that come out of her mouth, and Tessa will be stoked to get her back. She's been waiting patiently for Harper to come to terms with everything going on and reach out to her. I'm glad she finally did.

"Don't worry, babe. I'll be back in time to make you dinner." She laughs, kisses me, and heads out the door.

I pull my phone out to shoot Tessa a text.

Me: *Good idea having her tag along and do some wedding stuff. She needs something to keep her busy and occupied.*

Tessa: *I figured so. Plus, who doesn't love planning a wedding?*

Harper has made it abundantly clear that she doesn't want to be treated like a victim or broken. I try to remember that she woke up not remembering many years of her life and must feel estranged. Who wouldn't want to get their life back? Figure out who they are? She's just doing what she feels is necessary to get back on the path she feels is right.

Me: *Friends are exactly what she needs right now.*

CHERISH ME

BOOK 3

1

AIDEN

As my fingers wrestle with the tie, I pinch my lips together. *How much longer do I have to wear this*? This suit is from my Prom, and still fits me, but the material rubs against my neck, causing a red rash. A heavy sigh is relinquished and I make my way back into the rehearsal dinner.

The lodge is crowded with family and the wedding party. I know there are some individuals who enjoy weddings, but not me. They make me want to gag. It's not that I dislike Tessa for my brother, but *do they have to be so lovey dovey*? The only good thing that comes out of weddings is the cute bridesmaids and, against the wall, sex.

The area has soaring ceilings with banners up for the upcoming Newlyweds. Everyone is showing up dressed in their best and taking part in small talk. Fuck, all I want to do is take this ridiculous tie off.

Next to me is the punch bowl, and everybody nods as they fill up their refreshment and head on their merry way. A few have tried, but I'm not the mingling conversation type. It's all bullshit, and no one is actually listening to what's being said. They smile and nod.

Why don't they have any liquor? I'm not a social type of person without at least a little alcohol in my system, and right now I want to go to the bar and do shots.

"Can I have everyone's attention? Let's get into our spots and do a practice run for tomorrow," the officiant says.

I roll my eyes, wanting for this to be over, but being the supportive brother, I slap a smile on my face to pretend like I'm enjoying myself. Damon is happy again, and that's what matters right now. Even if I hate this, being here, I'll deal with it for him.

The wedding march starts and Tessa comes down the path, and the full room stops to offer her their absolute attention. This is the time women fantasize about, and husbands spend all their salary on, for them to have this one moment of being the center of attention. They say girls plan their wedding at a young age, and it disappoints most. The fairytale wedding is good, but most can't provide that. Hell, I remember one wedding where the bride and groom spent a lot of cash to have their wedding, and most didn't even stay to eat or dance after. It's like they came to see the ceremony and then took off. Think about the money saved if they would have invited less people and rented a smaller space? The bride still bitches about that day. So my suggestion; keep it quaint and limit the number of people that attend.

Or don't get married at all? I mean, consider this. They center engagements on the ring, which women demand to be this huge glittering rock, but most can't manage that either. Getting married is another way for the government and retailers to make more money by pressing the notion that marriage is the utmost end game. Almost like it's the only way for it to be treated "real." *Well, fuck that.* Save the money you would spend on a ring and wedding, and instead, go on a nice chance of a lifetime trip. I promise you, the week or two week trip will be something you will never forget.

The officiant goes through what to expect tomorrow, and I try to listen, but my mind keeps drifting off, thinking about the one and only time I've ever proposed to someone. Instead of making me smile, my knuckles turn white, and the optimism in my face drains. My biggest regret in life was made at eighteen.

Once it's finally over, I creep over to the punch bowl in the corner to people watch. I did agree to be here, but enjoying myself is out of the question. There's no alcohol and everyone here has dated one of my brothers or is related to me. *Where are all the cute, single women?*

My phone vibrates in my pocket, and after pulling it out, I see the notice that Hazel has posted something new on her Instagram. She doesn't post much, but it keeps me updated and frequently ends in regret. It's a picture of her inside an enormous office sporting a navy-blue pencil skirt, a white silk top, and black pumps. A smile is pasted on her face and I can't help but wonder if it's fake. Maybe she misses me, but doesn't want to be the one to say anything. Or she regrets turning me down and hasn't been with anyone seriously since?

"What are you doing over here?" Liam asks, approaching me. "Aren't you gonna go talk to anybody?"

I put my phone in my pocket, and groan. "Be content, I'm here. There's nothing to drink sight."

Harper joins us, wearing a lilac floor-length gown, and appearing a few inches shorter than Liam. The poor girl has been through so much in the last four months. My brother says she still has nightmares and doesn't like to be at home alone, which is reasonable after all that transpired, but she did go back to teaching, which is what she wanted.

"So, how are things going back at the high school? Excited to be back?"

Harper rolls her eyes and answers. "My sub didn't comply with my lesson plans, so assignments are all over the place."

"Damn, that sucks."

After her assault, the school board refused to let her come back until they found the person responsible. Yet, even after that happened, it took another couple of weeks to be cleared by a psychologist. Liam says it was because of the severity of the trauma, but the poor girl probably wanted to get her life back to normal.

"There are some people I'd like for you to meet tomorrow."

Is she serious? Blind dates are a tragedy, and what the hell makes her think I need help to find someone? "Not the dating type," I reply.

Harper shoves me enthusiastically. "How would you know? All you have is one-night stands. You'll get sick of them, someday."

And why should that be any concern of hers? She doesn't need to be worrying herself about my sex life or commenting on it. That's my damn business.

Liam steps in before I respond. "Let's leave him alone. He'll grow up one day and find someone." He grabs her hand and leads her over to Tessa's mom.

Asshole. He knows the reason I'm like this, and instead, he acts like I'm being foolish. Or I like not settling down. *Fuck him.* The only person I'm interested in being with left me. I have no plan of "dating" anybody and have made that perfectly clear to pretty much everybody in my life. If they don't support it, I could give a fuck.

My face flushes, and my jaw becomes tight. I don't want to be here another minute. It's not like I need to be here. The rehearsal part is over and now it's people standing around chatting to others.

Damon is across the room speaking with our Fire Chief, but I interrupt. "I'm gonna head out. Need a beer."

"Make certain you aren't late tomorrow," Damon says.

I wouldn't deliberately ruin the wedding. They might think I'm selfish, but not that much. Okay, so I have a dilemma with timing, everyone knows that, but an alarm is already set for two hours before I need to be here tomorrow. As much as I hate weddings, I ain't about to screw his up. He's come back from losing his first wife to cancer, delve into depression, and fought his way out. If anyone deserves some happiness, it's him.

After leaving Damon behind at the lodge, I jump in my truck and head over to Dixie bar, where it's Karaoke night. Maybe I can find a girl to take home and get Hazel out of my mind. Instagram is the only way I can check up on her, and when I get a notification, I can't help but look. Is it wicked to want to see if she's doing better without me? From her posts, she clearly is, and it fucking kills me.

"Where have you been?" Natasha asks. She brings me my drinks most nights.

The one and only reason she prefers when I come is because I tip well. Bartenders are paid hourly, but tips are their bread and butter. The more alcohol we consume, the bigger her tips, but that doesn't mean she hasn't cut me off before. We have a love-hate relationship.

"Damon's rehearsal dinner was tonight," I respond, lifting the shot glass. "Doesn't love make you sick? People turn into sloppy, high-pitched babies."

Natasha has been serving me and my brother drinks since before we were legal. If anyone knows our shit, it's her. Girls have their hairdressers to talk to like a therapist, mine is my bartender. And let me tell you, she gets paid well to listen to me bitch and moan.

"Whoever is responsible for making you like this, they did a damn number," she says, before pouring me another shot. "Love is supposed to be magical. Not sickening. Only you would be the one to think that way."

She has no idea. I roll my eyes and take the shot. "Keep em' coming."

I hate Friday nights at Dixie because you have to scream for anyone to hear you, even if you're a couple feet away since the music is always way too loud. Yet, it's the best night for there to be plenty of girls. Listen, I'm not a womanizer. Every girl is informed that I'm not the "dating" type, but I'll take them back to my place and make their night. So far, none have had a problem with it, because contrary to popular belief there are as many women who want just sex as men. Sure, love and connection can make sex a million times better, but relationships aren't for everybody.

"Listen, I know you got your heart smashed into a gazillion pieces, but don't you think it's time to move on? Like how long has it been?" Natasha asks, using a rag to wipe the bar down and look busy.

"Eight fucking years. It's pathetic, right?"

It's not like I haven't tried to forget about her, but when you meet your soulmate early on in life, you don't listen to other people. So many of my friends in High School told me we wouldn't last into college, most relationships don't. I didn't want to listen, and brushed it off.

"I'm moving over there," I point to the far side of the bar. "Keep the shots coming."

The spot in the corner is away from all the foot traffic, but I can still see everyone as they arrive.

An hour and six shots later, I hitch an UBER home solo to crash. My drinking only continues to grow worse, but it's the only thing that keeps my mind off her. Sure, meaningless sex is nice too, but won't make me forget about her. *The one that got away.*

Hazel understood me on a deeper level, and made me a better person, not some pretty boy athlete. That was, until she turned down my proposal and hauled off to Massachusetts to attend Harvard. The most fucked up thing; we were together for four years and she walked away on graduation night and never spoke to me again. How the fuck is my heart expected to heal after that, or crave getting close to someone again? *She crushed me.*

Every once in a while, I think about texting her, but I don't want to seem desperate. Plus, she's probably happy and kicking ass in some court somewhere. Maybe one day I'll get my second chance, but until then, meaningless sex it is.

Obviously, Damon didn't mean to bring up all this old shit on purpose for me, he's getting married, but it did, and now it's stuck in the forefront of my mind. I try to push Hazel out of my mind as much as I can, because who wants to be the sappy loser still hung up on a girl from almost a decade ago? Honestly, it's embarrassing, but when you know, you know. Sometimes, life can make us jump through hoops before we get to the final buzzer. I understand why she went to Harvard, and left me behind, but long distance could've worked. If her dad stayed out of our relationship toward the end, things might be better now. Yet, he voiced his apprehensions about dating while in college. It's not like he didn't like me. She could be dating a worse guy than me at the time, but he didn't want her to mess up her chance at becoming a lawyer. Why he thought I would do anything to deter her away from her dream is beside me. If anything, I would have pushed her toward it with love and support. If he would have kept his mouth shut, my whole life could be different. Hell I would've moved to Massachusetts. We would be happy right now, having lots of sex, and she'd still be a kick ass lawyer. But instead, she's there and I'm here drowning my regrets in shots and fucking thirsty women every night.

Sure, some might refer to me as a player, but I'm upfront and honest with every woman I take home. Hazel fucking broke me, and after that, relationships aren't something I'm even remotely interested in. My heart and soul was left on the table for her, and she walked away from me and never looked back.

After Hazel pushed me away, I didn't leave bed for weeks. My brother checked in on me, and made sure I didn't do anything stupid, but I thought about it a couple of times. Young love is amazing and terrible at the same time. After about three months of her not returning my calls or texts, I stopped trying to reach her and move on with my life.

Here I am, eight years later, and she still runs across my mind almost every night. They say those that are together in high school never end up together, but I hope that's false. I might be drinking my life away, but I still have hope that one day I'll have another shot with her. When that day comes, I will do everything in my power not to fuck it up. Treat her like a queen, support her fully, and make her happy. That is what she deserves, and if only she would give me a chance to prove it.

When my opportunity comes, I need to be ready for her, and show her she needs a man that is caring, supportive, and can make her laugh so hard she snorts.

And that man is me.

2

HAZEL

Everything happens for a reason. I keep telling myself that as I board the plane to Dallas. The things that have happened made me the strong willed person I am today, and yeah some of them were awful, but I have to stop and think what kind of person would I be if all those things never took place?

Damon, for example, lost his wife, and this wedding wouldn't have happened if he didn't save Tessa from the fire that day. They wouldn't have crossed paths in such a way that threw them together and forced them to get to know each other and fall in love.

The wedding invitation came three weeks ago, and I hold off on replying because there are many things I need to consider. Aiden, for example. Sure, I've known all the Jackson brothers for over a decade, but I only dated and fell in love with one. Grapevine will always be my home, but I didn't stay in contact with anyone besides my dad and brother once I left. It might seem trivial, but we all have lives and Damon didn't hold that against me. We chatted on social media a couple of times since I left, but I never had the heart to ask how Aiden was doing. The fear that he has moved on and found someone, scared me. Sure, I did him dirty, but can he really hold what happened at eighteen against me? People make mistakes, learn from them, and then try to do better.

The thought of seeing Aiden causes my stomach to tighten. What the hell am I going to say to him? Sorry I left you, but look at me now? I'm not the type of person to rub my success in someone's face, but I did bust my ass to get where I am today. I didn't exactly have the best upbringing before I met my adoptive parents.

I spent most of my childhood years in foster care bouncing from home to home until I was thirteen. That's when I went to stay with Donald and Regina. Not long after, Jeremy also got assigned to them. I didn't bond with them for a while, because that's what us foster kids do; hold off because it's only a matter of time before they send us back and request a younger kid. Yet, they acted like how I wish my parents were. They made their home feel like just that-- a home. Unlike the homes before them, they cared for us and didn't take us in for the check.

As a kid, grades were important. The only way to go to Harvard to study law would be to have straight A's, lots of volunteering, extracurricular, and high SAT scores. Law became important to me when I discovered a documentary on individuals who were charged and convicted of crimes decades ago with no concrete evidence. It lit a fire under my ass and every moment after was spent working towards the goal of making a difference. One guy was in jail for almost thirty-years before they finally overturned his conviction. That's where my love for true crime began.

Landing in Dallas makes my head spin. Maybe I should've said no, sent a gift and continued on my merry way, but it's also an opportunity to visit my dad and brother. It's been way too long, and my dad isn't getting any younger. I really need to make more of an initiative to visit more often.

I wonder what all the Jackson's are up to now. Sometimes, it's nice to see where everyone has ended up. My thoughts turn to Aiden and what he might be doing now? Is he married? Does he have kids? My stomach tenses at the thought. Sure, it's been eight years, but you never forget your first love.

The cars are whizzing by me, causing a breeze as I stand outside the terminal, fidgeting with my bag. My brother, Jeremy, is supposed to be picking me up, but he should be here by now. Everyone I see, the excitement amps up and then I realize it's not him. Where the hell is he? My eyes scour through the array of vehicles and toward the back I see

Jeremy wave. The only luggage I have is a small carry-on because the last time I flew and checked my bag, it got lost. It rolls behind me as I move past the crowd on the sidewalk to his truck.

"Jump on in," Jeremy says.

My ass hits the seat, and my carry-on is placed in front of me on the floor, not leaving much wiggle room. As we wait to get back into the flow of traffic, I lean over and give him a hug.

"So, how long are you staying?" he asks.

I hesitate because I don't actually know. I did take two weeks off from work to take care of some things, but I might not be here that whole time. Instead of answering, I ask him about Dad.

"Get this. Some women hit on him, and he told her he was happily married."

"Well, in his mind, he is. Just because mom died doesn't mean he wants someone else. Can't blame him a bit."

After she died, our case worker tried to move us to a different home and separate us, but dad wouldn't stand for it. He ended up making our family official and adopted both of us.

Conversation keeps us busy for the thirty-minute drive back to Grapevine, and it's barely nine. My stomach growls and Jeremy takes that as a sign that we should stop and get some breakfast before heading to Dad's. The only place in town I used to frequent is Lacy's diner. Jeremy, the Jackson trio, and I used to come here after school and football games.

The bell atop the door sounds as we walk inside, and grab a booth toward the back with glass windows showing main street. It's reminiscent of being back here, in this booth.

"So, how is it being a big shot?"

I laugh because he's far from the truth. "That's not me yet. Maybe someday."

The menus are already on the tabletop, so I browse like I'm not going to get the same thing as usual. Black coffee and a breakfast sampler, always.

A young woman comes over and takes our order, and flirts with Jeremy. I almost forget that he lives here, and it's a small town. Everyone knows he's a bachelor.

"Wow, you got an admirer. Why don't you ask her out?"

He laughs, and shrugs. "Don't really have time to date right now."

The diner doesn't look like it's changed a bit. The walls still have old signs hanging, and the booths haven't been upgraded since it opened. We didn't come here for the way it looks, but more about the people. They are all friendly, and give you that small town vibe. Reminds me of that bar Cheers, where everybody knows your name.

"Hazel, is that you?" Patty asks, pulling me in for a hug. "We wondered if you were ever gonna come back."

She has worked here for as long as I can remember, and ninety-percent of the time she was our waitress.

"Back to visit dad and go to Damon's wedding."

Her eyes search mine. "He and Aiden were here last week. I take it you haven't spoken to him?"

I toss my hair behind my shoulders. "Not in eight years."

Instead of responding she smiles, gives me another hug, and walks away as our waitress brings our food. Jeremy picks up his fork and smooths out the dollop of butter on his pancakes and his eyes keep darting over to me and then back on his food.

"What?" I ask.

He drops his fork like he's pissed. "You know he'll be there tomorrow, right?"

My eyes roll. "I'm not an idiot. What do you think I've been stressing over?"

His head shakes before he goes back to eating. Yet, I can feel his judgement. My brother and dad don't know everything about me since I left, and right now, maybe that's a good thing.

After eating a few minutes in silence, he starts up again.

"Listen, I know the history between you two. You left him and he's never gotten over you, but it's Damon's wedding. So, try to be civil."

Wait, how does he know he's not over me?

I grab two twenties from my purse and put it on the table as I stand. "I'm ready to go see Dad."

Civil? The whole ride over I think about that. Does he think I'm going to cause a scene? Not knowing what he meant by that is irritating the fuck out of me. Sure, we broke up but we are both adults.

The tires crunch on the gravel leading up to his driveway, alerting him of our arrival. The front door opens and when he sees me, a smile shows. *It's been too damn long.* His hair, what he has left, is white and it looks like he's lost some weight. He's never been much of a cook and when mom died, it was up to me to step in. I'm hoping Jeremy has been helping out in my absence.

"Let me take a look at ya," he says, pushing me back a bit. "Gosh, you've grown, sweetie."

A single tear falls and I try to gain my composure. There are so many reasons I haven't been back to visit, but those are years I'll never get back with him. This man took me into his home and never gave up on me. Yet, I took off and never came back. My chest becomes tight around that thought.

Jeremy and I follow him inside where he starts a pot of coffee. It's his typical morning, and he seems to have just gotten up, still in his plaid pajamas. I take the time to browse the array of old family pictures, and the many wonderful holidays I spent in this house. The kitchen has been changed, and an island put in. Why would he do that? It's not like he cooks very often. His version of cooking is throwing something in the microwave, or a premade meal into the oven.

Dad cruises into the living room, and sits down in his recliner. I know he must have so many questions even though we talk on the phone regularly.

"How's Roger doing?" he asks.

I shut my eyes. "We're divorced. What about him?" My ex-husband never met my father and honestly, I'm glad. That piece of shit can rot in hell with his assistant for all I care.

"I-," he struggles, running his hand over his head. "Divorced?"

Jeremy looks over at me and then back to him. "It's okay. Remember the doctor said this is going to happen."

"What doctor?" I ask, my gaze going back and forth between my dad and Jeremy. "What's going on?"

My dad's demeanor changes almost like he is afraid of himself.

"So, I guess we should talk," Jeremy says. "Let's go fix us a cup of coffee."

Before I go into the kitchen, my palm is resting on dad's shoulder, and I give him a quick kiss on the forehead. "It's okay. Do you want some coffee?"

"Yes, black please."

Jeremy is leaning against the granite countertop with his hands folded against his chest.

Honestly, I want to slam his head into the cabinet, but I don't. What the hell is he keeping from me? And why?

"Spill. What the hell is going on?" My voice jumps up a couple octaves.

"Dad has Alzheimer's," he pauses for a moment. "Found out about five months ago. He's gotten worse in the last two months. It started where he couldn't recall recent stuff, like if he ate and now as you can see, it's affecting his memory."

Five months ago? Where the hell was the phone call to tell me? He never mentioned this when we talked. My hand is over my mouth, trying to refrain from screaming at him, but also holding back the tears. For the last eight years, dad has asked me to come visit and I declined. What the hell is wrong with me?

"When we found out, he made me promise not to tell you. He wanted you to follow your dream and not worry about him," he says, with his hands up like I might punch him.

My dad worked two jobs when my mother passed to make sure we had everything we needed. How could this happen to him?

"Please. Don't kill me. I'm sorry."

The anger inside me isn't because of him. It's at myself. I should have been a better daughter. If I hadn't blown off visiting him, maybe I'd get some of that time back.

"Hazel?" Jeremy's voice is low.

"I'm processing. Give me a sec," I say, my finger elongated.

After clicking on the browser icon, I type in Alzheimer's and gasp. Reading up on the disease is only going to make it worse. Just like they tell you not to search your symptoms on the internet. I continue reading anyway. As it advances, he will have problems with language, disorientation, mood swings, and behavioral issues. I close my eyes, trying to keep my shit together.

"When were you gonna tell me? Or were you gonna try and hide it?" My hands wave in the air, and then cover my mouth.

"He made me promise to let him tell you."

"And I get that, but it's been months. Not a week. That's time you got with him and decided to keep me oblivious. We have no idea how fast this disease is going to mature and I'll never get that fucking time back, Jeremy."

"I-."

My hand is up in a stop position. "Typical life expectancy is three to nine years. And you kept this from me for five months. I wanna punch you, kick you, scream! I don't understand why you would keep something like this from me for that long? Whether he made you promise or not."

Tears start to pour from his eyes. "I'm sorry, but he's my dad. It's his business to tell and he didn't want you rushing back and giving up everything you've worked for."

I flick my wrist. "That man has given me everything. If not for him, and his constant support and believing in me, I would have never made it to Harvard. He did it. I owe him everything." My voice cracks and I pat under my eyes.

My feet pace around, and I try to keep my voice down so as not to disturb my dad. He is going through enough right now, especially dealing with this, and we don't need to add to that stress.

"What are you gonna do? It says he'll need constant supervision," I ask. "Do you even have a plan?"

He runs his fingers through his hair. "Honestly, I've not thought that far ahead yet."

My feet continue to pace while I chew on my fingernails. "You two can move in with me. Between the two of us, we can take care of him."

The offer is sincere, but it won't work. My hours are anything but reliable. I can work eight hours or fourteen hours a day, depending on the case we are working on. It's possible I could work out a leave of absence, but that only lasts so long without losing my job. But I would give up everything for him, after what he did for me.

"I'm not sure he'll go for that, sis."

"We'll talk when it comes time. Until then, all we can do is enjoy our time with him," I say, pouring coffee into two cups and going back to the living room.

"Here ya go. Hot and black."

Dad takes a tip, puts it on his side table, and goes back to watching Lethal Weapon. It's like he doesn't even remember what happened ten minutes ago.

The guilt is going to weigh on me, and it should. What kind of daughter leaves for college and never comes to visit? I'll do everything I can for him. He's my dad. *I owe him everything.*

3

AIDEN

The chaos of my alarm screeches and I almost shove my phone off my nightstand trying to make it stop. Eyes barely open, the sunlight is seeping in through the drapes, and it only means I need to get up. *Is it already eleven?* Maybe, I shouldn't have drank so much last night. Today is Damon's wedding and that only means more headaches for me. Who knows what kind of mood he is going to be in? Will he be stressed out or carefree? Lucky me gets to find out.

A groan escapes as I push myself up off the bed to take a quick shower. He will kill me if I'm late. I turn the knob to let the water heat up and go on a search for a towel. Afterward, I step in and hang it on the bar outside and start to lather body wash against my skin with my blue loofah. Mornings aren't complete without a warm shower to wake me up. Shampoo is next. I'm trying to hurry up and get out before he calls me. I get all of it out of my hair, and then turn the water off, and wrap the towel around my waist. The hand towel from the bar is used to dry my hair a little bit before I brush my teeth. Luckily, I set my clothes out before going to the rehearsal dinner. A pair of jeans and Luke Combs concert t-shirt. The suit is still in the original garment bag, hanging on my closet door, and it will stay in that until the last possible second. We have hours before the ceremony, and Tessa will kill me if I get anything on it and ruin her pictures. *Bridezilla in the house.*

With one foot out the door, my phone rings with Damon's name scrolling across it.

"I'm on my way to you," I answer and hang up.

He only lives two miles from me, and there's still thirty-minutes to spare, so I stop and grab a Starbucks to help give me some extra energy I'll need for today. The drive thru line is nine cars deep, but I know I won't survive the day without a good amount of caffeine, so I wait and take my chances. Normally, they are pretty fast, and there's only one in the town. It takes about ten minutes to get to the speaker, order my Caramel Macchiato with two extra shots of espresso, and then wisp out of the drive thru.

Liam's car is in Damon's driveway and it appears I'm the last one to the party. What kind of smart alike remarks are fixing to come my way? I don't even make it out of the vehicle before Damon is standing outside his door, yelling at me.

"What the hell took so long? The ceremony is in two hours."

He acts like we have so much to do. What all does he have planned before the ceremony? Don't the guys kind of hang out? It's not like we have makeup and hair to do.

"Calm down. I got a coffee. And still have five minutes to spare before you told me to be here."

He waves his hand, and I follow him inside, where Liam is sitting on the couch. His eyes get big, and then I look at Damon. "Are you okay?"

"It's just – I want this day to be perfect for her. She has been stressing about it since I proposed. It needs to go off without a hitch."

It's understandable that he wants the wedding to go well, but no one can ensure it goes perfect. Something always goes wrong on a wedding day, but it's how you deal with it that affects the memories.

"Harper's already called twice and seems frantic. The flower arrangements still haven't been delivered to the venue," Liam says.

Maybe this is my chance to show support. "I'll call the flower company and see what's going on. Instill the fear of god in them."

Damon nods, and then heads upstairs to take a shower.

I text Harper to get the company's name. Let's hope it isn't dreadful news.

"Thanks for calling Sharum Flower's. How can I help you?"

"Yes, this is Aiden Jackson. I'm calling on behalf of the Jackson wedding scheduled for this afternoon. The bride said the arrangements have not been delivered to the venue."

The woman gasps and asks me to hold on while she goes to check on the arrangements. "I'm showing the date as tomorrow, not today."

Fuck, what the hell am I going to tell Tessa and Harper? She's going to shoot the messenger for sure.

"It's today and we have a bride freaking out. Can I come pick them up? The ceremony starts in less than two hours." The skin is starting to peel on my thumb from picking at it.

She puts me on hold again, I assume to talk to an employee to see if they can have everything together in time.

"We can have them ready in twenty-minutes. I apologize for the misunderstanding and will give a discount to the bride for the inconvenience."

Instead of responding, I hang up to update Harper. She didn't sound too pleased with the answer, but it's better than not having them at all.

"Don't worry about it. They're both stressed to the max today. It's not personal," Liam says.

He will be the next one to be married and I feel sorry for him. After seeing the way Tessa changed once the wedding approached, I can't imagine having to deal with that again. Maybe Harper won't be as bad. Or maybe, they will elope.

Instead of waiting around to pick up the flowers, I head out and grab some lunch from Lacy's Diner right around the corner from the shop. This place holds so many memories; including me and Hazel back in school. I pull out my phone to check her Instagram to see if she has uploaded anything new since yesterday. A picture of her in an airport. Where is she flying to? Am I a little jealous of her? Yes. Only because she seems happy with her new life, and I'm not a part of it.

A familiar voice sounds behind me. "To go for Jeremy."

I sit my phone down, and get up to say hi, since I haven't seen him in months. He still hangs out with Damon and Liam occasionally but I'm usually busy. "How ya been?"

"Oh, just visiting with my sister."

Wait, Hazel is in town?

"How is she doing?" I ask, trying not to seem too interested.

"Good. We'll see you later at the wedding," Jeremy says before walking out.

I go back to my booth, and can't finish eating. My hands are shaking and I don't know what to do. Should I be nervous or excited? People change the most in their twenties or so I've heard, and she might not even be anything like the girl I fell in love with all those years ago. This image in my head of us being happy someday might not even be achievable.

I take one last bite of my food and then leave a twenty on the table-top. It's time to head over to the flower shop and deliver them to the venue before I get more rude phone calls from Tessa. She isn't usually like this, but the stress of a wedding can be a lot for women. They care so much about how everything looks and honestly, I don't think Damon is really worried about any of that.

The bell dings above me, alerting my departure from the Diner as the cold nips at me.

Sharum's Flowers has customers coming and going, so they must be busy today, which is normal for a weekend.

The door shuts behind me, and there are arrangements of flowers piled up. "Are these for the Jackson wedding?"

"Yes. I put the bouquets in this bag and tied it up to keep them fresh, but be careful with them. They're fragile."

Everything is safely loaded into my vehicle, and the whole backseat is covered in fresh flowers. It's going to smell like these damn flowers forever now. The venue is only about five minutes away, but Harper's name is now scrolling across my dashboard alerting me to her call.

"Hello?"

"Did you get them?" Harper asks, frantically.

"Yes, I'm on my way to the venue now. Crisis has been averted."

"Thank you," Tessa screams into the phone.

My vehicle pulls into the unloading zone and the wedding planner is waiting outside, hands across her body, looking like it's the end of the world. They are flowers. What's the big deal?

I open the back door, and that's when she helps me take the boxes inside and she takes over to set them up. I'm happy she didn't ask me to help, because I know nothing about flowers or decorating. Plus, the last thing I need to happen today is for me to be blamed for anything being messed up. I'll let her handle that. *No, thank you.*

It's now only an hour before the ceremony starts, and Damon should be here anytime.

Me: *Where are you? I'm at the venue.*

There's no point in driving back to his house since we are due to be here in ten minutes. So, I grab my garment bag, and head back inside.

"Do you know where we are going to be until the ceremony?" I ask the planner.

"Back there," she points her finger.

I smile and go to the back where there is a door, and inside is a small room with a bathroom, hooks on the wall, and a mirror. This must be like a Groom's room where we can change and chill until we are due out at the altar.

Damon: *Pulling up in a second.*

It might be best for me to be dressed when he arrives here in case he needs me to do anything. So, I take my garment bag in the bathroom and start stripping down. The suit fits perfectly. The only thing I didn't like about it is the damn tie.

"Aiden, you in here?" Damon asks.

"Right here," I reply, coming out of the bathroom.

He's already in his suit, and so is Liam. They look around and to my surprise, Damon asks if I brought anything to drink with me.

"I wish, but the liquor store is down the road."

"Can you go get some bourbon?" he asks,

Wow, he must be nervous if he wants to drink before the ceremony, but I won't complain. I nod, and pass through the venue, seeing the planner and Harper talking, but don't acknowledge. Damon probably doesn't want it to be widely known that he is going to have a drink. No need to make Tessa stressed more than she already is. So, I sneak out of the venue, and down the sidewalk to the liquor store. When I come out with a brown bag, people start to look at me, although I'm the brother everyone knows is an alcoholic so it's no surprise.

I open the door and peek inside to make sure Harper is with Tessa, and walk swiftly back to the groom's suite before anyone noticed the brown bag in my hand.

"Alright, here it is. I grabbed a couple glasses from one of the tables in the reception area."

Is he wanting a drink to celebrate or to take the edge off his nerves? Tessa seems like the perfect woman for him, and Emily is one of the sweetest kids I've ever met. He loves her like his own. I brush it off, and say to hell with it. Who wouldn't be nervous on their wedding day?

Liam pours some in each glass and then we clank them together before taking the first sip. I would've chugged it, but then they would have both looked at me weird.

Hazel comes back to mind, and I wonder if she still has that quirky laugh? Does she still wear her hair up in a bun all the time? I remember the first time she wore her hair down, to the Homecoming dance, and it took my breath away.

"So, has anyone talked to Harper or Tessa in the last hour?" Liam asks.

"I did when I got here," I replied, taking another swig.

A knock sounds at the door.

"Come in," Damon says.

Emily walks in with her hair curled and wearing a purple dress. "Mommy asked me to give this to you."

She hands him an envelope. "Also, they want to take pictures in a minute and will knock when they are ready for you."

"What is it?" I ask.

He shakes his head and opens it to find a note inside.

Liam and I stand idle as tears start to spring from his eyes. Obviously, it's something sweet she has written for him before the ceremony. This will help him with his nerves.

Another knock sounds, and the photographer pulls us out of the room.

"I would like photos of you and the bride. You won't get to see her, you will be blindfolded."

As a man that's never been married, I'm not sure why the blindfold is necessary. Are they afraid he's going to peek? Tessa would kill him and he's not that stupid to piss off his wife on their wedding day.

They bring her out, and she puts her arms around him, and pictures begin. She kisses him, whispers something in his ear, and then they are done. How many pictures can the photographer take in less than two minutes? After they are done, I grab Damon's shoulders and maneuver him back to the suite.

"Alright, you can take the blindfold off."

We pick up our glasses to finish before the ceremony starts.

"When were you gonna tell me Hazel is coming to the wedding? Or, did you think I would freak out?" I ask.

Damon smiles. "Why did I need to tell you? She was my friend, too. I didn't know you had to be notified. Is this why you have been drinking more lately?"

"I just found out. My drinking has nothing to do with her coming."

So many things are running through my mind now; like what if she doesn't find me attractive anymore? I think about all of the women I've used to try to get over her. What if she brought someone with her? Fuck, if she did, my whole night will be ruined. Hell, the rest of my life. The only thing I've been holding on to is the chance to be with her again someday.

The planner knocks, and then opens the door letting us know it's time to get in our places.

The three of us follow her lead and stand at the altar, waiting for everyone to be seated, and the bridesmaids to make their way down the aisle for the final reveal of the bride. Damon is fidgeting with his fingers, and swaying.

I keep my eyes on the door, wondering when she will arrive. What will she be wearing? Will her hair be up or down in curls? The anticipation is killing me, yet my focus should be on my brother getting married.

Damon is right. He didn't have to tell me she was coming, and honestly it's for the best. Since I found out, all I can think about is what I am going to say to her? What do you say to someone you still love, even though she rejected your proposal eight years ago? Hazel and I might not be eighteen anymore, but I'm confident our connection is still there. Tonight will only prove that.

Jeremy walks inside, talking to a woman in a short floral dress and a pin-up hairdo. That can't be her? My eyes squint trying to see from that far, and then her eyes meet mine and my body freezes. *It's her.* I'd recognize those bluish grey eyes anywhere. She continues talking to her brother, but her eyes stay on mine. They break away only for a moment to look over my body.

Her legs are short, but perfect and the dress comes down to about her mid-thigh. The bright red heels she has on only makes me want to push her up in one of these corners and have my way with her. My dick starts to harden, so I look away, trying to focus my attention back to the ceremony and not Hazel when the doors open.

We accompanied the bridesmaids down the aisle, and even then my eyes are fixated are her. How is it possible she is more beautiful? Emily begins down the aisle, throwing the flowers to the sides of the walkway, and then the wedding march commences. Everybody in the audience stands, and then the door opens. Damon's eyes start to water, and I know he is going to be emotional. No one thought he would find his second chance for love, until Tessa. I pat him on the shoulder, and when she makes it to the altar, they hold hands, and give their attention to the priest.

This is when my attention fades back to Hazel. So, she did come alone. If she knew I would be here, then her outfit reflects her wanting to look her best. My attention is all hers.

4

HAZEL

The venue is covered in flowers, almost too many. The chairs are comfortable though, which means my ass won't be numb when we head to the reception. I've only been to three weddings so far, and the chairs are usually old and worn, and when everyone stands up, they squeak. These are new and have some back support too.

Up at the altar, Aiden's eyes are boring into mine, and for a minute, I smile, but then look away as my mind thinks back to his proposal, and turning him down. The moment that haunts sometimes even to this day, eight years later. Sometimes, I think about what our lives would be like if I said yes. Would we have raised Jake, and then had more kids? Would I have still become a lawyer? Things could've worked out perfectly, or went majorly wrong.

We were both young, and it's the best decision we could've made at that point. At eighteen, we had no business getting married.

Damn, he look good up there though. His chestnut hair, perfectly tailored suit that accents his broad shoulders, and don't get me started on his deep brown eyes. The sadness instilled in them at the sight of me, only leaves me to think he isn't quite over our past.

Honestly, there have been times I thought of him, but we live across the country from each other now. It wouldn't work. Yet, in this moment, there is a want between my legs, a need for him to pleasure me like he's always been good at doing.

Sure, Aiden was my first, but honestly, no one has compared to him since leaving Grapevine. Angela always told me that being in love with someone will make sex better, and to wait until I find that person, and I did. Aiden never stopped supporting me, and pushing me to chase my dreams. This is the type of man I dreamed about ending up with, and now with me being back here, I don't know if we are ever going to work out. Both of us have changed since being teenagers, and might want different things.

As the wedding march begins, a woman comes out wearing a stunning gown, nothing too crazy, but simple and elegant. That must be Tessa. Damon's eyes don't come off her the whole time, and neither does his smile.

It's nice to see him happy, especially after what happened to Carol. Honestly, in high school, we always thought they were end game. You couldn't separate them even if you tried. After hearing about her passing, I don't know how he dealt with it, because if something happened to Aiden, even though we aren't together, I wouldn't be able to get out of bed.

My attention goes to Damon and Tessa as they say their vows, exchange rings, and then kiss for the first time as husband and wife. It is weird for me to say that I truly thought one day that might be us. Young and in love, Aiden and I did talk about a future together, but my dad made some important points about not letting anyone stand in the way of me achieving my dreams, and that my focus should be on Harvard. At first, there was some resistance, but after carefully thinking about it, he was right. College was going to be hard, and on top of that, it's Harvard, an ivy league school and I only had one shot.

My thought process was simple back then. Aiden and I would find our way back to each other someday. There are many things I need to talk to him about while in town, and things might get complicated.

After leaving Grapevine and arriving at Harvard, things started to spiral. I found out I was carrying a child, and had no clue what to do. As a young girl, I couldn't raise a child, especially living in Massachusetts away from Donald and Jeremy. After a couple of weeks, I told Aiden, and he was ecstatic. It literally took him two seconds to ask if I had thought about his marriage proposal. Just because I was pregnant doesn't mean we were getting married.

After a long phone conversation, he disagreed with my decision to give the baby up for adoption. How the hell would two eighteen-year-old college students going to provide for a child? Neither of us had jobs.

So, I had to be the sinful person and made that decision. Aiden reached out over the next year through texts to check on me, and when he found out Jake was adopted to a wealthy family-- he ghosted me.

Looking back, I understand his frustration. Never in a million years did I anticipate getting pregnant and giving my baby up for adoption, but it was the best choice I could make at that time. Do I regret it? Hell yes, but it's too late to change anything. Every year on his birthday, I light a mini cake and sing him Happy Birthday.

I can't say that since receiving my degree, the thought of raising him doesn't cross my mind. Should I have pushed through the hard times and kept Jake? Married Aiden and became a family? Our salaries now are more than enough to raise a child, but we didn't have these things back then. Who knows if I would have even finished school?

Don't beat yourself up. You did what you thought was right, at that time.

Is Aiden still pissed off about the adoption? It's hard to tell considering the regret for me is still there. Did he tell anyone? His brothers?

The closed adoption made sense back then, but now, I wish I would have pressed for an open one. How is he doing? What does he look like? Is he getting good grades in school? There are so many questions and likely I will never get answers unless Aiden gets on board with my plan.

Now, I'm here at Damon's wedding, seeing Aiden for the first time, and all I want to do is be that eighteen-year-old girl again, tucked in his arms, recklessly in love, without a care in the world. But I can't. That girl isn't around anymore.

Everyone starts to go to the other side of the venue for the reception, and champagne is already being poured into the glasses at each table. Jeremy and I find ours and take a seat.

"You okay? Eyes look puffy."

"It's a wedding. Girls cry, okay."

I take a sip of my champagne and glance around the room,

wondering how long it's going to take for him to approach me. In this dress, probably not long.

My confidence might be high, but not enough to approach him first. Who knows what might come out of my mouth, and this is not the place to blab our business. No scenes at weddings, it's my rule.

The music starts and everyone is enjoying their drinks while waiting for the bride and groom to make their entrance. Weddings are always such happy events, well except when they are left at the altar, but we won't talk about that today.

I haven't seen Aiden, but Liam walked in with a girl on his arm. Is this his new girlfriend? She's gorgeous. At first, I think about waiting to introduce myself, but maybe it's better to say hi before the party ramps up.

"I'll be back," I tell Jeremy, scooting my chair out, and walking over towards them.

The girl is laughing and then kisses Liam. They are so cute together.

"Holy crap. It's been too long," I say, putting my arm around Liam and bringing him in for a hug.

"Hazel. You look great."

His girlfriend clearly doesn't know what to think. Some random woman she has never seen is hugging her boyfriend.

"I'm Hazel. Grew up with the three of them."

She extends her hand out to me. "Harper. His girlfriend. Nice to meet you."

It's hard to know if she is being genuine, or if she secretly wants to claw my eyes out for hugging her man.

At that moment, Aiden walks in, and his eyes fixate on me. *Fuck*. I'm not ready to talk to him yet. My hands start shaking, and I try to carry on a conversation, so he doesn't approach.

"So, how've you been?"

He runs his fingers through his hair. "Oh, you know. Firefighter. Fell in love. Getting old."

I laugh. "When are you guys getting married?"

"We aren't engaged," Harper replies.

Aiden starts heading my way.

"I'll talk to you guys later."

Before I can get away, Aiden's voice calls my name. My body freezes wondering if I should pretend like I didn't hear him over the music, but instead I spin around. "Hey, stranger."

It comes out more awkward than I intend, but what about this isn't making me nervous.

"I didn't know you were coming." His eyes take in my body, and it fuels me.

"Yeah, wanted to visit Dad and Jeremy while I was down. Seemed like a good opportunity to catch up with them, too." I stand there, smile on my face, not knowing what else to say.

"It's been a long time. We should catch up later. You look beautiful. Red has always been your color."

"Thanks," I reply, shyly looking down at the floor. *Girl, bring that head up.* "You free later?"

He scratches his chin. "No plans. Nine at Dixie's for drinks?"

"Sounds good."

I walk away, butterflies in my stomach like he asked me out on our first date, or the first time he kissed me, or when we made love in my long, red prom dress. The crazy thing is that I'm already debating on what to wear.

I have no idea what tonight is going to entail, could be fighting or two old friends catching up after almost a decade. Either way, it's time for us to talk about Jake. That's my mission.

5

AIDEN

The black suit jacket hangs over my chair, and I try to hold my composure while the reception continues. My eyes meet hers a couple more times, and it's confirmed. The spark is still there, surging through my veins.

It irritates the piss out of me that after everything we shared-- a child, a bond, that she stayed away for all this time. Why can't I get over her? Believe me, I've tried, for many years, yet no matter what I do, she is still there in the back of my mind.

"So, what was all that about?" Liam asks, handing me a beer.

I never told my brothers about the baby, because I was worried about what they might think of me. Fucking stupid, but it's not like I didn't want to keep him. Was I ready to be a parent at eighteen, no, but didn't want him to be raised by strangers. He deserved to be raised by us, loving parents, who created him.

"Seeing her later. No big deal."

He turns to look at me, eyebrows arched. "You've got to be kidding me. Are you crazy?"

I take a step back, a little irritated from his reaction. "What's the problem?"

His eyes find her on the dance floor. "Don't get sucked in again. She's only visiting, Aiden. Be smart."

He acts like I'm an idiot. I can't turn down the opportunity to catch up with the one woman I want to be with more than anything. Massachusetts is where her life is now. I'm not naïve, but that doesn't mean I can't enjoy the little time I have with her and get some answers. I still consider her a good friend as well, and friends catch up when they are in town. Right?

"Stop acting like I'm that kid again. I can handle it."

Liam shrugs his shoulders. "Just remember, I advised against it."

Hazel must have a sixth sense, because she's staring at me with an inquisitive look. That's when some guy puts their hands on her hips, and they start swaying. Whoever this man is, he better get his paws off her. My primal instinct to pounce kicks in, wanting to pummel his ass, but I chug my beer and go see the newlyweds instead.

The fact is, she's not mine which means she is free to dance with whoever she wants, without me interfering. Nothing good will come from me confronting the guy, it will only piss her off more and our meetup would be cancelled.

"Enjoying yourself?" Damon asks, not taking his eyes off Tessa, who is making a fool of herself dancing.

"More than I thought."

"And could that be because of Hazel's attendance?"

He knows how I feel about her, and even more so how being around her affects me. Even in high school, I never had eyes for anyone else. Hazel was it for me. Many people told me I was being dumb back then, believing that Hazel and I were soulmates and nothing would break us a part. They always said, "no one stays together after high school. Who wants to go to college with a ball and chain?" It irritated me for a while, until graduation day came and Hazel proved them right.

"You don't have to answer. It's obvious, brother."

Her being here tonight and the fact she agreed to dinner means she missed me, right? No matter what though, I must be careful. We aren't getting back together and she's going back to her life in Massachusetts. So, I need to reel in my excitement a bit. If anything, this dinner will at least give me some insight into her new life, and if she is happy. That's all I truly want to know.

Of course, the hurt is still around from her denying my proposal, but it's been eight years and it's time to get the fuck over it. This can be my chance for closure.

Liam and Damon have been telling me for years to move on it's not that easy. Why would I want to date anyone else? My heart is still hers, whether she wants it or not, and stringing someone else along is a fucked-up thing to do. I might like to sleep around, but I always let them know it's not going to turn into anything serious. My brothers can say what they want, but I'm upfront and honest when it comes to that.

I try to keep my attention away from her and that guy. It makes my blood boil to think about his hands being all over her like mine once were.

"Why aren't you out there picking up girls?" I ask, sitting down next to Jeremy.

He laughs. "That's your thing, not mine, remember."

I guess he's right, but with Hazel in town, the urge to find someone to take home tonight is gone. Usually, the reason I do that is to keep my mind off her.

"How's your dad doing?" I ask, trying to make conversation. Anything to occupy my time. The last time I saw their dad was when she left.

"Fine."

Jeremy didn't seem in the mood to talk, so I moved on to Harper. She came off the dance floor, and is sweating profusely, chugging a bottle of water.

"You better get out there. Reception's almost over and I haven't seen you dance with one girl. Not like you."

I cross my arms, and shake my head. "I'm good. Better view from here, anyways."

She glares at me and heads back out, using her finger to try to get me to join.

It's a quarter to seven, and with only fifteen-minutes left until the reception ends, the newlyweds should be getting ready for their big exit.

The DJ cuts in and announces that, and everyone lines up in front of the doors with their rice to throw. Such a weird tradition.

Damon and Tessa smile and laugh as they make their way to the limo waiting for them to cart off to the airport and then to Jamaica.

After that, everyone starts to leave, little by little, until it is Liam, I and a couple others cleaning up a bit before leaving.

"I'll see you later," Hazel says.

I smile, but don't respond, because she doesn't need to know how excited I am. Hazel is a persistent woman, and will work hard to get what she wants, like obtaining her degree from Harvard. To be able to do what she loves, and help people in the process, it has to be so fulfilling. So many people are stuck in dead-end jobs that give them no satisfaction. We are both lucky we have found something we love.

"Alright, the planner said to leave the rest, and let the paid cleaners to handle it. We are being kicked out," Harper says.

"Are you seriously still out of breath from dancing?"

"You try doing that for an hour straight... it's harder than it looks."

Liam comes up, and gives her a kiss on the cheek. "So, you coming over to hang out still or bailing because of Hazel?"

Fuck, I totally forgot about hanging out with Emily. Liam and Harper are babysitting while the newlyweds enjoy their honeymoon.

"Nope. I'll meet you there. But only staying until eight-thirty."

Liam smiles, and scoffs to Harper. "See. Now he is going to start breaking plans and putting all his time and energy into impressing Hazel. A girl who isn't going to stay in Grapevine."

"Fuck you. We are catching up. Why are you and Damon making such a big deal about it?"

"Cause we know you."

Okay, so maybe they do. Deep inside, I'm wondering how life would be if she moved back, but I know that would never happen. I'm hopeful, not naïve.

"Obviously not if you don't think I can go catch up with her without begging her to stay. That's ridiculous. This isn't a damn romantic comedy," I reply.

We all start heading to our cars, and nothing else is said. My brothers need to stop making such a big deal out of this. I can see Hazel and not think we are going to run off into the sunset together.

This meet up might be the kick in the ass I need to finally realize that she isn't the girl for me, and things aren't going to work out between us. This might be my only shot, and I've got to take it. I deserve to be happy, too.

Damon and Liam have both found their soul mates and it's my turn to do the same. And maybe tonight, I'll be able to finally find out if that's Hazel or someone else entirely.

6

HAZEL

*D*amon's wedding proved to be a good event, and I found out a lot of information I wouldn't have otherwise. Out on the dance floor, lots of women were talking about Aiden, and from experience. Has he been sleeping around all these years? It shouldn't bother me because we aren't together, but it does. Some part of me thought maybe he is still hung up on me, and as shitty as it sounds, it made me feel wanted. My heart will always have space for Aiden, but sleeping around isn't my thing. It doesn't seem from the way they talked; he has any interest in settling down or being with one woman, and they might be fine with that, but I'm not.

Jeremy drives us back to my dad's house, and I relieve the woman we hired to keep an eye on him while we are out. He isn't liking the babysitting, but at this point, we have to be safe. Jeremy moved in to help, but he has to work, and can't be here all the time. So, help is necessary.

"So, are you excited for your drinks?" Jeremy asks, leaning into the open fridge.

My butt hits the granite countertop as I lean over and cross my arms. "We're catching up. Regardless of our dating history, we've known each other for many years."

He can see right through me and has always been good at that. Okay, so maybe I'm going to drink to find out more about him, and what's going on in his life since I've been away. Is that so bad? He acts like I'm going to seduce him and leave him again. I'm not that much of a bitch.

Yet, we are both adults, and I'm not going to lie, if he wants to take me back to his place and have his way with me, I'll be inclined to say yes. It's been too long since a man has touched my body, and I won't have many opportunities to be with Aiden while living halfway across the country. Hell, maybe that's the closure we both needed to move on and find someone.

"All I'm saying is to be careful. Neither of you needs to get hurt again. Adults or not."

I know he's looking out for us, and it's sweet. Blood might not relate us, but he's the best brother I could have ever asked for in my life.

"I've got to go change. No way I'm wearing this dress to Dixie's," I say, wisping out of the room and up the stairs to the guest bedroom.

My suitcase lays open on the bed, and I start going through all the items I brought with me. What the hell should I even wear? Jeans and a t-shirt might be to blah, but a dress seems like a date, and I don't want to send the wrong impression. Screw it. Black jeans and a red V-neck with black flats will be fine. It's casual enough for it not to look like a date, but still reminding him of all the great things we have done in red.

As I'm walking down the stairs, Jeremy is waiting for me at the bottom, arms crossed.

"Don't stay out too late. An UBER is waiting outside. I've got to work tomorrow," he says, trying to keep a serious face.

"Okay, dad," I say, sarcastically.

He rolls his eyes at my comment.

After exiting the house, and slipping into the car waiting outside, my hands start to sweat. Tonight might be a disaster or what both of us need to move on. Either way, I have to go into it with hope that he will be willing to help me with my plan to see Jake.

"We're here, ma'am."

I fumble with my seatbelt and get out of the car. "Thank you."

I have never been inside Dixie's, but my dad used to come here often. *You can do this.*

A couple of girls head toward the door, and I go in behind them, looking around for Aiden. My eyes search around the room, and then land on the corner table, with his eyes locked on me.

My mind starts to wonder how many girls he has picked up in this bar and taken home? Probably a good number, considering his charm and good looks. *Don't think about that. Focus on what you are here for, damnit.*

"Hey! It's so loud in here," I say, joining him.

"Yeah, you get used to it, though. You wanna drink?"

"Vodka Tonic."

He holds his hand up and gets the attention of the bartender to order mine. "So, how the hell have you been?"

Instead of taking it slow, inching into conversation, my mouth starts blurting out information. "Graduated from Harvard, and work at a law firm now."

"That's freaking incredible. I always knew you would do something great. Are you happy?"

Isn't that a loaded question? Happy in what part of my life?

"Like, do you like what you do?" he reiterates.

"Oh yeah. I worked on a case that helped get a man out of prison. Was there for over twenty-years and wrongfully convicted. I'm making a difference."

He smiles, and nods. "That's how I feel. Fighting fires and helping keep the community safe is what I was brought up to do."

His family goes back generations for being firemen and to carry on that legacy from his father is amazing. He always talked about it when we were younger, and I know it meant a lot to him.

"So, are you seeing anyone?" he asks, after taking another sip and setting it back on the table.

"Divorced. Not sure I'm up for anything after that douchebag."

His brows furrow. "What idiot didn't want to be married to you?"

My eyes fall to the table. "He cheated on me. So, at that point it was mutual."

It's weird to talk about my ex-husband with Aiden, but it also makes me feel good to know he still thinks highly of me after everything.

"What a fucking moron. Men never notice a good thing when they have it. He'll regret it."

The waitress brings me my drink, and I start to chug it. He's wrong. Aiden always made me feel wanted and needed, and my dumbass is the one that walked away from that. So, he might sleep around, but at least he would never cheat on me.

"Enough about me. So, what's going on with you?" I ask, the straw still in my mouth.

He runs his fingers through his hair and looks around the room. "Nothing really. Single. Oh, I bought a house and traveled a little bit. That's pretty much it."

Is he leaving around his risqué lifestyle on purpose? Maybe he's scared of what I might think, but he shouldn't be. It's not like it matters.

"Dating anyone?"

"Nope. To be honest, I never quite got over you," he starts to back-track, "but that's not why we are here. I'm not like expecting anything to happen between us or anything."

I try to keep my excitement inside, but a smile takes over my face. "Listen, we left things pretty tainted after graduation and there isn't a day that goes by that I don't feel horribly for that."

He gets the bartender's attention again to get another round of drinks, or maybe to change the subject.

"Let's not talk about that, okay. We can't change the past. All I care about is my present and future. No more harping on that."

He changes the subject by telling me about some duplexes he and his brothers purchased to help out Grapevine. Apparently, they are all saints, and every time I think they can't surprise me anymore, they do. Who knows how much they spent to get those, and they aren't even charging rent or anything? That's noble.

Aiden has always been a good guy, but no one ever noticed. They always thought about him as the stuck-up jock, but they never gave him a chance. Matter of fact, we officially met while volunteering at the homeless shelter. He probably didn't announce to the world he was doing it, but still. It's there that we started hanging out, and then blossomed into more than friends. So, Aiden wanting to do something nice for the community isn't surprising to me at all.

"You know, I still don't understand why some woman hasn't snatched you up yet. It's insane."

And then he opens his mouth but stops.

"What?"

He shakes his head. "Nothing. When do you head out?"

"Not sure yet. Got some things to take care of first."

"Like what?"

My hands fall into my lap, as I start to play with my fingers. This is a good of a time as any.

"There have been some things that I need to take care of while in town..."

"Well, don't let me keep you. Go get that done, and we can meet up another time before you leave," he says, getting up from the table.

"Oh, no. I mean, you."

He sits back down, and his eyes are searching my face for answers. "What do you mean?"

Shit. I'm not ready for this. The man I still love is never going to forgive me.

"Just fucking tell me. You being quiet is only making matters worse."

I fill him in on the situation about my ovarian cancer. Not many people know about it, including Jeremy or my dad. I don't want them to worry about me.

"Holy shit. Are you gonna be okay? Can I do anything?" He grabs my hand.

"I'm okay now, but won't be able to have children."

I might've given Jake up for adoption, but it never crossed my mind that I wouldn't be able to have children later in life. It only makes me regret my decision even more.

"What do you need from me? I'm confused."

I look deeply into his eyes. "There is a way that we might be able to see our son. And the only way it will work is if you are on board."

"I was wondering when he would come up in conversation."

He sits back, and motions for me to continue.

"So, you didn't sign any of the adoption paperwork."

"And I wouldn't have," he replies.

"Well, that is going to help us. You can write a letter to the adoption agency requesting information. Just claim you knew nothing about it until now, and want to know how he is. They might send it off to the couple."

"And why would they let us see him? It's been eight years. He's only known them."

"They might not, but it's worth a shot. To see Jake. I'll give anything."

Aiden's fingers tap on the table, as he looks around the room. "Why didn't you just keep him? I know you were young and all that, but we could've done it. And we wouldn't be in this fucking situation."

Coming into this catch up session, I knew that ill feelings are bound to come out. Did I prepare myself for it? A little bit.

"Listen, I regret it every day, but I can't change it. I've come here to beg you to help me."

"Did you not think I would be a good dad?" His eyes closed for a minute, and then his fists clenched.

"I'm so fucking sorry, Aiden. It was stupid and I should have never done it, I know that."

His eyes open, and fueled with fire. "He's eight years old and never met his real parents. Hell, he probably doesn't even know that he's adopted. Out there with strangers instead of us."

The music is too loud for most of the drunk inhabitants to even notice our conversation, but it didn't make it less embarrassing.

"I," I start to respond, but he cuts me off.

"I would have taken care of you and our child..."

This time his fists hit the table, and he stands up.

Tears start to fall from my eyes, I've never seen him like this. Frothing with rage. It's scary.

"I'm done with this conversation for now."

And just like that, Aiden walks out of the bar, leaving me there balling.

Did I expect him to react like that? In a way, but not so loud. It's not like he would hit me or anything. All our history has been wiped and who knows if he will ever talk to me again.

I pull myself together, order an UBER, and go home. If I can't get him to help me, we might never get to see our son. He needs some space, I get it, but he has to talk to me. The only way we are ever going to know how he is doing is if we work together. He might hate me, but Jake is his son, and he isn't the type of guy to let that go.

7

AIDEN

*T*he carpet is going to have a rut in it after I'm done. My mind keeps going over why in the world she would come to me with this now? She said we would never be able to contact the family, and so the hope for it has dwindled down slowly over the years of ever getting the chance to meet Jake. Yet, here she is, saying I can write a letter and they might let me meet him. What the hell? He's eight years old, why didn't she say anything about this before now?

Sure, I wasn't ready to be a father then, but I sure as hell would've stepped up. It irritates the piss out of me, that my child is out there being raised by someone else. He is going to grow up and think I didn't want him, and that couldn't be further from the truth.

My mind goes over all the things I've missed out on as his parent. All his firsts as a baby, plus first day of school, and probably first sports game. So many things I would have never missed if I was able to be a part of his life. Hazel took the chance away from me, and now she wants my help. I understand her regretting the decision, but why didn't she think of this sooner? Why now?

I love her, but I never put two-and-two together about how enraged I have been since the adoption. Listen, I get it, being eighteen and finding out we were going to parents' was scary, but I still think we could have provided for him. If Hazel would've let me, Massachusetts isn't such a bad place to live, and I could have watched him during the day while she was in school, and worked at night. Instead, she never even gave me the option and I think that is what infuriates me the most. I didn't let myself see the repercussions of her decision that would affect my life.

My life would be different had we raised Jake. I'd be a proud dad, and we would play catch out in the yard, and watch football games together. Maybe Hazel and I would have worked out, and she would still have graduated. The *what if* is what gets everyone. Not knowing what would of happened, but wondering what if about all our decisions.

My hand swipes across my face, trying to pull myself together, because at some point, we are going to have to work things out. I'm going to have to talk to her about this, and say some possible harsh words, but if I keep it all bottled up inside, it's only going to eat at me.

The inherent drinking problem of mine is getting worse, and as much as I'd love to stop, it's not that easy. It's how I ease my pain, and deal with stuff. Is the fact that this has been eating away at me silently the reason for this problem? It could be, but I can't take that out on Hazel.

The possibility of getting any sleep tonight is gone, and the only thing that will calm my brain will be getting answers. My eyes look at the time on the clock, thinking she might already be asleep, but I pull up Instagram and ask for her phone number.

It might be late, but there are things I need to say to her, and if I don't do it now, who knows if I'll ever say them. Hazel might be the girl I've never gotten over, but we still have our qualms.

My phone dings, and a notification with her number leads me to call her.

"Hello?"

"It's Aiden."

The silence on the other end tells me that she isn't able to sleep either. Maybe this is fucking with her as much as me. "Can we talk? In person?"

"I'm staying at my dad's."

"I'll send an UBER." Hazel doesn't respond, but I can hear her breathing. "See you in a bit."

Hazel coming over is the best way for us to work through this, and yes there might be some arguing and possibly screaming, but it is needed. She needs to tell me what made her make this decision besides Harvard? Why didn't she trust me? Even if she didn't want to be with me, though she never said that, I never would have abandoned my son. Sometimes, I think back and wonder why I didn't stand up for myself. Legally, I could have talked with an attorney and gotten custody possibly, since she didn't want to keep him. Why didn't I? If I did, then neither of us would have these regrets right now, or have to fight to even know how Jake is doing.

I go to the fridge and grab another beer, knowing I'm going to need it with the conversation that's coming ahead. Hazel will undoubtedly tell me things that I might not want to hear, but both of us need to get this off our chests while we can. Once she's back in Massachusetts, who knows how long until I hear from her again.

A rap sounds at my door, and I hustle over to open it.

"Hey."

Hazel walks in, staring down at her hands, not making eye contact, and takes off her coat, sitting it on the back of the couch.

"Have a seat. I think they are some things we need to discuss. And not just about our son."

She sits down on the far end, and covers her face with her hands briefly before pulling them away. When she finally faces me, her eyes are red, and her makeup smudged. Fuck. I hate seeing women cry.

"Go ahead. I'm a horrible fucking person. I know," her voice breaks.

My hand waves around, and my pulse elevates. "No, but it should have never happened. We could have raised him. Or just me."

"How the hell did you plan on taking care of a child, Aiden? Neither of us had jobs. Besides college dorms, we lived with family."

"I would have changed my whole world to have Jake in my life. You didn't even give me a chance!"

Tears start spilling down her face, and she wipes them with her shirt sleeve. "Listen, I can't take back what I did. It's done. That's why I'm here asking you to help. Do you want me to beg?"

Hazel isn't acting like the same girl. She would have never begged for anything, let alone bawl in front of someone. When we were younger, her emotions were in check, and half the time I didn't even know if something was bothering her. Adulthood has definitely changed her. Is it evil to say I like being able to see her emotions?

"All you have to do is write a letter stating you didn't consent to the closed adoption and would like the parents to reconsider. They may reject it, but we won't know unless we try. Aiden, please. You have to do this."

I scoot closer, only a couple inches away from my leg touching hers. "I'll do it."

The laptop is retrieved from the counter and I bring it over to the coffee table. What do I even say? *Sorry my old girlfriend gave our baby up, but I want to know him now.* I sound like a douchebag. My eyes run over the blank screen opened on Word and my fingers hesitate. "I don't think I can lie and say I didn't know about it."

"Then what are you going to say?" she asks, scooting closer to me.

"The truth."

My fingers start typing away, letting my heart and soul spill out onto the page, hoping this would be enough for them to think about letting me see Jake. If they don't, at least I can say I tried to be there for him.

Hazel is right about one thing. We didn't have jobs, and this couple had the means to provide a good life for our child. Instead of thinking badly about them, we should be thanking them for giving him a life that at eighteen we couldn't provide.

After ten minutes of combing through the letter, trying to come up with better word usage, I read it aloud to her.

Dear Jake's Parents,

You may or may not receive this letter, but my hopes are that you do. I have some things I need to get off my chest.

My name is Aiden Jackson and I live in Grapevine, Texas. I am the biological father of your son. First off, I would like to thank you for supplying him with a stable home and providing him with everything he has needed over the last eight years. The regret of giving him up is weighing heavy on my heart, and I want to make sure he knows that we did want him. I wanted him. However, at eighteen, neither his mother or I could have given him the life we wanted for him. Hazel made the hard decision for both of us to let you adopt him.

My letter to you is to ask for something. I understand she agreed to a closed adoption, but I would never forgive myself if I didn't ask to at least receive a picture or updates on how he is doing. Just to know my son is being taken care of, and in a good place.

I understand this is completely up to you, and you have every right to say no, but please consider it for both Hazel and I's sakes. We are worried that Jake will grow up and think that we didn't want him, and that's not the case.

Before the adoption was finalized, Hazel did tell me that you had been trying with no luck to have children and that Jake would be a blessing in your life, and I hope he is your ray of sunshine on a bad day.

Even if you don't want to communicate with us on his behalf, please tell him when the time is right that we loved him and still do every day. We would be happy to meet him and get to know him if he ever wants that.

Here is my cell phone number in case you want to talk. 818-856-8954

Sincerely,

Aiden Jackson

Our eyes meet as I finish the letter, and tears are present. I only get one shot at making a case for us, and it might be long, but it gets our message across. We deserve to at least have a picture of him, even if we never get to meet him.

"I think it's perfect. Never knew you were so great with words."

"There are still some things you don't know about me," I laugh.

I send it to the printer, and fold it up nice. "Here you go."

"I'll put a stamp on it and mail it tomorrow. Thank you for doing this," Hazel says, getting up from the couch and grabbing her jacket.

"Listen, it's late. Why don't you crash on my bed?"

"I don't think that's appropriate." Her eyes glance at me, but not for long.

"I'll sleep on the couch."

She nods, and follows me into my bedroom, which is not neat, and sits on the bed. "Could I borrow a shirt to sleep in?"

The thought of her in one of my shirts arouses me. What is it about seeing women in our t-shirts that is sexy? There's something about it, especially when they aren't wearing anything underneath.

I walk over to the closet and grab a Longhorns t-shirt, and toss it to her. "I don't have anything long, sorry. Get changed. I'll see you in a couple hours."

My eyes avert from her, and I close the bedroom door behind me. Did I want to sleep on the couch? Hell no, but it seems presumptuous to sleep in bed with her. Sure, we have done it plenty of times, but that was when we were younger.

As I sit down on the couch, it occurs to me that I never changed out of my suit from the wedding. I should've changed while in there, but it slipped my mind. Is she already asleep?

"Hazel?" I say, knocking lightly.

"Come in."

"Hey, I need to grab some night clothes." I gesture to my suit. "Can't sleep in this comfortably." A pair of grey sweatpants and a t-shirt is found and I leave her be again.

As I lay on the couch, wishing I could fall asleep, having her this close to me makes me think about how things were between us before graduation. I grab my phone off the coffee table and pull up social media to scroll through old photos of us. Every waking moment was spent together, in between classes, at lunch, after school studying, and when we weren't in the same room, texts were exchanged. There was something about her that kept me intrigued since I met her volunteering at the homeless shelter that summer. My dad had already passed, and honestly, I was still grieving and trying to figure out how to help my mom around the house and take any pressure off her that I could. Hazel became my rock quickly. I could talk to her about anything without being judged like the football team. They all called me a pussy and told me to stop crying. She never did that. When my mother passed away, she stuck by me all night, holding me, and listening to me cry inconsolably.

This is when my feelings peaked, and I never wanted to let her go. You see, my parents, they were great, but there is something about having someone intimately know you and still continue to come back around. I was fucked up when she met me, between the loss of my dad, and trying to figure out who I wanted to be. Everyone at school referred to me as the jock quarterback, but I was more than that, and Hazel was the first person to take the time to get to know me.

What would have happened if I didn't sign up to volunteer that summer? I went back and forth on it for almost a month. My high school years were undoubtedly better because of Hazel being by my side. Would I have ended up that dumb jock everyone thought I was? Who knows.

Up pops the pictures of us on prom night, one of my fondest memories. Honestly, prom is the signification of the end of high school, and becoming an adult. I was foolish and never thought we wouldn't stay together, and maybe that's my fault. I shouldn't have assumed. Yet, the night went as well as could be expected.

Some couples have sex in high school, not knocking it, but Hazel was the type of girl who wanted it to be with someone special. I get it, you only have one first time. She mentioned that she was ready, and when I showed up at her house and she walked down the staircase in that ravishing red dress, I started to drool. She knew what the color red meant, and the night went perfect. That's why I always compliment her when she wears red. It brings me back to that moment in time, when we were young and in love. Oh what I wouldn't do to go back to those days and have her in my arms again.

8

HAZEL

My eyes burn from all the crying I've done tonight, but that's what happens when you keep your emotions suppressed for a long time. I should have known Aiden would still be upset about the adoption. After all, I didn't give a choice in the matter, and with my regrets making the decision, I never stopped to think how he would feel. Now I know that he's outraged, and he has every right to be. If I could go back and keep him, I would. The nights I've stayed awake, wondering how he is doing, or if he looks like me, those will never go away.

I curl my knees up to my stomach, and snuggle the blanket closer, trying to get comfortable. His bed is nice, but what I wouldn't give to be in my own bed right now. The smell of him from his t-shirt reminds me of our happy days. This is the same cologne he wore in high school, and it brings back so many memories.

Our first actual date, at the diner, we snuggled up in the booth, and talked about life. We ended up hanging out there for almost three hours, and that's when I found out more about him. His dad's passing, the family of firefighters, and his aspiration to get a college scholarship playing football. At the end of the night, he walked me back to my dad's house, and kissed me on the doorstep. Afterwards, he pulled me in close, and told me he was going to marry me someday.

Why couldn't I be wrapped up in his arms again? I think about it, and before I can talk myself out of it, the bedroom door opens.

"Aiden, you awake?"

His head peeks up over the back of the couch. "Everything okay?"

"I can't sleep. You might as well sleep in your own bed."

"No, I'm fine here. There's no way I'm making you sleep on the couch, Hazel."

"Okay, then we can both sleep in the bed."

He runs his fingers through his hair, and stares at me. "Are you sure? I don't want to make you uncomfortable."

"If anything, it will help me sleep. Come on."

He gets up, and walks past me to the bed. "You sure?"

I nod, and take my place on the right side, raising the covers up to my shoulders. Would he get upset if I slept on his chest? I roll over, laying my head on his chest and he doesn't move or say anything. Instead, his hand rests on my arm and brings me in closer.

Why did I leave this man behind? He could have been a wonderful husband, but instead, I'm divorced already. Even with the regrets, and pain from the adoption, he still cared for me. It is mutual.

"I'm so sorry for leaving you behind. We would have been great together."

He rolls over, to look me in my eyes. "Listen, I'm still in love with you. Please don't lead me on. You are going back to Massachusetts," he says, before he puts me back in position and closes his eyes.

He's right. This is not the time to be confessing my feelings. Massachusetts is my home now, and the law firm makes me work to the bone every day, and focus on the case primarily, with little time for any relationships. And as much as I would love to see if we can make it work, we live too far apart. The commute alone isn't going to work, and neither one of us is going to leave our jobs to move. Long distance relationships never work, especially when you work as many hours as I do every day.

AROUND SEVEN IN THE MORNING, I leave without waking him up, as I figure he is still not a morning person, and dropped the envelope in my father's mailbox to be picked up today. Jeremy is waiting for me on the porch.

"Seriously? Did you go back out last night?"

"Yes. I'm twenty-six-years-old, you know. I don't need a babysitter."

"I don't know about that. Assuming you were over at Aiden's perhaps?" He takes a sip of his coffee and side eyes me.

"So? It's not like we slept together or anything."

He laughs. "Well, I would hope not. No need opening old wounds for only a visit."

I walk past him, and inside to make myself a cup of coffee. Jeremy has always been great at reading me, and that means he knows my feelings for Aiden are still there. It's hard to miss.

My hand reaches up into the cupboard to grab a mug while I brew a new pot of coffee and then pour some French vanilla creamer into the mug. Another comical thing, I never drank coffee until I met Aiden. This obsession with it is all his fault.

Jeremy comes inside, and leans against the counter. "I love you, sis. What's going on? I know something was up and you're going to tell me eventually, so might as well tell me now."

God he's good. Should I tell him about Jake? He's going to be so pissed at me for not informing him sooner.

The brew stops and I pour it into my cup watching the steam rise. "Okay, but you can't get mad at me."

"So, you did sleep with him?"

"No. It's something else. Happened after graduation. No one but Aiden and I know."

He sets his mug down and crosses his arms. "You didn't even tell me? I'm offended."

Instead of beating around the bush, I jump right in and tell him about Jake, the adoption, the parents, and how I haven't seen him since the day of his birth.

"Why wouldn't you call me? You shouldn't have gone through all that alone."

"Aiden knew and wanted us to keep the baby. Of course, now, I think we should have, too, but it was too late."

He pulls me in close and hugs me. "I'm so sorry you had to go through that. So, did you know anything about him? Any pictures?"

"Nothing. Aiden wrote a letter to the parents, hoping that they will at least send us some pictures, or something. We want to know how he is doing, and that he is okay."

"Don't blame ya. You know, you could've told me, right? I wouldn't have judged you. In the end, it was your decision to make."

We stand in the kitchen, enjoying our coffee, and chatting. Jeremy is seeing a girl named Abbie. His concern is between working and taking care of dad, he won't be able to spend a lot of time on a new relationship and he's worried she won't understand. If she gets upset about it, then Abbie obviously isn't the right woman for him. Plain and simple. If anything, it should make her like him more for taking care of his father in his time of need.

"I know you guys aren't too serious yet, but I'd like to meet her before I leave."

"We'll see."

Things haven't been easy for Jeremy while I've been gone. We have both been keeping things from each other, and that needs to end now. Blood or not, we are siblings, and that means I'm there for him, no matter what. He shouldn't feel the need to keep things from me anymore. The chances of him and Dad moving to Massachusetts are high once he starts getting worse, and he can't keep an eye on him by himself anymore. And I need to be able to leave her knowing he is going to be truthful and keep me in the loop.

He leaves to get ready for work, and I slump down on the couch to enjoy some old westerns with my dad, and finish my coffee. I don't know how many more times I'll get him like this; in a good mood, and coherent. Right now, I need to focus on spending some time with him, and enjoying the last times he'll be like this. Everything I have read, it shows to be a significant jump in demeanor, and the fact he has already had it for months means I have even less time than I thought.

"So, now that you are retired, what do you think about moving up with me eventually?"

His eyes narrow. "What do you mean? This is my home, kiddo. I spent most of my adulthood here with your mom."

When mom passed, he did everything he could to keep us going, and sometimes he dropped the ball, but we never faulted him for it. She is the one that kept us afloat between working, cooking, and laundry. We all had to relearn priorities when she was gone.

"I know, dad. Just thought it would be nice to have you around up there. That's all."

This isn't something I would push for right now, but when he gets worse, there won't be a choice. He isn't going to want to be in a home, and don't think I could fathom someone else taking care of him. I've heard way too many heinous stories about retirement centers.

"You staying for a couple days?" he asks.

"Probably until Monday."

9

AIDEN

My heart races after my hand sweeps the covers, finding her gone.

"Hazel, are you here?"

I sit up looking around the room, and notice her clothes are now gone and my t-shirt at the end of the bed. Why did she leave without saying goodbye? I could have made breakfast. A laugh escapes, cooking isn't my strong suit, but I could've tried.

The clock shows it's barely nine in the morning, and I'm never up this early. When did she leave? Hazel snuggling up on my chest basically put me into a coma, and I didn't wake up once, which is abnormal for me. Usually, I wake up a couple times a night, and toss and turn.

Being next to her, the aroma of sweet pea in her hair coupled with her body warmth just made it that much easier to sleep. I always sleep alone, because even when I have women over, they leave before I go to bed. This prevents them from getting the wrong idea. Yet, I wish Hazel had been here when I woke up. She is the only girl that has ever slept in a bed with me.

I grab my phone and type out a message.

Me: *You didn't have to leave.*

Things might be a little crazy and emotional, but that doesn't mean we aren't still friends. We did start as friends, and that will never go away.

Hazel: *I took my dad his favorite donuts. You know, like you used to do every Saturday morning before we went to the diner.*

She's right. Saturdays were always so much fun. I'd head down to the local bakery and pick up a half dozen of blueberry cake donuts for her father. He loved anything blueberry. It's almost an obsession. We would have a cup of coffee, eat, and then head over to the diner for some more coffee the two of us. Most of the day, we goofed off, studied or whatever needed to be done.

Me: *I'm sorry for being a jerk. We both have regrets. Let's work together.*

Things did get a bit crazy and emotional yesterday, and I can't fault myself for that. I've been holding that shit in for eight years, and needed to get it off my chest. Am I worried that it might have been too much for her? I don't like that she perceives herself as a horrible person because of the adoption. Girls get pregnant at young ages, sometimes. Many of them regret giving up their child later on, but it's hard to know what your life is going to be like. At that point, she did what she thought was best for Jake.

How are we supposed to know how our lives were going to turn out? Things could be different, yes, but it's not like we can do a compare and contrast on which set of parents would make him become a better person or give him what he needs? Each of us is going to feel like we could have done it better. My thought process is this, he's our son, but they are raising him. We need to remember that the bond they share is as important as the one we hope to gain with him one day.

I know Hazel's past in the foster care system is probably another reason why she regrets her decision, but she isn't her parents. She found parents who can provide him with a good life. They have money and careers. Unfortunately, the system is paying some parents and they only take in children for the extra money. As she has told me in the past, her first couple homes, she didn't even see that money. Yes, I know, it is not hers, but the first two homes, the parents were alcoholics and once that check came in, they would be drunk for the whole next week. Binging and ignoring the children. This is not what the money should be spent on. I'm she got out of there and got adopted by a great family.

If the letter makes it to the parents, I hope they will reconsider the closed adoption. I know it's a long shot, but have to take the chance. Even if they only give me pictures of him, it's better than nothing. There is always a chance of getting to know him after he's an adult. Ten years is a long time to wait, but I'll do it if I must.

It's time to get up and start my day. Sitting here, worrying isn't going to do me any good. My arms stretch, a yawn escapes, and then my feet hit the ground, taking me into the bathroom to start the shower. The steam always helps me wake up faster, so I brush my teeth while waiting for the water to heat up.

My phone starts to ring, playing Liam's ringtone, and I hesitate whether I want to answer it or call him back when I'm done.

"Hey brother. What's up?"

"What you got going on today?"

"Nothing so far. Just got up and about to take a shower."

"Thought it would be nice for you, me, Harper, Jeremy, and Hazel to meet up while she's in town. You game?"

First, he's telling me to stay away from her, and now he wants to hang out? What's gotten into him? "Sure. Just tell me when."

"We are meeting at the diner in about an hour."

Jesus, an hour? Why is he just now calling me then? "Okay, well I'm getting off here to shower then. See ya in a bit."

My happy ass runs to the shower and jumps in, lathering the body wash, and letting the warm water cascade off my body. For a moment, I thought someone is running their fingers down my back, but it's a memory. One weekend when her dad went out of town, I stayed over at their place, and we showered together. It only happened once, but I can still feel it.

After all the soap from my body is off, I take the shampoo into my hands and lather it into my hair, letting it soften, for a couple minutes before washing it out. Am I the only one that has the most unique thoughts in the shower? Like how come we never know it's the best days until it's over? Now, to be fair, I didn't know Hazel was going to turn my proposal down, but I wish I knew to savor and drink up every minute before graduation. You know, recognized them as the good days.

After washing the shampoo out of my hair, I grab the towel and wrap it around my waist. Even when I'm alone, it's weird to walk around naked. Technology these days can be hacked and I didn't want myself posted all over the internet from some hacker using my laptop webcam. Maybe I'm a little paranoid, but it pays to be cautious.

Inside the closet is a row of hung up t-shirts and then a dresser with all of my bottoms. What should I wear today? I pull up the weather that shows it to be chilly today, so I grab a long sleeve t-shirt and jeans.

My phone buzzes.

Hazel: *They picked up the letter. Fingers crossed.*

I don't reply, because we are meeting up in like twenty-minutes, and we can chat after. Has she told her family about Jake? My brothers have no idea about it, and wondering if I should wait until Damon is back before saying anything. I can hear them now, they are already think I'm immature and reckless. This is going to give them more ammo.

I grab my keys off the counter, and leave my house, heading to the diner. We will see how this goes. It's the first time Liam has seen her, too, so who knows what kind of questions he is going to ask and what answers she will give. Is she even going to talk to me?

The diner isn't busy yet, so I park on the street in front, and go inside, seeing them already in a booth in the corner. Just like old times.

"Hey guys."

I haven't eaten yet, and my stomach is growling.

"Have a seat. Hazel is telling us about Massachusetts and her fancy job as a lawyer at this law firm."

Let's be real, here. I always knew she would reach her dream. Hazel is nothing but persistent. Her dream of helping innocent people overturn their convictions has been around since before I met her. I love her thirst to make the world a better place, and to help rid the justice system of its racial misconduct. When we were only fifteen, she made me watch a documentary about a man who spent fifteen years behind bars for a murder he didn't commit. It took him fifteen years to get a judge to over-turn his conviction. The evidence was circumstantial at best, and the jury only took half an hour of deliberating before finalizing the guilty verdict. The lawyers worked together, finding jury bias and tampering evidence, and were able to finally get him out of prison. The man ended up getting a four million settlement for being wrongfully convicted.

She looks at me, and continues to talk. "I work a crazy amount of hours. Half the time I forget to eat. But I love it."

Hazel is one of those that let passion lead them. It's a good thing. It's what is going to make her a wonderful lawyer, because she is persistent and won't give up until she gets the truth or justice that her client deserves. As much as it pains me to remember that she left me behind, it was for good reason. Look at what she has become. A lovely, confident, strong willed woman who has followed her dream and continues to do so every day.

"So, I have so many questions," Harper says.

Those two start talking about true crime cases, and Liam and I smile. As a man, we know that sometimes they consider another woman around a threat, but not Harper. Like she needs to worry anyways. Their relationship is solid. Liam would never cheat on her. He's not that type of man. Our daddy taught us better than that.

Liam jumps in the conversation and changes the subject. "So, you seeing anyone?"

Hazel looks at me, and chuckled. "No. Just got divorced a little while ago."

Liam's head cocked back. "Oh, I'm so sorry. I didn't know."

The mood shifts and everyone is silent including Jeremy. He has been eyeing me, and that means Hazel has probably told him about Jake. Does he think I'm a piece of shit? Hopefully he knows the whole story, and that I didn't want to give him up.

"Well, I think it's time for me to go. We don't like leaving dad alone too long by himself anymore," Hazel says.

What is she talking about? "Why?"

Jeremy gestures for her to go, and then tells us about their father. Why didn't she mention that last night? Poor thing is dealing with all these regrets and now this. It makes sense how emotional she is right now, given the situation with her father, finding out she can't have kids, and Jake. All that together is bound to fuck up your head.

The conversation continues, but I dip out early. We used to tell each other everything, and not knowing about her dad's condition hurts. Why wouldn't she tell me? She is the only one that kept me sane when my mother passed. Without her, who knows what kind of trouble I would have gotten into. Right now, she is going to need a support system, and I need to make it clear that I'm a part of that.

Friends until the end.

10

HAZEL

*A*s I open his front door, I can hear shuffling going on upstairs. My feet take me as fast as they can up to his bedroom.

"Dad, what's wrong?"

He is on his knees, sobbing into his hands. We shouldn't have left him alone.

"What happened? Where is she?" he asks.

I look around the room and his closet is ransacked with clothes thrown all around. If I didn't know any better I'd think he got robbed. "What are you looking for?"

"Did she leave me? Where is all her stuff?"

It's at that moment it hits me that he is talking about my mom. My father is having an episode and he doesn't remember her passing. How am I supposed to tell him and break his heart? I should have done more research, like how long the episodes last, because there is no sense in rocking his world if he is going to snap out of it quick.

"It's gonna be okay."

I grab my phone and text Jeremy to come home.

My arms wrap around him as he sobs.

"What did I do? I can't lose her."

That's when my eyes start to water. I console him and let him cry.

They met in high school, and both ran for student council president, and that's how their relationship started. The campaign only brought them closer together, trying to take down the other, and in the end, it forged a friendship that turned into love. Before she passed, they were married for fifteen years, and every day we could see how much they cared for each other. Still deeply in love. Their relationship gave me something to look forward to, and helped me have high standards for the men in my life.

I hear the front door open. "Jeremy, we're up here."

Footsteps sound up the staircase and down the hallway, but it isn't Jeremy.

"Are y'all okay?" Aiden asks, kneeling down next to us.

I shake my head, and the tears fall. He brings in me for a hug, and then turns his attention to my dad.

"Why don't we get you some coffee, Mr. Grey?" he asks, and helps me pick him up off the floor.

What is he doing here? Where the hell is Jeremy?

And just like that, my father is back to normal. It's like a switch in his brain clicked and brought him back to reality. I've never been around someone that has had Alzheimer's, so this is a first. Later, I will be doing some more research on episodes so I can be aware of his nature. Are there warning signs or triggers?

"What the heck happened in here?" he asks, looking around his room.

"I was looking for something. Don't worry, I'll put everything back."

It's crazy to see him go from distraught to normal right before my eyes. And to know it's only going to get worse as it progresses.

Aiden looks over at me and back at my dad. "You still want that coffee?"

"No thanks. Already had four cups today."

As we come down the staircase, Jeremy walks in. "What's going on?"

"Nothing, everything's fine," I say, and then bob my head toward the kitchen.

My dad takes his regular spot in his recliner and switches to the discovery channel.

"I rushed over here. Why did you text me?"

"I'm gonna go hangout with your dad and let you two talk," Aiden says.

I nod, and cross my arms. "I came home and found him sobbing on the floor thinking mom had left him."

He doesn't say anything, looks at me, and sighs.

"We need to figure out a plan. I can't leave without knowing he's going to be okay."

"I can handle it. Dad isn't going to a home. I hear horror stories about sending people there."

"Wouldn't dream of that. We do need to figure out how to have someone here with him while you work though. He could've hurt himself."

Aiden steps into the kitchen. "Sorry, grabbing a drink. Not to intrude, but I can help out. Just say the word."

"You don't have to do that."

"I know, but he watched after my parents passed. It's the least I can do."

"Are you sure?" I ask.

Things between us are up in the air, but I don't want him to think he needs to help.

"Hazel, I'd like to help. No big deal."

Jeremy smiles. "See, we can handle it, sis."

I follow Aiden back out to the living room and sit down on the couch. With me leaving soon, spending time with him is a priority. Especially, with him already having episodes.

"Have you seen the new Bruce Willis movie?" I ask.

"There's a new one?"

I take the remote and switch to the movie. "Let's watch it. I know how much you love him."

I press play and drink in the time I have left with him like this. His normal, cheerful self, and enjoy this atrocious movie. See, I can't stand action movies, but he loves them. I'll suffer through it.

Two hours later, I couldn't believe it. Normally, I would've fallen asleep, but it actually held my attention pretty well. Plus my dad kept screaming, "come on, Bruce."

"Well, that was a good movie. Good pick."

Aiden is still sitting on the couch and hasn't moved an inch. I can't believe he stayed.

"What are your plans tonight?" I ask.

"An action movie marathon with your Dad. What do ya say, Mr. Grey?"

Aiden is showing me more and more that he hasn't changed since we were teenagers. He is still polite and well-mannered.

"Sounds like a great idea, but I don't stay up late. We can probably get two more movies in before I crash for the night," he replies.

Using his day off to spend time with my father means the world to me. Aiden is a considerate guy, and coming back here only makes me validate my feelings for him. There's a reason they are still this impactful after all these years. It might take some time for us to work up to it, but I'm not going to let him be the one that gets away. Someday we can be happy together, not right now.

We all sit down on the couch while Aiden puts on another action movie. Instead of finding something else to do, I stay and watch it with them. Jeremy orders pizza and we all scarf that down while trying to finish the movie. So far, I've liked both of the movies we have watched. Can we go three for three?

The next movie is a little older, and not up my alley. I stick by and watch it, but didn't enjoy the last one. When the credits start rolling, they both look at me.

"So, what'd you think?" Dad asks.

"It was alright."

"Kiddo that was a 10/10 movie. It's time for me to head to bed. I'll see you in the morning," he says, stopping to kiss me on the forehead.

Now, Aiden and I are alone. It feels like high school again, being back on this couch together. Yet, so many things have changed.

"You want to watch the new Ryan Reynolds movie?" I ask, picking up the remote and flipping to it. "I've heard it's pretty good."

He smiles, and puts his hand on knee. "I'd love to."

Grapevine has always been home for me, and coming back to visit everyone has had its perks. It's incredible to see the man Aiden has become, Damon and Liam happy, and my brother looking for his happily ever after. Sure, Aiden and I have our qualms, but he isn't holding it over my head and judging me for it and that means everything.

For the duration of the movie, we remain close. He does the smooth trick of putting his arm around me, and I lean into him.

"Listen, I know I'm going back soon, but can we stay in touch? It's been nice seeing you," I say.

He swings his foot over onto the couch, and takes my hand in his. "I'd like that very much. No matter what, we are friends."

When he says that, I feel jaded. Friends? He isn't acting like he only wants to be my friend. "One day, maybe we can try again. When there isn't a thousand plus miles between us."

He nods, and plants a sweet kiss on my lips that leaves me wanting so much more.

"I'll wait as long as I have to. You're worth it."

11

AIDEN

Things between Hazel and I have gotten better ever since the night of the wedding. I think getting all of my regrets and questions off my chest helped us move forward and connect on a deeper level over these past few days. Yet, she is leaving soon and now I find myself wanting her to stay, and be with me, but I'm not selfish and won't do that. She has a whole life up there, and I can't ask her to leave that behind, especially everything she's worked hard for, and move down here with me.

I haven't seen her in two days, and it's probably for the best. My heart is wanting more and right now, but she can't give that to me. We can see how moving on in the past hasn't helped. One thing I'm hopeful for is now that I've spoken my truth, the drinking can slow down. There is no pain to numb anymore.

My grey sweat pants hang off my hips as I pop a sausage egg and cheese biscuit into the microwave for a quick breakfast before heading into work. Today, Liam and I are scheduled, which means I'll be asked a million times if I anything has happened between Hazel and I since she's been back. It's none of his business, but he was there for me after she broke my heart.

I hear my phone start to ring from the kitchen, and I rush to it, hoping it's her.

"Hello?"

An unfamiliar voice is on the other end. "Hi, my name is Mary. Is this Aiden Jackson?"

I take a minute before responding, thinking it's probably a telemarketer. "Yes, who is this?"

She clears her throat. "We received your letter."

Holy fucking shit. It's Jake's mom.

I fall to the floor, and gasp. "I'm so glad you called. Didn't know if I would ever hear back."

"Listen, my husband and I talked and we would like to meet you. You can bring Hazel along, too. We can't make a decision until after that."

They want to meet me? Does this mean they might consider us meeting Jake? A smile plasters on my face. "Just let me know when and I'll ask off work and fly out there."

"Is Tuesday okay?"

I technically work, but I'm sure Aiden would cover for me, but then I would have to tell him about Jake. Am I ready to do that?

"I'll make it. Thank you so much. Let me know the details and we will see you Tuesday."

The phone disconnects, and cheeks are wet. Never in a million years did I think they would call me. Yet, I needed to at least try. The state of shock has not worn off yet, and my hands are trembling. I might get to meet my son. The realization of this is overwhelming, but never would have happened if Hazel didn't come down here and talk to me. I have her to thank for that.

I throw on jeans and a t-shirt and make a pit stop over at Hazel's to let her know the good news before heading to work.

Me: Come outside. Got news.

The front door opens and shuts behind her, and then her arm hooks on my window. "What is it?"

"They called," I say with a smile.

"Who?"

"Jake's parents. They want to meet up on Tuesday. So, looks like both of us are heading to Massachusetts."

For a minute, she doesn't respond, almost like she thought I might be joking. "Wait? Are you screwing with me?"

"No, I'm dead serious."

She spins around and her hands fly up in the air. "Thank you, Jesus."

"So, I'll go on and book the flights in a little bit. Can I stay at your place while I'm there or?"

"Of course. I can't believe this is happening. I told you your letter was good," She says, hitting me in the chest.

She sticks her head through the open window slot and kisses me. "Thank you."

My alarm goes off for work, and as much as I'd love to stay and celebrate this victory with her, my job awaits and if I need to have Tuesday off then I have go in today and talk to Liam about it.

"I gotta go to work. Talk later?"

She nods, and heads back inside.

On the way to work, I think about all the horrible things Liam is going to say when he finds out I have a son that I've never met. How is this going to change his perception of Hazel? I don't want them to fault her for it. And I will stand up for her if Damon or Liam have a problem with it. It's over and nothing can change that decision. No sense in harping on it at this point.

I park my car, and head inside the station. Things can get hectic sometimes, but we haven't had many fires lately. Not that I'm complaining. I hate to see families lose their homes and all their memories. So every shift that goes by without a fire, is a good day in my book.

"Look who is here. Thought maybe you were going to call in and hangout with Hazel instead," Liam says.

"I'm an adult, you know. My decisions, my consequences."

He laughs. "Sounds like something happened. I told you to stay away from her. You can't take another heart break, brother."

I love how he thinks he knows it all, and yet, Jake is unknown to him. Should I tell him or ask for Tuesday off? I haven't made up my mind yet, but if we are going to fly out tomorrow afternoon, that doesn't leave me a lot of time to make a decision.

"Can you work for me Tuesday? I've got to go out of town and take care of something."

"Like what?"

"It's a long story, and I'll explain when I get back. Can you or not?"

He nods, and walks away, possibly finally getting my frustration. I know he wants to know everything but that doesn't mean he gets to. There are some things I like to keep to myself, and even that's hard in a small town.

Pedro walks over, and sits down at the table. "Wanna waste some time playing cards?"

"No, not really. I gotta make a call," I reply, getting up and heading outside for some privacy.

The phone rings three times before she answers.

"Hey, I'll cover the flight. There is a flight that leaves Dallas around two tomorrow afternoon and gets in around eight."

"That works."

"I'll stay Tuesday and come back Wednesday afternoon as long as you don't mind staying an extra day," I say. She can say no, but is it wrong that I want to soak up as much time as I can with her?

"Nope, that's perfect. You gonna take us to the airport or are we going to UBER?"

"I'll drive and leave my truck there. That'll make it easier when I come back to drive home," I reply.

The conversation goes silent, and I want to tell her how excited I am about getting the opportunity to meet his parents, but I don't. Her feelings regarding Jake eat at her, and I don't want her to think I despise her for it. Do I think we could have raised him? Yes, but nothing I can change now. So, all we can do is be on our best behavior when meeting them, and hope they allow us to meet Jake.

"So, when do you go back to work? Aren't you on vacation?" I ask.

"In a week or so. So, I'll be coming back most likely to spend more time with dad before I have to be back at work. Just don't know how much lucid time he has left and it seems to be getting worse. Episodes are getting more frequent."

Hazel doesn't need to stress about going back to Massachusetts because Jeremy and I can handle it. Yet, I know how she is, and she will stress about it anyway, no matter what we say. That's how she is.

"I'm gonna do everything I can to help your brother. We can handle it. You go be a big shot, and make a difference. Talk to ya later."

After I hang up, the flights are booked and the countdown starts. I haven't exactly had anything to look forward to in a long time, so this is exciting. Not only will I be meeting the people responsible for raising my son, but I'm going to do it with Hazel by my side. I'd be lying if I didn't say spending a couple of extra days with her doesn't sound great. Having her close means a lot.

"So, Pedro said he overheard you talking about Massachusetts? You aren't seriously going back to be with her, are you? What the hell has gotten into you? She's only a girl. One that lives thousands of miles away. Do you want to have a long distance relationship? Especially, at twenty-six?"

There he goes again, getting into my damn business. "It's got nothing to do with being with Hazel. Stay out of it until I get back. Fuck."

The end of my shift has finally arrived, and I get in my truck and get the fuck out of there. Liam is pissing me off, sticking his nose where it doesn't belong, and assuming he knows. What is his fucking problem? Why is he so worried about me getting back with Hazel?

Me: Flights are booked.

I set my phone down in my middle console and take off toward my house. The last time I traveled was when I went to Europe, and I still hadn't unpacked my suitcase from that trip all the way. Guess that's what I'll be doing tonight.

As I start up my winding driveway, I see someone standing at my door. Elena? What the hell is she doing here? It's been months. I park my truck and get out. "What are you doing here?"

When she turns around, I see it. The bump. Oh shit. Wait, we never slept without protection and she said she was on birth control, too. There's no way it's mine. Yet, I don't come right out and say that because I'm not that douche that doesn't want to claim a child.

"You're glowing. Congratulations," I say, putting my arm around her.

"Don't worry, it's not yours. We were careful. Listen, I know you guys have those duplexes. Any chance you have one that I can stay in for a couple months?"

"What happened?"

"Well, my boyfriend kicked me out and wants nothing to do with the baby, and I don't have enough to cover a new place yet. Need somewhere to be until I get enough saved up and then I'll be out of your hair."

The last time I saw Elena was about four months ago, it's a small town so everyone pretty much knows everyone, and she came to Dixie's upset that her boyfriend wasn't acting right, worried that he was cheating on her, so drunk me talked her into dumping him and coming home with me. Douchey move, I know.

"Of course, we have one that doesn't have anyone in it right now. Give me a few minutes to change and you can follow me over and we can get you settled in."

She smiles and wraps her arms around me. "Thank you. I didn't know if you would want to help me after I went back to him."

"We all make mistakes, Elena. No sense in me holding it against you. Love is love. I'm going through some struggles right now, too. Why don't you come inside while I shower, it's too cold out here for you to sit in your car."

She follows me inside and takes a seat on the couch. "It's a lot cleaner than I remember. Expecting company?"

"Nope. Barely been home in the last week. I'll be back in ten."

I hurry into my bedroom and turn on the shower, getting the water warm for me while I grab a change of clothes and a towel.

Elena is a nice girl, and yes we have slept together, but like the others, she knew it wouldn't turn into anything serious. I'm glad she still came to me in her time of need.

I slip inside, and the warm water streams down my back as I lather soap all over, and then rinse it off. Normally, I don't take quick showers, but didn't want to leave her out there unattended for too long. She could try to snoop or get into my stuff.

"I'll be out in a second," I scream, while wrapping the towel around my abdomen.

Before I can change, the doorbell rings, and it almost made me jump. I hear the door open, and then Hazel's voice. I come out of the bedroom, and as soon as she sees me, she runs away. Elena shuts the door.

"What the hell is her problem?"

Great, another thing to add to the list for today. Now, I'm going to have to go see her once I get Elena settled and explain. I know exactly what she's thinking. Elena is here and I come out in a towel, freshly showered, she thinks we are having sex. Oh god, she probably saw the bump and thinks I'm the father too. I run my fingers through my wet hair, and shake my head.

"Why did you answer it? You don't live here."

"I'm sorry. Habit, I guess."

I go back into the bedroom, throw on my jeans, t-shirt, and converse. "Let's go. I've got some things that I need to take care of once you are settled in. Follow me over."

The door shuts behind us, and she follows me six blocks over to the two sets of duplexes, me and my brothers own. She's lucky there is one available because usually they are occupied.

"Here you are." I turn the key and open the door. "It's already furnished."

She walks in, and turns around. "These are nice. Wow."

"Here's your key. Make sure you get in touch with me when you leave so I can get it. Do you need help carrying anything in before I go?"

She takes me out to her car, and I lug in the two suitcases into the bedroom. "Let me know if you need anything else."

Right now, I want to go over and make sure Hazel isn't making up stories in her head. We are in a good place right now, and of course, she would show up while I have another girl at my house. If Elena would've not answered, then none of this would've happened. Ugh.

I race over to Mr. Grey's house and knock on the door, and when it opens she doesn't look happy.

"What do you want?"

"Listen, it's not what it looked like. She needed a place to stay and I took her over to the duplexes. There is nothing going on between us."

"Likely story. She's pregnant. Why would she come to you?"

"We slept together a while back and her boyfriend kicked her out after finding out about the baby. She knew I had property. That's it. Don't make this out to be something it isn't."

Her arms fold, and I can tell she isn't believing me.

"We aren't together. So, I'm not sure why I am even defending myself right now. You are going back to your life there and I'll be here. I know I said I would wait for you, but I need to know if you ever see us being together again. We both deserve happiness and I don't want to be strung along like some sad puppy dog."

I put myself out there, because even though I love her, she can't get mad about a girl being in my house if we aren't together. Yet, it seems to have upset her, and that means she still has feelings for me, which is great, but only if we can be together. Maybe it's time for us to have that conversation.

"I know you worked hard to get your position at the firm, and it's everything you have ever wanted, but what I want is you. Honestly, Grapevine is my home, and I can't imagine leaving it behind, but if it means I get to be next to you every day then I'll do it. Say the word."

I don't wait for her to give me answer, instead I walk back to my truck and take off. She needs to think about this because it's a big decision and I don't want her making it too fast. Her answer will determine our future, or lack thereof. I refuse to sit around and wait for a possible future relationship with her, instead of finding someone who can make me happy. All these years I've been fixated on my second chance with her, but it only works if I get it. Otherwise, I am waiting around for someone I'm never going to have a shot with, and ignoring women who actually want to be with me.

One way or another, Hazel is my first love and hopefully, she will make the decision to be my last love, too.

12

HAZEL

*A*s he speeds away, my heart drops. What the hell am I going to do? Jumping back into a relationship with him can be dangerous, especially, when I haven't been divorced long. Of course, I still love him, but what if I screw everything up? He doesn't understand how much I work, and the little amount of time I spend outside the office. It ruined my marriage, and the last thing I want it to do is drive a wedge between Aiden and I.

I sit down on the porch swing, and rock back and forth, trying to figure out what I'm going to tell him. Do I love the idea of being with him again? Yes, but there are so many things we need to talk about. Are we going to be in a long distance relationship? I can't move back to Grapevine yet, eventually maybe, but right now it's not an option. Would he move to Massachusetts and leave his family behind? I find that hard to believe.

It's selfish for me to ask him to move away from Liam and Damon to be with me, and his brothers will see it that way too. Liam has made it clear he doesn't like me and Aiden seeing each other while I've been in town, but he's not my boss. I'm not a teenager anymore, and can make my own damn decisions and so can Aiden. It seems like he has his mind made up.

The next few hours are spent thinking about scenarios and outcomes which only scare me more. If I say yes, and he moves, what happens when or if we don't work out? Our friendship will be ruined, and I could lose him forever. On the other hand, if I don't pursue a relationship with him, it might make him resent me.

The front door opens and Jeremy steps outside. "What are you doing out here? It's like midnight."

"Trying to figure some things out."

"What's going on?" he asks, sitting down beside me. "Let me help."

"Not sure if you want to be a part of this decision."

"I'm your brother. Try me."

I explain everything that's happened since being in town and how Aiden and I are still in love, but with me going back home, he wants me to tell him whether we have a future or not. For the most part, he sits there and listens to me, and doesn't interject. It's actually kind of nice, because it helps me think about things and talking about them out loud makes it more real.

"So, you still love him?"

"Very much."

"Sis, I'll say this. As your brother, it hurt to see you leave for college, and then seeing Aiden broken up about it, too. The whole time you have been gone, he hasn't dated another woman. Might've slept around a bit, but never found a girl worth his time in that arena. I truly believe he loves you with all his heart, and that is hard to find."

"So, you think I should tell him, yes?"

"If he is going to make you happy, then of course. But the decision is yours to make," he says, smiling and slugging my shoulder before walking back into the house.

We leave tomorrow, and that will give us a chance to be alone and see how things go between us. After our trip, I think I'll be able to make a sound decision, but not before.

Me: *I'll have an answer for you after our trip.*

The next day consists of me packing my stuff up, and explaining to Jeremy and dad that I would be back in a couple of days. Jeremy knows about Jake, but dad doesn't. Honestly, with his condition, I don't want to cause him any stress or worry, so it's better if I don't tell him. Although, he would be ecstatic to find out he has a grandson out there in the world.

Aiden: *You almost ready?*

Me: *Yup*

Aiden: *Good. I'm outside.*

We haven't talked since I texted him last night before bed. I'm sure he understands how big of a decision this is and that it will take me some time.

Jeremy takes my suitcase down to Aiden's truck while I give dad a big hug.

"Don't worry. I'll see you in a couple days. Don't watch anything good without me."

The front door opens, and Jeremy and Aiden are talking about something and then cease when I walk up to the truck. "Talking about me?"

"Why would you think that?" Jeremy asks, with a smile.

"Whatever." I jump into his truck. "We've got to get to the airport. Liam said to call him if you need him to come over to help with dad while we are gone."

"Ten-four. Have a good time, lovebirds," Jeremy says, as we are pulling out of the driveway.

We are going to be stuck with each other for the next two days, and hopefully, we don't get sick of each other. This is a good test to see if we still work like we used to.

"So, since we don't meet them until tomorrow... I was thinking we could go out to a nice dinner tonight."

He side eyes me, trying to pay attention to the road. "Oh, really. Are we going Dutch or you going to allow me to pay so it can be an official date?"

"It's still a date even if I pay. Plus, then I don't feel compelled to sleep with you."

Who am I kidding? I'd love for him touch me. Dinner might be what we need to get back into the groove of things. I already know the perfect dress to wear, and he's going to love it.

We get to the airport after a drive of mostly listening to music, and Aiden takes my suitcase from me as we check in and then go through security. The flight isn't that unpleasant, and once we get to my place, he seems shocked.

"You live here?"

I nod, and put the key in the door to open it. "Why?"

"It's nicer than I expected. Don't lawyers usually have to pay back all their loans before they technically make any good money?"

"Scholarships, remember? I didn't have to take any loans besides at the end, and it's not that much."

The home is a recent build with pillars in front of the house, and my favorite part about it is the vaulted ceilings. I've always wanted them. I let him take in the living room, and the grand staircase before he moves into the kitchen.

"Now, this is a kitchen that makes me want to cook."

The double island kitchen has all stainless steel new appliances and granite countertops with radiant navy blue cabinets. The pantry is the size of my old bedroom, and off to the side is the laundry room that could handle a whole team's clothing. It's nice to know I can afford nice things, but other than the house and my car, I spend very little.

"Wanna see upstairs?"

He nods, and follows me up the staircase. "This is the master bedroom. It has a shower and jetted tub in the bathroom with walk in closets and a double sink. The other bedrooms down this hall are nice too with a bathroom in each."

"Exactly how much money do you make now? Holy crap. This reminds me of that show Cribs on MTV a long time ago."

I'm not going to discuss my salary with him, but it's not like he's hurting. He got that trust fund from his parents, and should still have the majority of it. Does he not remember I've been to his house? He's living good too.

"Let's get settled in, unpack our stuff, and then we can go out to dinner," I say. Honestly, traveling always exhausts me, and a nap sounds great, but if I take one, then I know I wouldn't sleep later.

We go back down the staircase and retrieve the luggage. I let him choose which room he wants, and I lug my suitcase on top of my bed to put everything away for now. I'll take new clothes and shoes when I go back, and then I'll deal with the laundry once I've returned from this whole vacation. Normally, I am a very tidy person who doesn't like to leave things lying around, but I am not going to be home for long, and don't feel like doing laundry yet.

After all my things are put away, I take a shower and get cleaned up before we head out for dinner. The water warms up as I gather my outfit to drive him crazy. He loves me in the color red, and a couple months ago I bought this shorter red dress with a lower neckline that accents my long legs, and this will do the trick. He'll be drooling.

Expectations for this date are simple. We are both adults and have history, but we aren't going to jump into anything if we both aren't ready. My body tells me to walk into the bedroom right now, and screw his brains out, but that would be overkill. As a woman, I like to feel wanted, and if anything Aiden is good at doing that with his eyes.

I step in the shower, and let the warm water run over my breasts, as I lather my body wash in my hands and then disperse all over my body. It's his favorite scent of mine; sweet pea. Between this and the dress, I'm totally getting screwed tonight. My thighs quiver thinking about his fingers running down my collarbone, kissing my stomach, and then his lips on areas that haven't had attention in so damn long.

As I get out, I wrap the towel around my breasts and blow dry my hair before getting dressed, as it helps with the waves in my hair. I could straighten it, but that's how I wear it normally and want to go with something different.

A knock sounds on my bedroom door. "You ready yet? I'm starving."

"Give me about ten minutes. Just gotta get dressed."

The towel drops to the floor as I slip on the red dress, black heels, and then line my eyes before opening the door. He's standing there in black slacks and a blue button-up that is bringing attention to his broad shoulders. I wonder if he still has those sculpted abs? I used to love running my hands down them.

"Okay, I'm ready."

His eyes drink me in, and slowly look down my body. "Fuck. That dress is hot."

I smile, and start going down the staircase, and let him follow me, knowing he is going to stare at my ass the whole way to my car. It didn't bother me, because getting all hot and bothered is expected. It makes the night more fun for when we get back.

We close the door behind us, and get in the car. "So, where are you talking me?"

"One of my favorite places. Sit back and enjoy the ride," I reply.

His hand rests on my thigh and every time I go over a sliver of a bump it moves up, leaving me taking a deep breath. The attraction is real and the sexual chemistry we will find out later. Of course, that's a big part of a relationship, and being able to adequately please each other. I have zero doubts in my mind that Aiden will be able to fulfill my every need. Sure, he was my first, but since then we have both slept with other people and learned new things.

I pull into the parking lot of Giovanni's and turn the car off.

"Alright. Already have a reservation so we should be seated quickly. My stomach won't stop growling," I say, opening my door to get out.

"I'm definitely hungry right now," he says, winking at me.

The restaurant is not packed since it's only Monday night, and we get seated within a couple minutes of arriving. Aiden pulls my chair out for me, and then sits across.

"So, what's good here?" he asks, looking over the menu.

"I've tried about everything and haven't found something I didn't enjoy."

He nods, continuing to look it over while the waitress brings us our drinks and bread. And it's to die for. It's like a mixture of Olive Garden breadsticks and Red Lobsters' cheddar bay biscuits. Some of the best bread I've ever had anywhere. If he isn't careful, I might eat it all myself.

"Have you two decided on a main course yet?" the waitress asks, holding her pen and pad. "Any questions about the menu?"

"I think I'm going to have Linguine all'Aragosta o all'Astice," he responds.

"Tonnarelli alle Uova di Riccio for me, please."

The waitress hurries away with a smile to put our order in and this gives us some time to chat before we scarf down our delicious food. Instead of jumping right into a complicated conversation, I start small by asking him how things are going between him and his brothers? It seems that they aren't as close as when I first met them. Or maybe, I'm reading too much into their body language, especially with Liam. When we all met at the diner, he didn't seem that enthused with him or his questions. Or maybe, he is trying to watch out for me. Liam never liked us together, and to be honest, I always thought he had a crush on me.

"Things between us have gotten better over the last year or so. We try to hangout more often, but they still think of me as a child. It's like they are my parents, you know. No matter what, they always think of us as their little babies and not adults. That's how they are."

He goes on to tell me more about things happening lately. Apparently, Liam's girlfriend, Harper, was attacked and put into a coma. When she came out, most of her recent memories were gone, and she couldn't even remember meeting Liam. How scary. I'm glad they were able to work everything out and she gained her memories back. It gives me bad vibes thinking he would have had to get her to fall in love with him all over again. Tessa has problems with her child's father, who apparently kidnapped her from school one day, and had the Jackson's on red alert. They might not get along one-hundred percent of the time, but they are there for each other when it counts the most. Each one of them have their own flaws and problems. Yet, they are practically saints.

"I'm glad to see all of you are firefighters now. Your dad would be so proud," I say, grabbing another piece of bread.

The next question is one I didn't think he would ask, especially at this dinner, but oh well. He asks about my divorce and what happened. The reason behind our failed marriage is exactly why I'm scared to take this leap with Aiden. How do I tell him that I don't want the same thing to happen? My job requires so much of my time, undivided attention, and I love him.

"Sorry, if it's too much to ask."

"No, it had a lot to do with my job. He didn't like the fact that I worked very long hours and didn't give him all of my time. Towards the end, he made me feel like a bitch for spending my time beefing up my career to make a better future for both of us, but he was secretly sleeping with his secretary. He says I made him do it, but I call bullshit."

Things between Roger and I started to go downhill after I took the job at the firm, and he worked as much as I did. Towards the end, it seems like he has a problem with women holding down good jobs. He almost outright said one day that I should be at home when he is, and that my job should never affect my time with him. Yet, I never asked him to do that for me? There are so many reasons why we wouldn't have lasted, but the biggest one is the infidelity. It's one thing I don't forgive.

"Any man who cheats on you is an oblivious asshole who doesn't realize the good thing he has. It's common with people that are insecure. Luckily for me, that opens up the chance for us. And don't worry, I won't let your job affect our relationship. If you chose for us to have one."

His hand is on mine, and our eyes lock. Why can't I answer him? I know he is looking for a decision in the next few days, and this trip is going to help me. Hell, this dinner is already showing me that Aiden has always been and will always be my first love. He knows my struggles and how hard I fought and what I gave up to get where I am today. If I walk away from the firm, all that is for nothing.

The waitress sets down a tray and sets our plates on the table. "Can I get you anything else right now?"

"No, thank you."

Things between us are smoothing out and there are going to be many conversations about our past and what we want for our future. Jake is a big part of that future-- I hope. Tomorrow will determine if we get to meet our son, and that can drastically impact what comes next in our lives.

13

AIDEN

As she opens the door, and we slip inside, the first thing I want to do is push her up against the door and fuck her right here, but I don't. For the first time, I am wondering if not having sex is better right now. We are trying to work out things, and our sexual chemistry is off the charts. It's not something I want to affect her decision.

"That was a wonderful dinner. I'm stuffed," she says, sitting down on the couch, and taking her heels off. "Never disappoints my appetite."

The red dress is hiked up and from where I am standing, I can see the black undies underneath. Fuck.

"I'm not still hungry, that's for sure."

I think about it. Sex. It's something that we are able to enjoy without feeling ashamed about it. It's a way to de-stress and the chemicals it releases help with the feeling of being happy. We both deserve to de-stress, especially with how big of a day tomorrow is, and if she wants to, I'll ravish her all night.

She pats the spot next to her and looks at me with hungry eyes. "You don't have to be scared to sit next to me."

I sit my ass down, and turn toward her, resting my elbow on the back cushion. "So, what do you have in mind for tonight?"

Hazel paid for dinner, so I figure I'll let her call the shots tonight. Wherever she wants it to go.

She moves and inches on top of my lap. Her breasts are sitting right in front of my lips, begging to be in my mouth. This dress is going to be fun because I have direct access to everywhere I need without having to remove it. Something about Hazel in red gets me ramped up.

Hazel has definitely changed. No more making the first move, she does it. Her lips press against mine, as she tugs against my buttons, undressing me. Holy fuck. This is hot, having her take charge. My erection is noticeable by now, and I'm sure she can feel it pressing against her.

"Looks like you need some attention," she says, eyeing my pants. "Those need to come off first."

I smile as she works her way down to the floor, and unbuttons my pants and slides them down and off. Her eyes are hungry and it makes me want to pull up on this couch and fuck her right now, but instead, I let her do whatever she wants. It's a nice change of pace from what I'm used to.

Her eyes glance up at me right before she takes me in her mouth, and starts to work her magic. She used to be able to get me off in under five minutes, a pro at this. Can she break her record? I find myself, head leaning back against the couch, closing my eyes, trying to relish in the fact that I'm with her, here, and never thought it would happen.

When the inching toward my release starts, I wrap my fingers in her hair and let my arm move with her, instead of forcing her on me. I always felt like that was possessive of men to do. Instead of stopping, she smiles with me still inside her mouth, and goes even faster.

"Fuck. How is it possible you are even better at this? Your mouth is fucking temple."

She laughs, and after I explode and instead of her turning her head or taking it on the breasts, she lets it go in her mouth. That's a first.

As she gets up from her knees, she lays down on the couch and spreads eagle. "You wanna taste?"

During that sucking session, she must have taken off her underwear, because she is naked underneath that dress, and I can see all her glory, waiting for me. Instead of going straight for it, I bite her inner left thigh, and make her moan, then kiss her clit.

"Don't tease me, damnit."

My tongue circles around her clit, and a smile up at her. "I'm not, taking my time. Enjoying you."

She lays back down, and as I start to lick her aggressively, she arches her hips. We have always been great together sexually, and know exactly what the other wants. Of course, that's because we were together for years, and spent all of our time together.

"Don't stop!" Her hand flies to my head and practically pushes me into her. "Keep going."

I do exactly as she asks, except I go faster, and within thirty-seconds she is writhing under my touch, begging for more.

Now that we have both gotten the first time out of the way, we can enjoy the night. It's time for us to explore each other, what we like now, compared to back then. I wonder if she has any kinks?

I pull her down on the couch a little more, and ease myself inside, and a moan erupts from her chest. That's what I like to hear. While in sync, I kiss her, trying to soak in all I can of her before she makes her decision. This might be the last time I get to be this close to her, and I want to savor it. Her supple breasts are aching to be in my mouth - so I oblige. Each thrust is like heaven, and her eyes are begging me for more.

I pull out, and take her hand and stand her up.

"Let's make this fun. Where in this house do you want me to take you? Kitchen, washer, shower... you name it."

She bites her lip, and looks around. "Definitely the island."

I grab her hand and lead her into the kitchen and give her a boost up on the island. God, she looks magnificent up there, waiting for me. As I maneuver myself up there, she pushes me on my back, straddles me, and puts my hands on her breasts.

Hazel's hips swivel in the perfect motion, and I let her take control again. We both want to savor these moments, and I can't be selfish. Who doesn't like a woman who knows exactly what she wants in the bedroom? Hell, that's my ideal woman.

"Hazel? Are you okay?" The front door opens, and I hear someone rushing up the staircase. "You aren't answering your phone."

She must be in the moment, because Hazel doesn't stop, but continues to ride me with her hands rushing through her hair. I'm not going to leave her wanting. So, I start thrusting into her, fast and steady, with my hand over her mouth. Her eyes stare at me, wondering what the fuck is going on. And then we both let go, and accept the release given to us.

"There is someone here. Didn't you hear them come in and go upstairs?" I ask.

"Fuck. We are naked and our clothes are in the living room." Her hand flies up to her forehead. "It must be Kate. I forgot to let her know I made it home and she can be a little paranoid."

She rushes out of the room, and comes back with our clothes. We can hear her yelling upstairs, but Hazel doesn't say a word until she's fully dressed. "We're down here, Kate."

I hear the rushing of footsteps, trying to race against the clock to get dressed before she walks in, but I only manage to get my pants on.

Kate's eyes drink me in. "Oh, I didn't realize you had company."

"Hi, I'm Aiden," I say, as I put on my shirt.

"The Aiden?" she asks, eyeing Hazel.

"I guess. Nice to meet you, Kate. I'm going to go lay down and let you girls talk. See you in the morning," I say, and then give Hazel a gentle kiss on the lips before departing the room.

Kate had no idea I'd be here which means Hazel hasn't told her what's going on, and I can only assume that she will now. Who knows maybe her friend can help her come to a decision. Although, she has obviously talked about me, because she called me, THE Aiden. Hopefully, I can live up to Kate's expectations.

I shut the door behind me, and lay down on the bed, reveling in the fact that I slept with Hazel, and it was better than I could ever dream it to be.

14

HAZEL

The first thought that comes to mind is did she hear us? I'm not exactly quiet when I'm getting pounded by a hot ass man, especially Aiden, since he knows exactly what I want. It's so nice to have a man that can read my body.

"So, what the hell? You couldn't at least call and tell me you were okay? You had me worried sick."

Honestly, I did forget before dinner, and then we went to pound town and it's not like I'm going to stop him and say, "sorry, I forgot to call my friend. Wait a second." Yeah, that's definitely not going to happen, sorry.

"At any rate, what did I interrupt? Please tell me you came at least twice."

"More than that, girl. He's unbelievable," I reply.

Kate knows about my past with Aiden, and it's nice to have someone to talk to about everything. We met when I started at the firm, and became instant best friends. We are only six months apart in age, and she is so vivacious. It's always good to have someone who will tell you straight if you are being an idiot, and that is Kate.

The woman has saved me from so many screw-ups and making a fool of myself, like too many to count. She always seems to have her shit together, but also is the first person to take big risk. Honestly, I'm blessed to have someone like her by my side, because sometimes I need that little push to go over the edge.

"Listen, you deserve some happiness after that asshole. You have never said an ill word about that guy. I like him, and of course, I'm not saying that because he made you come many times and looks fucking fabulous without a shirt on," she says, tucking her hair behind her ears and smiling.

Things between us are going smooth right now, after we worked out some kinks, and I'm sure there are plenty more ahead. No relationship is perfect, and it's important to remember that going forward. The history is apparent and in some cases, it is the foundation of our relationship and where we could be headed in the future. Did I want to gamble everything and say yes to him though? It's a hard decision because of our history, my failed marriage, and if things end up going south, what are we going to do?

"Don't do it. I know you. Going through all the reasons you can't. Hazel, don't listen to it. You deserve this. If he makes you happy, then fall head over heels for him. You can't let what Roger did affect your happiness. Promise me you won't let that asshole ruin your chances at having someone make you happy," Kate says, taking my hand in hers.

I nod and make my way to the front door for her to leave. It's late and tomorrow is our meeting with Jake's parents. Sleep is needed if things are going to go well, and right now isn't the time to make a unfavorable impression. Aiden would kill me if I screw this up.

"I'll call you tomorrow night," I say, leaning against the door.

"Yeah, like you said you would tonight?"

"No, seriously. Talk to you tomorrow," I say, as she walks outside and I shut the door.

Kate isn't one of those girls that kids around when they say something. If she tells you she will come over to your house if you don't call her, then she will. Tonight is all the proof I need. It's not like I meant to do it on purpose, but once Aiden and I got back here, things escalated quickly. Surely, she understands after seeing him.

The staircase creaks as I make my way up the stairs toward my bedroom, ready to faceplant against the cold comforter and bid the day a 'due, but before I shut my door, Aiden yells goodnight.

"See you in the morning."

THE AROMA of freshly brewed coffee is how I like to start my morning, and Aiden's smiling face makes it twice as good. He hands me a cup of coffee and sits down on the edge of the bed. I take a second to make sure this isn't one of my dreams, because normally our clothes are already off and going to town. I think I'm safe.

"How'd you sleep?" I ask.

"Like a man who took sleeping pills. Too nervous about today to fall asleep without them.

"Well, if I was in their position, the first thing I'd question is why now? It's been years and I've never reached out. So, if you think about it, it seems sketchy, right?" he says, pacing around the room now, while I drink my coffee. "My mind is going crazy right now, and I can't get it to stop. They must think we are terrible."

Okay, so maybe they are wondering why we are now reaching out to them about Jake, but they made it clear from the get-go about it being a closed adoption. "Technically, we were respecting their wishes, and they can't hold that against us."

I place my feet on the ground, sitting on the edge of the bed, with the coffee cup in my left hand, using my right hand to run through my hair which must look a mess right now. A shower will make me feel better, and plus it's time to wash my hair. My hairdresser did give me some advice last time I went in, to not wash my hair more than once every three days. At that time, my hair had been so dry, and now it's nice and shiny again.

Aiden is clearly having a conversation with himself in his head, because he continues to pace around my room, even after I get off the bed and head to the bathroom. I leave the door open in case he wants to talk some more, but it's time for me to get a move on for the day. The proper start is always warm water cascading on my skin, and then picking out the perfect outfit. Usually, that is easy because I would be going into the office, but today's outfit is for pleasure not business. I have to admit I've been enjoying not having to wear heels all the time, but sometimes I find myself wishing I could wear my red pumps again. Everyone loves those in the office, and I get compliments all the time when wearing them.

I can hear Aiden mumbling to himself outside the door, and instead of engaging, I let him hash it out with himself. There is nothing I can say to make him feel better, and if Jake's parents have a problem, they will address it at the meeting later.

"What time are we meeting up with them?" I yell from inside the shower, rubbing body wash all over.

"They are supposed to call me today. I haven't heard from them yet."

Hopefully, they don't change their minds after Aiden agreed to fly out here. My brother seems to think he has been depressed, and something like this could send him over the edge. He doesn't seem down, besides about messing up this meeting, but I could be wrong. I've only been around for a week and he might be good at hiding things. Although, I've always been able to read him well.

I turn the water off, grab the towel off the bar, and wrap it around my breasts, tucking the end inside. The second towel is used to dry my hair a little bit before twirling it and tucking the end inside around my ear. Aiden always found it weird that I do this, but I can't be the only girl that uses two towels. I find it weird to use the same towel I used to dry my hair with to use on my body. What if hair is all in it, then they will stick to your wet body. No thanks. I'll pass.

"You still do that, huh?" he says, peeking into the bathroom.

"And you still like to sneak up on me... some things never change."

The smile drops from my expression, and I bend over, taking the towel from around my hair, and using it to dry it more thoroughly. There's another thing I recently stopped; blow-drying my hair. Instead I let it air dry, which means I always have to shower way before I need to be somewhere so it's possible to do that. It already makes the world of difference. After getting most of the water out of it, I take my scrunchie and throw it up in a bun to finish drying while I get ready.

I hold the towel around my breasts and make my way to my closet.

It's a pretty big walk-in, with many shelves for purses. Most of my wardrobe consists of nice dresses, heels, and purses, but that's mostly for work. Today is a casual day, and I find myself perusing my jean collection. Even though I don't need to, I still occasionally go into thrift shops to see what I can find for a good deal. My hand wanders over the bottom of the jeans. I found these bell bottoms at the end of a sale rack close to a year ago, and still have not worn them out of the house. It's time. After putting on some underwear, I shimmy them up around my waist, and the fit is perfect.

"Wow, that's something I never expected to see you in," Aiden says, sneaking up on me again.

"Jesus, can't you announce yourself? You are going to give me a heart attack."

He rolls his eyes. "They just called. Meeting at one at a place called Mon Ami. Wherever that is."

"It's a French restaurant. An expensive one. They must still be doing good," I laugh.

It's not like I'm hard strapped for cash, but how do they know we can afford a place like that to eat? People who are wealthy don't think about things like that. They don't look at the prices on the menu, they just order whatever they desire. I'm not to that stage in the game yet, but would love to be someday.

Aiden is leaning against the doorframe of the closet, watching me. I would ask him to stop, but I kind of like it. So, I bend over, and take a look at what shoes I am going to wear with the jeans, they have to have at least a little bit of a heel since the bell bottoms are long. There you go. I pick up my black wedge booties and slip them on and pair them with an old Rock N Roll t-shirt.

"Is that the t-shirt you got from our Aerosmith concert sophomore year?" he asks, coming closer.

"Sure is. Looks practically brand new, don't it?"

I never wear it around the house, and it's been hiding in the back of my closet for who knows how long. "That was a great concert. You asked me to be your girlfriend that night."

This is one of my fondest memories of us. At that point, neither of us had come clean about how we felt, and when he asked me to be his girl-friend, my heart nearly exploded. There I was, wondering if I was being stuck in the friend zone, and would never have a shot with him, and then he turned around and asked me to be his girlfriend officially. The rest of the concert we held hands, but he didn't kiss me goodnight. Even then, the night was still perfect.

I look at the clock, and get a move on. I only have thirty-minutes to get ready, and get us to the restaurant. We can't be late. So, I hustle past him to the bathroom to finish putting some product in my hair to help with the curls, then lined my eyes, and roll on some lip gloss.

"Is that what you are wearing?" I ask.

"Of course, not," he says, almost like he didn't understand my question. "I'm going to put a Polo on. The jeans are okay though, right?"

I nod, leaving him to change, while I rush downstairs to put my coffee cup in the sink to wash later. There's no time.

"Come on, let's go. It's about a twenty-minute drive there, more if we hit traffic," I yell.

He runs down the stairs, all the muscles in his arms and shoulders flexing underneath his polo, and then out the door he goes. I jump into my car, push to start, and then back out of the driveway. If I take Heather Lane, I can cut out the traffic on Elm street. It's still lunch hours and everyone will be scrambling to get food right now. Better if we miss that entirely. So, I turn left and cut across onto Elm and then take it all the way down until we hit Strozier and hit a red light. Once it turns green, I make a right turn, and pull into the Mon Ami parking lot.

"It wasn't that far."

"Yeah, we got lucky. I've been here a bunch and knew the back way."

I stop the engine, and unbuckle my seat belt. "Everything is going to be great. They've met me. From what I remember, they are nice, but they are wealthy, so don't overreact about the menu prices. I'll cover lunch."

"Are they that bad?" His eyebrows wiggle.

"For someone who lives in a small town, yes. Let's go."

I open my door, and shut it behind me, taking a deep breath before approaching the front door. This meeting can determine whether we get to know anything about our son, and that makes me nervous, but on the same side, I know how Aiden feels, and he is going to need some support. He clams up easily, and it'll be worse knowing this will hold the future of his relationship with his son.

He stands at the reception, and I put my hand in his and whisper in his ear. "Everything's going to be fine. Just breathe."

15

AIDEN

I close my eyes as her hand reaches for mine, and it calms me down. Why am I so nervous? It's not like I'm meeting the president. I doubt they are going to ask a million questions like an interrogation or anything. Right?

A young girl approaches the reservations desk, "what's the name?"

"Last name is Kaser. Should be party of four. We are a little early," I reply.

She checks the computer, and nods. "It looks like they are already seated. Follow me."

I take her hand again, and follow the young lady until I see a couple that looks like they have money. The man is dressed in a business suit and she in a fancy dress with diamonds around her neck. Hazel is right, they must be loaded.

"Good afternoon," Hazel says, sitting down in the chair across from the woman.

I sit in silence for a moment, not sure of what to say, it's not like I know these people. Hazel seems okay, talking away. They asked if she graduated from Harvard and how things are going, and were pleased to hear that she is working with a firm now.

"We had a good feeling you would push yourself to finish. We are proud of you."

Hazel becomes silent, looks over at me, and raises an eyebrow. "Aiden is a firefighter, runs in the family actually. All the Jackson's are."

"How rude of me. You probably don't even know our names. I'm Mitchell and she's Veronica," the man says, extending his hand.

"Aiden," I reply, shaking his head.

They both kind of watch me during lunch, and not in a pleasant way. Almost to the point where it did feel like their intention was to interrogate us after all. Hazel and Angelica continue talking about her career, while I look over the menu to appear busy. Hazel isn't kidding about the prices, and this isn't the sort of place I would normally come to if by myself. An appetizer is over thirty bucks, and that's ridiculous. I go to the drink section, and get a beer, just to lighten the nerves.

"I'll be your waitress this afternoon. What can I get you to drink?"

I order my beer and Hazel a glass of wine. Mitchell and Veronica order a glass of wine also. Good thing, too, because I didn't think about it being early in the afternoon and wanting a drink. If they didn't, it might make me look like a drunk.

"So, let's get down to business for a second. We got Aiden's letter and wanted to reach out. With it being a closed adoption, we didn't want to make matters worse for you, Hazel. Mitchell wondered if reaching out to you might upset you. Then we got the letter, and we were happy to hear from either of you," Veronica says.

Does this mean she has thought of letting us see him before? Why didn't they reach out?

"So, you aren't against us meeting Jake?" Hazel asks.

"Things are important in a child's life and knowing that he wasn't abandoned and adopted by us is a big thing to consider. He should get to know his birth parents, and the fact that you guys want to be in his life makes it all the better."

I scratch my head, overwhelmed by this, and the fact I could have met my son years ago, yet there's no time to focus on that. They are going to let us be in his life.

"When can we meet him?" I ask.

Our drinks arrive, and the waitress interrupts our conversation to take our order.

"Let's talk about arrangements. We would like to start off small, so we don't overwhelm him. We were thinking once a year for now, possibly more often down the line, but we would send pictures to you. We don't want him to be confused, you know," Mitchell says, looking over at his wife, like he's seeking approval.

I want to speak up and be stingy, but once a year is better than never. We need to take what we can get right now.

"Whatever you want. Hazel and I want to meet him, see how he's doing, and get to know him. Things didn't work out when we were younger, but we want him to know we are here for him."

The conversation turns into them wanting to know more about my profession, and why I chose to be a firefighter. Of course, my grandfather comes up, and the fact that since him all the men in my family have taken on the job without any regrets. I take this opportunity to ask what they do, and the answer is not what I expected. Mitchell is one of the highest regarded Defense Attorneys in Massachusetts and Veronica is the CFO of a cosmetics company. Our little boy surely has everything he wants and then some. A lot more than we could provide.

We sit around and talk about Jake over lunch, and they say he's getting straight A's and plays in little league. He seems to enjoy sports right now, and they are happy to see him get out and be active. How I wish I can attend his games and cheer him on.

Lunch is a success in my book, because I will finally get to meet my son. Mitchell and Veronica seem to be nice, and love our son like their own. They have provided a great life for him.

"So, would you guys like to meet him today?" Veronica asks.

"Yes," I say, my voice going up an octave.

She smiles. "I'll call you once we get home and head that way. You know where Geren Park is?"

"I do," Hazel replies.

She drops a hundred dollar bill on the table to take care of our lunch and follows him. Today is the day. We say our see you laters and get into the car. I let out a long breath.

"You okay?" Hazel asks, starting the car and pulling out of the driveway.

"Are you kidding? I get to meet my son today. This is the best freaking day ever."

Honestly, going into this meetup I was scared that they might not like me, and it would prevent me from being able to meet Jake, but instead, they liked me. Without their approval, I couldn't ever be a part of Jake's life until after he turns eighteen but here we are.

I take Hazel's hand in mine, and don't say a word. If she didn't come to Texas and ask me to write the letter, this would have never happened. Sometimes, you have to take risks to get what you want, and this is a perfect example. Do I wish she would have mentioned it sooner? Yes, but oh well. All that matters is now.

We arrive at her house, get out of the car, and go inside. She sits down on the couch and turns on the television while I pace around the kitchen, waiting for the coffee to finish brewing that I started. Normally, I don't drink it this late in the day, but want to make sure I'm fully awake with energy to play with him at the park. We only get one first impression and I want to make the most of it.

My brothers are going to be livid when they find out that I have a son, and never said anything. Liam will probably hate Hazel for a while, and make it out to be all her fault. I still don't understand why he dislikes her so much. So she turned down my proposal in high school, so what. That was many years ago, and we need to move past it.

The Keurig beeps and I grab my coffee and migrate out to the living room with Hazel. She's watching True Blood and officially is obsessed with it apparently. Not a show for me, but I sit down next to her and use it to pass the time until the Kaser's call.

Before we know it, two hours have gone by, and we have binged three episodes of her show without even realizing it. Okay, so maybe it's not that deplorable, and I should have gotten past the first season. The second season is actually pretty good so far. Although, I'm not a big fan of vampires and the stigma around them being with humans. Girls are into that crap, though.

My pocket starts to vibrate and I pull my phone out. "Hello?"

"Available to meet in twenty-minutes?" Mitchell asks.

I turn to Hazel to confirm the time frame works, since I have no idea how long it takes to get there from here. "Yes, see you then."

After hanging up, my chest gets tight, and my hand flies up to my heart.

"Don't start that now. We have both been looking forward to this. He's going to like you, no worries there."

Hazel is such a sweet girl, and has been good at calming me down, and discovering my potential even when I can't see it myself. I think that's why I've always stayed in love with her, and have never found anyone else. Things between us are worthy of a second chance and after this trip, Hazel will have to make her choice. I'll respect her wishes either way, but might take me a while if the answer's no.

"We better start heading that way."

I wonder if Jake looks like me?

We hightail to the park, and get there with about four minutes to spare, but don't see the Kaser's yet. Good. Being late isn't a great first impression for Jake. Should we stay in the car or sit down at the one of the picnic benches and wait?

"Let's go sit down by the jungle gym. It'll help us look more approachable," I tell Hazel, opening my door.

A brand new Mercedes pulls up, and we look at each other, knowing that's them. A deep breath is taken, and then we stand up and smile. The back door opens and out pops this little boy and a tear falls from my eye. It's him, and he looks like me. Dark brown hair, sparkling chestnut eyes, and a smile that could brighten anyone's day.

Jake waits for his parents to get out, and then takes Mitchell's hand. Did they tell him we are meeting? Or, is this like a surprise situation?

"I'm Jake," he says, putting out his hand.

"I'm Aiden and this is Hazel." I try to contain my smile as if not to be creepy.

Jake looks up at his parents. "So, you are my real parents?"

The Kaser's did make it clear they have never kept the fact that he is adopted from him.

"Yes. It's a pleasure to meet you finally. Would you like to go with us on the jungle gym?" I ask, trying to gain confidence.

Instead of responding, he runs and we try to keep up. All we want is a chance to get to know him, and if it helps him feel better by playing then so be it. I chase behind him, and try to beat him to the slide, but secretly let him win.

"Aw, come on. I thought I was going to beat you. Redo?"

Maybe I should give them a moment together alone, since she's been so quiet. I head back to the bench and sit down with his parents. They are both on their phones, not paying any attention, which scares me because what if we weren't good people.

"He seems like a wonderful kid. You guys are doing a great job with him," I say.

"It's the sixty-thousand dollars a year private school. Does wonders with kids and their grades," Mitchell replies, not even bothering to look up.

So instead, I focus my attention on them, running around the playground, chasing each other, and laughing. It's a sentiment to what life could be like if we didn't give him up all those years ago, and how our daily lives would be.

Things aren't as they should be, but at least we have him in our lives now.

I get up and leave them to their own devices and join Jake and Hazel back on the playground. We run around, chase each other for a while, having a good time, until the Kaser's approach us and let us know it's time to get Jake home.

"Am I going to see you again?" he asks.

I look over at his parents. "Yes."

Of course, I don't want to say it's up to your parents, because that seems like I'm putting the pressure on them, and don't want them to get upset.

Jake wraps his arms around my torso, and then Hazel's, and his parents shuffle him off as he waves to us.

"I wish we had more time," I say. "It'll be easier for you. Living close."

We leave the park and go back to the house to hope they continue to let us see him.

"I know we leave for Texas soon, and my brothers deserve to know. They might be pissed at you for a while, in all honesty. Just want to forewarn you."

Things are going to be rough once I tell them, but I won't let them talk ill of Hazel for her decision.

We make our way upstairs to repack our bags, and head to the airport to catch our flight back to Dallas. There are so many things I need to get straightened out to be the best dad for him I can be. I need to focus on those things first.

ONCE BACK IN TEXAS, the first stop is to Damon's house because he is having a dinner to thank Liam for watching Emily while they were gone on their honeymoon. The whole plane ride I mulled over exactly what to say when I tell them, and it doesn't matter how. Either way, they are going to be upset with me. As we get closer, the nervousness sets in, and Hazel takes my hand.

"Listen, who cares what they think. All that matters is that Jake is in our lives now. Remember that."

I park in the driveway, and knock on the red door.

"What are you doing here? Thought you wouldn't be back until tomorrow?" Damon asks.

"Nope, just got in. Heard you are making dinner. Care to have two more?"

He smiles, and opens the door wide for us to go inside. My brother loves cooking for people so it's unlike him to say no.

As we make it to the kitchen, Liam and Harper are drinking a beer, while Tessa is preparing our meal.

"So, I have something to tell you and would rather do it now," I say, grabbing Hazel's hand. "I have a eight year old son named Jake."

Damon and Liam glance at each other, and then back at me.

"What do you mean? How is that possible?" Damon asks.

"Hazel found out she was pregnant right after Graduation and we gave it up for adoption. However, we reached out to the parents and they let us meet him today."

Liam slams his beer down and gets up from the barstool. "You've kept this a secret all these years? How could you?"

I become defensive. "We did what was best for Jake at the time. Instead of being pissed, why don't you ask about him?"

Tessa stops preparing and walks over to me. "How did it go?"

So, I tell them all about meeting the adoptive parents and then going to the park to meet Jake. How much fun we had and he didn't want to go home. I wish I did have more time with him but they are his parents and we have to respect their wishes. Upsetting them means they might cut us off.

"So, when do you get to see him again?" Liam asks.

I don't know how to answer that question. "Well, that's something else I want to discuss."

Hazel looks at me, and arches her brow. "There's more?"

"I'm going to move to Massachusetts to be closer to Jake. You probably think I'm crazy and haven't thought this through, but he's my son. Any chance I can get to see him, I need to be able to do it on a moment's notice."

It's a on-the-fly-decision, but the right one. If moving there means I can see my son more often, possibly attend his little league games, then so be it. I'll give everything up to have him in my life. Eight years without knowing him, or how he was doing, and now I don't want to go another week.

"Are you sure about that?" Hazel asks, squeezing my hand.

"More than anything."

Liam separates me from Hazel and pulls me to the side. "Don't make a rash decision. Where are you going to live? What are you going to do for work?"

"I have money to buy a home, so that's not concerning, and I'm sure they are always looking for firefighters. Why are you so against this?"

"Hazel has gotten into your head. You don't need to get your heart broken again."

"This has nothing to do with Hazel. I'm doing this for Jake."

I push him out of the way, wave to her, and we leave Damon's. Liam is not going to push me around anymore. I'm a grown ass man and able to make my own decisions. He still thinks of me as that thirteen-year-old kid when dad died, and I'm not.

"They took it better than I expected," Hazel says.

I don't respond, but focus on the road and getting back to my place. She talks me into going to pick up something fast to eat, and taking it back, because we haven't eaten since lunch. I only agree because my stomach is growling fiercely.

As we scarf down our burgers and fries, the room is silent, basking in everything that has happened today. Things are beginning to look up, and maybe it's time to start attending AA meetings. My problem with drinking needs to stop so I can be the best father to Jake possible, and I don't need any ammo for the Kaser's to use against me in the future.

After dinner, it's time to discuss her decision. The trip is over and a choice needs to be made. Whether she wants to try this for real or not, I'm moving to Massachusetts, and we would still be friends. When I ask her, she looks at the ground.

"Listen, we had a great time on the excursion, but this is real life. I can't keep pining over you. We both deserve to find happiness, and if that's not with each other then we need to start looking elsewhere. Please just tell me."

I hate to be so damn forward, but now more than ever, speaking my truth is important. Grudges won't be held, but I don't want to waste any more time saving myself for her if she isn't going to want to be with me. And her the same.

Sometimes, love isn't enough.

16

HAZEL

*T*he last couple of days have been wonderful seeing the man Aiden has become and showing me how much I mean to him, but is that enough? I know he wants my answer now, but what if I need more time? Things can't be so black and white, that's why there is a grey area, right?

"You're moving. So, can't we see how it goes without putting all this pressure on it?"

He blindsided me with his decision to move to Massachusetts, but maybe this is a good thing. Liam won't be able to forge a wedge between us, and we can find our groove again. This can be our second chance and I would hate for it to be ruined by anyone, including myself. There are so many things that can go wrong even with him living near me. I work constantly, which means, I won't have the time to spend building up a new relationship, and I'm already divorced because of my career. Will Aiden understand if I am never home? If I continue to go the route I'm on, they are saying I could make partner before I'm thirty which never happens. Can I be in a healthy relationship and have a career?

Aiden takes my hand, and tucks a stray hair behind my hair. "So your answer is you are willing to give me a chance?"

I close my eyes, and picture my life without Aiden now. Working hard is only worth it when you have someone to share it with and come home to. My mind pictures us happy, having dinners, and watching movies on the couch. He is the man I picture making me happy.

"Yes."

He picks me up off his couch, his hands on my ass, and my legs wrapped around his waist, and carries me to his bedroom. I know where this is going and honestly I couldn't think of any other way I would like to spend my night. We have been away from each other so long, that not having him close is like having withdrawals.

Aiden gently places me on the bed and lays over me, his hands caressing my hips, and his lips on mine. He lifts his shirt off over his head, and then does the same with mine. Normally, I never go out without a bra but today I did. My breasts are exposed and he doesn't waste a minute showing them attention. His tongue circling, and causing them to get hard. But so is he.

"Looks like you're ready," I say, smiling.

"Always with you."

I unbutton his pants, and he kicks them off to the floor, and then inches mine down and then flips me over. The perfect position and one my favorites. It's the right angle for me to get the best release. And fuck if Aiden doesn't make me scream a couple times before he's finished. That man is a god.

He eases into me, my ass up in the air, and his hands holding onto my hips. *Fuck.* The pure ecstasy of feeling him inside me. Aiden starts to move, and with each pump, he gets harder and harder, which sending me into a frenzy of begging him to fuck me harder, and do all kinds of dirty things to me.

Right before I get my release, a knock sounds at the door. Are you fucking kidding me? Aiden stops, but I keep going, moving my body against him, not wanting to lose it.

"Be quiet. I'll give you thirty-seconds and then I'm answering the door," he says to me.

"Be there in a minute," he yells, to whoever the hell is here.

I don't hesitate and our bodies start to synchronize, both of us wanting to get our release before finding out who is on the other side of that door. We move faster, quicker, until I move his pillow under my face to keep the visitor from hearing me scream. Once we are both done, he smacks my ass, gets off the bed and throws back on his pants.

"Let's see who this could be."

When he opens the door, the first thing I see is a baby bump. It's her. The girl that I saw him with. What the hell is she doing here?

"Hey, sorry to drop by. Wanted to give you back the key. I've decided to move in with my parents back in Iowa. Everyone keeps telling me it's important to have a support system being a single mom."

He glances back toward the bedroom, where I'm still laying on the bed, peeking out at the door. "That's true. Well, if it doesn't work out and you need somewhere to stay, if it's available you can use it. Drive safe, okay?"

Elena smiles. "Thanks, Aiden. Have a good night."

Okay, so maybe inside I'm furious that this girl stopped by his house at ten o'clock, but at the same time, it didn't look like anything is going on between them, and I know how Aiden likes to help people. I can't get mad at him for helping a pregnant woman. I'm being ridiculous.

Aiden waltzes back into the bedroom, and lays down next to me, our elbows on the bed, and our hands on our chins.

"Do you remember when we used to sit on your bed like this for hours, talking about stupid stuff, and fall asleep?" I ask.

"Some of the best moments I'd say."

I want to bring up the move, but don't want him to think I'm trying to talk him out of it. It truly is the best thing for Jake. He can have a relationship with him if he's closer. Although, we haven't heard from them since they left the park. Hopefully we didn't do anything to piss them off.

"So, I am going back in two days. Gives me time to spend with my dad and Jeremy. How long until you get things settled here?"

He laughs. "I already told the fire chief that I wouldn't be coming back to work and explained the situation. I'm going to keep my house here. So, I'm going back with you, gorgeous."

"Where are you going to stay?" I ask, but it comes out bitchy, so I try to redeem myself. "You can stay with me if you need to for a little while. I've got plenty of room as you've seen."

Honestly, it's not a terrible idea, because it would be stupid of him to buy something out there. If things work out between us, then we would be living together anyway. No need to go through all that nonsense.

The conversation continues about how things are different where I live, and things are more expensive for everything. You don't find any mom and pop restaurants there. It's all fancy, usually over-priced food, but you get used to it, too. I go ahead and bring up my work schedule and make sure he understands that he won't see me a lot, especially when I have a case.

Emphasis on the amount of hours, because I don't want him to expect to see me all the time. My job isn't a forty-hour week kind of position, it's a work your ass until you win the case job. Sometimes, I work twelve hours days without barely eating because I'm on a crunch. Other times I might actually be able to take a day off before I get handed another case.

"I'm not Roger and I would never cheat on you, Haz. You're the woman for me. I love you."

17

AIDEN

*A*s I contemplate how my life is going to change once I'm no longer in Grapevine, things start to creep up. I won't see my brothers anytime I want, although I can still fly down for holidays. No exceptions there. Even though this is the best decision if I want to be close to my son, it's still a little scary. There is no guarantee Hazel and I will work out, but no matter what, we are friends first.

She is still lying in bed in my t-shirt, and I wouldn't want it any other way. My sleeping patterns have improved and now I get six to eight hours of sleep without the consumption of alcohol. Before Hazel's return, I was lucky to get four hours.

"So, are you going to say bye to your brothers? I know they freaked out but they are still family."

Hazel has a way of helping me not be so petty, but Liam needs to grow up. I get wanting to protect me from getting hurt again, but he doesn't get to control my life. If Hazel and I don't work out, it's not like I'm going to go back into a depression. A second chance with her is all I ever wanted, and now is my shot. Nothing, not even him, is going to ruin it for me. He might not like her for what she did to me, and now for everything with Jake, but his opinion on that doesn't matter to me.

I pull my shirt over my head, and reply. "Probably see them tonight. I've got a lot of things to handle before we leave tomorrow."

She crawls to the end of the bed, tugging on my shirt to come closer, and then pecks my cheek. "Me, too. Going to spend it with dad and Jeremy. Speaking of, I should probably get dressed and head over there."

I step out of her way as she gets off the bed, and starts for her overnight bag.

"I'll go get some coffee made," I say, heading for the kitchen.

There is so much that needs to get handled today before I leave, because who knows when I will be back, Thanksgiving I suppose. If my brothers want me to come back, that is. We will see. Damon isn't so much being a jerk, but I understand how frustrated he must be that I kept Jake a secret from him. Hopefully, he doesn't let this ruin our relationship, especially when we have gotten closer in the last year.

The pot of coffee is ready, and I pour into two mugs and add some milk and sugar before taking Hazel her cup. She accepts it with both hands, and takes her first sip. There is nothing better than fresh hot cup of joe in the morning. Okay, maybe a nice morning wake up, but I digress for now.

I turn on the news to watch while we finish our cups, and enjoy our last moment of silence for the day before we are both going to say goodbye to our family. She hasn't mentioned anything, but I can tell she is going to have trouble leaving her father behind, especially after finding out about the Alzheimer's. Jeremy promises to keep a good eye on him, and my brothers will help whenever they can. Our families are already bonded. If anything happens, I can fly back and help also. My job is not as time demanding as hers, and if she wants to fast track to partner then she has to do whatever they say. This is her dream we are talking about, and I don't want anything to get in the way of her achieving them. My job is to support her and help her stay focused on the end game.

As a partner, she won't have to work an obscene amount of hours, because that's what the subordinates are for, and you get paid a hell out of a lot more, with doing less. We can all get behind her until she hits that spot, and then there will be more time for visits, traveling, and everything else she wants to do. I'm here for the long haul.

After the morning news, she sets her cup on the coffee table, and heads to her dads. I hope she gets a lot of time with him today, and maybe it will make a sliver of difference in saying goodbye to him. I can't imagine what she's going through, and knowing how fast it progresses, and he might not be himself the next time she's down here.

As the door shuts behind her, I set my cup down also, and start making a mental note of everything I want to get done today.

First up on my list, clean out of the refrigerator, freezer and cabinets. They are full of food, and don't want any of it to go to waste. So, I get a few of the reusable shopping bags from my pantry and start filling it up with canned foods, and things that are going to expire soon, and plan on taking them down to the homeless shelter so they can get a few meals from all of this. No need in throwing it all away when someone else could use it.

After removing everything from my refrigerator and freezer, I grab a washcloth, run it under some water, and wipe down all the interior. You know those pesky spills or left behind food that always end up on the shelves? I don't want mildew or mold forming while I'm gone. It's worth the extra twenty-minutes to clean it up real good now. The white interior is now pristine and sparkling white without any flaws. That's how I want to leave behind the house.

I grab the bags of food with one hand and my keys with the other. This might be the last time I get to help people within my community, and I can make a small difference in someone's lives that might not get a meal otherwise.

My phone rings, and it comes through on the Bluetooth, and I hesitate to answer it after seeing Liam's name.

"What do you want?"

"Jeez, I know I overreacted yesterday. Can I come by later?"

"I'll text you when I get back to the house. Out doing stuff right now," I reply, before hanging up.

My truck comes to a stop in front of the shelter, and seeing all the individuals wrapped around the building waiting for lunch to be served. We do food drives for the shelter every month as a community, but sometimes it's not enough. I wouldn't say we have a lot of homeless in our area, compared to those of like cities in California, but seeing one person homeless is more than I'd like. The numbers have dwindled down since the shelter started inviting companies to do interviews on site for those that need one. When the recession hit in 2008, many people lost everything including their entire savings, and some still have not recovered from it.

I slip inside, walking past the crowd, and straight to the kitchen. "Brought some things. Hopefully, you can make something out of all this."

A young man turns his head, and looks at me. "You brought all of that for us? Where did you get it?"

"Just from my house. I'm moving and didn't want good food to go to waste. Thought you all could use it."

The man embraced me, for about ten seconds, and then his hands stopped on my arms. "Thanks to you, we might be able to feed everyone in line today. We were running short on food since the last drive didn't go so well."

I've never been good at cooking, but would like to at least offer my service. "Do you need some help? I can't cook to save my life, but don't do so badly under instruction. Tell me what to do and I'll help."

So, for the next hour or so, he would hand something to chop, or ask me to boil water, or stir something while he worked around the kitchen. You could tell he has been cooking here for a while and it makes me curious as to what he does outside of the shelter. Would it be weird to ask?

"Looks like the line is starting to come through. It's noon," I say.

"Time for lunch. Grab some big spoons and put a little of each thing on their plate."

I did as he requests, and help him serve every single person in line. This takes about an hour or so, and by the time we are done, he has made two plates for us and asks me to sit down with him.

"So, where are you moving?" he asks, as he stuffs some bread into his mouth.

"Massachusetts to be closer to my son."

"What do you do for work?"

"Firefighter, but not sure what I'll be doing out there. Haven't secured a job yet."

We continue conversating over lunch, and I find out he is a marketing executive. Is it rude to say I didn't see that being his profession? I think it's great that he volunteers to cook here for everyone. Selfless people seem to enjoy their lives immensely more than those that have everything. Normally, the rich folks seem stuck up, and don't want to deal with the people that are less fortunate. Yet, Craig, as he finally told me his name, is nothing like that. I learn he comes down on every Tuesday and Thursday to prepare lunch, as those are his days off from work. He usually spends the afternoon talking to everyone, and seeing what he can do to help them.

"You would be surprised at what they ask for. Once I had a man tell me all he needs is a good pair of shoes as he walks everywhere, and his feet have permanent blisters from having worn out shoes. So, that afternoon I took him to get some new ones. He could have asked for anything, but instead all he wanted was some new kicks."

"Wow," I reply, wondering if I could possibly help some of these people before I leave. One last way to help the community flourish.

"The people here aren't worried about getting a hundred bucks, they want somewhere to live other than sleeping under a bridge or on a street corner. Heck, some of them need a break."

I nod, and ask to be excused, as I walk around the tables to the front of the room.

"Hello everyone, I hope you enjoyed your lunch. I am looking for someone who can be an on-site maintenance technician. If this is something you are qualified for, and you can provide a reference for a similar job, please come see me."

It didn't take but thirty-seconds, before a man walks up to me. The stereotype that homeless don't want to work is bullshit. There might be some that enjoy that life, but there are still people who want to work and can't catch a break because they have been unemployed for so long. He introduces him as Jason, and formerly worked as a Maintenance Coordinator at a local complex.

"Do you have a number to verify your employment?"

"Yes."

He hands me a card that looks to be years old. Wear and tear noticeable. "Thank you. Let me give them a call, and then I will come back and talk to you in a little bit."

I leave there, and head straight to the complex since it's a couple miles away, to talk directly with the apartment manager. If his employment checks out, and he's not lying, I can talk to my brothers about bringing him on board to help with the duplexes upkeep. We would be able to provide him a place to stay while he looks after the others. I am sure they both agree that it's less for us to have to worry about and helping someone who needs it makes it all the better.

The apartment office is up front, and a bell rings as I open the door.

"Hello, I'm here to talk to you about Jason Cox?"

An older woman is sitting behind a desk. "He is a former employee. What do you need?"

"I'm looking to hire him to help with maintenance. Can you confirm that is what he did here?"

She gets up from her chair and comes around the desk. "How is he doing? I felt so rotten for having to let him go, but when so many people lost their jobs, tenants started having to be evicted and we didn't have enough work to keep him."

"He is doing okay. So, can you confirm?"

"Yes, he was one of the best maintenance guys I've ever hired. Tell him that Sandy says hi, please."

I nod before heading out the door. As soon as I get in my truck, I dial Damon and it starts trilling over the Bluetooth.

"Hello?"

"Hey, not that I think you would be against it, but I'm wanting to hire someone to take over maintenance and upkeep of the duplexes. I figured he can stay in the vacant one and that takes it off you and Liam's plate while I'm gone. Sound good?"

He laughs. "I was actually thinking about this while I was on my honeymoon. Will be easier that way for both of us. You got a guy in mind?"

"Yeah, going to meet him now. If you and Liam want to meet me at the duplex in twenty minutes, you can meet him."

He agrees and hangs up to call Liam.

There you go. We will be able to help Jason get on his feet. Sometimes, you need to be there for people who need it instead of judging them. I see this all too often.

He is still inside, sitting at the table talking to some guys, when I approach him.

"Jason. My brothers would like to meet you. Are you free?"

"Yes, sir."

He follows me to my truck, and off we go to the duplexes. Jason is playing with his fingers.

"Don't worry. They will like you. So, we were thinking that maybe you would like to stay in one of the duplexes, so you can be close if something needs to be fixed. Is that okay with you?"

His head turns and eyes lock on me. "I don't have money to pay."

"No, the place would be free. You are doing us a favor," I say.

It looks like Damon and Liam have already made it, and are waiting for us as we pull up into the driveway of the vacant duplex.

"Let's go, so you can see your new place."

My brothers introduce themselves, and shake his hand, before we take him inside. You could tell it has been a long time since he has had a proper place of his own.

"All of this is mine?" Jason asks.

"Yes, sir. When can you start?" Damon asks.

"Now!" he yells, and covers his mouth. "Sorry, I'm not sure how to thank you."

"No need to. I'll come back by in a little bit to drop off some groceries, and a phone. We will need to be able to contact you if a tenant calls. See you in a bit," Liam tells him.

We all stop by our cars, and Liam turns to me. "You sure have grown up a lot. Nice of you to help this guy find a job."

I don't respond, but get into my truck and head back home. There is too much to be done right now, and not enough time to get it complete.

After getting back inside, I start cleaning everything, the bathroom, the living room, and bedroom. I take off my shirt, and sweep, mop and vacuum whatever needs it. To be honest, it's probably been months since I vacuumed the carpet in the living room, but I don't spend a lot of my time in there, so that makes sense. I hear my phone going off, and rush to grab it.

"Hello?"

"Just wanted to let you know I made it to Iowa. Thanks again," Elena says.

After she hangs up, someone knocks at my door. Jesus, doesn't everyone know I'm trying to get shit done around here.

"What?" I say, opening the door.

"I told you I wanted to talk. Damon just wanted to join," Aiden says, walking past me into the living room and taking a seat on the couch.

"What is there to talk about? I get you guys are pissed about keeping Jake a secret, but it's not something I wanted everyone to know. You guys already think little of me, didn't want to make it worse."

"Is that what you think?" Damon asks. "Don't be an idiot. Have you done some stupid shit? Yes. Do you still have a lot of growing up to do? Definitely, but we are proud of you, Aid."

"Then why do you guys freak out so bad? Liam practically had a heart attack about my moving away. Ever since Hazel showed up, he's been acting like I'm a seventeen-year-old kid again."

Liam puts his hand up in front of him. "Fault for me looking out for you. I was the one who watched you sit on a damn couch for months after she left you. You have never been the same. Just be smart, damnit. Make sure you are thinking with the right head this go around."

Honestly, I don't really want to hear about what happened in the past, right now, it's time to focus on my future. Whether Hazel and I work out or not, my son lives in Massachusetts and that's where I need to be.

18

HAZEL

*A*part of me is scared about this move for him. What if it doesn't work out? Or, the Kaser's decide they don't want us anywhere near Jake? I guess it's good he's keeping his house here, so he can always come back. Cambridge isn't a place for everyone, and unfortunately there are many stuck up individuals that live amongst me. It's more about what you have to show, than anything else. A new car every year, what you wear, and how nice your house is and how many you have? I've actually had a neighbor ask me if I am ever going to buy a house in the Hamptons? Apparently I'm good at playing the type, but that doesn't interest me at all. What I do isn't about the money, it's about helping the people who need it the most.

I show up at Aiden's and it's spectacular. He wasn't kidding about cleaning the place.

"Ready for today?"

"You know it," he replies. "Just gotta finish packing up these boxes. Whatever I can't fit in my truck, my brothers will ship to me."

I guess maybe I haven't been paying attention or something, but why would they need to fit in his truck? We are flying back today. "Are they driving your truck out there too?"

"You're comical. No, I'm going to drive out. No sense in flying when I'm going to need my stuff and the truck. Might as well drive and enjoy the scenery on the way."

It's only a four hour flight nonstop from Dallas, but instead, he wants to drive? I pull my phone out and map out how long it will take if driving. Holy crap. twenty-eight hours without any stops. It's going to take us almost two days to get there.

"You are more than welcome to drive with me, but I know you have to be back to work on Monday. Might be too much. I'm planning on doing some stopping for cool stuff on the way."

He's got a point. If we leave today, we will get back sometime on late Saturday, early Sunday. However, I haven't been on many road trips and being stuck in a car with him might be sort of fun. I pull the map back out and look at what is on the way. Nashville is some place I plan on visiting someday, as I'm an avid lover of country music, and everyone says it's a great place to travel to. I wonder if he would be interested in that being a stopping point. It's about a ten hour drive, so it would fall into the category where we could stop in for the night and explore possibly.

"So, what if I want to drive with you, are you against Nashville? It's the only place on the way I'd like to stop."

"Anything for you. Remember I don't have a job waiting on me, so we can stop anywhere you want," he says, taking my face into his hands and giving me a sweet kiss.

Saying goodbye to my dad broke my heart, but soon enough he will be coming out to stay. Jeremy won't be able to handle it by himself for long, not with how much care he is going to need once it gets worse. It scares me knowing the next time I see him, he might not remember me at all, but I'll be back for Thanksgiving and Christmas.

We finish putting everything from his closet into boxes, and carry them out to the truck. The whole backseat is filled to the brim with boxes and we can't fit anything more. The rest will have to be shipped or picked up when we come back out for the holidays.

He takes one last look at the house before shutting the door, and locking it. It's a big deal for him to move across the country and leave everything he's ever known. I know he is trying not to let me know how it's affecting him, but he doesn't have to hide it from me. I'll understand.

"All aboard. Let's get this show on the road. It's already nine in the morning. If we make good time, we can be in Nashville by eight tonight. We can get something to eat and look at whatever else you want. Sound good?"

"Wonderful," I reply.

He starts to back out of his driveway, but a call comes through from the Kaser's.

"Hello?"

We are both shocked to see their name pop up, but want to know the reason they are reaching out. It seems weird since we haven't heard from them since the park and they took Jake home suddenly when we were having fun. It's been bothering me trying to figure out what we did.

"He's got a little league game on Wednesday and asked if we would invite you," Veronica says.

Aiden answers. "We'd love to. Wouldn't miss it. Text me the details. I don't know my way around that town yet, so I'll have to use Maps for everything."

"See you Wednesday. Have a good morning," she says, before hanging up.

We look at each other, and smile. So maybe, I read too much into them leaving and nothing is wrong at all. Surely, they wouldn't be inviting us to his game if they didn't want us around.

"Let's get the hell out of here. Nashville, here we come."

It's interesting to see everything on the way, it's so pleasing. Arkansas has so many mountains and it's so red and orange from Fall. Sometimes, you can go forever without seeing a single house, instead nothing but fields of trees. We play music, so I pair my phone to the truck, and put on a Road Trip playlist on Spotify. What's a trip without some old school music to bring back your teenage years, right? You know, the guilty pleasure songs, that everyone sings when they come on, but they weren't the popular ones when they were first released. Shania Twain comes on, and of course, I know every single word. That woman is amazing, and still singing. I'd love to attend a concert of hers one day. Right now, it seems she is only doing them in Las Vegas, and not a fan of going there. It's a tourist trap with two long streets chalk full of hotels, casinos, and attractions that cost way too much money. My mother, Regina, once surprised Donald by taking him on a last minute vacation about a year after I came to live with them, and all they did when they got back was complain about how much money they spent and how unpleasant the experience. The one thing I remember from that conversation was a salad that cost $26. Who the hell charges that much for a salad? No thanks. Although, most restaurant in Cambridge are that away.

Aiden hasn't been talkative, but honestly I think it's because we have been enjoying the sights, and all the colors that surround us. It's peaceful, and the windows are down enjoying the wind through my hair. We have been driving for about two and a half hours, and the gas light came on. This truck definitely doesn't get as good gas mileage as my little car. I can fill up and get like three-hundred-and-fifty miles before I have to fill up again. He only gets about one-hundred-eighty miles. I see a gas station coming up on the right, and it's a little mom and pop looking one, and for some reason it creeps me out. It's an old tin building, in rough shape, but who knows when we will see another gas station. The next major city is Little Rock in Arkansas and we still have about two hours before we hit that. So, if we gas up here, we won't have to stop again until we hit there.

The tires hit the gravel, and it crunches underneath his tires as we come to a stop beside a gas pump. "I'll pump. Take this and pay for gas and snacks. I'm getting a little hungry but no time to stop and eat an actual meal."

"Anything specific?"

"Road trip food. Beef Jerky. Chips. Whatever."

I peck him on the check, grab the money, and run my happy butt inside. The bell on top of the door makes noise, alerting the man at the counter of my arrival.

"Good afternoon, darling."

"Hey," I reply, slipping down the first aisle where the beef jerky is, grabbing a bag of regular and then teriyaki. I don't know which one he'll want. The chip aisle is next where I falter between Sour Cream and Onion Lays or Cheddar and Sour Cream ruffles? I say fuck it and grab them both, and a couple cherry coke's to last until we stop again.

I lay all of it down on the counter in front of the man, and he continues to stare at me. "And whatever is owed for gas on Pump 1, please."

He rings everything up. "That'll be one-hundred-seventy-two dollars and sixty-three cents."

I get the cash out of my pocket he handed me and realize it is two one hundred dollar bills. "Here you go."

Gas prices are ridiculous right now, and only getting worse each week. I can't imagine spending one-hundred-fifty dollars to fill up my car. Although, I have to remember he has a huge tank, and the miles to the gallon are poor. I'll never understand why men like trucks so much. They could save so much money driving a small car. Or maybe, it's an ego thing.

He hands me the change, and I run out of there as fast I can, feeling like he's staring at me the whole time. *Creep.*

"You in a hurry?" he asks, as I get in the truck.

"Let's get the hell out of here."

Once we are down the road, he asks me what the hell is going on. I told him about how the man was staring at me, and made me extremely uncomfortable, but maybe that's from the scary movies Jeremy had me watch yesterday. I'm not a scary movie fan at all. Never have been, but he talked me into watching a movie about a sister and brother that get run off the road and murdered. Not my cup of tea, and maybe it's making me paranoid.

He pulls me closer to him, and puts his arm around my neck. "Nobody's going to mess with you. I'll make sure of it. Sit back and relax."

Before we hit Little Rock, we stay on the interstate and go through so many little towns, and it's interesting to see the different style types of homes and barns in the middle of nowhere. We make it maybe twenty-minutes before we bust open a bag of beef jerky, the teriyaki kind, and start chowing down. We should have eaten before we left, but oh well.

"So, be honest, are you excited about me being in Cambridge?" he asks, but keeps his eyes on the road.

Yes, but nervous, too. This is a huge jump from not even talking a month ago. The thought of possibly rushing into things is going through my head, but I try to keep myself from harping on it too much. "Of course. The plan was always to find you after getting my degree but then life happened. Things changed, but here we are now."

I never planned on meeting someone in college, and getting married, but I did. Maybe it's best things didn't work out, or I never would have gotten another shot with Aiden. Sometimes, I wonder if I should have caught on to his ways earlier than I did. Sure, I was overloaded at work, but he stopped being intimate with me as much, but I think I played that off as being exhausted from working all the time. I'll never understand how movies depict women as being ready all the time. I'm not going to lie, there are some nights where I want to curl up in bed and close my eyes with no thoughts of getting laid. Who has the energy for that after working fourteen hours? Not me. At least, not with Roger. Maybe that's why he started seeing his assistant, she was accessible to him all the time, and I wasn't. No excuse though. He's an asshole, through and through.

"Turn it up!" Aiden says.

Backstreet Boys comes on and no matter where you are, when *I Want It That Way* comes on, you have to sing it with all your might. He starts belting out the lyrics and it's like I fall for him all over again. The way he feels okay to be himself and not worry about what anyone thinks, it's freeing. He might have cared in high school but now.

The next two hours are spent bingeing Backstreet Boys and N'sync albums and finding out we still remember almost all the lyrics to all their songs. Go figure. I like all music, and not picky on what I listen to, Rock, R&B, Country, Pop, or whatever else. If I like the beat and the message of the song, I'll give it a chance. I'm an Equal Opportunity Listener.

We stop and get gas in Little Rock and then again in Memphis. We are on the last stretch before hitting Nashville and shouldn't have to stop again before making it there. I go ahead and try to find a hotel for tonight. I type in Luxury Hotels in Nashville and a bunch of listings come up. Some cost as much as one-thousand dollars a night, but that's ridiculous. I keep scrolling until I see Margaritaville Hotel. It's cheaper, but still nice and runs three-hundred-fifty dollars a night. I want to stay somewhere that going to be close to things to do, and restaurants, but then I see they have a fancy on-site restaurant and only a five minute walk to Broadway. Done deal. I pull out my credit card and go ahead and book the room.

"We have a room booked, and I'm so ready to have an actual meal, it's not even amusing," I say, patting my stomach.

He smiles. "I'm ready for dessert."

19

AIDEN

The traffic coming into Nashville is worse than Dallas and that's saying something. We have been stuck in a standstill for almost fifteen-minutes and have moved past one exit so far. The one we need to get off on is about four up, and it might take us another two hours to get there at this rate. What the hell is going on?

"I wonder if there's an accident or something. No way it's this bad on a weeknight," Hazel says.

Cars start to move a little faster at a time, and about fifteen-minutes later, we are finally getting off on the exit to the hotel. My mind might be fixated on dessert, but it's definitely time to eat something besides jerky and chips.

I follow the GPS and when it has me approach this hotel, I eye Hazel. "How much did this cost?"

"It doesn't matter. I covered it."

"You don't have to pay for everything. I'm perfectly capable of paying for our hotel room."

I try not to get to bent out of shape, but this isn't how our relation-ship is going to be with her always wanting to pay for everything. This must have cost at least two-hundred bucks. I would have been perfectly fine staying in a small hotel and walking over to all the stuff she wants to do. Hazel seems to like fancy stuff, and that lifestyle. While I admit, I love my big house and my truck, spending that much on a hotel for one night is insane.

The truck comes to a stop, and she gets out to check us in, while I grab our two small suitcases with two extra pairs of clothes and personal hygiene items. We figured we would stop tonight and drive most of the day tomorrow. To be honest, my eyes are starting to burn from staring at the road so long, and don't know how long I'm going to be able to stay awake for sight-seeing tonight, but I'm going to try my best since it's something she has been looking forward to all day.

I meet her in the lobby, which looks like a freaking resort catered to rich people, with probably a million dollar chandelier hanging above. Too much for my taste. I follow her to the elevator, and then to the room door.

"Next time, let me pay, please."

She smiles, opens the door, and ushers me inside.

"Let's get changed and go get something to eat. There's a Steak and Oyster place close. It's got good reviews on Yelp. Or, do you want something else?" she asks.

When does a man ever turn down steak? I already eat it a lot, but what's one more time? "Fine, but I'm paying for dinner. No arguing."

I drag out a pair of black slacks and a blue button-up to wear for dinner, since most likely, it's going to be a fancier steak place, only because that seems to be where she gravitates. It's around eight thirty and if she's lucky I'll be awake until eleven or midnight. Probably not going to last much after that. Especially, if we are driving all day tomorrow.

The bathroom door opens and she is fucking teasing me with a cute almost floor-length summer dress and black flats. The only reason she's wearing those is because we will be walking everywhere tonight, and I'm not an idiot. Why wear heels if you don't have too? Am I right?

"Fuck. I wish I could ravish you right now."

"We should get dinner first. Dessert later."

I take her hand as we exit out of the lobby, and the GPS takes us to the restaurant. The way we are dressed is a little overkill, because as we walk in, it's a chill environment. Most patrons are wearing jeans and a t-shirt. Most steakhouses where I'm from are considered on the fancy side. The hostess takes us right to a table, and takes our drink order.

"This place is actually cozy. I love all the wood," Hazel says.

The waitress brings our drinks and sets down two menus. "I'll be back in about ten-minutes to see if you are ready to order."

We both nod, and pick up a menu. I don't know about her, but my stomach is growling so loud, it's embarrassing.

The prices aren't too atrocious. I take a look at the appetizers and spot deviled eggs with caramelized onions and Canadian bacon.

"I'm gonna get an order of the deviled eggs to start. Probably the Dry-Aged Strip Steak." It's described as being twenty-one day dry-aged with cracked peppercorn garlic butter, chive whipped potatoes, and grilled asparagus, and fried onions. I'm practically frothing at the mouth right now.

"Help me choose. The Nudie Suit or the Belle?"

My eyes cut to the menu to see if she's fucking with me. Nope. There is actually a menu item called Nudie Suit. "You know which one I'm going to pick by just the name."

The waitress comes back and takes our order, and then the live band starts playing. It's an open environment, because you still see everything going on outside with the big bay windows, but still feel like you're in the old south because of the saloon feel. She moves closer to me, my hand resting in her lap, as we enjoy the country music.

The waitress comes by and drops off a basket of garlic rolls and our deviled eggs, which are delicious and my stomach thanks her silently.

In walks someone that I know is going to get Hazel freaking out. Instead of telling her, I wait to see her reaction as he gets up on stage.

"Hey everybody, just wanted to stop in and do one song for ya guys," Luke Bryan says.

Hazel's eyes grow wide, and then she turns to me. "That's Luke Fucking Bryan. I must be dreaming. No way he is here right now."

I pinch her. "He's here. Stop being a psycho groupie."

She stands up and yells, "I love you."

Everyone laughs, and he starts to sing one of his best hits. I don't recognize the song, but I am not someone who listens to music all the time either. Hazel seems to know it and I watch her idolize over him for about three minutes until the song is over.

"Thanks for listening. Have a good night everybody."

What are the chances that he would walk into this place out of everything in Nashville and just play a song? Hazel is one lucky girl.

"Here's your steaks," the waitress says, and then asks us to cut them to make sure they are cooked right.

"Perfection. Thank you."

We practically eat our food without chewing it seems like because within fifteen-minutes we are full and fat. Hell, I don't think I've ever eaten so fast in my life.

"I'm almost reconsidering going anywhere else. Pretty sure I just gained like ten pounds," Hazel says.

I jokingly tell her she's still the most stunning woman in the room. These little things I am getting to experience with her means a lot. Sometimes, people get caught up in the big things and forget about all the small things that give us joy, like enjoying a nice dinner with someone you love. Or, watching her fan-girl over a famous country artist while on a date with you. Sure, I could get jealous, but I'm the one she's going home with tonight.

The waitress brings the check, and I hand her my debit card before she even sits the billfold on the table. "Thank you."

"So, what's next?" I ask.

"Country Music Hall of Fame?" she says, her shoulders going up.

She's so cute, and I know she's scared that I'm going to go say no. And I could, but who knows when she is going to get another opportunity to come here, so I pull myself together, and will find somewhere that sells coffee. I'm not going to keep her from doing anything.

The waitress brings back the check, I leave a thirty-dollar tip, and we head out onto the street toward the Museum, which conveniently has a Starbucks on the corner. It's like they know me so well. I ask her to wait while I grab a cup before we head in. If I didn't get some good caffeine in my system, I'm not going to last much longer.

The line is about six deep to order, and so instead, I pull up their app and do a mobile order, hoping it will be faster than waiting in line. I go basic with some regular coffee plus cream and sugar. It takes about five-minutes for them to call my name, and I run out of there to find Hazel. She is standing in front of a store window, eyeing a dress.

"If you want it, just go buy it."

"It's not that simple. It's like thirty-five hundred dollars. Maybe someday," she says.

My first thought is to walk inside and buy it for her, but with things going with moving, and Jake coming into my life, I should save my money since I don't know when I will be getting a call back on a job. Normally, I wouldn't even think about stuff like that, but I must now.

She takes my hand, and buys the entrance passes to the museum. I won't say I love country music, but I'll listen to it if it's playing. This is more for her, but I'll make sure to show some enjoyment throughout the place. It's huge, and has halls and halls of famous country artists that have been inducted into the Hall of Fame. Many of which I've never heard of. Hazel is so excited every time we walk into a new room, almost fan-girling about everyone. She's so cute like this.

"You know, if I had known this would get you hot and bothered, we'd have come here a long time ago," I say.

"Haha. So funny."

We continue dipping in and out of halls until around an hour had passed, and we are at the end of the museum. She seems bummed, but I'm overjoyed at the thought of shutting my eyes for more than a few minutes. We walk out of the museum and head back to the hotel room. Hazel snuggles up next to me once inside, and its light out for us.

AFTER BEING scared awake by my alarm, we have been on the road all day, and only have ten minutes until we hit Cambridge. The traffic hasn't been obnoxious thus far, and hoping it continues that way. We found some new artists to binge like Green Day, Blink 182, and Journey. They keep us company all the way to Hazels' house. God does it feel good to finally be able to get out of the truck. My legs feel like putty.

"It felt like we were never going to make it."

Obviously, I know, I'll be staying in the guest bedroom, and I don't mind. The last thing we need to do is be stuck in the same room as each other twenty-four-seven. I don't want to become a mooch and have her get sick of me or anything.

I leave all my boxes in the truck, and only grab our luggage to drag inside, and then up the staircase. Hers is dropped off in the master bedroom, and then I roll mine to the guest one. I don't even wait to see if she needs anything, instead I turn off the light, take off my pants, and slide under the covers. It's been a long ass day and I don't have much energy for anything right now.

Things are going to get more complicated after tonight since we will be living together, but this is a good test to see if we can stand each other after the honeymoon phase ends. Of course, the first couple of months is always all sex and perfection, but after is when you get to see if the relationship can survive. With all the time we spent together prior to her leaving, I think we can handle it, but also know that we have both changed. Things are different when you are living together, which is why I've always been an advocate for moving in together before you get married. Sure, in some countries you don't even have sex before you are married, but to me, that means you are marrying someone you don't know if you are sexually compatible with, or how their personal hygiene is. These are big things you need to know before getting married to someone.

I know I've talked before about never wanting to be married, but Hazel is the exception. Of course, I already proposed to her once and she turned me down, so I need to be damn sure she is going to say yes next time. Or maybe, she doesn't ever want to be married again? As long as I get to be with her, marriage doesn't matter to me.

"Are you asleep already?" Hazel says, turning on the light.

I cover my eyes with my hands. "Well, I was about to be. That's bright."

The light turns off and then the bed squeaks, and she lays down next to me, her palm landing on my chest. "Do you mind if I join you?"

It's kind of a stupid question since she is already pressed against me, her warmth only makes me eyes want to close.

"Goodnight, Aiden."

I turn to kiss her, and whisper. "Goodnight, love."

20

HAZEL

Of course, my alarm goes off way to early, reminding me that today is the day I return to work. I wish I could stay in bed with Aiden all day, but duty calls. There's no telling what I've missed while being gone, and the amount of things I have to catch up on. I'm already stressing over whether or not I will be able to go to Jake's game on Wednesday. All I can do is work extra hard to catch up to earn the time to be off a little early.

My feet hit the arctic, hard wood floors causing me to tense up, forgetting to keep my socks on last night. I like to sleep cold, but it sucks when you are trying to gain motivation to crawl out of bed. I leave Aiden sleeping, and tip-toe to my bedroom to start the shower. It's only like six in the morning, and he's probably exhausted. The road trip did sound fun in theory, but yesterday we spent like twelve hours in a car with minimal stops only to retrieve gas to make sure I made it back in time for a good night's sleep before work. Aiden did that for me.

I strip down, my clothes hitting the tiled floor, and step into the shower letting the hot water cascade down my body. Nothing like a morning shower to wake me up, and prepare me ready for the day ahead. Hell, I already have the start of a migraine and haven't even left the house yet, but I know how hectic things are at the firm, and being gone for two weeks only makes my return worse. Lydia did win my case while being in Grapevine, but a new case will start today.

The two-in-one shampoo and conditioner comes out of my hand as I massage it into my hair, and then wash it out quickly. I'll need at least thirty-minutes to prepare for the date. I wrap one towel around my body, securing it around my breasts, and then the other around my hair, and tucking the excess into the side by my ear. Hopefully, it won't still be soaking wet once I'm dressed and put my makeup on. The light in the closet is on, and I go to the left side which is where I keep all my work appropriate clothing and accessories and start browsing through. My eyes land on an emerald-green mid-length dress, and pair it up with some classic three-inch black pumps. The outfit sits on my bed until I'm ready to put it on. Is it weird that I feel like I'm playing a role? You know, the good little office woman, and even though there's nothing in the dress code about women having to wear dresses, skirts and heels, it's almost implied. There are about fifteen other women that work for the firm, and I've never seen them in a pair of slacks before. Most are always dressed to their nines, decked out in expensive jewelry, and holding their head up high.

Without taking my hair down, I apply some black eyeliner on both my upper and bottom lids, and then some subtle gold eyeshadow, then finish it off with a touch of a light red lipstick. It's important to look our best, and when I was hired, there was actually a conversation about how what we wear is how we are perceived, and the firm didn't want anyone to come to work in less than Business Professional attire. Of course, I wouldn't do that anyway, and it is weird they had to specify that to any adult, but I'm sure there is always that one person who pushes the boundaries to see what amount of work is required to keep their job.

My feet drag against the tile, until they hit the carpet, and I stand in front of the end of the bed, and put the dress on first, and then the black pumps. I don't even feel like the same person anymore. Something about these outfits gives me confidence. I grab the small gold hoop earrings and put them in, before massaging some mousse into my hair, giving it some extra hold for the natural curls to come through. It's drying pretty quick, so hopefully, by the time I make it into the office, it will be dry enough where it won't be noticeable.

I peek in on Aiden who is still passed out, wrapped up in the sheets, and face down. He is tired, so I don't want to wake him, so instead, I leave a note on the nightstand. The stairs creak a little as I walk down, and then put two scoops of coffee into the maker and press start. There is no way I'm getting through this day without some caffeine. I grab a banana to scarf down for some breakfast, until the coffee is ready and fill my to-go mug and head out the door, setting the alarm behind me.

The traffic is insane, everyone trying to speed their kids to school on time, and on top of that the eight o'clock workers trying to make it work without being late, too. Sometimes, I go in early to beat all this, but not today. If this new case comes in today, I'm going to need about five more cups of coffee. I pull into the parking lot, step out, and head toward the front door, and then straight to the elevator. When it dings on the fourth floor, people start to welcome me back with smiles, and I try to seem polite, but don't want to stop and talk to anyone yet.

After making it to my office, I set down my briefcase, and fire up my computer to catch up on emails and chug my coffee. Hopefully, no one will bother me for the first hour, so I can rummage through and see what I have missed in the last two weeks. The firm can obviously run without me, but I like to keep up with my cases and being in Grapevine, I tried to keep myself from checking in at work, and use the time to take a break from it all. I'm a workaholic, but as a new lawyer I have to be, if I ever want to make partner, they have to see I'm willing to do the hard work and give up having a social life. And for the most part I have, but now being able to have a relationship with my son, I have to tread lightly because the one thing I'm not willing to do is sacrifice growing our relationship.

It's easy to accumulate emails, and I can spend half my day trying to answer them. Surprisingly, no one comes in until around one in the afternoon, and it's Jayden to give me insight on my new case. He has been keeping up with it while I've been gone without even being asked.

"So, we are going to write a formal appeal. I've been digging, and I think you will be surprised on what I've found. I took the liberty of putting all in his file for you to look over," he says, slamming the file on my desk.

"You know, you really didn't have to do all that. But thank you. I'm almost done catching up on emails and then I'll look it over."

He leaves my office, and the intrigue sets in to where I can't focus on emails anymore. What did he find? I press control, alt, delete and then lock my computer. Our firm has represented him on multiple appeals and so far, each trial has been a mistake and only furthered his guilty charge. It's not only me handling this case, but about twenty others. We are all looking into old case files of the prosecutor, and their careers to see if there is anything that stands out as far as when selecting jurors or any allegations brought up against him. My official role on this case is project manager, and I'm supposed to go through any material the others find and determine if it can be helpful in getting the charges dropped.

I open the folder, and for the next two hours, cipher through all the notes Jayden has taken, as I comb through them. So many things stand out, and even though we have to do more research to be able to use them in another appeal, these might be what we need to finally overturn his conviction. Being a lawyer isn't all about the money for me, it's about helping people who can't help themselves, and legally speaking this man needs people who believe he is innocent and will work their asses off to prove it. That's me.

The thing is, none of this is confidential, trial records are public knowledge, but there is so much paperwork to sift through, it takes forever to find anything worth a damn. I have been focusing on this case since I started with the firm, and the partners are dedicated to getting this man out of prison. A couple times, I've wondered if it's personal, and one of them knows him or his family.

My phone vibrates against the wood desk, and I look over to see it's Aiden. Surely, he's not waking up. It's like three in the afternoon.

"Good afternoon, sleepyhead."

"Hey there, gorgeous. You going to be working late tonight?" he asks.

"It's looking that way. Groceries will be delivered to the house shortly. Put the order in when we were still in Grapevine."

"Okay, great. I'll make some lunch. Hope your first day back isn't too deplorable. See you later," he says, before hanging up.

The more I get done today and tomorrow, the better my chances at leaving early enough to go to Jake's game. So, it's crunch time. I continue to shuffle through the folder, and make two piles. One requires more documentation and research before we can use it in court, and the other is not enough by itself to present. I didn't want Jayden to feel like he didn't do a great job finding all of this, but being a lawyer is hard, and unfortunately most times you have to do some digging before you find gold.

Jayden comes into my office, and asks what he can help with, and I hand him the research stack of papers. "Look into these. If we can gain more supporting evidence, we could use it in court."

He nods, and leaves my office.

"Hello, miss. I've got a delivery for you," a young man says.

"Oh, thank you."

He sits a vase of flowers, chocolates, and a notecard down on my desk and has me sign a paper to confirm I received the delivery. I smell the flowers, open the chocolates, pop one in my mouth, and then open the card.

Hazel,

I'd like to request a quick recess from work around dinner time. You have to at least eat dinner, right? I'll make a reservation so we can get in and out in an hour.

Love,

Aiden

He never ceases to amaze me, and it's nice to have someone who is romantic. My ex-husband is definitely whatever is the opposite. I pull out my phone and text him, yes. He's right; I might have to work late tonight, but if I don't eat, then I'll be worth nothing. It's nice to know he's thinking about me. I hate that I have to jump right into work when we got back, but that's what being an adult is all about, right? Of course, I wish I could be laid up on the couch, snuggled in his arms, watching whatever binge-worthy tv show, but I'm not.

Aiden: *Reservation for Bon Ami Gai at six.*

I smile, and try to focus on work until dinner. The stack of papers that needs more documentation is slowly dwindling down between me and a few others that are still here to help with the case. If we can score more documentation to prove his incompetence when selecting jurors, this could be something that can blow the bottom out of the prosecutors case. This could help overturn his conviction. How has no one read more into this until now? Although, if you aren't searching for it, most wouldn't think to look into his past cases and allegations against him.

My alarm goes off at five-forty-five to alert me that our reservation is soon, and as much as I want to continue the deep dive into the prosecutor, I can't bail on him the first night we are back. So, I lock my computer, put the pile of papers into my locked cabinet, and try to think about something else.

I always keep a spare outfit in my office, and right now it's a mid-thigh black and white polka dot skirt from Macy's and a pair of red booties. The black blouse I currently have on will match perfectly. My hair is up in a cute up-do, but I consider letting it down for dinner. Is he going to nibble on my neck? Earlobe? Maybe back me up into the wall and have his way with me? I shiver as the memories of us fling around in my brain.

Work is going to be stressful this week since picking up a brand new client, but even I have to eat. It makes it better that I will have good company for the hour. Aiden has been supportive so far of my career, and long hours, but Roger was too before he started cheating on me. *Don't go there.* Aiden and Roger are not the same man, and I can't fault Aiden for what he did. He's one hundred percent a better man than Roger will ever be.

I leave my hair up, and throw on some red hoops I found in my top left drawer of my desk. Some might find it weird that I have a stash of extra clothes and jewelry, but you must. You never know when you are going to need to change, and it's always better to be safe than sorry.

It's ten-minutes until our reservation and traffic should be light this late, but I hate being late to things. I take one last glance at myself, and strut out into the main walkway to the elevator. As I wait, my foot taps and someone in the desk closest to me starts to stare.

The elevator finally arrives, and it's chalked full, leaving enough room for me to squeeze in. Normally, I would wait until the next one, but I didn't think I could spare the extra few minutes. My nervousness has gotten worse since we both arrived in Massachusetts, because now there is more riding on this. Our personalities have changed a little since we separated and now it's interesting to see what makes him tick, what excites him. Some is exactly the same, like seeing me in red.

The bell rings, alerting us that we have reached the lobby, and the restaurant is down the street from my office. I could have taken a cab, but that's silly. The exercise won't hurt me. As I enter Bon Ami Gai, Aiden is nowhere to be found, so I tell the receptionist I'll be at the bar when he arrives. I tap the bar, drumming on it, and ask for a vodka and sprite. It's not like him to be late, and it's now pushing ten minutes. Did he forget?

I pull out my phone, click on his name, and the line starts to trill.

"Hello?"

I sigh. "On your way? I'm waiting at the bar."

The line is silent for a moment. "I'm a couple minutes away. No, I didn't forget. See you soon."

The bartender slaps my drink down on the bar top and then places a small straw inside. Long work weeks always involve at least a bit of liquor. Stress is a killer and we all have our ways to cope with life. Some weeks are harder than others, but having Aiden waiting for me when I get home makes it all seem a little less dreadful.

A pair of arms wrap around my waist, and then lips are on my ear. "Hi, love. Sorry about that. Ready to eat?"

I spin around and embrace him before the hostess takes us to our table. Something seems off with him.

"So, what were you doing today?"

His hand runs across the back of his neck. "You know I believe I have a drinking problem, and so I went to an AA meeting. I don't want anything to jeopardize my relationship with you or Jake."

He has mentioned his love for alcohol, but didn't realize it has been that hard to quit drinking. Aiden has been nothing but honest with me about that since moving here, and the fact he is willing to attend meetings means he is taking this seriously. This makes me so proud of him.

"That's great. You know I'm here for you if you need to talk. Or anything," I say, flagging down a waitress to take my drink away. Alcoholism is a hard thing to quit and it's not right for me to be drinking in front of him.

She returns back with a notepad and pen to take our order, and we both order the garlic and herb salmon with a side salad and grilled zucchini. One thing I do is order the chef's special almost anywhere I go because it's usually highly rated and the best thing on the menu. Even though it's also the most expensive.

The topic is changed by him when he asks how the case is going. The problem is it's going to be a hard one to win because it's a higher profile case from 1989 where my client, an African American male, was accused of murdering four people inside a family owned general store. All the evidence is circumstantial, and the eyewitnesses that place him around the scene of the crime are convicted felons. It's hard for a felon to turn down a reduced sentence in exchange for information, even if that conversation never happened. The prosecutor has been accused of jury tampering in other cases, but not this one and it might be about time we hit on that. Every single juror on this case was white, and race played a huge part in convictions during that time period. Our justice system is about having a fair trial and innocent until proven guilty, but for him, the first time he was brought in by the local police, it put a target on his back, and he was the talk of the town. Now, of course, most of his case is public knowledge and has been followed by the media since his first trial, and this is no exception.

"Can't you have everything thrown out since there is no DNA evidence that ties him to the murder?" Aiden questions.

If only it were that simple. "I wish my job was that easy. There are still many eye witnesses who place him there, and a fellow inmate who testified to him confessing to the murders while being in the same cell."

This is all public knowledge so I'm not telling him anything he couldn't look up himself.

"That's such shit. How do people get away with that?" he asks.

"If only I had a definite answer for you, babe."

Our dinner arrives and we focus on devouring it instead of talking about my job. It's not something I like to go into depth on, because I spend enough time worrying about it in the office and don't want it to interfere with our time. I think that was Roger's biggest complaint that I couldn't leave it at the office and always brought it home and never spent time with him.

Aiden starts raving about how good his meal is, and I agree, is my favorite from this restaurant by far, and worth the price. Normally, when you come to upscale restaurants the portions are small, and you leave wanting another meal, but not here. It's just enough.

My alarm starts to go off as I am taking my last bite, and I scoff. "It's time for me to head back. One of the partners wants an update on the case, and it's not something I can be late to." I wipe my mouth with the napkin, and then move over to the other side of the table to give him a kiss. "I'll see you in a couple of hours."

21

AIDEN

I watch as she leaves the restaurant and heads back to work, but sit and enjoy the rest of my food before leaving. Hazel's house is not as fun to be in when I'm by myself, and without a job currently, I might be going a little stir crazy. My application has been put in with the fire departments around the area and waiting to hear back about a position. With my experience, I doubt I'll be overlooked, but never know these days.

A part of me feels like a mooch, living in her house, and not working, but it's not like I'm broke. I thought about looking for a house to buy, but then if things work out between us, we would both have a house here, and that would be pointless. I am keeping my house in Texas because when we visit my family or hers, we have a place to stay. It's already furnished and everything.

I know sometimes it takes a minute to find a job, but don't want that to affect our relationship? She hasn't said anything, but a part of me wonders if it bothers her? I almost asked her the other night but stopped myself. We are starting back in the groove of things and don't want my doubts of something stupid to hinder our progress.

After the bill is paid, I head back out to my car, and take off toward Hazel's house. Tomorrow, I plan on going out and exploring the city.

Might as well take advantage of the downtime and learn where things are and what there is to do around here. If for some reason, I can't find a job as a firefighter, there is still my business degree. Yet, I'm going to hold out for a couple of weeks before jumping into a whole different profession. It's in my blood.

I see a car in her driveway, and when my car halts to a stop next to it, I can see someone standing at the door. The porch light isn't on so it's hard to make out anything.

"Can I help you?" I ask, walking up to the door and that's when I see a man, dressed in a suit, and holding a bottle of wine.

"I'm sorry, I must have the wrong house. She must've moved."

"Are you looking for Hazel? She still lives here."

"Oh, uh, who are you?" the man asks, eyebrows narrow.

"I'm her boyfriend, Aiden. I'll let her know you stopped by..." I stop, waiting for him to tell him his name.

"Roger. Just wanted to bring by a bottle of wine. It's our anniversary, well would've been."

Why the hell would he show up here? Hazel wants nothing to do with him. Maybe his mistress left him and now he's trying to crawl back to her.

"I don't think she's interested. You can go now," I say, brushing past him, unlocking the door, and then shutting it behind me.

Do I need to be worried about him? Hazel wouldn't ever go back to him, would she? And there go my insecurities, wondering if I'm good enough for her, and if this is going to work between us. It's a bitch. Of course, you see on television women talking about insecurities, but no one ever thinks about men when it comes to things like that. We might not voice them, but every man has something they are insecure about, believe me.

I plop down on the couch, and my phone dings. It's a message from Hazel warning me about Roger coming over. So, he is still trying to contact her, and she hasn't said a word to me? *Okay, wait, back down a bit. You are not the over jealous type.* I ponder over how to reply, because being a jealous person isn't something attractive.

Me: He's already been here and left. Didn't know you were dating anyone. I set him straight on that. Shouldn't show up again =)

I add the smiley face because, hopefully, that will make it seem less possessive. That's not who I am. Yet, the thought of him showing up angers me, and if he is smart, he won't do it again. Although, not sure he's that intelligent if he cheated on Hazel with an assistant. Dumbass. She is one of those that you hold on tight to and don't ever do anything to lose her. His loss, my gain.

I'm not going to let Roger coming here affect my relationship with Hazel. She's with me, and that's all that matters.

THE DOOR SLAMS and I startle awake, realizing it's now morning, and I must have fallen asleep on the damn couch. She didn't even wake me up when she came home, but there's no telling what time that was either. She's hitting it hard, and she might have received pushback from her ex about how much she is working, but I think it's admirable what she is doing for her clients. She loses some of her home life to try and set them free. Hazel is one hell of a woman. How insecure of a person did Roger have to be to cheat on her because she wasn't home often? Honestly, I think he would have ended up cheating on her regardless.

My feet drag up the staircase, and I jump in the shower real quick and then throw on some clothes. I'm not going to sit around the house all day today, instead I'd like to get out and see some things. I've never been to Cambridge before and the only thing I know about the city is that it's home to Harvard.

The search engine shows there are many museums, but I'm not that type of person. Harvard Square seems to be close, and has restaurants and stores to gawk at and get out of the house. I can only sit in the house for so long without going crazy. Not working is not like me, but I don't regret moving here.

I take the spare key, and lock the door behind me, and jog over a couple blocks to where Harvard Square is located. It reminds me of a town's main street with local restaurants, small bookstores, and boutiques. The coffee shop is my first stop because I can never have too much coffee.

"A black house coffee blend with two creams and three sugars please."

She takes the two dollars from my hand and then hands me the cup. Coffee is nice and warm, and it's about sixty-one degrees or so outside with a breeze. I should have grabbed a jacket, but oh well. The door closes behind me, and I saunter down the street, looking into the windows and seeing if there is anything inside that might interest me. At the end of the square, I cross the street and go down the other side, stopping at a small bookstore along the way. Many don't know that I do like to read. I rarely have the time or energy too.

Upon entering, there is a short older gentleman, petting a cat, and standing behind the counter.

"Welcome to Sam's. Everything is one dollar."

Is it weird that giddiness takes over as I start looking over the shelves to see where the murder mysteries are located. My mother used to read them when I was little, and when she finished one, she would leave it on my nightstand next to bed for me to read next. I didn't get to read all of them, some were inappropriate for my age, but I devoured book after book. When dad passed away, she didn't get much time for reading. It's the first section I search for, and start grabbing books and reading the blurbs on the back. If it catches my attention, I turn to the first page and read it, if it still piques my interest, then I intend to buy it. This isn't a good idea because after about twenty minutes, there are already ten books tucked underneath my armpit and it will take me a while to finish these. I better go ahead and get these and then come back when I'm done.

"You've got a good selection here. You read?" I ask, realizing it is stupid question if he owns a bookstore.

"Actually, no. My wife did though. Big lover of these books," the older man replies.

For some reason, I become intrigued with getting to know about how he acquired the store and his plans for it. When I ask, he seems almost taken back.

"Well, it'll go up for sale. I've got no family around here to pass it off to."

Poor guy doesn't have any family around, and the only social interaction he gets is with whoever comes into the store.

"Well, I'd love to know if you ever want to sell it. It's a great location," I say, picking up my bag of books and turning around to leave.

"I've been looking to sell it so I can officially retire, but no one seems to want it. You have serious interest in purchasing?" he asks, his chin dropping toward his chest. "If so, it's been on the market for about three years. Everyone that had any interest wanted to convert to a boutique or some crap, but I want someone who is going to keep it as a bookstore. There aren't many of us left."

It seems out of the blue, but owning a business isn't something I'm opposed to. "How much are you wanting?"

"All I'm asking is what I paid for it. Fifteen-thousand dollars."

"And all the books and things come with the place?"

"Yes, it's a steal deal, but with the stipulation it stays a bookstore. Most run when they hear that." He extends his hand. "Name is George, by the way.

"Aiden, sir. Good to meet you. I would like to buy it. Have your realtor draw up the contract and I'll be back on Thursday to chat," I say, taking the books and my coffee and heading back out to the square.

Is Hazel going to think I'm crazy when I tell her about purchasing the bookstore? It's an easy investment, and after some improvements, I can hire some staff and do some new things to attract more customers. If I end up getting a firefighter job, then I can still do that and help run the business on the side. Who knows, maybe I can be happy being a bookstore owner and it might prove to be easier working hours than being a firefighter. Most times, you start working overnights and on call on the weekends. I hated that when I first started at Grapevine, but didn't have a choice.

I stop and sit down at an outside table, and text Hazel.

Me: *So, I think I'm buying a bookstore. Call me crazy?*

She's at work, and won't see the text until later.

Hazel: Uh... details. Free for a quick lunch at that bistro down the street from my work on the corner? Twenty minutes?

A smile takes over my face, and I quickly reply as I start to walk that way. I stop by the house to drop off the books and grab my jacket and I'm still early.

City Bistro is a quaint little place on the corner with outside seating, and since the breeze has stilled down a bit, that's where I'm going to sit down and get a drink. The coffee dehydrated me, so my mouth is dry as fuck.

"So, tell me about this store. I'm so confused," Hazel says, slipping me a kiss on the cheek, before sitting across from me.

I know she is probably wondering why the hell I'm suddenly buying a bookstore, and maybe I am, too. It's not like I don't have the money and it's a great way to become part of the community, without having to work crazy hours as a firefighter. My brothers will probably say I'm going through a mid-life crisis, but that's not it. Running a business isn't an easy task. It takes hard work, dedication, and a good mind to keep a business afloat, but George isn't in the headspace anymore it seems like and I promise to do it justice for his wife.

"Just feel like, maybe this is my opportunity to have my own business, and learn more about the community. Who doesn't love an old bookstore? There are so many things I could incorporate to make it better, especially for the younger generations. I mean, think about it. Instead of just being a bookstore, we can have trivia nights, family game nights, and even karaoke."

Saying it out loud makes it more real, and sounds like a good plan, but what does she think? I study her face for a reaction, wondering if she thinks I'm nuts, but there's a smile.

"I think it's a wonderful idea. You know I love to read, but never have time for it anymore. You could make a wonderful addition to Cambridge."

Hazel used to always have a book in her hand in high school, and in study hall, she would be devouring the latest pick up from the local bookstore in Grapevine. It almost feels like with becoming adults, neither of us have been doing much reading anymore. Maybe this can change that. Help us get back into our love for reading and escaping to an alternate reality even if for a couple of hours a day.

I take her hand in mine, and look into her eyes. "It's never too late to get back into it. Today I bought ten murder mysteries and plan on reading them in the next week or two. Even if it's a couple chapters a day, it's enough to escape a little bit. Everyone can use something to keep their mind off the everyday stress.

The waitress finally comes and takes our order, which ends up just being two club sandwiches, and we continue talking about the bookstore. I have so many ideas already, and the next step is to work out how to execute them. I have about a hundred and fifty thousand left in the bank, and could use some of it to fix the place up, and make it more modern. Nothing against George, but it's dark and brooding inside right now, and not inviting. I have to change that. Open the place up, give it some color, and also places for people to sit, like reading nooks throughout the store. Hazel thinks it's a great idea, and I can't wait to start fixing it up. Of course, I'll have to shut down while I do the renovations and changes, but I think it will be fine. I must apply for my business license anyways.

After lunch is served, and all gone, Hazel heads back to work and me to the house to start mapping out where I want to change things and how. It's always good to have a vision before starting a project. The bookstore has three levels, and until I maximize space, there are things that will need to be done like new bookshelves, paint the walls, redo the counter area, and possibly install a coffee machine. Who doesn't like to drink coffee while reading their new story? It's almost a given. I could get some reading chairs or like reclining arm chairs to put in a couple spots throughout the store for people to curl up and read in. I haven't been this excited about something in a while.

A part of me wants to call Damon and tell him the good news, but decide to wait until after everything is finalized. Only because if I wait, he can't talk me out of it. Thursday, I'll go back and talk to George and see what we can get done and agree on. Tomorrow is Jake's little league game. Being a dad and meeting Jake showed me how much I need to grow up, and start taking risks, because without them you are never out of your comfort zone. The best things happen when you step out and enjoy.

Take Risks. Do things you wouldn't normally. They can payoff in good ways.

22

HAZEL

Crap! The exhaustion from working crazy hours has set in, and it's six o'clock. I slept right past my alarm and need to arrive at the office early. We are coming up on the wire of being able to obtain all the documentation for the hearing in front of the judge to have the case overturned, so the team is working nonstop. I pray we can get this finished before I have to leave to go to Jake's game tonight.

I hit the ground running, throwing on a black pencil skirt, white blouse, and black pumps before throwing my hair in an up-do bun since I don't have time to do anything with it. It's an early day to get a head start on finishing all the documentation for the high profile case. It's going to require my teams undivided attention today since he goes in front of a judge in two days. All of the evidence and documentation needs to be fool proof to give him the best chance at getting out.

After putting on the finishing touches, my feet scuffle down the staircase, and then into the kitchen to brew some coffee to take with me. While waiting on that, I go into the living room to put everything back into my brief case, before the coffeemaker beeps. I pour it into my to-go mug and make a beeline for the front door. I'm lucky because it's only six-thirty, so I will be able to miss all of the school morning rush traffic. The roads are empty and I make it to the office in less than five minutes.

Stepping out of my car, I see Jayden heading for the front door, and walk fast to catch up to him.

"Hey, you think we can get this all done today?" I ask.

"I'll update you hourly on the team's progress. This might keep some butts into gear to work faster. The partners are breathing down our necks to dig up anything we can to use in this hearing. I can't be the only one that feels like it's up to me to get this guy out after looking at his past cases."

Jayden and I have been working for the firm for almost the same amount of time, and this could be drudging up things from his personal life. His grandfather was prosecuted for a murder, and was sentenced to life without parole. At the time of his sentencing, he was already in his sixties, and instead of spending his final years with his family, he died in prison. A couple years after his death, evidence came forward that proved he did not commit the crime, and someone else ended up being put on trial and convicted. So, this case might hit close to home.

"Listen, if you need to step back from this. Everyone will understand," I say, as we step into the elevator.

"Hell no. If anything it makes me work harder to prove he's innocent. My pops wouldn't want me to sit by while another man rots in prison for a crime he didn't commit."

As the elevator door opens to our floor, we smile, and part our separate ways. The team working on this case with me is dedicated and most are trying to prove their worth to the partners, so none of them want to fuck up, especially on this case. The whole world is watching, and waiting to see if the firm is able to overturn the conviction, and I can't wait to see their faces when we do. The people who testified against him, spilling bullshit testimony to have their sentences lessened, or the racist hypocrites who didn't actually see him anywhere near the store, but assumed he did it. They are all going to see that justice will be served for our client.

Jayden keeps his promise and every hour, he comes into my office and gives me an update on the progress of the team with a folder of the things they completed documentation on. It makes things flow smoothly, and that gives me something to turn into the partners to keep them updated on our progress as well. Josh, Adam, and Linda have been working all day on the most effective strategy, since they have such a short amount of time to plead their case. When I turn in a folder, they choose two things that are the best to use. At the end of the day, they will go through the ones picked, and then weed it down to the top six.

Linda has been emailing me throughout the day asking me my opinions on some of the stances they could take, and which ones I would choose to use if I was the one in the court room fighting for his freedom. Honestly, the fact that he has been accused of jury tampering, purposefully striking black jurors without proper excuse, and the fact that in the prosecutor's notes, it shows the police questioned several people before our client, and a fingerprint from the scene matched one, but still let them go and arrested our client. This is enough for reasonable doubt, and using all of these things together should be able to open the judge's eyes to see that the prosecutor isn't doing what's right by the law, but using his power as a prosecutor to fulfill his personal agendas. Although this proved to be a problem back in the eighties and many cases have been overturned because of racial bias. The thing that hurts my heart the most is many of those that could have gotten out died in prison before times changed. If only I was practicing law in the eighties, then maybe I could've made a bigger difference.

It's almost five and I'll have to leave soon, and Jayden has informed me that the team is almost done going through all of the documents and he should be able to turn in the last section before I leave. Linda has been staying on top of it all day, and I can't leave until turning the final file is in to the partners. I go ahead and change into jeans, a t-shirt and some converses and wait for Jayden to turn it in. I've caught up on all my emails and low and behold five minutes before I need to leave, he walks in and hands me the final folder.

"We did it. Go hand it in and enjoy the game. The rest of us are going out for drinks."

I run upstairs, hand it to Linda, and then rush to the ground floor to pick up Aiden. Halting in the driveway, Aiden runs outside and jumps in, not skipping a beat, because we don't want to be late. They have been nice enough to invite us to this and don't want them to think we don't care. I go the back way to miss all the traffic and make it with five-minutes to spare. When we arrive inside the gym, we find the Kaser's and take a seat.

"He's number eleven," Veronica says, pointing him out to us.

The game starts and at first, we don't do anything but watch, but by the last quarter, Aiden is standing up cheering him on. They are tied, and there's only fifteen seconds left and our son has the ball. He looks over at Aiden, smiles, and shoots the ball without even looking, and score! The team goes wild, and the parents rush onto the court to congratulate their kids. These are the things we would never want to miss; sharing in his victories, and helping him in his defeats.

Aiden picks up him and swings him around. "You did it, son!"

The Kaser's seems a little shocked by him calling Jake son, but what do you expect? That's our son, too. Jake didn't seem bothered by it and when his feet hit the ground, he enveloped Aiden into a hug. "Thanks for coming. You must be my good luck charm."

Veronica and her husband embrace him, and congratulate him. "Looks like celebrating is in order. Where do you wanna go, sweetie?"

"Pizza!"

Aiden and I step back and thank them for allowing us to come watch, but then Veronica asks us to join them. We didn't want to impose, but not going to turn down the option to spend more time with him. So, we tag along and meet them at the local pizza place. It's a buffet style, and Jake loads his plate up with six different kinds of pizza. I laugh because that was me at his age too.

The evening goes great, finding out more about Jake. He asks many questions about us; like what we do, and if we would like to continue coming to his games. "We wouldn't miss it."

This is the beginning of a great relationship between the three of us and it means so much for him to ask us to continue coming. The Kaser's might not trust us fully yet, but hopefully that will change over the next couple of years. All we want is to be part of his life, so he knows we didn't just abandon him.

On the ride home, Aiden wouldn't stop talking about Jake, and how he is so much like him. He would have made a great father, and it hurts to know I will never be able to give him another kid of his own. Yet, he knows this, and continues to be with me, and loves me unconditionally.

Sometimes love can conquer all.

23

AIDEN

*A*fter my morning coffee, I grab my jacket and head over to the bookstore to talk to George. I have so many ideas on how to improve the place like making it brighter, and more inviting to the customers. I ended up staying up way too late yesterday looking at book-shelves, a new counter, and what color I should repaint the walls. I already went on and have many books in my list to purchase for new displays. That's one thing that I would like to incorporate is new books. Sure, used books are great, but new ones are as fun. The walk over is chilly, and upon walking in, George is sitting behind the counter, drinking a cup of coffee.

"Good morning, Aiden. Was hoping you would be back today. Didn't know if you were actually being serious," he says, putting down his coffee. "The realtor has the paperwork drawn up and can be by when-ever you are ready. He asked if you were going through a bank?"

"Nope, I have the cash in my account. Can write a check or money order. Whichever you prefer."

He nods, and picks up the phone to call. "He's here. Can you bring over the paperwork? Okay. See you soon."

"Are we good to go?"

"Yes, go get the payment and we can sign the papers today. Although, son, I'd like to keep the store open today and enjoy one last day if that's alright," George says.

I'm not sure if George expected me to kick him out as soon as we signed the papers, or if he thinks I'm going to be ready to run the store tomorrow, but it'll have to closed for at least a couple of days. As soon as we sign, I'll call the local company to make the new business sign, and then everything has to get done before it reopens. "You're welcome here anytime."

I leave and come back with a money order, and the realtor is there waiting on me. "Hello, sir. Thank you for being so swift on this."

He smiles, and hands over the paperwork. "I have put a sticky note in every place that needs your signature."

I nod, and hand George the order. "I promise to give this place a good chance. Hope you'll come by and check it out next week when I reopen."

We all three shake hands, and the realtor leaves.

"So, here are the keys. I'll return next week to give you my set and I'll close up tonight. When do you plan on reopening, son?"

"Monday, maybe. I'm hoping I can get someone in here to repaint the walls and stuff this weekend and then the rest of the stuff can be shipped the next day."

"Wonderful. I'll be around Monday afternoon."

The door closes behind me, and I call the place that is making the new sign. "Hello, this is Aiden Jackson. I've got the go ahead on the property. Can we do a rush order on it? Have it made and up on the building by Sunday night?"

A young man asks me to wait a minute while he checks with his supervisor, and then comes back and gives me the go ahead before hanging up.

I'm officially a business owner, and my heart is racing. What if I fuck it all up? The bookstore could bomb and be a horrible business decision. Damon and Liam will find out eventually, but right now, I want to keep the excitement and rush to Hazel and I. Not everyone will understand the impulsive decision to buy the place, and right now I need to focus on getting everything squared away.

Me: *It's done. I'm officially a bookstore owner! Ah!*

I stop in at the coffee shop, and start putting in all the orders for the books that I would like to put toward the register for new releases. There are many authors that readers devour like Stephen King, Nicholas Sparks, and Colleen Hoover. There were several newer releases I order multiple copies of, and then some signage as well. The one thing I haven't decided on yet is how to decorate the floors. A smart thing would be to separate the used books from the new. Maybe we could let the bottom floor be all used books since it's bigger, and then the main floor be for all new books. What about the top floor? We could make it into a kids area with books and little tables and chairs. So, I impulsively add lots of Dr. Seuss and other authors to the shipment too.

Hazel: *That's amazing. Lunch in an hour?*

I am wanting to save some money where I can, and painting is something I can do myself instead of hiring someone.

Me: *I'll be there. =)*

I can go pick up the paint, and have it done myself this weekend, and possibly get the new shelving units picked out and ready to go. Most of this can be taken care of today before the end of her shift.

Hazel: *Of course. Meet me in fifteen at the bistro.*

My feet hit against the pavement as I jog over to the bistro. Hazel doesn't get a very long lunch break and I don't want her waiting on me. As I get on the street, I see her waiting outside for me, and sneak up behind her.

"Hey, babe. Let's go inside," I say, putting my arm around her.

After getting seated, we take our coats off, and she's asking me about the bookstore. She seems excited about this adventure to be asking if we are going shopping later for furniture or what my plans are. I would love for her to feel included in this process. "I'm going to go pick out the paint after lunch, and then I thought I'd go shopping for furniture so that way we could pick it out and have it delivered on Saturday."

A waitress stands next to me, and waits for us to finish before she starts speaking.

"My name is Lauren. I'll be serving you this afternoon. What would you like to drink?"

"Dr. Pepper," we both said in sync.

"And do you guys know what you want to eat already or need a few minutes?"

"The clubs, please," Hazel says, handing back the menus.

"Alright, I'll be right back with your drinks."

I do want to get this re-opened as soon as possible, and there is so much to get done. Am I going to be able to open on Monday? Hazel gauges my concern and tries to comfort me.

"We got this. Pick out the paint and we can get it done tomorrow. The furniture we can handle tonight, and then on Sunday, we can install the shelving units."

"Only problem is, all the new books won't come in until Monday, so we might have to open on Tuesday instead. Yeah, we will do Tuesday to make sure everything is set and ready to go without any hiccups," I reply.

The waitress drops off our drinks, and I start to suck mine down. It's nice to have Hazel be so supportive of this decision, whereas if Liam was still around, he would be talking me out of it at every turn. We continue talking and I pull up the shelving units I've found that I like and they have them at Lowe's. I don't necessarily need all new bookcases, but would like to get new ones for the upstairs kid area. I get a white, two shelf bookcase and end up ordering four of them.

"Here you go. Let me know if you need anything else."

We scarf down our food because we wasted almost thirty minutes looking at units and waiting on our food. It's good as always.

"Listen, I'll get back to work, and once I'm done with my emails, I'll head out early. We won't get another case until next week. Might as well take advantage of the free time by using me to pick out awesome chairs," she says.

"Okay, well I'll go to Lowe's and get the paint then."

I give her a kiss and head back over to the house to get my car and use the navigation to get to the store. There are so many streets that are the same, like Cambridge Street, Avenue, Terrace, and so much more. Why would they do this? It's too damn confusing when you aren't from here.

After getting inside, there are so many blues to choose from and I end up going with the color called blue eggshell. It should brighten the room without being too crazy. The damn curtains are coming off the windows, too, when I get back to the store. Why have windows and not utilize them?

I stop by the store, unlock the door, and slip the paint inside before locking back up. Hazel is off and meeting me back at the house to go shopping. Things are going to be more fun with someone tagging along helping me pick out things other people are going to love. They have to be comfortable, sturdy, but also able to be sat in for a long time. We are in search of the perfect chairs.

"Honey, I'm home," I say, walking in the front door to find her already changed into jeans. "Damn, already? Figured you'd need an hour or so."

"Nope, let's go," she says, brushing past me to the car. "I don't waste no time when it comes to shopping."

The next several hours are jampacked at store after store trying to find the right chairs at a decent price. We end up at K's Furniture and Hazel falls in love with this navy reading chair. It swivels and leans back a bit, and it's the width where you can curl up and read.

"This is the one. We have to get it."

I take a look at the tag and smile. "Just in our price range."

The manager takes the tag, and rings up for ten of them to put throughout the store to be delivered on Monday.

"See. I told you everything would work out. Stop stressing. This should be fun for you."

Hazel can see right through me, and I hate it. Sure, I'm stressed, but more so because George is counting on me keeping the store going, and don't want to let him down.

I close my eyes, and mutter to myself. *You can do this.*

Hazel's phone rings, and I can hear a man's voice. She walks away from me a bit and can't quite make out what she is saying, until her voice jumps an octave. "Wait, are you serious?"

"What is it?" I ask.

"Thanks for updating me, Jayden. I'll talk to you later."

"Is everything okay?" I ask, holding her hands, thinking something is wrong until I see a smile.

"It got overturned. He is getting out. We did it!" She starts squealing, and jumping up and down. All her hard work has paid off, and another innocent man is getting out of wrongful imprisonment because of her.

"Baby, I told you could do it. Do you want to go to dinner and celebrate?"

She bites her lip, and comes a little closer toward my ear. "I was thinking more along the lines of dessert first."

Your wish is my command.

24

AIDEN

Over the last several days, Hazel and I have worked our asses off to get the store ready to reopen. We ended up covered in paint, lots of papercuts, but it's ready. Everything is in place, including the brand new sign. As soon I set eyes on this place, it didn't take me long to come up with the name and stick with it. George has been by and actually teared up when he took a look at the changes, and told me his wife would love it. This means so much to me because this was her baby, and I didn't want to take away from the vibe she gave it. The bottom has been transformed into a used book basement with over forty shelves filled to the brim with books and all separated by genre. Hazel made a good point about organizing them by genre but not necessarily by author since there are so many. There will be no way we can keep up with thousands of used books being alphabetized. The main floor is now the new book area along with new signage specific to authors like Colleen Hoover, Stephen King, and Nicholas, Sparks who have them on shelves filled with their books. I even lucked out and found some signed copies and have them on display by the door.

The weekend has been spent busting ass to get everything done and ready to go so we didn't have to waste another day closed. Grand Reopening day is tomorrow and we have a special day planned. After finding Krista and Amy, students at Harvard, that have agreed to work part-time to help me out around the store. They worked in the campus bookstore for a while last semester and so they had experience, and both seem upbeat and sweet. I let Hazel do the interviews, and I trust her opinion.

"Okay, everything is ready for tomorrow. You ready to head out?" Hazel asks, holding onto a wrapped package with a bow. "We don't want to be late for Jake's birthday party."

The Kaser's have been so kind to invite us to his birthday party, and we wouldn't miss it for the world. The entire reason I moved up here is to be close to him, and they have been more than generous in letting us spend time with him. "Let's go."

I walk out, and lock the door behind me, following Hazel to her car.

The party is at a local pizza and arcade restaurant, and it's only a couple blocks away, so we are in the driveway ten minutes early. Although, Hazel isn't ever late to anything, it's not in her nature. She has been working what I would consider normal hours since her firm got the overturned conviction and it's been nice. She is home for dinner at six o'clock and after we eat, usually we are on the couch, snuggled up watching a movie. I never would have thought this would be me if you had asked me a year ago.

My AA meetings have been helping and I haven't had a drink since arriving in Cambridge. The urge to get wasted is gone, but I owe a lot of that to Hazel and Jake. It doesn't help when you bury things inside, and use liquor to try and cover it up, or push it down further. I refuse to go there anymore. Once I realized the source of my drinking, it helped me stop. Being sober has been eye-opening and to make it even better, I have a wonderful woman who loves me and a son who calls me dad. Never did I think I'd get to hear him say it, but once he did, I never want it to stop.

As we walk into the restaurant, there are kids everywhere, running around, and playing games. I gaze around the arcade, looking for Veronica or Jake, but don't see them. "Maybe, they are in a room. Never been here."

Hazel takes point. "We are here for a birthday party. Jake Kaser."

The woman at the desk, types away on their computer, and points us to the back of the restaurant. "Party room two."

Many people would find our arrangement with the Kaser's weird, but to me it's perfect. For the longest time, I never thought I would ever get to see him, so the fact that I am getting to celebrate his ninth birthday with him today is phenomenal. None of this would have happened if Hazel didn't come down and ask me to write that letter. We would both still be having regrets and I'd be drowning my sorrows in liquor. This is proof that sometimes you have to take risks to get what you want.

"Aiden!" Jake says, running up to me and giving me a hug. "I'm so glad you made it. Come on."

I follow behind him until we are inside the party room that is filled with parents and children. Most of them are dressed in business attire, so I feel out of place. You can definitely tell that we aren't rich like everyone else. The whole back wall of the room is stacked up with gifts, and here we are with the smallest gift of all. Maybe I should have gotten him more. I pull the envelope out of my back pocket and stick it on top of the box in the corner.

"Thank you for coming to celebrate Jake's birthday with us today. The pizza will be put in here at five-thirty and until then, go enjoy the arcade," Veronica says handing out cards.

For a minute, I wonder how much they spent on this party, but then I remember they have no budget when it comes to expenses, and not to go down that road. As long as Jake is getting the education and love he needs, that's all that should matter right now.

Hazel stays back in the room with Veronica to help set up and I take off with Jake to do the racing games. Of course, he schools me and comes in first place every time. Ugh, that kid is good.

"I bet I can beat you in basketball. Wanna shoot hoops?" I say.

"Yeah right. When's the last time you played basketball?"

I didn't respond because I always played football as a sport, but every once in a while, Damon would ask to play and I enjoyed it. All you have to do is put a ball into a hoop. Yet, he schooled me. To be fair, he has been playing, so of course, he'd beat me. We continue to play games until a voice comes over the speakers announcing to go back to the party room.

"Come on, son. Pizza must be ready. I don't know about you, but I've surely worked up an appetite."

All the kids run past us, and start gorging away on the ten large pizzas sitting on a long table. Hell, at the rate these kids are piling up their plates, there might not be any left for the adults. It reminds me of my eleventh birthday, when my dad hosted the party at our house and ordered pizza. We didn't get enough, and he had to go back out and grab more so the parents could eat too. Jake is like me in so many ways and it's refreshing.

"Veronica asked if we wanted to go to dinner at their place this weekend."

I glance down at her. "Really? I mean, we can't say no. It might be interesting to see where they live."

When I picture their house, I think like a five-million dollar mansion with way too many bedrooms, luxury bathrooms, and a basketball court in their backyard along with like three acres of land. The Kaser's and us have been getting along and we want to keep it that way. I don't think they would withhold Jake from us, especially after we have been spending so much time together, but people can sometimes surprise you.

I sit down next to Hazel and eat a couple pieces of pepperoni pizza while watching Jake interact with his friends. Rich people usually come with their own problems. They don't have any concept of money, how other people feel, and sometimes are downright rude. The Kaser's haven't seemed that way yet, but it always shows in the kids. So far, Jake has been polite to everyone, and doesn't freak out over tap water. I remember once overhearing a child ask if they had sparkling water at the diner in Grapevine. Damon and I laughed so hard.

"It's time to do cake," Veronica says, lighting the candles and we all started singing.

Everyone chimes in and by the end, Jake's face is blushed. Maybe he doesn't like all the attention being on him. He blows out the candles, and a single tear appears. *I am not going to cry at his birthday party. Get it together.*

Jake doesn't end up wanting any cake, so they let him open presents while everyone else enjoys the massive cake at the end of the table. Gift after gift, and the things he receives blows my mind. One of them is a card with three hundred dollars inside. Who the hell gives an eight-year-old three hundred dollars? Rich people, I guess. He also got a brand new PlayStation and Xbox, along with a bunch of games.

"Do you think he's going to like our gift?" I ask, getting cold feet. "Maybe we should have gotten him something else?"

"Shut up. He's going to love it," Hazel replies, shushing me as he picks up the card and opens it.

He reads the front of the card and when he opens it, his eyes light up. "No way." He turns to his parents, and then looks at us. "Are these real?"

"Yes, buddy. What'd you say? Wanna go see the Lakers floor side with me?"

He drops the card on the table and rushes over to me, giving me the biggest hug of all. "I can't wait. Is mom coming, too?"

"We are all going. Your parents, too, if they want."

"This is the best birthday ever!"

Hazel kisses me on the cheek and whispers *I told you so* in my ear, while we watch him open the rest of the gifts. None make him smile quite like ours did. By the end of it, he's gotten almost a grand in cash. Kid makes out like a bandit.

We did clear the Lakers game with his parents before buying the tickets, because that's being respectful. They agreed to let us take him ourselves. It will be our first trip together and that makes it even more exciting.

After we say goodbye, and get back to Hazel's, the excitement of the day gets to me. Tomorrow is the opening of the bookstore, and my mind is going over everything, a check list of things to make sure everything is complete for tomorrow. Amy and I will open at eight in the morning sharp and hope that the ads in the newspaper and the hype on social media is going to bring customers in. I want this to be a success, and the first day being opening is going to tell me if this has been a mistake. I look up to the ceiling and mutter, *please let tomorrow be a great day.*

25

HAZEL

*T*oday has been looming in my mind and hoping for the best. It will crush Aiden if opening day doesn't go well and he barely slept last night. He might not verbalize that he's scared, but I can tell. He has put so much money and work into the store in the last four days, cramming most of everything over the weekend, and paying contractors extra to get stuff installed, and it's now time to see how it's going to play out.

"Good morning," I say, coming off the last step of the stairs and seeing him sitting on the couch. "Couldn't sleep?"

"Nope. Big day. Want to get there early and take one last look at the place before we open. Girls are scheduled to be there in an hour."

This is one of the instances where nothing I say is going to make it better, and opening day should be great. The Facebook event shows over four hundred people have said they are going to come check out the store today, and that's great. Aiden has so many things planned today, and has been receiving astounding engagement on his business page through social media. Amy has been handling most of it.

"It's going to be a wonderful day," I say, pouring my cup of coffee, and walking back into the living room. "I'll be by to check on you. I love you."

As I walk by him, he pulls me close to give me a kiss, and then sees me off at the front door. I wish I could go and take the day off, but we might receive a new case today, and that wouldn't help my chances at ever getting partner, so I decide to go ahead and go in. The traffic is minimal, and Jayden is waiting for me at the front door again.

"It's the big day. Is he nervous?"

"Didn't sleep. Poor guy."

"I'll post about the opening on my page, and see if I can send some people over there. I hope it does well. He's a good guy," Jayden says.

They haven't formally met each other, but he knows a little bit about Aiden and our past. Company parties involve booze and well regrets usually come up. "Thanks. The more people, the better."

There's nothing wrong with wanting him to succeed, especially since he moved from everything he knew to come out here. And yes, it wasn't to be with me, but I still suspect that had something to do with it. Even though he won't admit it.

I plop down in my office chair, and press the power button to boot up my computer, and take everything out of my briefcase while waiting. As much money as this firm makes and we still have outdated computers that could've used an upgrade a decade ago. The first ten minutes of my morning is waiting for it to come on so I can start my day. Ugh.

After going through and responding to all my emails, I go fill up my coffee cup, and try to see if Jayden has heard anything about a new case for today. I don't want to sound bitchy, but if we aren't getting one then I can take a couple hours off and go help with the opening. A part of me feels awful for not being there to support him, yet he knows how crucial making partner is to my career, and he wouldn't ever ask me to jeopardize that. That's why I love him. See, we support each other, and that's what makes our relationship flourish. Both of us have goals and push each other to achieve them without getting jealous or feeling left out. It makes a huge difference when you are with someone who is as driven as you are.

"So, any news on that case?" I ask Jayden, who is standing in line for a refill.

"Nope, haven't heard anything. Maybe this afternoon?"

"Well, I'm gettin' out of here. Can you call me if you hear anything and I'll come back?"

He nods, and I go back to my office, grab my stuff, and head to the parking lot. If I hurry, I can make it before he officially opens. The car is put into drive, and I speed out of the lot onto the street without a care in the world. The world must be on my side because I don't hit a single red light there, and pull up with five minutes to spare.

There is already a line waiting for us to open, and that makes me giddy. Aiden must be so excited. I knock on the door, and he lets me inside, and that's when I see him sweating profusely.

"Are you okay, baby?"

"No, I am forgetting something."

"What?"

"I don't freaking know. I've been going through everything with the girls, but something seems off."

His hands end up in mine, and I try to calm him down. "Well right now, there is a line of people waiting to see your bookstore. Aiden, you did it. You need to get out there, and welcome them inside."

He takes a deep breath, before unlocking the door, and stepping outside. "Thank you for coming to the opening of Book Rebel. We hope that you like the changes and look forward to hearing your thoughts on how to make this your favorite bookstore. Come on in!"

The line files through the door, and split ways, some going downstairs, and the others making their way to the signs about new releases. You might think people are more apt to buy their books online because sometimes they are cheaper, but many want to be able to go to the store and receive it as soon as possible, not waiting two to seven days to receive it in the mail, and paying an extra dollar or two to a small business doesn't faze them.

The girls are walking around asking if anyone needs help, and I'm staying toward the front to welcome any newcomers that wander inside. Amy has made some print outs that ask for feedback about the store and what they would like Book Rebel to incorporate into the store to make it more inclusive. Feedback is always good to get when you are looking to bring in more patrons to an establishment, and hone is on what they want. Sure, Aiden wants to appeal to the community, but he has to make money too.

The Colleen Hoover shelf is a huge hit with almost twenty women, standing and gawking at her incredible cover on her latest release. She's one of those that I'll read anything she writes, even if it's not romance. Her voice is so appealing and she knows how to write wonderful characters and keep me intrigued until the end when the twist usually happens.

"We have a few signed books on a shelf near the counter, if you are interested."

"Are you serious?"

"And it's the first edition. What's better than that?" I reply.

Two of the ladies practically pushed me out of the way to hustle toward the counter to find them, and within five minutes, all her signed copies were sold. I found some of these at other bookstores and for a decent price, so I only asked a couple bucks over what I initially paid for them. Just something that can give us some buzz, because I know they are going to post that on social media, and then others will want to check us out, too. That's how things work in this day and age; you have to be talked about online to gain traction most of the time, and it can be good or bad. Although the negative things usually outweigh all of the good ones. Sucks, but the truth.

Patrons keep filing in, and some bring in their kids to check out the new upstairs area, and I follow to see their reaction. We put a couple small kids tables up there so they can sit down and read, and we have so many books for them to choose from, and that's how it should be. Inspire them while they are young and the joy of reading will follow.

The girls are checking customers out as fast as they can to keep the line moving, and then George shows up. He becomes speechless seeing all of the people inside and roams around to check out everything that Aiden has done to spruce the place up. When he comes toward me and Aiden, I greet him.

"You've done a wonderful thing. I never had this many people in my store at one time."

Aiden shakes his head, and he continues to roam around.

The rest of the day goes by fast with a string of customers coming in so the bookstore is never empty for the rest of opening day. As he suspected, the new releases are performing better than the used books, and he's glad he stocked up on so many. Around noon, another box of books is put on the shelves to fill the empty spaces of what's been sold. Business is booming today and about twenty minutes before we are set to close for the day, Aiden thanks the girls for helping him today, and then we go through and make sure everything still looks good for tomorrow. Books are left behind by patrons on the tables, and everything needs to be organized back on the shelves for tomorrow.

After everything is cleaned up, and six o'clock hits, Amy locks the front door while Aiden does the register closeout for the day to see how much they ended up making in sales.

"If you want to go home, I'll be there after I get this done. Thank you for coming today," he says, kissing my cheek, as he follows me to the front door. "I'll be home shortly."

This is the Aiden that I fell in love with all those years ago, passionate and driven to make something of himself, and he showed that side of him today. Sometimes, you lose sight of that, but not him. Seeing him so passionate about the place, and wanting to do good for the community, makes me love him even more.

Once home, I put my purse and jacket by the front door, and make my way to the kitchen to figure out what is going to be for dinner. Chicken alfredo because it's simple and doesn't take that long to cook. So I put the chicken in a skillet, water boiling for the noodles, and the alfredo sauce in a pan to heat up. While waiting, I think about all the things that our future holds together, and that Aiden being here in Cambridge has become the right move even for him to find something he's passionate about again. Sure, he did love being a firefighter, but now he is his own boss and that is freeing.

The front door opens and closes as I hear him say my name.

"I'm in the kitchen."

He walks in and smiles. "Guess how much we made today?"

"A couple thousand?"

"Six-thousand and twenty-three dollars!"

He rushes toward me, and picks me up off the floor, and spins me around. Aiden still had doubts leading up to opening day on if he would be able to pull this off, but hearing those numbers makes me happy.

He turns off the stove, and then sits me up on the island, starting to kiss my neck, as his hands move up my thighs. My fingers run through his hair, and then I work his shirt up over his head.

"Fuck dinner. Let's celebrate!" Aiden says, getting up on the island with me, and moving my panties to the side as his tongue does wonders making me convulse with passion. Fuck, no one is better than him at this. My hand cups the back of his head, as I wither in ecstasy wanting it to never stop, and when he bites the inside of my thigh, it sends me over the edge, but he still doesn't stop as I'm on the orgasm train, he keeps going, and throws me into another spat, and this one is even more intense then the first. Yet, I ride it like a wave, until my body crashes and electricity runs through my body.

He smiles, and then flips me over, leaving me no time to bask in the glory of the orgasm, but that's okay, because he eases into me, and then my ass is up in the air. The quartz on my knees hurts, but after a second, I don't even think about it, because he's inside me, pumping into me like a fucking rockstar, and all I want is for him to get his release. So I match his tempo, and go to town, moving my hips to help him get a better angle inside me, until I hear a primal growl erupt from his throat. So fucking sexy.

"You like that?" I ask.

He nods, and continues and I can feel him getting harder until it's about to combust. *Come on, baby. Let's do it together.*

We speed up, and work on each other until we both reach our climax and relish in it.

"What's gotten into you? Not that I'm complaining." I say.

He is dripping sweat, and lays down on the island next to me. "I just want to show how much I appreciate you, and what you have to look forward to for the rest of your life."

If there's one thing he's fucking great at, it's knowing my body, and giving me exactly what I want, and hopefully that will never change.

Since he arrived in Cambridge with me for good, we have come to know the adult version of each other, and I've only fell harder for him knowing that he is open and honest about his problems, and if anything it makes him more desirable.

"All the doubts I had about this working out have come and gone. We are meant to be together. I'm not going anywhere," I say, cuddling up to him.

ABOUT THE AUTHOR

Ashley Zakrzewski is known for her captivating storytelling, sultry plots, and dynamic protagonists. Hailing from Arkansas, her affinity for the written word began early on, and she has been relentlessly chasing after her dreams ever since.

She has opened a TikTok shop that you can get signed paperbacks that come with swag packs. Go follow her on socials.

TikTok: @lovemeashley
    Instagram: @authorashleyz
    Facebook: Author Ashley Zakrzewski

Made in the USA
Columbia, SC
09 October 2024

907ba07a-a699-44a2-9682-aea98098eb0aR01